CW01635776

SERY

1.

"Everything's gonna be just fine," said the man as he readied his gun. The click echoed in the ruined, abandoned room, and he slowly pointed the Glock towards the woman.

"Where's my little girl?" she asked. Her voice faltered as her mind struggled with consciousness. Her eyes were deeply blurred, her pupils pulsing. With her fingers she searched for his hand but only gripped air.

"She's with Abigail."

"Is-is she alright? I'd like to s-see her!"

He glanced at her wounds and tried to swallow the lump in his throat, but it stuck in his gullet like a glob of glue.

"I don't think that would be a good idea."

The woman had been bitten. Her clothes were ripped at the spot where she'd been mauled, and blood spouted from the open wound. A drying puddle of blood covered the two wedding rings that hung from her necklace. Her muscles strained unwillingly as her body battled with the infection.

She had no chance, and it was only a matter of time before she would transform.

"P-promise me you'll look after her!" She closed her eyes. "You m-must promise me!"

The barrel shook, and he wished he could do what she asked. There were times when he would have promised without hesitation. But not anymore.

"Close your eyes!"

"Please..."

She couldn't take it any longer. In her very last moment, she only wished for false hope, to be reassured about her child's safety, the child for whom she had given her life.

"I'm begging you... Do it for me!"

He bit his bone-dry lips and took a deep breath.

"I'm gonna take care of her... I promise!" he said, and they looked at each other. She was ready. He aimed at her forehead and only hesitated for a beat before he pulled the trigger.

The shot echoed in the room, then silence. Only the spicy, sour smell of gunpowder remained.

Deep breath.

Exhale.

He turned towards the others: four children stood in the upstairs room of the abandoned warehouse like ghosts among the dusty, faded office furniture. They watched him with eyes wide open, then...

...they looked at a panting fifth child.

The little girl lay by the wall at the other end of the room, her hands strained to her chest. Her hair was shaggy and bloody, her clothes ripped in several places. She struggled to stay conscious. She moaned quietly and her desperate limbs shook. It was the same feral that had bitten her. And she too had no chance.

The man stepped away from the woman's body, and the four children started backing away. The little girl was close to transforming, so they didn't have much time. The infection had quickly overwhelmed the fragile body. He stood before her and raised his pistol, but this time the trigger resisted more.

She looked up desperately from the shadows and her eyes still glittered behind the glassy look, the color of a roaring, crystalline ocean. He felt he would get lost in the waves any minute.

"Cassius, wait!" The eldest child, a teenage girl, gripped her shotgun. "Perhaps..."

"Perhaps what, Abigail?" he asked and stared at the rest of the children, but they were speechless. They just wanted the whole thing to end. Cassius's face turned red in anger. Now it was the hesitation that annoyed him. The same quarrel again, even though they knew there

WELCOME TO THE SILENT ZONE

VIKTOR CSÁK

WS

Based on the story by Viktor Csák and Krisztián Illés
Published in 2023 by Writing Systems

ISBN Ebook: 978-615-01-7400-6
ISBN Paperback: 978-615-01-7399-3
ISBN Hardcover 978-615-01-7445-7

Edited by Sherry Mooney
Translated by Zsolt Fekete & Viktor Csák
Cover design by Ádám Ludwig
Interior layout by Vanessa Mendozzi
Special thanks to Declan Hannigan, Andrea Kékes-Szabó

Writing Systems Kft.
Hungary | www.writingsystems.eu

FilmFinity Inc.

THE WASTELAND

It started with a whisper. Something was happening in the alleys of Headland. People mauling each other like rabid beasts. Crazed demons roaming the streets at night. Far away from danger people shuddered, but in this world news only lasts fifteen minutes.

Then rumor became reality, whisper turned to scream, and the crazed demons stormed out of the alleys. People watched the footage, horrified.

The sheer panic.

The unquenchable blood thirst and unbridled rampage.

The gouged, empty orbits and the ragged stumps.

The rest of the world sat back, waiting and hoping that the ocean would stop the devastation. It was the largest quarantine ever, enforced by unmanned warships and drones, since no country dared to send their soldiers to that earthly hell. No one mentioned solidarity anymore.

The vibrant, sparkling cities were silenced forever. The screams faded as time passed. The wasteland devoured everything.

One day the New World was standing tall, was thriving; the next it ceased to exist and was left to collapse. The handful of survivors had forgotten what life was like before the Breakdown. Unfortunately, hell always has a lower pit. Something unexpected happened in the empty, windblown plains. Something that was unlike anything else. New beasts were born in the heart of the wasteland, and no one cared about the survivors' screams.

Welcome to the Silent Zone… and good luck!

was no hope. "Perhaps you have another great idea? Well, fire away!"

Abigail squeezed her mouth shut and turned her head. She stared at the door, which they had barricaded earlier. She didn't want to witness what was about to happen.

"Thought so!" Cassius said, then he felt the weight of the gun in his right hand. For the last time, he gave the little girl a smile.

"Everything's gonna be just fine..."

2.

Jake Armstrong, or Cassius as his long dead friends used to call him, knew that the last feral would attack soon. They had fought back the first wave, but even the children knew that ferals would immediately reorganize themselves.

It didn't matter that, even with a struggle, they had killed the first three monsters. The fourth member of the pack was lurking somewhere outside, just waiting for the right moment. It was as hungry as the others, and now it could taste blood and flesh in its mouth.

"Ammo?" he asked, but Abigail was distracted by the blood stain on the wall. The splash pattern above the little girl's head was reminiscent of the wings of an angel. Abigail winced when Cassius rapped his gun against a nearby desk.

"Abigail! Ammo?"

"Six in the pistol and three for the shotgun. What about you?"

"Three in the Glock, seven in the Remington."

Not much.

"How the hell could this happen?" Abigail asked, but no answer came.

Cassius looked at the other kids and saw that he couldn't rely on any of them. The youngest, the seven-year-old, Lucas, was severely injured, and held his elbow tight. The pain pulled at his facial features with an invisible fishing line. The ever-grinning Nia was squatting beside him. The thirteen-year-old girl had carefully placed the boy's favorite Matchbox car in his hand, in the hope it might calm him. And, of course, there was Molly, who stood by the wall, dejected and staring at the floorboards as if it were her only task. Cassius saw that the quiet ten-year-old girl could not fight a feral. Especially not the one that was after them.

"I'm scared," Lucas whispered.

Nia caressed his forehead. Her encouraging smile looked as if it had been painted onto her face. It fell away slowly but surely. "Everything's gonna be fine, okay? We'll be headed home soon!"

"Yeah, for sure!" Molly rolled her eyes.

So, the only one left was Abigail. The spindly sixteen-year-old girl could barely stand but straightened her back as if she exactly knew what Cassius was thinking. Her deep-brown eyes had grown wide with shock, and the August heat had burnt a blush on her thin, pale cheeks. Her thick lips were half-open as she stamped on the rubble and spun her head around steadily, like an Energizer flamingo. She wiped her dirty hands on her favorite T-shirt: the first piece of clothing she had picked for herself. CHEER UP, read the ragged, over-washed letters.

"Now what?" Abigail asked, then quickly swept aside an unruly lock of hair from her eyes. Her shaggy blonde pixie hair was sweaty from the escape and waved in the afternoon light like a bundle of straw. It was only a question of time before Cassius would order her to cut it even more.

It's about survival... it ain't a fashion statement. He said the same thing every single time she felt like arguing. Of course, she knew that even though she was fast and smart, if she let them grab her they would never let her go. It didn't stop her from wanting to argue.

Cassius slipped the Glock into its holster and lifted the Remington from the floor. He stepped to the window and looked down from the height. His broad shoulders hid the sunshine, and his long, tense shadow ran through the room, hiding Abigail in the dark.

Where are you? Show yourself!

He was looking for the fourth one, but nothing moved outside in the weedy parking lot. He didn't let the calm and the silence confuse him. The woman's bag was still at the tires of the rusty truck where she had dropped it in fear; not far from it a teddy bear lay in the dust, hugged until it was threadbare.

Cassius looked to the side. At the blood-shaped angel wings.

Concentrate! You don't have much time left...

They barely had a couple of hours until sunset.

"What if it gave up?" Abigail asked. No reply came. His sharp contour did not move. "What if it escaped?"

"Has that ever happened?"

"No."

The answer was pure formality. Once a feral stalked its prey, it never gave up. It could smell uninfected blood from a distance and wouldn't give up the taste of flesh. Still, the parking lot was empty. Their horse, the last one not slaughtered by the ferals, had been frightened by attack and was already far away.

Cassius turned and the sunlight immediately broke its way through to Abigail. He saw that she was searching for his eye-contact so that she could read his expression.

"It's already in the building, ain't it?" Abigail asked, holding on to her shotgun tightly.

Cassius nodded.

"Then it knows where we are!" Abigail involuntarily crept closer to him. Her voice trembled with nerves. "If we split, we can search the building! I'll take the upper level, downstairs is yours..."

"You're not going anywhere!"

She stopped and spread her arms angrily.

"Well, what then? Wait for night to fall on us?"

"Better than walking into a trap!" It was Molly's plaintive voice, which, as expected, was followed by Nia's objection.

"We can't stay here! If night falls, we have no chance, even if we dig ourselves in!"

Cassius closed his eyes and tried to recall the attack. How and when it became a clusterfuck. They were headed home on the old Route 285 when they spotted the warehouse among the dry brown slopes and the fresh growth of pepper trees. They hadn't searched this building before, and they desperately needed supplies. The woman and her daughter meant there were two more hungry mouths to feed, and the lack of ammo had been a worry for weeks.

By then they had already been marching for at least six hours in the August heatwave, and the exhausted children had convinced Cassius to stop. Thinking back: they had made too much noise. The woman and her daughter were happy to be found and saved. They rushed in, but the ferals had been waiting for them in the warehouse. The one hiding behind the truck bit the woman first, and she immediately went into a shock.

"Did you notice anything about them?" Cassius asked. He already knew what he had to do, but something still bothered him. Their survival was at stake.

"Yes," Abigail said. "The first one was a Delta."

Delta, meaning it had been infected for a year. Signs of transformation were easy to see on its body and face: its cheek bones strained inside its skin like blades, its limbs grown frighteningly long. Cassius remembered first seeing a Delta, realizing that the virus had not only reprogrammed the ferals' brains, but their bodies, as well.

"The second was a Gamma."

Right... and the bastard didn't give up easily!

The Gammas had been bitten two or three years ago, and in the meantime the virus had forced enormous transformations. Long, thin, spidery fingers; abnormally strong, still delicate human jaws; faded yellow eyes. If you wanted to kill a Gamma, having a weapon was just a start; you also needed training and practice to spot its weak points. Firing at its legs and crippling it was the best course of action, so you could finish the job with a headshot or a bullet into the heart, for the Gamma's bones had not grown strong yet.

"The third was just a Greenhorn."

He nodded.

Just a Greenhorn, meaning it was only different from the ordinary humans by its behavior. That, however, meant a hell of a difference. The first symptom was frantic fury as the human body tried to fight the infection, even though the battle had already been decided.

Civilization suppressed the brutal animal instinct in all of humanity, but that instinct could never be fully destroyed. And sooner or later it broke out in those bitten with infernal devastation.

Cassius could only think of one solution: promptly send a bullet into the poor bastard's head to end its suffering. Transformation was accompanied by dreadful pain, and the longer it took, the more difficult it was to kill the feral.

"What about the fourth one?"

The last one, which was lurking outside.

"I couldn't see it clearly, but..."

Abigail clipped her sentence, which was enough for Cassius. He had hoped he was wrong. He had hoped he was mistaken, and perhaps he couldn't see it well, either, but even the distance was unable to hide the atrophied lips, the teeth behind them, the robust shoulders.

Abigail did not dare to finish. Cassius did it for her.

"The fourth one is a Beta."

3.

Fuckin' Betas! Cassius had every reason to curse, but he kept most of it to himself. He did not want to cause panic, so he straightened up. *Bring it on, we can handle this!*

A Delta or a Gamma could be beaten, but the Betas were so fast and so strong that there was not much hope in this labyrinthine, dimly lit building, especially not with machetes and half empty magazines.

The features of the Betas were unrecognizably distorted by the virus. Their bodies had grown as if invisible, infernal forces were pulling their limbs, and even the smallest one towered above their prey. They were seven-foot-tall, two-hundred-and-fifty-pound beasts. Their bony muscles were like knotted cables swelling under the skin, while their fingers were like sharp claws. Their lantern-jaws were a nightmare come to life with fang-like teeth and lips ripped open into the cheeks.

All useless hair and fat had vanished from their bodies, and with their sophisticated sight and sense of smell it was impossible to hide from them. The only thing that could kill a Beta for sure was a headshot or bullets (yes, plural) into their stomach. Their ribs and spine were like Kevlar. Most of the dangerous packs were led by Betas, but there was one thing worse.

An Alpha.

A monstrosity which had transformed in the first year of the pandemic and for some reason had not died from the endless deformation. Their existence had long been a rumor, but nothing more; they were just dark shadows in some traveler's tale. Cassius had never seen anyone who had met an Alpha face-to-face. Even if some poor soul had the ill fortune to fight one, they were unlikely to have survived the encounter.

"If it was really a Beta, we would all be dead by now," Molly said, while Nia shrugged her shoulders.

"Not necessarily! There were only four of the bastards. If there had been twice as many, then… yikes!" And the girl raised her fists above her head and let her tongue hang out, pretending to be hanged.

Molly shook her head, as she always did when she was not taken seriously, and curled up on the floor.

"What if it wasn't four of them?" Abigail asked.

Cassius hesitated.

"We would've seen them," he said and pointed to the cabinet cramped in front of the door. "Help me pull it away. I'll go look around."

"I've got an idea. If we…"

"You stay here and hold out!"

Abigail lost her enthusiastic look.

"What?"

"If anything happens to me, you know what to do."

"Bullshit!"

Cassius's face twitched. He heard Nia giggle in the background. *Here it comes!*

"You wanna go out alone?" Abigail continued. "Against a Beta? You can't be serious!"

"It won't have an advantage in these narrow corridors. I can shoot it if I spot it in time."

An obvious lie, both of them knew that.

"Shoot it with what? Your nine remaining bullets?"

"If I can't, at least I'll tire it out," he looked at the blocked door, "so when it attacks it'll come right at you through the only way in. No games, no tactics. That's your best chance."

"Or you'll be enough for it. Your fat guts…"

She pointed her sharp, stubborn chin towards him, but Cassius was not distracted by her game. He slipped his military bag under the table and carefully cushioned it with several empty boxes. He exchanged looks with the curled-up Molly, whose eyes were filled with helpless tears.

Cassius summoned his strength and stood up. Abigail waited for him, unbothered by the fact that his sullen, gray-green eyes looked down at her from a head taller.

"This is the greatest bullshit I've ever heard! You wanna know why I'm so sure about this?"

"No, but it's coming anyway."

"The reason I know it, wiseass, is that it's not what you taught me."

"We're doing it off the cuff."

"Hell no! You just don't trust me. You don't think I'm able to help!"

"Okay, let that be the answer." He silenced her with a gesture before she could continue. Cassius pointed to his bag. "Take good care of this! You know how important it is, don't you?"

"I do."

"Let me hear it then!"

All of her muscles strained with rebellion. She mustered a monotonous voice so even Cassius would understand how unpleasant it was for her.

"I'll look after the bag."

Cassius nodded, then straightened up. "Are we happy?"

"Yes, we are!" Abigail replied with arms akimbo.

"Awesome! Hold the fort!"

Once again, Cassius checked everything — his rifle, his armor, the kids in the background — then he moved past Abigail, towards the door.

Deep breath.

Exhale.

Go!

Cassius did not wait for the girl. He pushed the huge cabinet aside and slowly opened the door, gun held high. The half-shaded corridor was empty, and only the dust motes were moving in the thin beam of light. They heard the wind dragging metal against metal in the distance, and the noise covered the half-shadow with demonic echoes. Cassius bit his lip and hesitantly stepped over the threshold. There were no doors on the right side of the corridor, so he instinctively kept to that direction.

In his mind he visualized the building as if observing a blueprint. Just as he was taught. Seventy feet ahead up to the dark corner, then…

…a sharp turn left…

…about fifteen feet to the staircase…

…down to the right is the ground floor and the main entrance, straight ahead are office rooms, the diner, and a door to the other wing. To the warehouse.

"Cover me till the end of the corridor, then lock the door!" he said and slowed down his breathing.

"Are you crazy? I'm not going to lock you out!"

"Cover me!"

The sound of pounding from the ground floor disrupted them, then a desperate howl and scuffle could be heard.

They both winced and stood there dumbfounded, staring at the end of the corridor. Holding their breaths, waiting for what was inevitably going to happen, but nothing moved. Only the distant, painful howling echoed in their ears as some poor animal threw itself about, yowling and gurgling. The suffering seemed like it would never end; the butcher knew no mercy.

Cassius immediately recognized the sound. It was a dog being massacred by something much stronger. The howling reached its peak, then silence.

"What the hell was that?" she asked with eyes wide open. Cassius beckoned to her and pointed his gun at the end of the corridor.

Slowly, the last grain of dust fell on the rubble, but no thundering attack broke the silence as Cassius had reckoned it would. As it would normally happen, when a Beta sensed smell and sound.

Nothing seemed right. He wiped his face but couldn't move. He tried to calm himself, but inside he was terrified.

"Stay here and do as I told you!"

He slipped into the silence.

4.

The adrenaline immediately switched him into autopilot. He didn't even need to think: when he stepped into the corridor his honed reflexes took control. Cassius knew the biggest mistake they could make was to settle for defense. The only reason they had stayed alive so long was his lessons to Abigail: the fight must end before it could start. While he crept down the hallway, he found himself obsessing over mistakes that had led to their present situation. If the woman and her daughter hadn't been with them, it might not have happened. They would have seen the telltale signs.

I was right again. He blamed himself and swore that if they survived he would never make the same mistake again. He had clearly pointed out the risks they took if they helped others, but Abigail wouldn't listen, and it had happened just like he'd been afraid it would.

Cassius grimaced. He heard the girl's heavy breathing behind him, but the noise of settling rubble and rustling ratshit slowly overwhelmed it. He prepared all his nerves for what he knew would happen next. All he was focused on was taking back the initiative.

He reached the curve of the corridor as it faded into shadow. From then on he could only rely on himself. He knew that if he didn't pay attention, it would be over. Anything could have been around the corner; there was plenty of space in that uncleared sector for the Beta to hide.

Cassius slowed down and almost slipped in the dust as he shuffled forwards. He raised his gun and held it close. The pad of his finger rested on the trigger-guard and he planned his footwork to keep his body in perfect balance.

With all his strength he tried to control his breath, and he prepared himself for the final pinpoint step. In the last couple of inches, he heard his pulse hammering in his ears. His right toe reached beyond the corner, his left one simultaneously followed, and with that movement he found himself around the corner and into the next section of the corridor.

He pushed his gun ahead, his eyes looking for threat, but…

…the echoing space ahead of him was empty.

A few yards away on the right was a staircase leading to the ground floor and the reception area. To the left were offices and a break room. Trampled sheets of paper were scattered across the floor.

Above him hung partially fallen light fixtures and cables. On the wall was the symbol of the former Resistance, probably painted by the soldiers who had once been based in the warehouse.

In the distance, towards the end of the twenty-five-yard corridor was a metal door into the other wing. Leading to a dark, treacherous warehouse he wanted to avoid. To have any chance at all, he'd have to use himself as bait and then attack the Beta as it rushed at him, hoping to land a blow when he himself was most vulnerable.

Cassius sneaked to the staircase and looked down at the ground floor. He saw no significant movement near the industrial-style reception desk, just a draft waving the yellowed dust covers. The once-proud, masculine black metal surface was worn out, the plaster crumbling from the light-gray wall nearby.

He spotted something at the door leading to the courtyard. The torn-up carcass of a dog was lying next to some broken glass, cushioned in a fresh puddle of blood. A young German shepherd, its tan fur glistening with red droplets. A bit farther, an oddly shaped bloodstain led to the ground floor corridors and debris that could easily be used as cover. A grotesque, surreally drawn human footprint. A huge one.

Cassius swallowed and took his knife out of its sheath on his tactical vest. He had already found the hideout, but he didn't really feel like preparing the bait.

Something cracked in the debris near the dog's body, the crunch of broken glass. He raised his gun and waited with bated breath. No movement followed the noise, but Cassius heard the resonating growl. It must have come from downstairs. The Beta was waiting for him to attempt to escape outside. Most people, in a panic, would have done just that.

Cassius, however, forced himself to remain calm. He took a deep breath, cut a wound in his lower arm and soaked a piece of cloth with his blood. He tried hard not to hiss at the sharp pain, and once he had quickly bandaged the wound, he threw the bait on the stairs.

Slowly he started backing up towards the last office room. The hideout he had sought.

But he made a mistake...

5.

Abigail covered Cassius with shaking hands until he reached the end of the corridor. With every step he was closer to vanishing from her sight and she didn't want that to happen. Her throat tightened in panic that she might never see him again.

Only three steps left. Two. One.

Cassius halted before he entered the unknown, and Abigail saw him squint back before disappearing into the dark. Then she was on her own.

Abigail wiped her sweating, dirty brow and she felt the caustic perspiration as it dripped into her eyes. Her T-shirt was damp with the heat, and the bag strap chafed her shoulder. She would have thrown it off, but she didn't dare move.

The door, the bloody door... Lock that bloody door!

The instructions echoed in her head, but she was unable to step back. She tried to slow down her breathing so that at least she could hear what was happening. That was the only thing she could cling to.

She looked back. Back into the repulsive room, where she had to wait. Where the bodies of the woman and her daughter lay. Whatever Cassius said, they couldn't have left them behind.

Muffled clashing noises drifted up from the ground floor on the draft, but Abigail was still deep in her thoughts. She didn't even notice the noise – her eyes were glued to the woman's pale face. She wanted to picture the calm in the slowly freezing features, but her guilt shattered this image into pieces.

I did what was right!

Abigail looked back down the empty corridor. She tried to focus with all of her attention – not only on the instructions, but also the skills she had learned through the years, skills she needed to utilize right now. She desperately took stock, but her thoughts were flashing like lightning.

Gun on the target, fingers loose. *Do not squeeze the trigger! Damn... Am I even doing it right?* She was hungry and exhausted. Her legs were bouncing to a strange rhythm. *Come on, girl, take two steps back!*

She kept enough distance between herself and the end of the corridor just in case the Beta actually showed up. *Come on*, she ordered herself, but her legs obeyed only slowly.

What else is there? What the hell did I forget? If it attacks, you first have to shoot at the leg, and if it collapses, then at the head.

The commotion intensified in the distance, and she looked that way. Nothing happened for a few seconds...

...then a gunshot, and another. Sounds of a struggle. She could clearly hear the clash of the needle-sharp fangs and the jaws clattering. The Beta could practically taste its prey and attacked with a beasty growl.

The walls suppressed everything, but Abigail could imagine the uneven fight... and still she stood there. *This is not why I suffered through all that training, that struggle! Why am I standing here?*

She cursed Cassius and tears swelled in her eyes. Dread overwhelmed her body in waves: she feared losing him, but she was scared of the feral too. She had never encountered a Beta alone.

The noise of the struggle didn't lessen. Fleeing feet stamped. She gripped her gun. Perhaps now. If Cassius turned around the corner, she could shoot the Beta. She knew she was capable, she had practiced a thousand times. *No, don't be overconfident*, she murmured to herself in Cassius's grumble. Her own voice responded. *I know I can do it... I'm ready!*

But then she remembered that he would never bring danger to her. Abigail turned pale with the realization, as the stamping feet got farther away. Cassius was not leading the Beta towards her. He'd rather die to protect her.

And Abigail couldn't let that happen.

6.

It had seemed like a good idea, but reality rewrote Cassius's plan. The Beta wasn't waiting for him on the ground floor and he only realized this when he took a couple of careful steps ahead. He felt a shiver on the back of his neck. Others might have put it down to fear, but Cassius knew that his body worked with excellent precision. An alarm sounded in his brain.

He retreated and gave himself a second to listen. He smelled the rotten stink in his nose, and as he bent his head, he spotted the fresh traces: blood covered the dust by his feet and, farther away, a footprint leading into the room behind him. The old dining room.

Cassius spun around and instinctively held his gun high. The doorway was vast, and as he glanced into the room, he immediately found what he was looking for.

The Beta no longer needed to hide itself.

It didn't want to waste any more time on Cassius.

The worn tables were flung into the air when the demonic creature burst out of its hiding place. Wooden shards exploded and a blood-curdling growl split the silence. The room turned dark as the beast moved across the window and dust swirled as the Beta's claws slashed through the air.

Cassius immediately fired, but only one bullet hit. The shot to its shoulder slowed the Beta down, but only for a moment, and it was on its feet again quickly. By the time Cassius could even process what was happening, he was already running.

Towards the warehouse. Away from Abigail.

He didn't have to look back. He knew exactly what was happening behind him.

The Beta threw itself into the corridor with enormous force, hitting the opposite wall and knocking chunks of plaster to the ground. The beast didn't seem to notice the impact. Cassius heard its feet scrambling on the floor as the Beta tried to find its balance. Then it was after him.

Due to many years of deformation and transformation, the ferals moved and ran as no person could. A few steps ahead, Cassius recognized the pattern from the demonic stomp. The Beta had caught up almost immediately. *Jesus... it's gonna catch me!*

The door leading to the warehouse was at least ten yards from him.

Bang, bang!

He pulled the pin out of his last grenade and tossed the Lemon behind him, then crashed into the warehouse door with his shoulder. The rusty hinge and the weary lock let go, breaking into tiny pieces, and Cassius fell against the railing opposite the entrance. He felt the impact in his ribs but didn't hesitate. He had only a few seconds to get as far away as possible.

The walkway ran above a vast warehouse space, most of it lost in semi-darkness. Beneath him, on the other side of the railing, were a ten-foot drop and endless shelves.

A couple more steps... I can do it!

The spherical steel body of the grenade was torn to pieces and the sound of the explosion echoed through the warehouse. The air pressure pushed Cassius with elemental force. He lost his breath as he fell to the ground and felt his head bang against the railing.

For a moment... a vision returned Cassius to the past. He was in Headland again, on his way to the refugee camp. He was lying in the overturned bus holding little Abigail tight against the stream of broken glass, hoping the girl wouldn't get hurt. Beyond the screech of metal, he could hear screams and abrupt instructions, but then his survival instincts dragged him back to reality.

Clouds of dirt and fragments of plaster lay all around him, his ears ringing. He wiped the blood from his eyes and summoned his remaining strength to turn onto his back. His rifle lay in front of him, its barrel pointing into the depths. Cassius, however, kept his attention on the door and quickly put his right hand to his thigh, to the grip of his handgun.

A blast like that must have killed the Beta.

Please, he prayed and waited. He took a breath, his throat searing with ash, but he resisted coughing. *Get up, come on!*

He saw no movement in the gray chaos of particles. And then it happened, what he had feared the most. From the other end of the corridor, through the rubble and smoke, he could clearly hear

Abigail calling.

"Cassius?"

He grabbed his rifle and managed to pull himself up to his knees.

An enormous shadow appeared out of the dust cloud. The injured Beta growled and rose up.

7.

He only had a few seconds. Cassius saw frames of alternate futures pass before his eyes. He knew that the Beta cared about nothing else anymore, just Abigail, and it would immediately throw itself at her.

The cloud of debris began to clear, but he still couldn't clearly see what was happening. Cassius started to run. His breath came in painful gasps, but he kept going. He held his gun high as he stepped over the threshold of the ruined door. Blood thundered in his ears, but still he could clearly hear Abigail's scream.

Come on, Abigail! Shoot!

For a moment he thought he should duck down. He was in the line of fire, the shotgun pellets might hit him, but he didn't trust the girl. If he threw himself down on his stomach and Abigail started to run, any tiny chance they still had would be gone. Then finally...

Boom! Boom! Boom!

Cassius went down on his knees, ready to act. After the third shot had been fired, the smoke opened up in front of him and he spotted something in line with the staircase. The outline of a demonic creature. Cassius didn't hesitate. He fired.

The Beta fell to the ground and roared in pain. Abigail dropped her empty shotgun and took out her handgun and screaming, she fired the whole magazine into the tormented feral's body.

The dust slowly dispersed, and the corridor was quiet again. Just a high, whining sniffle could be heard. The putrid stink of swamp spread through the air. Cassius stood up and ran to the girl, keeping his shotgun on the Beta at all times.

Abigail was standing still in shock, the gun held high and frozen in her hand. A few muscles strained on her pale face while she gasped for air. Her eyes stared at the carcass of the Beta as if her mind still wouldn't believe the beast was dead.

A number of battles raged inside Cassius. The first was that he should fire a couple more bullets into the Beta, just to be sure, but then his cold blood won. The glazed eyes and motionless body were convincing enough on their own and the sticky brownish blood leaking from the skull gave him the certainty he needed.

On the other hand, he lost the second battle. He had lost it the second he heard Abigail's voice.

"Are you out of your mind? It could have killed you!" Cassius grabbed Abigail and shook her arm to bring her back to reality. In her eyes he saw panic and the first fat teardrops.

"I… I was only trying to help…"

"Help? I gave you a clear order to follow!"

That was the magic word to bring Abigail back. Her pride promptly blew away the shock and she quickly pulled her arm out of Cassius's grip.

"An order? I'm not a soldier!"

"This whole fuckup happened because you didn't listen to me again!"

"Really? I thought we were a team and we made decisions together. But nooo, you're the one giving orders here!"

"That's because I'm the only one that can think straight!"

He didn't get a chance to continue. Behind them, in the room where the others were hiding, a window smashed in with a loud crash. Pieces of the frame and glass hit the ground with a clatter, together with something else.

Cassius heard the thump. The rubble cracking under heavy bare feet. The children's screams echoing in his ears, just like that day…

His heart filled with fear, and he got a glimpse of Abigail as the pique froze on her face. They turned towards the sound. There was another feral. A fifth one.

8.

Cassius threw himself down the corridor towards the room. His only thought was that the more time he gave the beast, the bigger the odds were that they wouldn't survive the day. He had to draw the feral's attention to him before it could orient itself. He had to get it confused. That was their only chance.

"Cassius!" Abigail screamed desperately, but he didn't slow down.

He held his gun high, his finger straining on the trigger-guard. As he reached the door, he immediately spotted the figure standing at the window, turning its head as it searched for them. The sudden daylight blinded Cassius for a moment, so he acted instinctively.

He fired the last three bullets from his rifle. Two ripped into the Delta's body, which fell back helplessly, then tumbled out of the window. He heard the body thud as it hit the ground. He threw down his rifle and grabbed his handgun as he ran to the window. Down by the partially torn off fire escape, the Delta's lifeless body was lying exactly where it had landed on the ground.

Cassius turned around in a flash and switched into search mode. Worry strained his heart, but finally he found what he was looking for.

The children were huddled together under the table...

...next to them, his military bag.

He stepped closer and saw that apart from fright, the children weren't hurt. Once Cassius was sure the danger was over, Nia helped Lucas and Molly climb out from under the table. Lucas gripped his Matchbox car, while Molly held onto the lucky dolphin bracelet that she had gotten from Cassius. He had convinced her that while she was wearing it, nothing could harm her.

Then Abigail appeared in the doorway with a face that showed she was as scared as he had been before. She walked to the window and looked down from the height. She rubbed her eyes as if waking up from a nightmare.

Cassius turned back to the bag, and when he exchanged looks with Molly, the girl shook her head with quivering lips. He looked the other way and pulled the bag out from under the table with his right hand. Its contents were intact. He took a deep breath and held it in his lungs for a while before he slowly exhaled. He felt it was almost an unearthly luxury to let oxygen run through his body. He zipped up the bag and looked at Abigail. He nodded towards her gun.

"How many left?"

"None," she said, slipping the gun back to the holster. It didn't matter whether she kept the gun or not, since there were a few more at home that had run out over the past few months. "How about you?"

"Three in the Glock. Together with what's at home it's..."

"Fifteen."

"Awesome!"

Fifteen bullets and the machetes were all that was left against the world's most dangerous predators.

9.

Cassius did not want to take any risks, so he checked all the carcasses with Abigail. He didn't think there would be any more ferals hiding around the warehouse, but better not to tempt their luck. They had about two hours until dark, and he didn't know this area at night. He had no idea what other horrors might come when darkness fell.

The game bag was the last thing he checked. He had thrown it away at the entrance during the attack. As he crouched down to look inside, it was obvious from the torn-up bag and the blood traces that the ferals also hit that. Almost nothing was left from the deer.

Cassius gave himself a hundred and twenty seconds to process everything that had happened. He let the light summer breeze caress his face. Now that his thoughts weren't controlled by adrenaline, he felt the drying blood and the dirt on his hands. But he didn't care. He raised his gaze to the horizon and watched the clouds floating across the porcelain sky...

...ninety-nine, hundred, hundred-and-one...

He spotted something in the dust: a ripped and worn flier that had been thrown down from a plane during the pandemic to warn people. The faded headline evoked long-buried memories: BORDERS CLOSED, DO NOT SET OFF. Smaller letters below, as if they were meant to be hidden: SHOOT TO KILL ORDER IN EFFECT.

Cassius got up, dusted himself off, and glanced up to the zenith. In the distance, in the vast blue, something glittered, but as fast as it flashed, the metallic glow vanished. It could well be a mirage, or something watching from beyond the Silent Zone.

He grimaced then raised his middle finger towards the sky and the glow, as if he was trying to send a message to whoever. Right that moment it was all the same to him, whether God or any human saw it, the message was meant for everyone. He straightened up and turned to Abigail.

"Get ready, we're leaving soon!"

"Shouldn't we look around? We could spend the night here."

"Don't push it!"

"We need supplies. Anything would come in handy!"

It was a firm argument, but he no longer trusted her instincts. He started to think that he would even hold logical things nonsense if they were Abigail's thoughts. Foolish, and he knew it, too. He looked around. Two cars and a van were parked nearby. A bit farther, in the shade of a pepper tree, there was an old truck. He pointed at the cars.

"Check them, but that's it. I'll see what's in the truck."

He walked towards the ramshackle Freightliner, which was listing badly due to its punctured right front tire. Cassius checked the cabin then hunkered down in the front seat. He quietly closed the door. The lock clicked, the leather seats squeaked. He was in a familiar place. He smiled as his hands touched the wheel and from habit he flipped down the sunshade. A yellowing family photo looked back at him, just as he had expected from a fellow professional.

Just like he had done himself way before the Breakdown.

Outside Abigail checked the last car and as he glanced towards her, he caught his own reflection in the rearview mirror. His dusty-dirty stubble and the scar on his cheek… the grayish hair and the deep-set green eyes…

Exhaustion washed over him unexpectedly and he realized how worn out he was from the day. He had aches and pains all over, but he summoned his strength and quickly searched the truck cabin. There were three bullets in a Browning leaning against the passenger's seat and an old flashlight in the glove box. He pocketed a creased book by Tom Wolfe that was on his wish list. Everything else was useless junk.

He had a few minutes before Abigail finished with the van, so he closed his eyes and tried to breathe smoothly. Tried not to think about anything, to calm down and get ready for the long walk that was waiting for them up to the junction of Route 10 and 285. To the old motel where they had found shelter since spring.

For a flash he saw the images of the attack. He heard the little girl's scream, the crack of bone. His hand instinctively reached for his bag, and he thought to himself that maybe it was a sign: not to wait any longer, but to finally carry out what they had been planning for nearly a year. And it was high time to be tougher. From now on they couldn't risk their lives for anyone else.

"Cassius!"

First, he couldn't decide whether her voice was excited or scared, but when he saw Abigail at the van he knew that she had found something interesting.

The lock clicked and the door squeaked.

Cassius jogged over. She was crouching inside, watching a bundle of cloth on the floor with six tiny furballs happily cavorting. Uncomprehending, he watched the squirming, whimpering puppies. Then he put the pieces of the puzzle together.

10.

She had never felt so excited. Abigail watched the puppies with a wide smile and could hardly wait to show them to Cassius. She quickly nudged a little male with dark socks back into the litter and carefully caressed him. *Your name could be Soxy.*

Her heartbeat sped up when Cassius appeared and she saw the surprise on his face. Abigail knew he would object at first, but she would persuade him. She started collecting arguments. *We'll raise them! Even Cassius can't say no to these little ones…*

"The German shepherd in the hall… must've been their mother, right?" she asked, glancing at the mix of puppies. Cassius nodded.

"You know we can't take them with us, don't you?"

Just be cool, you're prepared for this, girl…

"But we can't leave them alone! They're gonna die."

"Without their mother they'll die anyway. They're only a couple of weeks old."

The smile on Abigail's face faded and raw disappointment took its place.

"I'll look after them! Just think how cool it would be walking with a whole pack of dogs. They'd sniff out danger from far away, we could train them to fight..."

"Don't you get it, Abigail?" he asked. His voice was calm and sad. "We don't even have enough food for ourselves? What would you feed them? Expired canned food? We only have a few of those left anyway."

Abigail stood up stiffly.

"We'll manage... I promise I'll take care of them!"

"Let's go!" Cassius said, and after stepping out of the van he stretched out his arm to help Abigail.

But the girl got stubborn.

"We can't do this!" Abigail was about to cry.

"I'm sorry, but no! They don't have a chance!"

"So, what then? We just pretend nothing's happened? Huh?" She got louder and more intense. "Or? You just wait for me to get out of the bus, then perform some kind of mercy killing?"

"No. We just go home."

"You're cruel!" Abigail hissed. She tried to be mad and begging at the same time. "I'll never forgive you!"

"So what? At least you'll live."

Abigail took a defiant step right, between Cassius and the puppies. He pulled his handgun out from its holster.

"I can still change my mind!" he said and touched his thigh with the butt of the gun. "But then you'll have to watch it!"

Abigail's eyelashes quivered as she saw the darkness in his look. Over the years she had learned the true meaning of this blink. Cassius was serious about what he said, and he was steadfast. No matter how determined she had been to stand up for herself, she still didn't have enough strength to defy him. It was always like this. Her shoulders slumped.

"Why are you doing this?"

"You damn well know why..."

"Don't use me like that!"

"Like what?"

"I'm not an excuse for you to be ruthless."

"I can do it and you can be angry with me as long as you like, I'll survive."

Abigail looked back at the squeaking puppies and felt the desperation waiting to burst out of her. One of the furballs whimpered. The one with the dark sock patches on its feet.

"No… Please…"

But her voice was quiet and high. She wanted more than anything to keep the puppies safe and sound, but she'd be ashamed for Cassius to see her cry. The battle was over and she couldn't hold back her tears.

Cassius knew the girl as well as she knew him, so he stepped aside. Abigail stamped her feet, a burst of furious despair, then stormed out of the van with her eyes brimming with tears.

Wiping her face, she grabbed her bag from the ground near the van and angrily headed to the main gate. She didn't even wait for him, hoping that instead of the gunshot she'd only hear the van door sliding shut. She didn't want this story to end now, in front of her. Not even if deep inside she knew: Cassius was right.

No, she reprimanded herself. *It can't be like this… we always have to try! Always!*

The aim is to survive…

…but at what cost?

"We're leaving in five minutes! When night falls, rabid rats will be swarming here," he yelled, but she didn't reply.

Do whatever you like! She knew what he was up to, but for the moment she couldn't care less.

11.

The woman and her daughter were lying next to each other in the middle of the room, their hands resting on their chests. Their faces were clean, their eyes shut. Cassius gently pushed the girl's body closer to the woman's, and once again he crouched down beside them. For anyone who didn't know him, the gesture could have seemed like a moment of prayer, although nothing could be further from the truth. He was simply observing the stiff features, trying to memorize the faces. He didn't move until he noticed something on the woman's body.

It was her necklace. With two wedding rings on it.

He took the necklace, then covered the bodies with the dust covers that he'd pulled off the reception desk. He tucked the cloth well under them as if he was afraid the first breeze would blow it off and make their devastation and passing visible again. He couldn't let that happen.

At his last tender touch, he felt the girl's cool cheek, and again he was reminded how fast children's bodies got cold. She was no exception.

When he finished, he took out a flat metal box wrapped in a striped linen rag from his bag. He carefully unwrapped it, and as he opened up the rusty, battered lid, he could hear the clatter of the tiny objects inside the box.

He gave a smile when he spotted the red Matchbox car. Its plastic left rear wheel was still stuck, and the paint scraped off from its start number. On top of the pile of junk was a battered USB drive. A lucky bracelet lay limp in the corner with its colorful pearls, and a tiny dolphin hung from a plastic fishing line.

The dolphin had brought the girl no luck after all.

It has been a while since he last saw them, but the objects didn't seem lonely. There was a gold-plated leaf-brooch with enchanting blue crystals…

…a tiny Swiss Army knife…

…a ragged hair clip…

…a fox on a crumpled postcard from a faraway island…

The proof of seven years of misery. The proof that it would never get any better.

Cassius stared at his palm. He was holding the necklace and the two wedding rings in his dirty, bloodstained fist. He softly placed them on top of the other objects and closed the misshapen lid.

He realized that the children had been standing in the corner the whole time, as if they were waiting for him. He could see them, even though they were long gone. Nia was still holding Lucas close. Molly was sitting on the floor, staring at him.

There was nothing strange in their presence. At least, he didn't think so.

He gave a forced smile, as if encouraging them. This is just the way of life, his weary grin seemed to say. If this was supposed to happen, well, then so be it. He tried to speak using only his eyes. *You were just as important to me. I cared for you as long as I could. But I'm so sorry…*

The children didn't move. Nor did they respond. Their looks flashed just like the day when Cassius last saw them…

…Molly angry, rejecting the destiny she had been given…

…Lucas with childlike incomprehension…

…Nia with her fear of death.

Cassius took out his flask and drank a sip. He wasn't even thirsty, but he had to do something to finally get that swollen lump to disappear from his throat. When he put the flask back down, his eyes returned to the corner where the children had been hiding. There was nobody there.

He was alone in the room, but he wasn't happy about it. He knew that they would come back to him whenever they got the chance. That was what shades of the past did.

Cassius didn't move for two long minutes. His thoughts were swirling, but he tried to focus on the same lie.

…ninety-nine, hundred, hundred-and-one…

Everything's gonna be just fine.

PACK OF WOLVES

1.

There were fifteen of them, and they all wanted the same thing. For days they had been attacking the colony between Deserter Creek and Keley Pond, by the old ranger cottage, and the people living there had used up all their resources in defense. A breach was imminent, but the members of the colony believed they were prepared for everything.

If they had known what they were facing, they probably would have fled on the first day, when the majority could have made it out. But the signs of the approaching danger triggered curiosity, not fear, in many of them. And on the last day it wasn't only their lives that were at stake.

The two-story lodge with its mint green roof used to be as a gathering place for Gen Z, where the youth of the neighborhood would go to blow off steam. No one would have thought of it as a shelter after the Breakdown. Not even old Nelson the Wise, as they mockingly called him in Liberty, would've realized it at first. In fact, he had a good reason to reject the idea.

Nelson had always wanted to travel, so when his wife died of cancer and his enterprise took its first hit after the pandemic, he gathered all their gold jewelry and bought himself a decommissioned oil truck. He figured for any man that could build a hundred and ten houses, even with the help of a construction crew, a task like this would be a piece of cake. So he made himself an armor-plated motorhome.

He tried to think of what was waiting for him as an adventure. Head on down south, preferably before they closed the borders, all the way down to Patagonia on the Pan-American Highway, hoping the pandemic wouldn't reach that far. Then find a place to park the vehicle for good, where he wouldn't be disturbed. He'd just roam the woods and learn to hunt, so that after a long, tiring day he could sit out above the canyon and listen to Merle Haggard, with a joint as the only company he needed.

Nelson had everything prepared: the truck had its own water tank, a spare tank for gasoline, a decent heater, a wide bed, a mini kitchen, and enough instant noodles and beef jerky for a platoon.

At first, he was considered a fool and a fear monger in Liberty, liable to freak out children, but he was more bothered by the fact that so many people still believed the lies of the press and the politicians. Then, in the middle of April, when the drugged, formerly-restrained infected broke out of the Presbyterian Hospital in Headland, Nelson was no longer "the Wise" but the prophet, and the neighbors would've given anything to be a partner in the old man's apocalypse-proofing business. The yield was survival.

Nelson had to choose: either he shut the truck doors and didn't stop until the border, which was open at that time, or he risked his own life to help anyone he could. Just a week later a dozen people were welding their newly purchased vehicles at the junkyard of his old buddy, Grant Wyers. Nelson even found an apprentice in the person of his neighbor's daughter, Aurora.

No matter how much the others believed in the Patagonian dream, however, nothing came of it. When the Army locked down the state borders and panic hit Liberty, the colony finally settled down in the junkyard for good.

The image of distant fields and babbling brooks under the mountains faded throughout the long lockdown, and because of the dark rumors that reached them, residents of the camp gradually accepted that faraway hills were not as green as they had previously thought. By the time the summer ended, most cities on both Coasts had fallen, while the southern border was still being protected by soldados, narcos, and coyotes. It was almost impossible to get through there, especially not without fighting the tens of millions of refugees and ferals who simultaneously stormed the roads.

And when there was nothing else left to defend, and the GI Joes were all gone, Nelson was sad to see that the drive of the others evaporated as well. The faint light of hope vanished when a mother and her son escaping from Chicago told stories for hours about what was happening on the roads.

The woman said if they wanted to hear the truth, they should get themselves a ham radio; they might get useful information from the amateur operators. Most of the frequencies were broadcasting news from Mexico, where the government had much bigger problems than dealing with unauthorized programs.

Nelson and his companions found out that only San Diego was still standing on the West Coast. The Navy was attempting to evacuate the survivors there, but in the meantime ferals were already attacking the refugee camps. Those fleeing towards the Florida Keys might have had better luck, but the fancy yachts anchoring there didn't wait for long. And staying on the islands wasn't an option.

The radio claimed that millions were stuck at the Mexican border despite the shoot to kill order, while both friendly and enemy military vessels appeared on the waters of the coastline…

…or that the smaller settlements had organized their own defense in the countryside. That armed militants helped nobody and let no one pass.

After hearing this, the colony voted, and the majority wanted to stay. Those who still wanted to go, demanding their own portion from storage, were forced to hand over their ignition keys and despite Nelson's begging, they were badly beaten up. The kind little colony by the edge of town turned into *Lord of the Flies* in a flash, where the ends ruthlessly justified the means.

Nelson pulled aside his favorite armchair, the one he'd gotten from his wife, from which he used to sit by the wheels of his truck and cast a happy eye on his empire. He pulled it into the cover of the shadows, where he was less visible, and where he was less tempted to see the doings of others. He sat more and more in the half-shade and locked his door sooner after sunset, so that nobody would bother him with anything stupid. He pondered the idea that this was not at all what he'd had in mind.

Maybe I should've left? Alone…

Meanwhile the colony became a self-organizing commune, and at the edge of Liberty, in the safety of the junkyard, it seemed as if things were getting back to normal. However, destiny was just taking a deep breath, and when it exhaled, the breeze disturbed their small-town tranquility. At the end of the second year, a reconnaissance team returned with a special package, and everyone in the colony could see the corpse of a feral which had been shot dead on the highway.

"Otherwise, no one would have believed us," the thin, scar-faced reconnaissance leader said, keeping his gun trained on the feral thrown in the dust. His silver Smith & Wesson was unwavering, as if the danger were not completely over.

The carcass stank and flies were swarming around it, but most people were upset because of the feral's distorted face. The scar-faced man lifted its arm and showed the elongated, deformed fingers.

"Not even God can explain this horror," Grant Wyers grunted out, scratching his forehead under his cowboy hat.

"Well, I'd be glad if someone tried to," Nelson said, but he looked around pointlessly. Everyone else was stunned into silence.

In a couple of weeks, they realized that the shocking souvenir wasn't an isolated case, and as the ferals became stronger, everyone admitted that in Liberty there were far too many sightings. By the end of the year, a few hungry ferals even broke into the junkyard, and a gang of thugs tried to snare one of the reconnaissance teams on the other side of town.

So, they voted again, and the majority wanted to leave. Everyone had ideas, but only Nelson's seemed useful, when he suggested that the hidden ranger cottage should be their new headquarters. He planned the fortress minutely, and they barricaded the cottage and the old well just like their ancestors had done in the laagers.

Then, at the end of the long, busy week of preparations, the Purple Urkle came out of his Saverette, deeply relaxing, sleep inducing, and a great option for full body pain relief. The smoke-snakes of the languid siesta blew Nelson away into the distant past. In front of the cottage, sinking into his favorite armchair, where everyone could see him and he could see everyone, memories of his youth came back to him. The first house he helped build; enjoying the fruits of his labor, receiving a paycheck for the first time; getting to know new people, making new friends. He had the same vibe then and now, that life was finally going somewhere, and they could turn their destiny around.

"It ain't hopeless," he growled under his nose, as he glanced through their new home. A pale smile appeared on his raspy face, under his white beard. "It ain't Patagonia, but it'll do..."

2.

The colony was still far from finished, but Nelson could finally do what he was best at and what he loved most, organizing the construction with precision. He had all the trees in the surrounding area cut down in order to build a fortress and a watchtower on pylons.

The cottage became a central space, and later not only did they add greenhouses and allotments, but also a small tract of land in the valley, where they grew potatoes, peppers and soy, although without much success in the beginning. They even solved the fuel problem with the help of David Carter, who was clear evidence of the fact that even the greatest fools of the old world get a second chance.

After a long dispute, David, who had flunked out of college, was taken in to maintain the vehicles. He was quite capable at it, despite a few misdemeanors here and there. A lot of people were angry because David hated working, but he was damn good at growing weed, so he was able to get on the right side of the old man. During a common smoking session, the idea of biodiesel popped out of their minds and took them out of their misery.

They didn't see it as a perfect solution, but nobody complained after the Breakdown. It was a miracle that they were all still alive, considering all they had seen over the years as the virus created and tormented the ferals. And what was even more shocking were the stories told by passing strangers they met once in a while on the neighboring roads, stories that couldn't be explained.

A grumpy man named John told them about ex-soldiers organizing a resistance in Boston during the second wave, and door by door they tried to reclaim the suburbs. By then, the provisional government only controlled a few military bases, and they were preoccupied by negotiations with the British, who were whining on the other coast of the ocean that the virus might spread over to them. The West Coast was under blockade by the Chinese, who shot at everything they could, while in the south the refugee crisis had resulted in chaos.

The Bostonians could only count on themselves. And, of course, the Icelandic smugglers who brought food and equipment in exchange for any American souvenir that they could sell in other parts of the world. They got the most for videos depicting ferals.

However, after the success of the first years, something happened. In the beginning they lost connection with the drones sent out for reconnaissance, but in later years entire troops vanished as if something had trapped the veterans not yet broken in Afghanistan.

"But the most terrifying is yet to come!" John warned, gripping his hot tea. "A few days later one of the troops found some wacky fool. He had curled up in an old apartment building. He was the type of guy who must have looked the same before the Breakdown: greasy hair, patchwork clothes. A real bum; I guess you can picture him."

"Sure I can," Nelson growled, waiting for him to continue.

"The guy had been watching something for weeks, but we had a hard time getting him to tell us what was so freakin' interesting."

"And?"

"He realized that the ferals that used to hunt in huge hordes have started to gather up in smaller packs and stalk their poor victims like wolves. And the packs were led by the ones bitten at the beginning of the pandemic. The deformed, I guess you know who I mean."

"Yep."

"And what's more, the packs started dividing the city amongst themselves… and our little fool said, if you want to live, you don't go to Revere. He believed some really ancient evil was hiding there."

"Bullshit!"

"That's what we first thought. Ancient evil, my ass! Then another patrol disappeared, but one guy just had time to report on his radio. You know what his last words were?

"No."

"He said that the bastard was damn right. Guess which part of town they were in."

"Revere?"

"Yeah..."

John was a real goldmine regarding news, but a few weeks later he ran off on them, as well. He was headed to the south, hoping he could cross the Mexican border. Even though Nelson told him they knew absolutely nothing about either the Brownsville path or the Hidalgo bridge, John did not want to stay, and set off the next morning.

They never heard of him again, just like the Boston resistance. Some time later they met an entire caravan from Massachusetts. The travelers had heard legends of hard as nails soldiers, but none had risked approaching the city or the evil it might have contained. The mystery seemed unsolvable, at least from the relatively comfortable distance of the colony, and in any case, it was far from the only enigma facing them.

The field radio stations in Mexico were silenced after a while, leaving only rare reports from amateurs in Cuba or Australia. They learned from a guy in La Habana that even if you could cross a slowly collapsing Mexico, survivors were being shot in both the Panama Canal and in the open waters beyond. The guy told them that naval ships and drones were patrolling near the coast so that no one could get out.

Nelson tried not to think about how hopeless the situation might be in a metropolis, where millions had locked themselves up in their homes waiting for the quarantine to end and then those same millions had set off after the watchdog report from Associated Press. The locked-down cities proved to be perfect incubators, where beasts came to life below the concrete jungles, thriving under infernal circumstances. It was only a matter of time before they would break the blockade.

The Zone, neglected by the outside world, grew on and became more silent than ever. Since help did not arrive from Beyond, most colonies raised walls, locked the gates, and made their own laws. Those who were clever enough or lucky enough would rise up only to sink into the waters of memory because of a careless moment or a devastating attack. There were colonies that they could talk to cheerfully on the radio one night, and then never hear from again. Success stories became increasingly rare. Only the boat-town in the east and the mountain colony in Idaho were able to properly develop because the issue of food had been addressed, so the people who steadily came to join them could all be fed.

Nelson and his company had no such luck. After they had looted the nearby shops and left no stone unturned in Liberty, the colony slowly ran out of opportunities. Following the previous year's poor harvest, they had a feeling that this year's wouldn't be enough to pull them out of their misery, and the last straw was decreasing their rations by half.

"What can we do?" Nelson asked, seeing the discontent.

"There is a colony, in the east… by the river. It might be worth a try," someone said, and more and more demanded a new vote. At last, Nelson also admitted that they needed a Plan B. But he didn't plan to act as chance directed.

3.

The task was simple. A smaller team would form a bridgehead along Route 10, thirty or forty miles from the cottage. By that time, they'd already been making contact with the boat-town for at least half a year. The colony was located on the eastern bank of the river, near Blue Springs. Nelson wanted to see how far they could get, but carefully.

Knowing their own limitations, it was tempting to think that the distant colony was a real river fortress: the people living there had pulled the ships together, some distance from the bank, and they provided food and living space for almost seven-hundred people. At least that was what they claimed…

However, the four-day journey seemed daunting. They couldn't go through the tunnel under the mountains, and they somehow needed to get through the city of Headland, which no sane person would enter. So, they decided to explore the roads and set up safe houses where they could shelter during the journey. Even though there were fewer ferals by then, the world outside the walls was still ruled by packs and thugs.

The first team, led by the now grown-up Aurora, would go around Liberty from the east to reach Route 10, but only as far as it was safe.

Then, a second excursion would move further, to the old motel by the junction of Route 285.

The only thing the old man asked Aurora was to take care. No unnecessary risk, no recklessness.

"Just be smart, lass!" Nelson told her, and she grinned like a Cheshire cat when they put their foreheads together.

The ironclad Jeep hit the road in the morning with four people on board, and even though the mission seemed routine, the group never returned. No one had the faintest idea what might have happened to them.

Therefore, on the fifth day they sent another unit after them, led by Grant. They found traces about twelve miles from Liberty. Aurora and the others were trapped and massacred. Due to the bites and the dismemberment of the bodies, it was clear that it could not have been looters. Nelson was taken aback by Grant's report.

The traces showed that the entire attack happened in a matter of moments, but the scouts didn't find any feral bodies. Aurora and her companions died in such a way that they couldn't kill a single enemy, although they'd fired at least a hundred bullets. Only a few limbs and dried puddles of blood remained, stretching like red canyons where the attackers had dragged away their prey.

And the report didn't end there: Grant opened up his leather-covered book and pulled out a folded up, smudgy sheet of paper, red with old blood. It was an imprint that Grant had taken from one of the victims: the red spots in a semi-circle corresponded to bite marks. Nelson stared at the imprint, astonished. The bite was huge, as if not even from human jaws.

"How is this possible?" the gathered crowd asked.

In the course of the following week, they started to understand the gruesome possibilities.

4.

The nighttime attack caught them off guard. The two watchmen were overwhelmed so quickly they were unable to raise the alarm. The attackers didn't get into the colony, although some speculated the ferals chose not to go further. Grant, looking at the evidence, was convinced that the pack were probing them, looking for weak points.

They climbed up to the watchtower in the darkest hour of the night and killed the watchmen so quietly that no one woke up.

"They could have massacred everyone," said Nelson.

"And we wouldn't even have noticed," replied somebody from the gathered crowd. Nelson suspected it was David, but he couldn't see clearly because the person immediately bent over to vomit in the back row with a loud retching sound.

Nelson watched Grant, puzzled, as he descended from the tower wiping his bloody hands. It was the first time the old man had no idea what to do. He wanted to yell at Grant to hurry up and speak at last. He needed answers. He had slept less and less since the first team had disappeared, and he felt panic pressing down on him more and more often. And the crowd started whispering.

"Easy, folks!" Grant said and tipped his taupe-colored cowboy hat up straight. Once again, he looked up at the watchtower, but simply scratched the edge of his lips with two fingers, as if his thick mustache was bothering him. His yellow teeth flashed as he despondently pulled up his gum. He had an unpleasant, rusty voice. "Well… I ain't gonna lie, we have a pretty wild situation here. It wasn't no bunch of Greenhorn who done that."

"Shit!" said Nelson. He could practically smell the panic in the air. "What are we gonna do?"

"You guys? Nothing!"

Somebody snorted in the crowd.

"Nothing? Then we're all gonna be massacred in our sleep?" A bald, bearded man in a flannel shirt asked, and others argued around him. Nelson desperately watched the terror infecting his people.

"What if it was the same pack?"

"Impossible!"

"Why would it be?"

"Because it's your idea, buddy!"

"You can suck it whenever I'm in the mood for your toothless mug…"

"Shut up!" Grant raised both hands, but the pushing only slowly subsided. "Y'all're fighting like a bunch-a-kids in a sandbox!"

Silence.

"Most idiots ain't gonna do nothing! Why?" Grant looked at the bald, bearded man in the flannel shirt, who dropped his eyes. "It's because you ain't got the courage in your limp dicks, that's why… and pardon my French, ladies."

The crowd grumbled. Mostly the ladies.

"Now everyone get some breakfast, if your stomach is fit for it, and I'mma go out and look around. Need me two volunteers!" Grant glanced at Nelson, who nodded. But before Grant could turn to the few eager, younger men, Nelson quickly added:

"I'll be one of them!"

After a beat of hesitation, Grant shrugged his shoulders.

"As you wish, boss."

Suddenly someone in the distance let out a desperate scream. Someone within their walls. The crowd immediately turned towards the sound, but Grant was the first to realize what was happening and he was the first to reach the van parked behind the cottage. A gray-haired woman leaned on the hood. She wiped the sweat from her forehead with her cardigan sleeve, then pointed her finger under the minivan, as if she was about to say something important: even more important than what had happened in the watchtower. Behind the wheels, in the dust, a skinny little boy was huddled up, his body shaking like a leaf.

Grant crouched down and immediately noticed the bulging eyes that looked into emptiness, a look he had seen a thousand times over the past few years.

"Sammy… can you hear me?"

He tried to touch the boy, who shook and cowered back. The stalled crowd hissed.

"He didn't get bitten, did he?"

"Don't think so," Grant replied and tried to catch the boy's gaze. But Sammy's brain was in shock and would not let go.

Grant hesitated, whether he should ask the obvious. Finally, he did.

"You saw what happened, didn't ya?"

The boy nodded.

5.

After the crisis meeting, they doubled the guards, but nobody would volunteer to go outside besides Grant and Nelson. After what Sammy said, a sane person would only have gone into the woods with an entire army behind them. But these people were not soldiers, and the colony was no training camp.

"I saw something... I hid right away, but it spotted me... I know it spotted me..."

The sobbing boy was comforted by David's sister, Megan. She stroked the boy's face with one hand and her round stomach with the other. "You know what, Sammy? I guess you deserve a bit of candy. What do you think?"

She looked up at the others with a smile, but her sky-blue eyes flashed seriously behind her long, chestnut hair. Grant nodded, went to the kitchen cupboard and took a Hershey's bar from a near empty shelf. The younger ones had jealous looks, but watched quietly while the adults started murmuring.

"And you? Don't you want a tiny bite for yourself, sweetheart?" the gray-haired woman in the cardigan asked scornfully, pointing her finger at Megan's stomach. "We all know, you need it now more than ever."

Nelson just shook his head in the background. Inside, he laughed ironically at himself, at what a fool he had been to think they could turn their destiny around with a couple of four-wheelers. Nothing changed and nothing got better.

But maybe the harvest... maybe now, he thought to himself while the crowd tried to shout each other down around him.

"That's enough!" Grant ordered and handed the chocolate bar to Megan.

"Thank you!" Megan whispered. She looked up at him gratefully, but Grant had already turned to watch the murmuring crowd, his face like stone.

Megan opened the chocolate wrapping and kindly slipped it into the boy's hand. "All right, Sammy, everything's gonna be just fine, right?"

The skinny boy nodded vaguely.

"No shit it's gonna be just fine!" said the thin, scar-faced man in the background. "What did the bastard look like? Ask him if he saw it!"

Grant crouched down by the boy and looked through Megan as if she wasn't even there. She watched him out of the corner of her eyes, and just like everyone else she was waiting for answers.

It can't be that bad! Nelson leaned closer as well.

"It was a needle-tooth..."

6.

Why didn't it attack Sammy? What did the bastard want? Nelson asked himself as he crept through the woods behind Grant and the scar-faced man. He was afraid the answer might be more frightening than anything he could imagine.

The trail was tough and he was wearing down from the strain. He felt the weight of the shotgun he'd been able to wear all day long just a few years before. He saw the scar-faced man observing the woods with shivering lips, the silver Smith & Wesson shaking in his hands, but somehow Nelson was neither worried nor scared. He remembered Aurora and her last glance; the tiny dimples that made her smile so peculiar.

Finally, he began to be honest with himself. Over the past few days he had tried to explain to himself the things that were happening, but this morning his conscience was straining his throat. *What the hell is the use of all this?*

The old man knew he had sent someone to their death, someone who had only lived a third of the life he had, all the while he preached hope and endurance to the others. His mind kept circling back to the idea that nothing would change if they destroyed this pack. Others would come the next day. They didn't even have to be ferals, and someone among them would die...

They found the remains of the younger guard in the valley around noon, near the brook, by a mossy rock. The guard was easily identifiable by his watch. The scar-faced man seemed about to get sick as he watched Grant examining the stump of the hand.

"How many can they be?"

"Eight, ten at most."

"Sure? Or are you also just asking, my friend?"

Grant pulled up his gum. He tried to smile.

"We ain't seen a larger pack so far, right?"

"Hope they know that too!"

"Shouldn't we get out of here?" the scar-faced man asked.

Nelson looked around suspiciously. He had lived through enough not to ignore others' concerns, and he felt some unpleasant shivers running down his spine. His eyes ran among the gray-brown trunks of the trees and the green curtain of leaves that impeded the view. The old man noticed that the birds had gone silent and the wind had settled. The tree branches above them weren't moving, and the babble of the brook masked any tiny, giveaway noises.

"Let's get the hell outta here!" the scar-faced man hissed, but Grant shushed him.

"Shut up! Nobody move!"

Nelson held his breath, but the forest didn't want to talk to him. Or didn't dare. Nothing moved among the trees, and he calmed himself with the fact that if the ferals had actually followed them, they would be dead by now. Still, he couldn't explain the shivering up his spine. He turned to Grant as slowly as he could and whispered as quietly as possible:

"Can you see anything?"

"Up there, by the rock!"

Nelson glanced towards the ridge, where the curtain of leaves along the horizon was intercut by a smaller slope. But he didn't see anything. "You sure about that?"

"What the hell are you whispering about?" the scar-faced man asked.

"Quiet, you idiot!" Grant shushed him, and carefully readied his gun. He watched the rock motionlessly, hoping he might see what he had sensed. "Go… but no running! Understood?"

Nelson immediately nodded. The scar-faced man needed some time for the words to reach his brain, then he swallowed.

It was only when they arrived at the cottage that Grant told Nelson what had been in his mind. Nelson silently listened as he explained that they had probably found the place where the ferals went to drink, and that they could potentially take advantage of the discovery.

"Do you think anyone would be stupid enough to give it a try?"

"You're the boss… So start bossing!"

After a few hours of thinking, Nelson admitted that Grant was right, and in the late afternoon they gathered in front of the cottage to vote. Everyone was terrified by the events of the past few days and by Grant's reports, so Nelson was grateful that the colony didn't panic and devolve into chaos.

"What are we gonna do?" somebody from the crowd asked.

Grant looked hesitantly at Nelson, who remained silent. It was Grant who finally told them about the plan.

"We're gonna set a trap for them bastards!"

7.

Megan Carter had something terrible in her past. It frightened everybody in the colony, even her brother, David. Most people would've already thrown her to the wolves; even Grant had had some similar thoughts, although he would have given almost anything to see his child be born. But not at this cost… not like this, ignoring the risks…

Nelson was more sober and fortunately there were others in the colony who thought that a pregnant woman (no matter her history) was untouchable. The old man would always say to Megan that what had happened was a miracle and that miracles were meant to be accepted, not destroyed.

"Yeah, a real miracle… And what've I won with that," Megan said when she heard this, because she had seen how the last two births in the colony had ended. Her companions were afraid of the horrible things she might bring about, a fear was aggravated by the fact that Nelson had ordered that her ration not only wasn't to be cut in half, but raised instead.

She felt the others' behavior towards her was unjust, but she was more focused on the fact that the baby shouldn't be born in a place like their patchwork home. Only the eastern colony, the boat-town, would be safe enough, and she felt they should go rather than stay.

"You know it, too. This isn't sustainable," Megan said to David over dinner. He winced. Even he was afraid to argue with her, particularly an argument they had already had.

"What else can we do?" he asked, and involuntarily lowered his voice. "The move can't be rushed. Nelson said so."

"Rushed? Jesus Christ, David, a herd of snails moves faster than we do!"

The clinking of the cutlery gradually got quieter in the cottage. David leaned closer to her and started whispering. He nervously wiped his hair back. "You can gripe at me, but you saw what happened to Aurora and the others!"

"One more reason not to wait until we're massacred too! Do you think the ferals will stop?" Megan burst out, which made Nelson, who was sitting at a distant table in front of the stone fireplace, pick up on the conversation. He meticulously wiped his lips and gave a slight cough.

"Is anything wrong, my dear?"

Megan and David darted a glance at him at the same time, like two children caught in some mischief. David frowned at her, hoping to silence her, but Megan glanced at the others' plates, at their rations split in half, and that was enough.

"Yes," she said, while David closed his eyes. "We all know how this will end! When will we admit that we need help?"

"Megan!" Grant's deep voice was a warning in the awkward silence. Nelson shushed him, then turned to Megan, who felt that this was her last chance to persuade anyone. She rose, huffing.

"Somebody has to say what everyone else is afraid to. If we stay here, we're all going to die!" Megan looked at her brother for help, but David leaned forwards, hoping that nobody would notice him perching in the background like a human question mark.

Everybody turned to Nelson. Grant watched the old man and waited for his reaction, elbows on the table, his head resting on his fists. Nelson cleared his throat.

"This is our home, Megan," he said, and when he spread his arms, his look reflected a sparkle of genuine wonderment. "Would you leave it so easily?"

"For the hope of a better life? Yes, I would!"

Some of them hissed, others exchanged looks, so she pushed her chair back and shuffled to the map on the wall. The map showing the southern waterfront was so old that the edges had ripped and curled, but the essence was still clear to see. The lower third was ruled by the blue sea of the bay and a couple of tiny islands, while the upper two thirds were dominated by a green-brown blend of land. Liberty was somewhere on the left side, and a long blue line on the right marked the river running to the bay.

Megan took a pin from the edge of the map and with a defiant movement she placed it onto the northern part of the river. Everybody could see that Liberty was hundreds of miles away from the boat-town.

"I know, it seems far, but they have everything we might need… a safe roof over our heads, food… doctors and medicine."

"How do you know they told us the truth?" Grant asked. Megan got distracted for a moment and gave a perplexed smile.

"Why would they lie to us?"

Someone laughed in the background, and Megan looked around ungracefully. She desperately tried to grasp back the reins, while the others shook their heads and grinned awkwardly. Megan turned back to the map.

"Their leader told us everything… If we don't want to, we won't have to live on the boats. In the upper part of the river, a cabin was put up on pylons for the fishermen, and they also have a farm, where they work in a field ten times as large as ours. They have plenty of water and food, and if we don't want to completely integrate with them, they can provide men to help us build another farm. They ensure protection, and we can trade with them… Say something Trevor!" Megan turned to the bald, bearded man in the flannel shirt who listened to her dully, his arms folded on his chest. Trevor took a deep breath and shrugged his shoulders.

"Yes, that's what we were talking about on the radio… of course, it could be bullshit."

"It's not what you said yesterday."

"No, but I told you we'll see when we get there! We've heard stories like this."

"That's right!" the thin, scar-faced man nodded at the other table. "We've worked like hell to make things better here!"

"And why would they want to help us?" the gray-haired woman in the cardigan asked.

Megan spread her arms.

"They want to help because they need us too! They have hardly any reliable mechanics. Just to have help from David, they would give us lots of seeds..."

"Huh!" the scar-faced man snorted, a sardonic grin on his face. "They're bloody idiots, man! They've no sense for business!"

"Hahaha... I'll die laughing!" David leaned closer, then looked down, embarrassed. Megan spoke more and more vigorously.

"We told them about you. Trevor, nobody knows more about radios than you... Tina, don't you think they need a teacher, when a hundred children live on the boats? And Linda, they asked twice about you, because their best tailor died in the spring..."

"Is that right?" The woman in the cardigan asked and blushed.

Megan nodded and spread her arms.

"Finally, we could live a normal life... but we can't wait for long. You know it, Grant! We already told you what they're planning."

All eyes turned to Grant, but he watched only Megan.

"What's this about, Grant?" the scar-faced man asked, but Grant didn't break under the weight of the questioning looks. He knew exactly what she was going to do and deep inside he grudgingly respected her for turning the tables so cleverly.

"You're doing great, Megan! Go ahead and steal the show!"

"I don't care who steals what, but say it, for God's sake!"

Megan straightened up.

"After the fall solstice they're going to blow up the Headland Bridge... And when they do it, we won't be able to cross the river. Then we might be stuck here forever."

8.

"They're going to blow it up? Why the hell would they do that?"

The grumbling grew louder and louder, so Grant cracked his neck and got up.

"All right, folks, that's enough! The boat-town is full of clever people, and if a bunch of clever people come up with a plan, it's bound to be brilliant, right?"

They looked at each other, scratching their heads.

"It ain't?"

"No, it's bullshit!" Grant promptly replied. "They want to blow up the bridge because they believe that the ferals can't cross the river."

"Is it so crazy?" Megan asked. "Within a year or two they could clear the whole area."

"And then what, Megan? You think you can have a nice walk with your baby in the wheatfields? Assuming that everything goes fine with the labor..."

"Enough of that!" Nelson burst out and got up. Grant raised both hands.

"All right, boss, all right... I'm also just saying what everyone else is afraid to!"

"And see what you've done with it!"

Nelson glanced at Megan, who was getting prepared to defend herself with quivering lips and flaming eyes. "Six have already died, Nelson! How many more need to die before you come to your senses?"

"Darling, what you're saying here is that we set off on a four-day journey with a bunch of old guys and some skinny kids to a colony where we'll either be welcomed or made into salami for the winter. You've heard those stories, too... And, by the way, do we even have enough fuel and ammunition for the trip?"

"No, boss, we probably don't," Grant said, staring straight ahead, not looking at Megan. Taking sixty people and cars into the unknown seemed like a real horror story to him. He'd much rather stay on home ground. "What's more, most of the trucks haven't even moved in the last few years. Not to mention the condition of the roads."

Grant slowly walked over to Megan. He looked at the map and shook his head.

"Do you even know what's going on out there, Megan?" he pointed at the long road that ran east to west, leading to the river. "Route 10 alone is a nightmare, and not only because of the ferals. It should've been cleared of all the rubble and other crap, and we can't even go through the tunnel, so we have to go around. Then, somehow, we have to pass the Pincers, but we don't know anywhere we could stop for the night. The motel at the crossroads could be fine, but who knows? And let's not even mention what'll happen when we reach Headland."

Grant took out a pin and he placed it on the city at the eastern part of Route 10. The others started whispering.

"What if we got around?" Megan asked.

Grant chuckled. "You don't just go around Headland. Did your friends at the boat-town not tell you that?"

"No," she answered.

Scornful murmuring intensified inside the cottage.

"Maybe it's not that dangerous anymore," said Megan with a huge amount of uncertainty. "Maybe the man-eaters moved or died."

Grant shrugged. "Maybe. And maybe my ma and pa are alive, just playing trick-or-treat somewhere."

"I wouldn't bet on that," Trevor sighed. "I mean that the man-eaters have bounced. The boat-town people say their patrol found strange trails at the bridge a couple of months ago. Traps and so little blood that it couldn't have been ferals. So, without recon it would be risky."

The scar-faced man and those around him started nodding. Grant continued.

"And if we cross the bridge, there's still at least a day's journey ahead of us until Blue Springs, where none of us has ever been. All we know is what your so-called friends said on the radio. The boat-town could be a goddamn lie... a trap, and we'd walk right into it without hesitation."

Grant took his hat off and combed back his thin, brown hair with his palm. He did this when he wanted to place extra emphasis on what he was saying. "If you weren't just huddled here inside, but would move beyond the walls and the fields once in a while, you would know. So don't tell us what to do."

They could hear the humming of the mosquitos. Grant clapped his hands. He looked around to make sure everyone was listening carefully.

"We all know the rules. Nobody will help us outside the Zone, trust no-one beyond the walls, and take nothing from anyone within the walls. We can only rely on ourselves!

Then he walked back to his seat.

Finally, Nelson broke the awkward silence.

"And let's not forget what would happen if you went into labor during the trip. In the worst moment, out there where we're all unprotected. You wouldn't want that either, right?"

Megan couldn't respond. The debate was over. Nelson glanced at her with a fatherly smile. She was disappointed to see the others' support vanishing.

"You see, Megan? As frightening the situation may seem, we must trust Grant's plan. If we can set a trap…"

"There is no if. We can!" Grant cut in, scrutinizing the faces of the others to make sure they believed what he had just said. Nelson cleared his throat, confused, then carried on.

"Well, yes. What matters is that we will solve this! Right?"

Some of them nodded, others chose to turn back to the poor, tasteless soup so that nobody could see their faces. Grant looked at his watch, then hurried to drink the last sip of his supper and got up, hoping that moving would help him forget about his hunger.

"All right, folks, we're leaving at first light! Until then get some rest!"

9.

It was a starry, humid night as the ten-member team passed through the gate loaded up with weapons and ammunition. They disappeared one after the other among the dark trees. Nelson and Trevor locked the heavy wooden gate behind them. Everyone except the children was milling around the trucks and vans, worried at the possibility that their loved ones and friends could disappear into the darkness forever.

Later, when they had all locked themselves up in their trucks, the old man sat down in front of the cottage, in his favorite armchair. He placed his shotgun next to himself on the ground and slid his hand towards his pocket, but in the end he didn't light up. He just scanned the dark-blue sky and the softly vibrating stars.

He inhaled the silence and thought about the team taking their position above the brook. Grant must be whispering commands, while his companions sought out the best hideouts. All motion slowly ceasing among the dark trees, and the hours of waiting to come.

This was the moment when hope hung above the abyss on a thin string, and there was no knowing yet whether it would fall or hold. He remembered the evening debate, and he became so depressed that he didn't have the strength even to try to persuade himself. *Who am I trying to fool? Even if we kill them… there's still no guarantee that everything is going to be all right.*

If they stayed, the pack would decimate them, he was sure about that, but if they set off, half of the group would die during the trip. Whatever happened, it would be held against him.

He didn't realize how much time had passed; he only noticed one of the truck doors creak open. Megan stood at the door, wrapped in a soft blanket. The fresh air made her shiver, so she pulled the blanket tight, careful not to fall, and shuffled over to Nelson with a frayed rug, which she lay over his bony back.

"You shouldn't be out here," he said vaguely. "You know, it's dangerous."

"And you?" she asked, then sat down in the grass and leaned back.

"What do you care about me?"

Megan didn't say a word. Instead, she watched the dawning horizon with her sky-blue eyes. Her long thin fingers held tightly onto the blanket at her stomach. She straightened out the blanket across her belly, and as the wind blew in her chestnut hair, Nelson could smell the delicate chamomile scent around her.

"David?" the old man asked.

"What do you think?"

They started laughing at the same time.

"Good for him… I don't even feel like sleeping."

A bird gave a frightening shriek in the distance and they both looked that way with their breath held tautly, scared expressions on their faces. Then silence returned. Nelson swallowed hard and smiled fitfully. He nodded towards the cottage.

"Have I told you that I helped build this?"

"You missed that somehow," Megan winked.

"I'm not saying I instantly fell in love with the smell of waste wood, but time brings back good memories... and makes it truly hard to leave a place that has so many memories."

"Did you tell that story to Judy, too?"

Nelson's face clouded over.

"Judy wouldn't have survived labor in the boat-town either, you know that."

Megan dropped her eyes.

"And what if you're wrong?"

"And what if I'm not?"

A dull sound intensified from the direction of the brook, as if the woods in the forest had suppressed the sound of a scream. Nelson and Megan didn't even realize that the crickets were no longer chirping and the trees above them weren't rustling anymore. The old man gazed into the distance and thought of Aurora. The last moment he saw her.

"You see, this is what I'm afraid of," he said at last. "There is no right decision, no right way, and someone is going to die because of me, that's for sure. I know. Sometimes I think, you'd all be better off with Grant, not a Dream Weaver like me."

"Perhaps you just need to rest a bit."

"Rest?"

"You know, go on holiday, like back in the old days. Far away from here. Somewhere there's peace and quiet."

Nelson grinned.

"You want to push me out of here?"

"If it helps, I can fire you myself. You won't even get your two weeks' notice, just leave!"

"And they thought I was the Wise."

They burst out laughing. Megan nodded at the trucks and vans. Her happy smile slowly faded. Her droopy nose trembled restlessly.

"Don't think I'm wise... It's just that I know you all well. I know what you want... what you're really longing for..."

"Do tell me."

"Most of you want safety, what else? They'll hold out here until the very end instead of having to face insecurity. And when enough people have died, they'll vote against you and betray you. But it might be too late by then..."

Nelson gazed at her, speechless.

"And what about me? Am I just a fool, too damn loyal to the home I built for myself?"

"This place is not our home, you know that... and there's a long road ahead until we find it," Megan said, and placed her soft, warm palm on his hand. "For you and for me."

The distant, desperate scream and the corresponding gunfire could no longer be hidden by the woods. It echoed among the first thin sunbeams of the dawn as if splinters of glass had been dancing in the wind.

Then more and more followed.

10.

"The gates! Quick!"

The chaos woke everyone up. Nelson and Trevor opened the wooden gates. They were covered by two women, and the others were prepared for the worst. Adrenaline blew the dreams out of their eyes, and people began whispering restlessly. A buck-toothed young boy ran up to the tower to get a better look.

Megan stood in front of the cottage holding Nelson's gun, which the old man had given her so that she could protect herself. David stepped out of the truck with a sleepy face, wiping his eyes.

"What the hell happened?"

"I don't know, but I have a bad feeling," Megan said.

Nelson pointed into the distance.

"I can see something."

As the gates opened wide, the dusty road paved with trees sank into the valley. In the half-light they spotted two people staggering along the road, slowly separating from the dawn light.

"Is that Grant?" Trevor asked as the two approached. Grant was supporting the scar-faced man. He kept glancing nervously behind him. His rifle was still smoking in his right hand.

"Cover me!" Nelson signaled, and the women raised their guns high.

Together with Trevor and Linda, he rushed to help Grant, but when they reached their compatriots they were taken aback. Linda groaned. Trevor stepped back and quietly cursed. Only Nelson wasn't bothered by the blood and the chunks of flesh. He put his arm around the scar-faced man to help Grant carry him to the gate. When they got there, they carefully laid him down in the dust. He was barely alive, short of breath, spitting blood. He had been bitten on the neck.

"Lock it, quick!" Grant gasped, then he grabbed a water bottle from somebody and took a big gulp. Trevor latched the gates.

The others, who had been standing around stunned, pulled away from the dying man one after another. Linda was playing with her cardigan sleeve, confused. The scar-faced man squirmed in the dust and raised his hands up towards them as if he wanted someone to touch him, it didn't matter who, just someone to pull him back into the real world. Festering spots had already appeared where he'd been mauled, and thin, black lines inched upwards, straight towards his skull.

Nelson watched his suffering partner, perplexed. He knew the poor soul didn't have the slightest chance. "And the others? What about them?" he asked, but Grant furiously dismissed his question.

"We had no fucking chance! It was a trap, and we were taken down one by one. Some of them were able to run off towards the valley… if they were lucky, they might have reached the fields and hidden in the cabin."

"Yeah, as if they're safe there." Trevor shook his head, then pointed his finger at the scar-faced man. "And why the hell did you bring him here?"

"Believe me, none of this mess was a part of my plan!" Grant took a threatening step, which made Trevor back off.

"A pack of ferals can't kill ten armed people. This is… impossible!" said Nelson.

"This was no ordinary pack, old man! Never in my life have I seen anything like this… There were almost twenty and I only managed to put a bullet in two of them!"

The crowd flared up, and Nelson looked around with a pale face. "Shouldn't we go down there? To see if anyone else survived?"

"I'm not going back there today!" Grant said, and the others nodded ardently. Meanwhile, a stubby guy pried the silver Smith & Wesson from the scar-faced man's hand, checked the bullets, and placed the revolver in his pocket. Grant took an angry step towards him, blocking his way. "Hey, hey! What the hell are you doing?"

"What do you think? He won't need it anymore."

"I don't give a damn! You know the rules," he nodded towards the two women. "The corpse is taken care of by the women, and they will distribute his possessions. There will be no looting here!"

Grant stretched out his hand, and the stubby guy reluctantly passed him the handgun. Megan pushed her way through the crowd. She crouched down next to the injured man and took a vial of morphine out of a metal box. She carefully gave the morphine to the crying, retching man. He let out a cry and tried to squirm, but he had hardly any strength. He spit blood and a couple of drops landed on Megan; then he slowly slid into a daze.

Grant gave his head a scratch.

"I hope it was worth the waste!"

"You're a jerk!" Megan got up and tried to wipe the blood off of herself, but instead she smeared it even further on her clothes and neck.

"Okay, and now?" somebody from the crowd asked.

Nelson looked his companions up and down, and saw most of them drop their eyes. None of them wanted to speak.

"Everyone barricades themselves in until harvest. Those of you whose home isn't safe enough will be placed somewhere else. Then we'll vote after harvest."

"If we survive!" Megan added.

Nelson lashed out. "We don't have any other choice, Megan, you have to understand!"

Just then, the buck-toothed boy exclaimed in the tower, pointing insistently into the distance. In the direction Grant and the scar-faced man had come from.

"Hey! Look! Over there!"

As fast as his old bones let him, Nelson scrambled up the tower to see what was happening. He froze when he saw what was in front of him.

"What can that be, Mr. Nelson?" the boy asked, lisping.

Thick, gray-black smoke was drifting from the direction of their fields, up towards the hills, but the trees made it impossible to see the source. Nelson had a bad feeling, and anxiety tied a knot in his throat.

"Get the jeeps ready!" he shouted to the others. "We're going down to the fields!"

The crowd started grumbling loudly. Grant waved to David and Trevor, who reluctantly set off to start the two remaining shellproof jeeps. The swirling smoke could now be seen even from the gates as it stretched its thick, dark arms into the sky.

Grant looked up at Nelson. Neither of them said a word, but their expressions gave them away. They both had a good guess about what had happened.

When the old man started down, Grant looked at the scar-faced man, whose body lay curled up and motionless in the dust, his head dropped back, his eyes glazed. He was no longer conscious. He suffered no more.

Grant took out his gun and pulled the trigger without hesitation. When the echo of the shot had ceased, he glanced at Nelson.

"Let's see if we're right!"

11.

By the time they reached the valley, most of the crops were on fire and the devastation seemed unstoppable. The fire turned the fields into a raging, hellish landscape. The first jeep, the old Mercedes, went as far as it could, then it braked beside the ruins of a newly charred cabin that coughed thick clouds of smoke.

David's hands had been shaking on the way over, but seeing one of the burnt remains as he sat behind the wheel, he couldn't take it any longer and opened the window, retching.

"Are you out of your mind?" yelled Grant from the passenger seat, but Nelson shushed him. David leaned back, coughing, and closed the window as he wiped his running nose.

"What the hell happened?" he asked, but Grant just shrugged.

"It could have been self-immolation. That's what I would've done… I'd rather choose death by burning!"

"Bullshit!" David whimpered as he sadly watched the flames eat up the crops. The fire reflected in his eyes and the gray-black fumes swirled relentlessly into the skies.

Grant turned back to Nelson, who was already bracing himself to go out there. "It's all the same what happened," the old man said finally and got out of the car.

David watched him, frightened, but Grant figured there was nothing more to worry about, so he followed Nelson. As they got out, the heat and the smell of the burnt crops hit their faces. The choking cloud of smoke irritated their eyes.

Grant glanced at the old man. Nelson shook his head.

"That's it… Everything we worked so hard for…"

"Let's go back, boss! We'll discuss it in the camp!"

Grant opened the back door of the Mercedes, but Nelson didn't move. He gazed at the fire, his lips quivering. Trevor edgily shouted at them from the second jeep, the rattletrap Wrangler.

"Are we waiting for the fire fighters, or what?"

"We're going back!" Grant replied.

Trevor nodded and started reversing, revving the Wrangler's engine. The spray of dust under the tires and the roar of the engine brought Nelson back to reality and he wearily sank back into the car. Before Grant could shut the door, they exchanged a look.

"What are we going to do now?" he asked, despondent, but Grant didn't say a word.

12.

When they arrived at the bottom of the hill Nelson had a bad feeling, even before the weathered, gray piles of the camp could be seen. A strange nausea caused him to squirm apprehensively as he gazed tensely at the dusty road. When he saw the gates were wide open, he knew immediately that something horrible had happened. And what's more, in front of the fortress, a couple of yards from the piles, there was something on the road.

"What… the… hell?" David craned his neck, but none of them could tell who had thrown a big brown bag in front of the gate, or why.

It was only when they got closer that they realized the brown bag was actually the stubby man's prone body. And when the two jeeps slowed down at the gate, the devastation unfolded. Life had frozen in the camp. Even those who had survived the attack were catatonic.

Near-demonic power had pushed one of the vans to the side, the windows of the cottage were broken, and the residents were lying hacked up in unnatural positions in the middle of the camp. About a dozen of them.

Nelson and Grant jumped out of the jeep simultaneously. David only left the vehicle when he saw Megan. She was standing at the door of their truck, shivering, with the old man's shotgun in her hands.

And as the morning sunshine tumbled over the fence from the east, all the tiny details of the horror revealed themselves…

…the torn female upper body caught on the wooden fence…

…an arm, ripped off and sunk into the bloody dust…

…a bloody palm print on the side of a truck showing that someone had tried desperately to get a grip before being dragged away…

…empty cartridge cases…

…and blood, blood everywhere.

Megan inched closer to them with shaking legs. Nelson and David had to catch her.

"What happened? I told you to barricade yourselves in!"

"We did, but… it didn't help! The monsters only wanted to kill…"

The anguished woman let her brother fully embrace her. Nelson took a few steps away and took stock. The suffering froze around them, and absorbed into the dust like drops of blood. Eleven of their companions had died in the attack, while they'd only managed to kill one feral. One that hadn't even begun to deform. A Greenhorn, as a traveler aptly named them previously.

"What kind of beasts are they?"

Nelson sat down in the dust. Grant threw his hat on the ground.

Most people were crying.

Seeing the devastation, nobody imagined that things would get better anytime soon. Not even Nelson the Wise.

13.

Finally, the members of the colony between Keley Pond and Deserter Creek packed up, but there was one among them who chose a different way. And no matter how hard they tried to persuade him, Nelson wouldn't change his decision.

"Don't do this, old man!" they said to him, but he just smiled. He had never been so certain about anything.

"If I don't do it now, when will I? I fear that more than biting the dust!"

The members of the colony took turns saying goodbye to him. Some with a few kind words, others with a simple handshake. David made his way over to him, wiping his greasy hands. He nodded at the old man's truck.

"I took a look at her. I'm not saying she's in perfect shape, but she might hold out. To be on the safe side, I've packed some spare parts, in case you need to replace something."

Nelson nodded gratefully, then patted David's shoulder. The young man just sniffled and wiped his nose in embarrassment. He was lost for words. "Thank you. For everything," he said finally.

Nelson raised his index finger, as if he had saved the most important for last. He dug into his pocket and placed his Saverette in David's hand. He held the plastic joint holder like a magic wand.

"For old times' sake. But don't waste it!" The old man grinned and David nodded emotionally before he hurried to the Mercedes.

Nelson glanced at Megan, who was standing in front of the cottage holding her stomach, with a wide smile but sorrowful eyes. She was waiting to be alone with the old chap.

"So, you'll finally sign up for that holiday, right?"

"Sure I will!" Nelson said with an honest smile. Like someone who can at last be really free, free from all burdens. "Promise me that you'll reach the colony safe and sound!"

"I promise!"

"And don't you worry about the others. We all know how special you are."

Megan bit her lip.

"Send me a postcard!"

They burst out laughing. Megan hugged him with tears in her eyes, holding him tight and close, then she got into the jeep beside David. She watched Nelson through the window with her head bowed.

Not having enough fuel, the group had only prepared half of the vehicles. The rest they took apart, packing everything useful in the convoy. They attached a plow to the front of the Wrangler against any obstacles in the road, and they fixed a machine gun on the tailgate of the Mercedes. Grant ordered them to leave enough fuel for Nelson's truck.

Once everyone was ready for departure, Grant dusted himself off and walked over to Nelson, who was smiling nervously.

"Get round the Pincers in the direction of the old quarry and don't stop before the intersection!" Nelson said. "If everything works out fine, you'll get there by tomorrow evening. The motel in the crossroads might still be safe."

"It might be..."

"God willing, it's far enough from this place. I can hardly imagine that anyone has moved in there since the winter, but if they have, just be careful!"

They shook hands, and held the gesture a long time.

"Is there anything else I can do for you?" Grant asked softly.

Nelson glanced at the Mercedes.

"Promise to look after them! Especially her," he said, nodding his head towards Megan. "I don't care about your stupid fears, that's all I ask of you. Get them to the boat-town!

Grant raised his gaze to the sky, then reluctantly shrugged his shoulders.

"And you? On to Patagonia?"

"You know me! Someone needs to check it out... so, I've decided to accept the mission."

They exchanged looks and nodded. Nelson's mind was flooded

with thoughts, but eventually he decided he'd given enough advice, and Grant didn't ask him what would happen if the old man reached the border. Their ways had parted for good.

"Keep the shiny side up, my friend, as always."

They said nothing else. They didn't need to. Thirty minutes after the handshake between Nelson and Grant, the convoy was on its way. Twenty-two people left and only Nelson remained behind.

The old chap waited for them to pass, and when he couldn't hear the engines humming anymore he sat down in his favorite armchair and looked around the ruins of the empty colony. The mounds of the dead rose in front of the cottage, at Nelson's feet, where they'd been buried.

He stared at the headstones, took a deep breath, and got up. *Time to leave*, he thought and believed that this could be the greatest adventure of his life.

His truck ran for a hundred yards, then broke down once and for all.

14.

The final attack came at dawn, and Nelson admitted that he could only delay his destiny, not stop it. He figured at least he'd give the others a slight chance and take as many ferals into the grave with him as he could.

When the first phantom climbed over the fence, the old man set the main gate and the tower on fire, hoping to slow them down, but the game was soon over.

There were fourteen of them.

At least, Nelson saw fourteen.

The members of the pack led an attack in perfect harmony through the burning camp, purely intent on destruction, seeking out anyone they could massacre, drag away, and tear apart.

By the time the sun had set, smoking ashes covered the ruins of the camp, where the residents had once really believed that they could change their fate.

And the members of the disappointed pack knew that the first and only bite was reserved for their leader.

Shivering, covered in bloody wounds, Nelson crouched among the phantoms, not quite sure why he was still alive. He held on tight to his shotgun even though he had fired all his shells. No matter where he tried to crawl, the ferals were everywhere.

As if they were leading him.

To it. The leader of the pack.

The half-light and the fire revealed a gigantic figure. Even as its demonic steps slowly approached, it radiated power. Its long arms and thin legs were clear to see through the smoke. It was at least eight feet tall, its body slightly stooped in constant readiness.

As if its life was all about attack…

…death and destruction.

Its muscled outline ripped the black smoke apart, and as it approached the ferals retreated.

The members of the pack howled, slavering. Their movements and voices were excited and fearful. Subservience. A Beta clattered its milled teeth, and an unearthly rattle broke out of its throat, but as the mysterious leader approached, it also backed away two steps, yowling.

That was the point when Nelson realized that his last moments could perhaps explain this whole infernal story. The answer came directly to him…

…and in the shimmering light of the smoldering fire he finally saw the pack leader's face.

He had never seen anything like it before.

His last judgment towered above him, a muscular, demonic figure. The virus had shaped its bony face to make it unrecognizable. Its sharp teeth nearly ripped its mouth open. Its eyes had a pale-yellow glint, blood mixed with mud on its bald, weather-beaten head. Its skin was like armor, its nose just two rotten holes.

It was an Alpha.

SWEET HOME

1.

"When are we gonna talk about it?"

The question surprised Cassius, who thought Abigail would not say a word until they got home. He knew her well enough to sense pouting from her defiant steps, her jaw grimly set, but inside he was glad that at least they would have a peaceful journey to the motel. He needed some extra time to consider their next moves.

Their last horse, Monty, had gotten so scared of the ferals that it ran off. Most of the collected supplies were lost, and they were low on ammo. The situation was dire, but Cassius's brain was working hard on the solution.

However, Abigail must have had enough of pouting. She changed her tactics, and he could hardly imagine what could be so sorely important.

"Talk about what?"

"The Great Plan, wiseass! What else?" Abigail nodded her head towards his military bag.

"I don't know what is there to talk about. We'll set off, and if we're good, we'll make it."

She shook her head.

"I thought, like, what if I don't want to go?"

Cassius slowed down involuntarily, but did not stop, because then he would only have taken up the gauntlet. "You'll be an adult soon, so do as you please."

Abigail stopped. She tilted her head like she always did when she didn't understand something. *Right,* he thought, and walked beside her.

"You're gonna let me go so easily? No veto, no talking me out of it?"

"Who am I to defy a strong, independent woman's decision?"

"Hahaha… I'm laughing if you hadn't noticed."

"Speaking of which, I'm curious about something."

"Hit me."

"How you're gonna push your fortune in life. You must have a plan…"

"I'll manage off the cuff!"

"Awesome, and I'll be thinking a lot about you at the beach!"

Abigail didn't answer, but Cassius heard the tight boots holding her long, thin legs hit the asphalt that bit harder.

He smiled, knowing that she couldn't see him, and he tried to enjoy the rest of the journey. After all, he couldn't solve anything until they got home. He watched the burning skies painted by the sun as it slowly descended behind a dark horizon furrowed by trees. The bare land showed its friendlier face at sunset, and the smooth wind slowly blew away the heat. He went around a wrecked Chevrolet Malibu with bullet holes in it, and cast a quick glance from the corner of his eye.

In the distance, on the top of the hill, the lonely oak tree was already waiting for them, the first clear sign of where the old motel rested in the middle of the plain. Cassius turned around and took a few steps walking backwards. Nothing moved in the distance. His eyes met hers, but Abigail angrily looked the other way, and Cassius turned back, facing the slope and the lonely oak. He closed his eyes as he felt the last sunbeams on his face. *It would be good to stay like this for a few more hours.*

He felt tired and old, with legs as heavy as lead from marching all day long.

"I know what's wrong with you."

He flinched. *So much for a peaceful journey.*

"And I know you won't leave me alone until you've said it, so just go for it."

"You think it was all my fault, don't you?"

"I never said that…"

"But?"

"The vanguard was your job."

"Oh, screw you!"

Cassius stopped. Abigail bit her lip and stood with arms akimbo.

"You had a job to do, but you were too busy chit-chatting, not paying attention," he continued. "Because if you had done your job, you would have seen the signs."

"So they died because of me, just say it to my face!"

Cassius wordlessly watched the girl, whose temple nearly exploded with her pulsating heartbeat.

"Thought so," Abigail puffed, then went around Cassius and took the lead. He waited for a beat, then followed her. He didn't feel like quarreling about the same thing over and over again.

After a long trudge uphill to the lonely oak, they finally spotted the motel at the crossing of Route 10 and 285. The building, accompanied by a gas station, idly sprawled in the dusk, just as they had left it a week before. It was situated farther from the junction, partly covered by a line of trees, its lots filled with rusty vehicles discarded after the pandemic. The labyrinth of cars and RVs took care of those familiar with the place. To prevent surprises, Cassius and Abigail had placed traps and alarms around the building. The most important part was a roof protected with barbed wire, from which the surrounding area could be seen perfectly.

Cassius took a deep breath and rubbed his eyes. It was time for the more pleasant part of the hike, down the hill, opposite the distant bay ruling the horizon with its big blue mass. He braced himself to look around thoroughly, to make sure there were no further surprises, and only after that could he have his well-deserved rest. He calculated that they would have fifteen minutes to inspect their surroundings, and by the time darkness fell he would be relaxing in the rusty leather armchair on the roof.

"The northern sector is yours," Cassius said, but Abigail didn't even slow down, nor did she turn back. "Got it?"

"I'm not deaf!"

"I replaced item twenty-two before leaving. Hope you remember!"

"I'm not stupid, either!"

Cassius nodded. He was hoping the girl would calm down by the next day, and things would get back to normal, but holding out an olive branch was not among his strengths.

The alarm in his head went off. First, only silently, vaguely, then louder and louder. The persistent siren, trained into his subconscious, eventually brought him back, and with so many years of experience behind him he knew there were no false alarms. Cassius frowned. He tried to figure out what was causing his apprehension and why his arm was shivering.

Then he found what he was looking for.

"Get off the road! Quick! To the trees!"

Abigail had learned the lesson. Without further ado, she huddled up and leaped into the dry bushes. To the left, about twenty-five yards from the road, a small line of trees spread to the east. Cassius and Abigail headed towards it. As soon as they found shelter, she pushed her back to a tree and peered at the motel, but to no purpose.

"What is it? What did you see?"

"To the right, by the main entrance," he whispered. In front of the two-story building, among the rusty cars and languid trees, there was something incongruous. Something that had not been there a week before. Abigail let out a silent curse.

"Isn't that a…?"

"A school bus," he finished her sentence, and indeed, it was a Blue Bird, parking in front of the propped open door of the building.

They had a visitor. Somebody was in the motel.

2.

They lay prone and unmoving in the shade of the trees, melding into the dusk, waiting for the mysterious strangers to show themselves at last. Cassius scanned the motel with the mounted scope on his Browning and a few minutes later he discovered what he was searching for. Movement at the entrance, protected by columns and a canopy.

There were two of them, uninvited guests from far away: a stubbly man and a withered woman, scruffy drifters wearing long leather coats despite the summer heat and sweaty singlets gone yellow. Their stringy hair waved as they rushed, their faces disfigured by stains of oil, and both of them were smoking home-rolled cigarettes. They awkwardly packed stuff into the school bus. The hobo threw gallons of water, while the tramp collected useful stuff into a box. They were very busy and in a great hurry.

Abigail watched them open-mouthed through her Vortex binoculars. Her ears went red as she saw the tramp sorting through her clothes.

"They're taking all our belongings."

Cassius readied the semi-automatic Browning. He inhaled deeply, slowed his breathing and letting his body calm.

He aligned his sights with the reticle held on the hobo's chest, using the fine lines on the scope to line up his shot.

Now or never! The hobo stepped beside his partner and told her something. Cassius followed his movement, holding the rifle securely.

"Hey, hey... What are you doing?" Abigail asked as quietly as she could.

"What do you think I'm doing? I'm not gonna wait until they've packed everything out!"

"You don't have to."

"Oh please, don't say you have a plan..."

"We'll simply stalk them. I go from the east, across the roof, and you go from the west across the car-maze. Surely we can handle two losers."

"And then what? We give them a warning and let them leave?"

"Still, we can't just shoot them!"

His sight lost focus. He only needed a couple of seconds to consider her plan and admit that it might just work. Might. He saw no guns with them, just two machetes leaning at the bus. They could do it in ten to fifteen minutes, but they didn't have much time and all Cassius wished for was the day to end. To shut his eyes and indulge in sleep – in the dark, dreamless depth which had been drawing him for days. He wanted to lose this battle. He did not want to feel, know, or remember. *On the other hand, who said it was worth the risk for two looters?*

"I'm not gonna fight with you about this."

"Of course not; this isn't a democracy."

His eyes flashed in anger, but eventually found their focus again. The reticle was back on the hobo's chest, and the stock of the rifle strained against his shoulder.

Deep breath, again…

…exhale…

Fresh air filled his lungs. Cassius knew he could not fail. He had three bullets in the Browning and missing the first shot could mean the beginning of a nightlong hide-and-seek. He tried to tune out his environment: Abigail sniffling next to him *(Is she doing it on purpose?)*, the drops of sweat on his forehead, the darkening dusk. His eyes hurt from focusing and he had a hard time seeing the target.

Something moved on the eastern side of the long building.

"Wait!" Abigail hissed. She saw the worst coming, a feral, which would have further complicated the situation, but then started to smile when she recognized the horse stepping among the bushes. "It's Monty! He came home alone."

Cassius looked away from the scope. His shoulders unwound, a slight smile appearing in the corner of his lips when he saw the pack horse. His brain instantly started working on a Plan B. After all Monty's appearance rewrote the scenario.

"Smart boy," he said, but the proud smile quickly faded. Monty was not as careful as them and he hacked towards the entrance of the motel. Cassius looked into the Browning scope again and pursed his lips. "Bad idea, Monty! A really bad idea…"

But Monty couldn't hear the warning and he didn't slow his forwards progress. The horse was headed towards the two strangers, who were stunned at his appearance. Their movements froze in the air, the cigarettes dropped to the ground. They exchanged looks. The hobo stroked his stringy hair and licked his lips, while the tramp was grinning as if they had hit the jackpot.

"Why are they so happy now?" Abigail asked.

Cassius closed his eyes. When he re-opened them, the hobo was gone and only the tramp remained within the reticle, dancing like a fool. She jumped and shook her hands as if she was praying for the rain around a campfire. Even from this distance they could hear her grating voice. The hobo finally returned with a shotgun.

The blood ran out of Abigail's face, her fingers nearly crushing the binoculars. Cassius was desperate to focus on the hobo stepping out from the cover of the bus, who checked the shotgun shells with clumsy movements, and immediately fired at Monty.

The bang of the gun drowned out everything. Abigail cried out, a teardrop appeared in the corner of her eye, and she turned her head aside from the binoculars.

Monty fell with a whomp. When the cloud of dust subsided, the tramp tore the bags off the carcass, and the hobo grabbed a machete to join the frenzy. Cassius did not look at Abigail, nor did he pay attention to her. Fuming, he aimed at the tramp who was fiddling with a bag, stamping her feet in excitement. He wanted to save the hobo for last. He had also planned out how he would do it…

"Give me the gun!"

Cassius glanced at Abigail, her expression wreathed in red mist. From behind her twitching facial muscles, the warrior was about to break out, the one Cassius had hardly ever managed to lure to the surface. At other times he would have been happy, but not now, not in the worst moment, when *sang-froid* was needed to end this nightmare.

"Not a good idea," Cassius said. "We have three bullets…"

"Three reasons why you shouldn't screw up!"

He raised his eyebrows, then cracked his neck.

"I appreciate your self-confidence, but…"

"At dusk, from a two-hundred-yard distance, who do you think has better chances? You know I'm better! In this, I am."

Cassius hesitated. His eyes were drawn back by the monocular sight, but he had already taken his finger off the trigger. The hobo and the tramp hadn't moved from their places, but he still found it hard to make out what the increasingly faded shapes were doing.

"Shit!" he growled. Carefully he rolled over while Abigail slid into his place behind the Browning. Cassius saw a vein pulsing in her temple. She pressed her lips together hard, as if she was about to bridle a hell of a hurricane.

"Breathe, just take it easy," Cassius whispered.

"I know the drill!"

"Nice and stable! Focus only on the reticle…"

"That's what I'm doing!"

Cassius grabbed the Vortex, and through them he watched things unfold. The hobo was working in the cover of the tall grass and the horse, so only the top of his head and his arms striking down could be seen. The tramp was crouching a few feet away next to the bus. She was packing out of the kit-bags. She even called out to the hobo as if asking how the stuff had gotten onto the animal. The hobo shrugged his shoulders, only interested in dinner. Fresh meat, which they had probably not had for a long time.

"Don't rush it!" Cassius said.

"I won't, but I'm not gonna wait for them to finish."

And before he could say anything, she gave a whistle. Long and loud enough to sound suspicious, but not to make their location obvious. Cassius shook with the force of his concentration shattered.

"What... the... f..."

He had no time to finish. The hobo jumped up at the sound of the whistle; he even dropped the machete. He never got the chance to pick it up again. As he straightened, his head reached the perfect position.

Abigail pulled the trigger just like Cassius had taught her. Slowly but precisely, as if she was scratching a line on a board chalk. Smoothly, firmly. The first bullet hit the hobo's skull, exploding it into a red cloud. The report made the tramp flinch, and she also jumped up, but before she could properly react, Abigail aimed at her as well.

Bang! The second bullet whooshed over Route 10, straight into the woman's neck. A few seconds later she was lying next to the hobo.

Abigail got on her feet. She strained her fist to hide the shivering.

"That's for Monty, assholes!"

3.

The bodies lay next to each other, with slowly drying blood puddles around them, a blend of awe and incomprehension on their faces. The two bullets had ripped their bodies like a wild beast, but it was still Monty who had ended up the worst off. His head was only attached to his body by a thin piece of skin. The kit-bags were lying scattered, cans and sacks everywhere, a broken bottle of cola in the distance, from which the blacktop eagerly drank.

The bus door was open, showing only darkness inside.

Cassius and Abigail broke through the wall of twilight with their flashlights. They held their guns ready and approached the bus as silently as they could. Her light rested on the corpses' hard facial features, but then she hurried around Monty and finally stopped at the bus door.

Cassius carefully stepped closer and thoroughly examined the rusty Blue Bird. Every mile was a gift for the worn-out vehicle, a jawless skull had been painted on the side and grids had been welded to the windows. It would have been a nice stalemate if the two had barricaded themselves in the bus.

He turned back to Abigail, who nodded. They both felt that something wasn't right, but neither of them could tell yet what was causing the weird tingle inside. Perhaps the smell, the strange smell that Cassius had already sensed in front of the vehicle. The stink of death spread towards them from the dark.

Meanwhile, everything went still around them; even nature was listening with breath held. The wind subsided.

Cassius stepped up onto the dirty stairs with his Glock held forwards, then swung quickly into the aisle, preparing for anything that might be hiding among the rows of seats. As he was enveloped by the bus, the putrid smell became so sickening that he lost his balance for a moment. He stopped himself from putting his hand to his mouth involuntarily and scanned the walls with his flashlight.

The Blue Bird was empty. Ragged things and boxes were packed on the front rows, while the back seats were completely removed. That was where the smell of devastation came from.

"Did you find anything?" Abigail called before pulling her T-shirt all the way up to her nose. She stood on the lower step; she had no interest in moving further in.

With the beam of the flashlight, Cassius pointed to where she should look, and the metallic shine left no doubt about what she was looking at. In the rear part of the stripped bus, chains were braced to the floor, each of which led to a pulley in the ceiling and hung down with handcuffs at the end. Stains of blood were all around the floor, and vomit and urine blended with the putrid smell.

Abigail winced when she realized what it meant. She looked up, hoping she was wrong. “Man-eaters?”

He lowered his light. Abigail swallowed and stepped away from the door, and Cassius gave her some time. They had the same thought: pull the trigger before it’s too late, because hesitation exacts a heavy price. Through the dirty bus windows, Cassius watched as the girl stepped over to Monty.

He felt distress spread through his limbs, and his eyes were excessively heavy from exhaustion. His head was pounding. As he slid his fingers across the leatherette seats, he recalled the moment when he had last traveled in a Blue Bird, and he was back in Headland, on the way out of town. He heard the squealing of brakes; he saw the driver desperately pulling the steering wheel over. From the mist of his memory Abigail’s face appeared; the face of the intrepid, scraggy child he had saved just a few hours earlier.

His fingers stuck in a dried puddle of blood. Cassius shook as he was dragged back to reality.

The flashlight suddenly caught on something on the seamed floor of the bus. He bent down and lifted a bunch of keys from among the junk and trash. One was the ignition key, sticky with filth and blood. He hopped behind the steering wheel, inserted the key in the switch, and turned it. The Blue Bird rocked. The digital display on the dashboard showed nothing; only the red battery indicator was on, and rhythmic rattle sounded from the direction of the hood. Oil pressure was in order, and the tank was a quarter full. Cassius shut down the engine, took out the key, and put it into his pocket.

“It’s a junk pile. It might roll down to the port, but nothing more,” he said. Abigail stood up, dusted her trousers, and turned back to him. Her eyes sparkled in the beam of the flashlight.

“Where did they come from?” she asked, pointing at the pair on the ground.

“Probably from Headland. Some of them are still there.”

“I’m glad we skipped that trip. Do you think it was only the two of them?”

Cassius wiped the dirt and the blood off his hands.

"I don't know, so tonight we sleep with eyes open."

"Great." She looked around. "Now what?"

Good question. The horizon eventually absorbed the thin red strip of light, and they had not much choice left in the darkness.

"Check the traps around the house. We'll deal with the rest in the morning."

"What about them?" she asked, pointing at the dead bodies. The ferals could sense fresh blood from a large distance; they had learned this lesson a long time ago. "They can't stay like this."

"I know. I'll take care of them."

Abigail's shoulders rose slightly as she stood up straight. Relief washed over her face.

"Really?"

Cassius nodded.

"Don't take long!" He smiled at her encouragingly. "Are we happy?"

"Yes, we are." She gave the thumbs up.

"Awesome, let's get going!"

Abigail lifted her bag carefully as if she was carrying fragile treasures, and set off, wiping her eyes. She hurried along the bus and only looked back when she reached the corner of the motel, but Cassius paid no more attention to her. He was digging the first grave far from the building.

Abigail got lost in the night. She had no thought about checking the traps around the house, and she was not headed to where Cassius had ordered her.

4.

Abigail stepped across the crumbling bones in front of the old gas station and climbed around the rubble to enter the building. Most of the shelves were empty, but some medicine, spare parts, and food were left over in the back rows; much more than in other shops. Evacuation of the neighborhood had happened so fast and in such a panic seven years ago that people drove frantically to the west, all the way to the Pincers.

A couple of years later, a pack of ferals set up camp in the shop, and they dispatched looters like the old lion in the tale dispatched the animals that strayed into his cave. Cassius and Abigail were the famous fox who discovered that the footprints led inside, but not back out.

She stopped at the cashier station and carefully placed her bag on the counter. She slowly undid the zip to check the contents and relaxed when she saw that everything was all right. It might take a few minutes until she found what she had come for and in the meantime it was better not to take any risks. She put the bag on the ground, and with a broad smile she started walking among the aisles. She scanned the shelves with her light and searched so absently that Cassius would probably have gone mad about it. *Pay attention, girl! Be aware of your surroundings.*

Then, finally, she found what she was looking for and quietly snapped her fingers.

"Bingo!"

Abigail had a smile from ear to ear, not only from happiness, but also pride. She took a few packets off the shelf, and bounded back to her bag. Even this small success felt like a complete victory. She might be able to save the day. She might be able to correct her mistake…

Mistake? *No, it was no mistake!*

Abigail shook her head. With their skills they could save dozens of people. They could even build up their own colony. *Cassius can train them, and I can help. At least we wouldn't be alone.* Because this was what she feared the most. She no longer wanted lonely birthdays, being bored on watch, wordless marching for endless miles, and she didn't want to stay alone. But Cassius decided otherwise, and doing nothing worthy was his choice, one he had made alone. Without the debate at the woman's hideout, they could have set off earlier and perhaps everything would have turned out differently. Then perhaps the woman and her the daughter would still be alive.

But that wasn't what had happened and she had no time to brood over the past. Duty waited for her.

Big smile! *We are happy after all…*

She returned to her bag. She crouched down and slipped the packets on the ground. With tender movements, from the bottom of the bag, she took out a padded shoebox that pranced and yowled as she placed it on the ground. Abigail glanced at the hairy ball inside it.

"There you go! Look, what I've found? It says," and she read the words written on the side of the packet as if they were a fairy tale, "this formula has everything that makes a puppy healthy, and see, the expiration date wasn't even that long ago. It's our lucky day, isn't it?"

Something moved outside, in front of the building. Rat-tat-tat. Abigail trembled hearing the patter of the tiny feet. She listened, motionless, then sighed with relief. By the minuscule soles... *It could only have been a fox!*

When all was still, she opened up the bag, and mixed a portion of formula with water. A first dinner for the puppy, who was squirming in the bottom of the box with his hungry mouth open. Abigail glanced at the spotty paw and she instantly knew: she would call him Soxy.

5.

After feeding the puppy, Abigail carefully placed him back in her bag and then set off towards the motel, almost blindly avoiding the traps and the alarms, most of which she had installed earlier. The sounds of the night suppressed her quiet steps, but she didn't forget her training. Reaching the car-maze she stopped, crouched down, and waited for a while, head turned aside to be able to hear every noise. She switched her light off and crept among the abandoned wrecks towards the motel; she stopped after a couple of quick steps and sought shelter.

Finally, she entered through the back door and inched all the way to the old reception desk, where she watched Cassius from the shadow. He was just pouring lime over the carcasses. When he finished, with a few fast movements, he buried the hole and dusted himself off.

Abigail knew she only had a few minutes left. Holding her bag gently, she hurried to the cold storage section of the restaurant. They considered it to be a panic room, which made it seem like a perfect hideout. The busted ventilator had been removed, so fresh air was free to flow in and the temperature inside was ideal in the summer heat. Not too cold and not too hot.

She snapped open the door lock and listened carefully for a while. She thought Cassius must still have been outside since she heard no steps and no snuffles. *Great!*

She put the bag on one of the metal tables and with delicate movements she unpacked Soxy. Silently yowling, the puppy mouthed her hand. His button-eyes were sleepy and unfocused; his tongue was licking her palm.

"All right, big boy, now we'll make you a nice little snug."

Abigail took a larger box from a shelf, tucked rugs in it, and carefully placed the puppy in the middle. She gave him a small dish of water to hold him over; she planned to feed him again at dawn. Soxy moved around fretfully.

"I know, I know," she said smiling, though her eyes were sad. "But now you'll have to make do with me. I promise, we'll be a great team."

She almost said she would be his new mommy, but she swallowed the sentence as her own past swamped her mind. The warm touch of her mother. The fresh lavender scent of her father's clothes. Her little brother's giggle.

The last moment she saw them…

…the screams, the blood…

…the time spent under the car and the rattle that she did not understand back then. *Mommy…*

Abigail knew exactly what the puppy felt when it watched her just like she had watched Cassius seven years before, when he had saved her.

"Trust me, it will get easier as time passes!" she said, giving Soxy a faint smile. Her eyes weren't shining anymore, and her hands didn't move on the puppy's head. She tried not to think of Soxy's siblings that they'd had to leave behind; she reasoned that she could only bring one pup with her. *We had no other option*, she kept repeating, yet she could hardly believe it.

The aim is to survive…

…but at what cost?

6.

Everything for miles around could be seen from the top of the motel, so on the first day Cassius took the dusty armchair that he found by the reception desk and collected a parasol — the one with the fewest tears and the least dirt — and took them up.

Until now the hideout had worked out well, but they had never stayed in one place for so long. Their secret to survival was to be constantly on the move. He had heard stories that the ferals observed the habits of a colony, and if the pack was big enough, they attacked without hesitation. If they did avoid some places, the residents living there ruined it over time. For lack of a common enemy, they tore each other up.

At the beginning, of course, they didn't have much choice: they roamed most of the country trying to find Cassius' family, who had been dragged away from him when the Breakdown began. They searched each and every colony where his wife and son could have gone, even those where strangers were not welcome. Even where their lives were in danger.

Cassius flopped down into the armchair and tilted his head back. He inhaled the scent of the night, and a few moments were enough for sleep to drag him in. His disturbed thoughts kept returning to the newcomers. As if he had stepped out of his body, he saw from behind his closed eyelids the hobo and the tramp standing tall above him with bloody, muddy machetes in their hands.

Fresh air filled his gasping lungs, and he stared across the dark blue horizon like a scared beast. *All right, I'm awake...*

He needed some time to calm his body. Tired, he rubbed his eyes and scratched his stubble in a stolid manner. Abigail was still nowhere to be seen. He lit an oil lantern and in the dim light he pulled his bag closer and took out a crumpled notebook. Scraps of paper with torn edges were sticking out of it. Maps, drawings, lists – he turned to the last page and took some notes with a blunt pencil. Then he reached into his bag and started pulling things out, things for which they had covered more than a hundred miles in the past couple of days.

Things without which there was no Great Plan, and – at least according to him – there was no future. They needed the cans, the sacks, and the boxes to survive, but very different treasures were to be found in the military bag. He was considering the long run, no matter the resistance. He unpacked everything beside him and carried on with his inventory until he reached the bottom of the bag. On the concrete around him rested plant seeds in jars, ropes, matchboxes, medicine boxes, portable solar panels, water purification bottles, and duct tape (a lot of it). Clothes, soaps, and fishing nets lay beside a saw and a magnifier.

They had everything they needed to gradually start all over. Not here, of course, but somewhere else, somewhere far away, in perfect safety, where they wouldn't have to flee any longer. Cassius looked through the items. Only a few were missing. *Little things...*

The soles of light boots knocked on the stairway up to the roof. Cassius didn't need to turn around to know it was Abigail coming.

"You didn't rush it," he murmured.

Without answering, Abigail threw herself on a sunbed. She dug in her bag and amidst loud clashes, she took out a soda can. The lid hissed open and she dropped her bag next to her and lay back. She didn't look at him, just stared defiantly ahead pretending to watch the mountains slashing against the northern sky and the stars, quietly sipping the soft drink.

Endless, motionless calm, until...

She spotted a quickly moving, shimmering light headed eastbound at an enormous speed, flashing against the deep blue zenith. A satellite. The sight also attracted Cassius's attention. He pulled out his Glock and pointed it directly at the moving spotlight. When he pulled it, the trigger made an empty click, but that didn't bother Cassius.

"Bull's eye," he said proudly.

Abigail could only hold it for a moment, then burst out laughing. Secretly she glanced at him. She hesitated, then asked:

"Do you think they're watching us? I mean out there?"

"Maybe."

"Julie said if there were survivors in other parts of the world, they would have already dropped nukes on us."

"Julie?"

"We talked last night, when you were asleep."

They both kept silent for a minute. As if they had recalled the motionless body and the angel's wing splashed on the wall.

"She also said that the leaders with nukes probably couldn't wait to press the button, especially after the Breakdown. And the fact that eventually nothing happened could only mean one thing."

Cassius grimaced and scowled. Abigail noticed it and turned to him with an uncomprehending look in her eyes.

"Don't you think so?"

"I'm too tired to think of anything now." Cassius glanced at the notebook resting on his lap. "Luckily, it's none of our business. We're headed to a place that nobody cares about, and nobody will either. By the way, we're pretty well prepared. We already have twenty-two types of seeds that are good for a subtropical climate. The rest we can get in Garden City. If we pack quickly, we can sail out in the next few weeks."

"An excellent plan, farming on a goddamn island in the middle of nowhere."

He scratched something on the back page of the book, then put it away and looked at Abigail like a teacher waiting for a schoolkid's correct answer.

"You got a better plan?"

"You bet!"

"I mean something that won't kill us."

Abigail angrily dropped the empty can beside her and shook her head.

"Do you really think you'll just hang out on the beach, and not miss this whole thing?"

"This whole thing? What? The constant dread?"

"No! The fact that we're fighting for something and we can help others."

"Others?" Cassius let out a sarcastic laugh. "We can't even help ourselves, never mind others! Trust me, this is the best we can do. We're alone and we can't count on anyone. I don't see why we should stay in this hopeless place."

"Yeah, sure…"

Cassius forced a fatherly smile to his face, but Abigail looked the other way. He slapped his thighs with his palms and stood up.

"Now get some rest. We're starting with some training in the morning. There's a lot more to master!"

"As you wish," Abigail said sulkily and stood up with her sharp chin high. She headed towards the ladder. "At least I don't need target practice."

"You'd better take it seriously. If I were you, I wouldn't be so proud of the last few days."

"You really are funny."

"I wasn't being funny!"

Her face quivered. She turned back to him.

"I shot them, as far as I remember."

"You were lucky, but the problem with luck is that eventually you run out of it. I've told you, Abigail, you're not ready yet, even if that's what you think."

"Oh, really? And what if I don't agree with you?"

"Then you're wrong.... and I'm afraid that by the time you realize it, it might be too late." He stepped towards the armchair, picked up his gun, and went to the ladder. "I'll go look around."

Abigail's raised palm stopped him.

"Just leave it to me! I can't sleep anyway. At least I'll have time to think about what a naughty little girl I was!"

Abigail disappeared as she descended, but the furious stomp of her boots still echoed in Cassius's ears for a while. His eyes dropped, heavy, and he felt remorse, even though he knew he was right. Still, he was ashamed.

7.

Cassius stepped up to a huge chest that was pushed to the edge of the roof and protected by a massive lock from any eager visitors. He crouched down, opened the padlock, and looked through their treasures. Nothing glittering, nothing worth envying, at least for others. Books on one side, dozens, packed closely on one another; even more jars with seeds on the other side, smaller agricultural tools, bows, arrows, multitools, and guns that had long ago run out of ammo, but perhaps in Garden City they could get some resupplies.

Everything needed for the Great Plan lay there.

Cassius packed their newly acquired objects. When he finished, he locked the chest and hid the keys in his pocket, then slumped back down on the armchair. He placed the Tom Wolfe book in his lap, but after the recent quarrel he didn't feel much like reading, and he couldn't turn up the light of the oil lamp. A low flicker was what he considered to be safest.

The blunt pain weighting his eyelids finally defeated him, and he shut his eyes. The dreams took him immediately. He saw the children sitting at the end of the roof. Molly was staring as if it was her only task. Nia was crouching next to Lucas and comforted the weeping boy. Cassius' body was filled with relief, but a strange, unexplainable feeling was in his mind. As if he knew that what he was seeing didn't exist, as if his brain was constantly warning him not to lose himself in the past. The rest of him didn't care. He felt the smile, the sense of freedom. *Here you are, nice and safe...*

There was no bus ride from Headland into the nightmare, no screams, just a frozen snapshot of the past. Then he heard her voice. In his dreams he could only hear her voice.

"Jake."

Since his parents' death, only she called him Jake. Nobody else.

His shoulders were flushed by a hot wave as the familiar fingers caressed him. He felt an unknown force turning him around, but the dreamless void finally drew him in.

8.

Abigail crept out of the building and climbed onto an RV parked in the front of the car-maze. She could have chosen any room, but eventually this had become her snug. She had the perfect view, and to make it truly homey she had dragged a mattress to the vehicle's roof and gathered all the magazines from the motel. Girlie, trendy, travel. It was all the same, as long as they were colorful. She tucked them under the mattress and excitedly browsed the articles. But only in the daytime; it was forbidden to use light during the night. She could only imagine what the old world had been like. She didn't have many memories to draw on.

The moon slipped closer and closer to its zenith, and since it was a cloudless night she could clearly see her surroundings. She knew she had to leave her eyes open because they could be ambushed any time, but she didn't feel like it. Abigail gazed at the stars until she fell asleep. She dreamt of Europe, of the Paris that she had seen in magazines. She was wearing a bell-shaped dress, a photo of which she had cut out and pinned in her notebook. Her long hair was floating in the breeze, and she could smell the scent of the perfume she had once tried in a dusty store. She imagined cabs honking happily around her, just like in that picture where the smiling woman turned back and waved towards the road. She heard someone calling her name. Some people were waiting for her. She was not alone.

It was still dark when she woke up, and the puppy was expecting her, whimpering in his soft box.

"All right, big boy, don't be a drama queen," she said with pretend rigor, and prepared the next portion of formula. Soxy wolfed it down and this time he didn't drop like a wheat bag, but kept playfully licking Abigail's hand.

She giggled.

"I bet I'll have a hard time with you. You'll be a real rascal."

Soxy quietly whimpered and restlessly turned his head around.

"Hey, what's wrong?" she asked and turned back, but nobody stood in the cold storage doorway. "You don't need to be scared of Cassius… I don't know how we're gonna tell him, but now you're a member of the team, right?"

Abigail smiled at the puppy, and when Soxy was nice and cozy, she smoothly covered him. She caressed his fluffy noggin and crept onto the roof.

Cassius snored softly and steadily, one hand hanging from the armchair, the other held strongly to his chest. She creeped to the wooden chest and opened it. On one side there was everything they had collected…

…on the other side were almost a hundred books piled up. They were not only about survival practices, agriculture, and first aid, but about sailing and geography studies, as well. Cassius had tried to gather as much knowledge as he could: he had entire encyclopedias on how to survive in the subtropics.

Abigail crouched down and started sorting. When she found what she was looking for, she gently closed the top of the chest and headed towards the ladder. The first lights appeared in the east, and Abigail was hoping she could read a bit before Cassius woke.

She climbed back onto the RV roof, lay down on her back on the mattress, and opened the book. She didn't have to search for long to find the part about bringing up puppies. It was short, but better than nothing. *The rest,* she thought, *we'll figure out on the way.*

9.

With a single jolt, Cassius woke and sat up straight in the armchair. It was early in the morning. The sky had turned to light blue and the sun crept over a gray horizon. He took a deep breath of fresh air and got up. His body needed time to muster energy, so he just stood there and tried to figure out what date it was, but the days had gotten messed up in his head.

Sunday the twenty-seventh. Maybe.

He walked to the edge of the roof. He raised his binoculars to his eyes and looked around carefully. Abigail was nowhere to be seen. He sighed and, at an easy pace, walked down to his room to wash himself. He took clean clothes out, a comfortable pair of jeans and a dark-colored T-shirt, then set off to find the girl. Abigail, wearing a gray T-shirt and dark jeans, was searching the bus.

"Have you found anything?"

"Just junk."

"I'll take this watch, if you want to get some rest."

"And what about practice? I was so excited, I could hardly contain myself in the evening," she said with a sarcastic smile at the edge of her lips.

"Don't worry, we'll make up for that. But you're no good to me if you're tired."

"It's good to know that at least I'm of some use."

So, she's still mad!

"Look, about last night…

"Just leave it!" Abigail said and spread her arms. "I got it. I'll try as hard as I can. Perhaps one day you'll be proud of me."

They heard the stifled sound first, an echoing, distant pop, which grew into a deep boom. Twittering birds flew up from the trees. Cassius and Abigail shivered and turned around at the same time, unsure where the sound could be coming from. Abigail spotted it first and raised her hand to the west, towards the Pincers.

"Look!"

Cassius turned in the direction Abigail was pointing, but he knew they were standing in the wrong position to truly see anything. Within a minute they were both on the roof, short of breath because of the run. She watched impatiently as he gripped the binoculars. The line of smoke got thinner and high above the glowing orange sky a rocket slowly descended. The flare that had been discharged in the distance eventually vanished behind the trees.

"The old quarry?" Abigail asked.

Cassius nodded.

"What do you think it means?"

"Nothing good."

He handed the binoculars over to her. Abigail grabbed the Vortex and glued her eyes to the device. Nothing additional happened over the mine, and eventually the thin line of smoke dispersed.

"There's someone at the old quarry, right?" Abigail asked.

"Yep," he replied.

"We should check it out!" Silence. "Shouldn't we?"

Cassius's jaw tightened impatiently, but he didn't want to answer. What he should do and what he wanted were two different things.

"I wouldn't say it's a good idea. We don't know what it is…"

"It doesn't matter what it is!" she exclaimed. "If there is somebody at the mine, they're likely to be headed to our place. It's better not to find out here who it is and what they want."

Cassius hesitated. He glanced at the school bus and was mad at himself for rejecting the possibility that the hobo and the tramp hadn't been travelling alone.

"They could well be man-eaters, signaling to the two idiots," Cassius said, and nodded towards the shallow graves.

"And? Does it make a difference?"

No...

Cassius scanned the sky. The frightened birds were flying high, and the lights of the morning were gray. The air seemed dry. There was unlikely to be a storm. He glanced at his watch, a solar-powered G-Shock. It was past seven o'clock. His body strained as he made the decision and acknowledged the potential consequences.

"Pack the usual gear, we're leaving in ten minutes!"

INSTINCT

1.

By dawn, the pain was unbearable.

The adrenaline boost evoked by the massacre had long passed. The smell of blood had evaporated and it was overtaken by suffering. Its head was pulsating with blood-thirst. Its limbs were strained by the spasms. Its teeth were aching with torment. All it desired was to bite flesh and taste blood again.

Without adrenaline, the pain kept coming back, and only the beauty of destruction could ease it. It was a vicious circle, and the spasms came more and more frequently. More often than in the beginning; and much more often than for other members of the pack.

The Alpha stopped. It shouted when it could not take the pain anymore.

Its fingers strained and the air escaped its lungs in a rasp. All it wanted was to end the suffering. No matter how… Images of longing spread through its brain. Biting into soft, living flesh, taste-buds caressed by the metallic flavor of blood. Taking a deep breath of its victim's fear.

Angrily, it smashed its injured wrist against a nearby tree. The watch, strapped on seven years earlier, stayed intact. This was the only thing remaining of its old life, and it had almost melted into its skin. No hair and no clothes remained on its distorted body any longer.

The pack slowed down and looked at each other. One of them stepped up: a female. It used to be an ailing girl; now it was a muscular, six-foot-five Beta. It flashed its serrated teeth as it sensed weakness, but the Alpha was on alert. It stood up straight and struck down backhanded. The Beta fell into the bushes, yowling. The Alpha rattled towards the others, then turned away from them, short of breath.

Rampage eased its pain for a short while. It felt its heart beating faster and it could breathe easier. Its pupils were wide, its jaw muscles quivered, and the noises of the outside world grew more intense. Euphoria spread in its body like a hot wave. Its mind craved impulses rather than words. Destruction, joy, blood, death.

Its sight cleared and the fog vanished from its head. When the grip of pain subsided, it felt their smell. The prey smell. The Alpha started to run. A desire for killing moved it forwards and thinking of the prey made its mouth water. It slowed at the edge of the woods, and immediately spotted what it was looking for.

2.

The truck stood in the middle of the road amidst a scattering of junk. It was clearly abandoned, its hood open, oil stains and spare parts lying everywhere. A bit farther, cans and empty plastic bags. Those who escaped had eventually stopped; out of necessity, judging by the truck left behind.

The Alpha sensed the aroma of the stale canned stew and the diluted instant coffee, mixed with the smell of human perspiration and of biodiesel, which resembled the scent of fried potatoes. Its eyes scanned for motion against the dawn twilight, but no signs of life were to be seen on the road. It let out a short, guttural grunt, and the rest of the pack ran one behind another out of the forest along the road. They approached the truck from two sides, faster and faster, with ceaselessly clashing jaws and a blood-thirsty rattle.

Only the Alpha slowed down. It let the others search the truck's surroundings. The Beta stopped beside the Alpha with head held low. Saliva was pouring from its mouth, directly towards its chin. It was watching the Alpha, which bared its teeth angrily at the disappointed ferals.

They were late. The truck was empty, no humans anywhere.

The Alpha looked around. It was aware that the survivors of the colony could only have gone one way. It gathered momentum, tossed a careless Delta aside, and leaped onto the top of the truck. The fiberglass caved in as if the Volvo had been made of plasticine, and the windshield broke into pieces beneath the Alpha's steel claws. It gazed along the southern horizon and quickly noticed sparkling lights. They were shimmering red and white spots, easy to recognize in the faded semi-darkness.

The convoy they were after was headed south to get around the mountains leading to the ocean. It would be impossible to reach them, unless…

The Alpha turned its head towards the hills. Hidden in the distance, the tunnel was waiting for them, the one which the humans steered clear of. But the pack had nothing to fear.

The ferals growled impatiently. The Beta looked up. Its ghastly voice roused the Alpha, who gave the command. They set off together. They did not rest, nor did they slow down.

All they wanted was to bite flesh and taste blood.

BROKEN PROMISE

1.

They were close. The noon sunshine slowly blew the fresh morning air away, bringing back the sweaty August heat. Reaching the Pincers, they got off their bikes and walked the rest of the way. They carefully nosed among the rusty vehicles with guns held high. Abigail carried the Browning while Cassius managed the Remington, but they didn't have much chance with sixteen bullets in the magazines. The playbook for situations like this was active hide-and-seek, which meant to find out what had happened without anyone noticing their presence. But she hated actively doing nothing.

They stopped at the dirt road leading to the quarry, where it all started seven years ago.

At the Pincers, traces of the fight could clearly be seen: thousands of wrecks jammed into each other, burnt out, paved with bones and abandoned suitcases. The ferals, Greenhorns at that time, had gathered into a huge horde and cracked the line of vehicles crowded before the tunnel from every side. The cars tried to get out, cutting each other off. Some of them even drove up onto the dirt road, but most of those eventually either flipped upside down or crashed into trees. The dried bloodstains on the seats gave away what had happened to the passengers. Abigail could still hear the screams of death, the exploding windshields and the squeaking brakes. For her the memory was about sounds. However hard she had tried to press her palms to her ears, huddling up in the backseat of the car, she couldn't reduce the noise.

After the failure of the quarantine in Headland, the massacre at the Pincers was the second coffin-nail. The outlying areas were flooded with thousands of refugees, who were slaughtered one after another by the ferals. As dread rose from the crowd, the monsters leaped from one victim to the next, often after only a single bite, as if the virus at that time had only worried about infecting the most people.

Quiet but rhythmic knocking drifted from the distance. Metal crashed against metal, which mixed with snatches of conversation.

Abigail glanced at Cassius, then doubled her pace towards the ridge, staying in shadow all the way. She moved quickly and hunched before reaching the top of the hill. *I know my job*, she exclaimed to herself, though her companion said nothing. She could only hear the quiet shuffle of his feet.

On the hilltop they crouched down behind a dry, rotten tree trunk, just before a chasm. Motionless, they watched what was happening in the manmade, rocky valley that had once been excavated by machines.

Most of the quarry was covered in weeds and some scrubby trees towered here and there in perfect harmony with the wrecks. The cars' former owners had escaped from the Pincers only to reach their destiny in this cauldron. The old service road could also be seen, now only trails; one led left, towards Route 10, the other wound up to the hill on the other side and disappeared to the east at the edge of the quarry.

They immediately spotted the movement. There was a jeep among the twigs, refracting the red-brown expanse of sand. An old Wrangler, the hood of which was being shut by a bald, bearded man in flannel shirt. He wiped his greasy hands with a cloth and checked the plow attached to the front of the jeep, then packed his tools. A barrel-chested veteran stepped out of the cover of the Wrangler and spat on the ground.

"They don't seem like man-eaters," Abigail said, and wiped her sweaty brow.

"I don't see no nametags."

Abigail let this new wisdom pass by, which made her feel like she was sitting at a classroom desk. *I told you, the only thing certain in life is that nothing is certain, blah-blah.* She frowned.

"What are they doing?"

The bald guy jumped into the jeep, made the engine roar, and set off towards the slope leading out of the quarry where there was a rusty SUV halfway slipped off the road. The barrel-chested man watched from the background as the Wrangler's plow pressed against the wreck. The SUV finally yielded to the pressure and slanted off the road, cracking in half in the dry bushes.

"They're preparing the ground. Probably for their mates. Hence the flare."

"Do you think we should talk to them?"

"What would we tell them? Let's just stay down here and hope that they don't stop at the motel."

Abigail was thinking about Soxy. Her heart filled with dread that the mysterious travelers might rummage their hideout. The sound of the engine brought her round. The bald guy backed out with the jeep and, not caring about the stirred-up dust cloud, he jumped out of the car. He gave the barrel-chested man a five and took a swig from a bottle with transparent homemade spirit in the bottom.

"Are you thinking what I'm thinking?" Cassius asked, and the girl nodded.

"They're nincompoops. I wonder how they're still alive!" Abigail crawled back and got on her feet. "Let's go back!"

But Cassius's hand stopped her and firmly pulled her back.

"Don't move!"

He was watching the rim of the quarry. Abigail was reading his gestures and huddled up; only her eyes danced impatiently, understanding that Cassius had noticed something worrisome. Then she saw it as well: something moved among the trees, about a hundred yards from them, headed directly towards the two men, faster and faster. Cassius and Abigail simultaneously readied their guns and turned them to the valley. The bald guy and the barrel-chested man were unaware. They drank the last gulp from the bottle, which flew into the bushes with a loud clash. They even whooped.

A Delta broke out from the trees and promptly threw itself onto the barrel-chested man. Its teeth sank into flesh, then blood squirted and bones cracked. Its victim shouted in pain. The feral mauled him until the bald guy emptied his handgun into them both. The Delta's body strained, then fell lifelessly onto the barrel-chested man, whose mouth was filled with seething blood. His body made a final tremble.

"Goddammit!"

Through the Browning scope, Abigail watched the bald guy kicking the Delta off his buddy. Time stopped. Only the red sand whirled around the carcasses. The bald guy went to the jeep, his movements those of a puppet controlled by clumsy hands, collapsing with every other step. He took a box from the back seat of the jeep and desperately poured its contents into the sand.

Cassius gripped the Remington.

"Eleven o'clock, at the white rock."

Abigail turned her head. Dust and leaves swirled at the edge of the quarry, and the trees below the cliffs were bowing like in a storm. Something started moving towards the bald guy from that cover, chopping branches and bushes in front of it. It was another feral, and not just any.

"Don't fart around!" Cassius hissed, but the bald guy was still crouching by the box, trying to refill the silver Smith & Wesson with shaking hands. The bullets kept dropping out of his fingers.

The trees then opened up behind him, and a Gamma threw itself out of the shrubs. A female. It smoothed the fall with its strong arms, and immediately began leaping yards at a time, closing the gap to the bald guy. Its pale-yellow eyes flashed as its jaws clapped with bloodthirst.

Abigail took a deep breath and her hands stiffened on the rifle. She didn't have much time if she wanted to act. The Gamma was only a few seconds away from the jeep.

"I can get it," she said.

"Wait for it!" Cassius shushed her while observing the trees, looking for other ferals. The Gamma wasn't slowing down. Fifteen yards...

"Wait for what?"

"There's one bullet in your Browning!"

"And? Otherwise it's gonna kill him!" Abigail aimed at the Gamma and softly placed her finger on the trigger. The feral was in her sight, and she didn't hesitate. She pulled the trigger. Everything seemed perfect; she did exactly as Cassius had taught her. Nice and stable, focusing only on the reticle. However, she couldn't see that the bald guy had also noticed the danger, and had immediately reacted. He jumped to his feet and threw himself towards the Gamma with his handgun halfway loaded. In the blink of an eye he stepped into Abigail's sight, and she couldn't do anything. The bullet split the air at a speed of three-thousand feet per minute, then hit the bald guy's shoulder, ripping out pieces of flesh and bones in a spray of blood.

The impact floored the man and the monster at the same time. The bald guy grabbed his shoulder and as he hit the ground, his saliva mixed with the red dust to cover his face like a mask. When he came round, the Gamma had already taken the initiative. Instincts overrode its sense of danger, and the feral bit into his shoulder. Agonized gurgles blended with the screams. The bald man tried to defend himself, but he only grasped at the air while the Gamma tore more and more chunks of flesh out of him.

"No, no, no!" Abigail's face turned ashen. For a second she thought all it was a nightmare, that it couldn't be happening. She couldn't have made such a huge mistake. Someone would die because of her.

Cassius did not hesitate. Inhale, hold it, aim… and he fired, twice to be sure. The feral's spasming body fell to the ground next to the bald guy. The whirling dust slowly settled. The voices of agony echoed no more in the quarry.

Abigail's mouth was still open, her snub nose trembling. Cassius observed the valley and he waited. No motion among the trees. No noises. Nothing suspicious. When she tried to get to her feet, he raised his hand to stop her. Minutes passed, and the sounds of nature multiplied around them.

He swallowed hard, threw his rifle onto his shoulder, and started downward. "Let's go!" he said to her. "We have some things to clear up."

2.

The ferals and the barrel-chested man were dead, only the bald guy in the flannel shirt gasping in the dust. His injuries were severe, but not so bad that he would die before transforming. A bite on the neck meant they didn't have much time left. Cassius stepped closer to him and looked around once again, but there were no movements at the edge of the quarry. Only the intensifying wind blowing through the trees.

"We have to hurry!" he turned to Abigail, who did not come closer. She stood stubbornly beside the jeep and balanced on the verge of tears as she watched the bald guy. "Abigail!"

She winced and looked at him with glazed eyes.

"Check the car!"

Abigail opened the jeep door on the other side, and through the window she watched Cassius leaning closer and closer to the downed man. She tried not to hear his gurgling struggle for breath. Cassius attempted to catch the poor soul's gaze, but the latter was already fighting with the shadow world. His right hand spastically scratched the dust beside him and Cassius finally realized what the guy was looking for. The silver Smith & Wesson.

"You no longer need that, buddy," Cassius said, and before he took the revolver, he checked the bullets. *Four more...*

He took out his flask, held the bald guy's head and poured water in his mouth. The poor soul could hardly swallow those few gulps. He turned his head and gasped.

"Where are you coming from?" Cassius asked.

No answer. The bald guy's body shook as he struggled with blood loss.

"Hey, buddy, stay with me. Where are you coming from and where were you headed to?"

Just gargling. *Damn!*

Cassius stood up. His eyes stuck on the Gamma's lifeless body. The alarm sounded in his head, but so silent and uncertain that at first he didn't understand why all his bones were flooded with restlessness. *Something is very wrong!*

A bird flew up from a branch with a loud shriek. The wind stirred up the red sand. Cassius bit his lips.

"There's nothing here... just stink!" he heard Abigail from the jeep, and for a moment he saw as the girl's head rise higher, watching events with curious, worried eyes.

Cassius took out his machete and pointed it at the maul wound.

"Sorry, but we can't waste any bullets." Before he struck down, he saw the bald guy's boots. They were barely used. "Nice pair. May I have them?"

The bald guy didn't reply, just watched with bulging eyes as Cassius waited for a second, then:

"Thanks, buddy!"

It was over in a beat.

3.

The inside of the worn, dark-blue jeep was sticky with dirt. It hadn't been properly cleaned for years and there was junk on the floor and thick dust on the dashboard, while old food stained the upholstery. Abigail secretly watched Cassius as he took a deep breath and struck down. Then she turned away, pretending to continue her search of the car, trying not to give herself away. Unfortunately, her thoughts wouldn't rest, and in her head she kept desperately repeating the question: *What have I done?*

She pushed some bags over on the back seat, but found nothing valuable in either one. Nothing on the floor. In the front, the only useful thing was the ham radio, but she already knew how Cassius would react, so she left it there. She found some cans of food and two wrapped sandwiches. She packed the tins, but tossed even the flask aside. He had taught her what food and drink they could trust and what they shouldn't bother with because of the high risk.

Cassius showed up at the driver's side door. Abigail saw the drops of blood on his face as he looked through the filthy interior of the jeep.

"Have you found anything?"

From the glove compartment, she took out a folded map marked with X's and lines. She handed it to him, and he carefully examined it.

"So, they were headed towards the motel," Cassius said, and turned the map over to Abigail. The dot indicating the motel had been circled, and an arrow showed which way they would move on. Towards Headland, on Route 10.

"Headland? What the hell did they want there?"

"No idea. Anything else?"

"Apart from this? Nothing interesting. Some food, some clean cloths that could be useful, and of course the radio."

"Does it work?"

"Guess so," she shrugged her shoulders, and started turning the dials, but heard nothing but static noise and cracking. Cassius started to lose his patience.

"Just leave it! We'd better get going."

She nodded and quickly collected the useful things. In the meantime, Cassius tied the bald guy's boots to his bag, involuntarily watching the rim. Abigail sensed what he was thinking.

"They were just scouts, right?" she asked, and pointed at the two ferals.

Cassius nodded.

"So the pack must be nearby." She winced as she considered what that meant. "Could they have heard the gunfire?"

"They surely could." Cassius signaled to set off. "We got to carry all the stuff up to the roof by noon, although if their companions are as stupid as they were, they might not even notice that we're there. Perhaps they'll soon move on," he looked back at the beheaded body. "Hopefully they will shit their pants seeing what happened to their buddies, God bless their souls."

Abigail sped her steps and tried to catch up with Cassius, who was at least twenty-five yards from the vehicle when…

…the radio came to life. After a sizzle, the voice of a young man crossed the ether.

"Trevor! Can you hear me? We're nearly at the mine. What's up with you guys?"

Cassius and Abigail stopped at the same time. She stared at the jeep with bright eyes. The questions and the possible answers kept rattling in her head. She felt her heart beating faster from the excitement, even through her concern about who the mysterious strangers could be and what she would tell them. *Everything's gonna be all right… They'll understand!* She thought if they warned these new strangers, she could right her wrong.

Cassius, however, was just standing, motionless. When they finally exchanged looks, he pointed towards the road.

"Let's hurry up!" He wanted to leave to get back on Route 10 as soon as possible. Abigail was standing stunned.

"And the pack?"

"If we're fast enough, they might not see us."

"But they'll see them!" she shouted and pointed at the radio. Cassius still didn't slow down, he simply added:

"None of our business. I don't want to die because of their idiocy."

The radio hissed. The voice on the other end became less and less patient.

"Trevor, what the hell's going on?"

Abigail ran after Cassius, and tried to get in front of him, but he simply moved faster. She shouted, almost screamed. "We have to warn them!"

"Really? And what do you think their first question will be when they find us here?"

"They'll ask, when are the others coming." Abigail pointed at the ferals' carcasses, but in her hurry she almost tripped in her own feet.

"They'll find out. But I'd rather they didn't even know that we exist!" he said and took a worried look around. She angrily shook her head.

The radio in the background did not fall silent.

"Fuck, Trevor, where are you? We need to know whether the quarry is safe. I don't want to go round it." Beat. "To hell with these idiots, I bet they..."

Hissing suppressed the rest of the sentence. Abigail stopped. *Now or never!* Cassius gripped her arm and turned her in front of him.

"Enough of the nonsense for today!"

Abigail pulled her arm free from his fist.

"Is this what we're gonna do from now on? Just leave everybody to die?"

"If we want to stay alive, then yes! We're not responsible for anyone, only ourselves."

Abigail wanted to reply, but Cassius shushed her. She immediately realized that he had noticed something. The wind blew the sounds of vehicles from the other side of the quarry. Slowly but surely, the noise got louder, and Abigail expected the vehicles to arrive within a minute or two. Her entire body was vibrating with excitement. She knew the only right solution. *They'll understand that it was an accident...*

"Let's go!" Cassius ordered, but in vain. She headed back towards the jeep, her steps moving faster and faster.

"Abigail!"

He angrily dropped his bag, then tucked the silver Smith & Wesson in his belt at the small of his back and went after Abigail with his rifle held high. Just in time. As he reached her, an entire convoy appeared at the other side of the quarry, with trucks and vans. The first car, a Mercedes jeep suddenly stopped on the top as the travelers saw what had happened down below. Brakes squeaked and a thick cloud of red dust covered up the vehicles.

Cassius raised both hands, holding the Remington in one, and the Glock in the other, showing that their intentions were peaceful. She followed his example but noticed the silver revolver attached to his waist. *Just don't do anything stupid, old man!*

The convoy didn't move from the top of the hill and Cassius threw a cutting glance at Abigail.

"I hope it was worth it, smartass!"

4.

The first two vehicles started towards them: the Mercedes in the front, on the flatbed of which a buck-toothed boy gripped the mounted machine gun, and behind it an armored Transit. The rest of the convoy stayed on the rim, but more and more passengers got out of the trucks to see what was happening. Cassius signaled to Abigail to wait, then he took a few steps ahead so that the travelers would have to deal with him.

The jeep and the van stirred up a large cloud of dust on the narrow serpentine, then stopped at a safe distance. It took a lifetime until the doors opened: three people stepped out of the vehicles, and without any questions, they pointed their guns at them. The fourth one, the buck-toothed boy fiddled with the machine gun until he was able to ready it. *There is at least one noob among them... but why did they put him there?*

"Hey, take it easy, we're all friends here!" Cassius said, and allowed himself a slight smile. Still, he held the Glock in his right hand ready to use if necessary. When the travelers lined up in front of him, eyeing him distrustfully, he tried to figure out which of them was the leader.

"Weapons on the ground!" the young man driving the jeep said.

Classic stoner disgrace, Cassius thought when he noticed that the young man's shotgun wasn't even readied. The lad tried to act with confidence, but his tight shoulders and twitching eyes gave him away.

"You heard me."

"We heard you, buddy," Cassius replied calmly, and held a long pause, "but there is a slight snag. We don't like to be eye to eye with gun barrels."

"And we don't give a shit about what you like!" A shoulder-bag woman stepped closer. The revolver glinted in her hand, but she was holding it so awkwardly that Cassius was certain she had never fired a live weapon. The woman glanced vaguely at a man with a cowboy hat and mustache, who was standing on the other side of the jeep with a semi-automatic rifle. Cassius took a deep breath and clenched his Glock. A good old Mexican standoff.

"All right, we'll do what you want," Abigail said in the background, and to Cassius' great surprise she dropped her gun on the ground and put her hands in the air. She moved forwards, she might even have passed Cassius if his outstretched arm hadn't stopped her. They exchanged brief looks, his eyes narrowed, the muscles in his forehead strained.

"They have to see that they can trust us," she whispered and tossed away his arm. "Or do you think you can outrun a machine gun?"

The shoulder-bag woman swayed her revolver.

"You, too, big boy! I don't want to say it again!"

"Why, what happens if you have to?" Cassius hissed to himself, but eventually he also dropped his guns and carefully lowered his hands. He was prepared to grab the silver Smith & Wesson hidden by his waist at any moment.

"What the hell happened here?" the stoner young man asked. He seemed to have been calmed by the fact that the guns of the opposite side were lying in the dust.

"We're peaceful travelers," Abigail said, and bowed a bit as she spoke. *Not to him, he's not the boss*, Cassius thought. Abigail, however, continued. "Your friends were attacked by ferals. We were trying to help."

"Oh, really?" the man with the cowboy hat asked, then nodded his head towards the young man. "David!"

David bristled up. "Me? Why me, Grant?"

The shoulder-bag woman snapped at him: "You coward piece of shit!" Then she started towards the Wrangler. As the woman walked past them, Abigail wanted to say something, but Cassius shushed her. It would have been useless to explain herself any longer. He was just hoping that the travelers would put the puzzle pieces together. After all, two ferals were lying in the dust. *But if they don't...* Cassius glanced behind them to search for escape routes. The Wrangler was just a few yards away, and if he could draw one of the idiots closer, they would even have cover. Meanwhile, he tried to stand so there was no way the shoulder-bag woman would see the Smith & Wesson hidden behind his back.

Abigail didn't wait for the verdict.

"We'll explain everything, but we must hurry now!" she sputtered. David, whose face had flushed at the earlier indignity, stepped closer.

"Shut up!" the young man said, but Grant snubbed him.

"Easy, dummy!"

The shoulder-bag woman crouched down to Trevor's body, then retched loudly and vomited. When she looked up, she just shook her head with tears in her eyes.

"So, you wanted to help us. Who are you? Mother-fuckin' Teresa?" Grant asked with a sarcastic smile, then pointed his finger at Cassius' bag. Right where he had tied Trevor's boots. "I might even believe you, but I'm not really keen on looters."

His companions immediately raised their weapons higher, and the shoulder-bag woman also went back, even though her body was still shivering from what she had seen. Grant had a superior grin on his face.

"And we do the same with every scumbag like you. We rip them off, break their knees, and leave 'em there to fuckin' rot, so that the birds would shit around their bodies."

"You don't understand." Abigail's voice got thin, as she began to realize the difficulty of their situation.

"Oh, we don't, kitty cat?" David asked and his face was burning.

When he looked over her shoulder, his eyes were caught by Trevor's beheaded body. The skin strained on his neck. "Hmm? What don't we understand? Was that a feral that cut off our friend's head and stole his stuff?"

Abigail clenched her fists at the scornful remark. David carelessly stepped closer and pushed his gun between Abigail's eyes. He wasn't afraid of her. He should have been.

"Huh? You don't say nothin', kitty cat?

Oh, shit! Cassius closed his eyes and prepared for the worst.

A defiant shadow ran across Abigail's face, and her hand immediately swung. She grabbed David's arm, and while she pulled him towards herself, she also pushed him aside, and when he lost his momentum, she beat the barrel of his shotgun directly into his nose. The beat was followed by a frightening crack and a squirt of blood, and David fell into the dust and cried out. She turned the shotgun around and pointed it at the stunned travelers.

Cassius did not want to give them time: he ripped the revolver out of the woman's grip, and with his other hand quickly took out the silver Smith & Wesson hidden behind his back. By then, everybody was shouting, but neither Abigail's nor Cassius's hands shook.

"Hey, hey, hey! Drop them!"

"Weapons on the ground!"

"Don't you dare! I said now..."

Abigail readied the shotgun, and when David tried to get up, she kicked his shoulder with one move.

"That's how you do it, dumbass!" She stepped forwards with the gun held high, aimed directly to Grant. He wasn't insane; he held both hands up and spat on the ground. He probably knew now what he was up against. Not Sunday drivers for sure.

"Take it easy, folks," he said.

Cassius looked to the side and watched the rim of the slope. He sensed motion, but when he turned, he saw nothing among the trees. Still, he hadn't had much time to look around.

"Was it gibberish what I just said?" Abigail asked impatiently. "Your friends were attacked by ferals. We tried to help, but we couldn't."

"They're lying!" the shoulder-bag woman snapped. "They shot

Trevor."

"Yes, and I'm sorry." Abigail's voice quavered. "It was an accident, I swear! We didn't mean any trouble."

"An accident, I see," Grant nodded. He spread his arms and grinned, as if it was the most natural thing in the world. "And the boots?"

"Should I give 'em back? Will that calm you down?"

The travelers standing on the rim of the quarry started whispering in excitement. By then, at least two dozen of them had grouped up in front of the trucks and vans, and they watched the events holding their breaths. Of course, none of them wanted to intervene. Nobody ran back to their trucks to bring guns, and none of them tried to organize themselves to circumvent Cassius and Abigail from up there. *Amateurs... luckily,* he thought, but he was worried that a finger on a trigger might do something stupid.

"It would be best for all of us if you just laid down your guns," Grant said. "If you're telling the truth, there will be no trouble."

"Do I look like an idiot?"

Cassius's hands tightened on the guns, but before they could continue their argument, the Mercedes door opened and a woman in a baggy dress stepped out of the jeep. By the time she had slipped out of the cover of the door, everyone was watching her shamble.

"Megan!" David turned back and hissed like a snake. "What are you doing?"

Cassius was astonished as the traveler's figure unfolded: a beautiful brunette, just about ten years older than Abigail, with a belly so big that there was no doubt she was only weeks away from giving birth. Grant turned back angrily.

"That puts the lid on it!" he murmured to himself. "Put your butt back in the car, woman!"

Megan, however, took no notice of him. She stretched her arm out directly to Cassius, with eyes filled with desperation.

"Please, calm down! We don't mean to hurt you!"

Cassius was mesmerized by the woman, whose soft, booming voice distracted him. Her long hair, played with by the wind, brought back a memory of a long-lost moment, an image he believed he'll never see again. He tried to force some words out of his mouth, but was unable. Megan continued:

"I'm sure you meant no harm. Please... Put down your weapons!"

Cassius didn't want to fall for any tricks, but he couldn't escape her gaze. A cold sweat ran down his back, making him shiver. The alarm bell was already ringing wildly in his head, but he couldn't decide why. Was it because of the woman standing in front of him, her hand on her stomach, or because something had moved at the edge of his vision, on the rim of the quarry? Cassius lifted his head, his gaze fixed on the trees. Abigail must have noticed his unease because she had resorted to other tactics. She turned to Grant.

"We just wanted to warn you."

"Warn? Warn us about what?" Grant asked, raising an eyebrow. The mask of confidence seemed to have finally melted away.

"'That there might be more ferals lurking around" Abigail replied. "We gotta get out of here!"

The travelers froze. Grant looked around in fright. For a split second, the wind seemed to stop, and Cassius could hear the dust grains scratching the vehicles. From the edge of the quarry, muffled snatches of speech grew louder; someone got out of a truck and slammed the door loudly; the whispering of the trees died away, replaced by an unearthly rumble. It climbed up Cassius's spine, clutching his throat, leaving a bloodcurdling resonance. The alarm bell went off in his head, louder than ever before, and then it fell abruptly silent.

And that silence was more frightening than anything else.

Movement flashed through the trees, then another, on the other side. A strangled, animalistic guttural sound followed.

"Too late," Cassius said, and pulled himself up, as if preparing every inch of his body. He didn't have to wait long for the first wave of the attack.

Above, at the edge of the quarry, a passenger standing by one of the trucks turned back in shock and then disappeared behind the vehicle with a muffled scream. Something terrible had dragged him down, leaving only a grunt and the sound of carnage. Those standing nearby screamed and began to flee back into the trucks. One of them fell, and the others trampled over him without thinking. No one waited for each other. Panic immediately engulfed them, and they escaped down into the valley, towards Cassius and Abigail.

Abigail helped David up and handed him back the shotgun. The hurt in the young man's eyes faded and was replaced by terror as he looked desperately at them. Cassius tossed the shoulder-bag woman his revolver and stepped towards Abigail. He grabbed her shoulder and pulled her towards the Wrangler. They both knew that what had happened so far was just a distraction, and that the pack was somewhere in the woods waiting for the perfect moment. *The ferals are herding everyone into the valley!*

But Grant and his companions had no idea of any of that. They were frozen, watching the panic above, unable to tear their eyes away from the edge of the quarry. Grant ordered his people to get back in their vehicles, but they were distracted by the roar of an engine and a crash.

What the hell? Cassius looked up. One of the trucks had found a way for itself and was speeding down the dusty service road. *Too fast! Slow down!* A feral emerged on the top of the cabin, swinging on the bumpy road and immediately slammed into the windscreen, which exploded into tiny pieces. The driver screamed, braked, and jerked the steering wheel, causing the vehicle to overturn. The truck crashed into the reddish-brown sand, the grille creaking and screeching as the twenty-five-ton doom pushed a thick cloud of dust towards them.

Cassius and Abigail pulled themselves together, Grant ducked into the cover of the Mercedes, and David threw himself to the ground. The overturned truck stopped ten yards away. The dust particles swirled around them, and only Megan's wails could be heard. Then the desperate sound of brakes and horns, as the overturned truck was slammed into by another behind it with a deafening crash.

"Back to the jeep!" Cassius pulled Abigail to her feet and headed for the Wrangler. It was their only chance to escape. The driver's side door was open, they just had to jump in and shut out the world. Abigail hesitated. She glanced back at Megan, who was hunched over the wheels of the Mercedes, but before she could speak, Cassius shoved her angrily. "Now!"

A lanky shadow emerged from behind the Wrangler and with

one giant leap landed on top of the jeep, cutting off their only escape route. The Gamma snarled at them, its teeth chattering with bloodlust. Its sinewy body contracted, ready to pounce. Abigail screamed and fired all five bullets from her Glock. The Gamma screamed in pain, but the two hits that tore into its shoulder were not fatal. The beast threw itself to the side, and when it landed, ripped the door off the Wrangler in one furious motion. It threw the door at them as if it were a ball.

At the last moment they leapt aside and the Wrangler's door crashed, deformed, into the sand between them. Cassius and Abigail looked desperately at each other, but the Gamma gave them no time. It swung its clawed arm towards them.

Cassius sprang up first to leap between the girl and the feral. On a sudden impulse, he grabbed the torn door as a shield before the Gamma could tear him down. He had to control himself so he wouldn't close his eyes instinctively. He tightened his chest, but wasn't prepared for the pain that struck him.

On impact, Cassius felt as if the last gulp of air had been sucked from his lungs, and then he hit the ground with a groan. He had the rusty, metallic taste of blood in his mouth. His face was covered in a red-brown mask of sand, but he fought his way back up. His weapons had scattered as he fell, his fingers only touching the handle of his machete in the sand. He summoned all his strength to strike at his attacker. Blood spurted and he heard the unmistakable tearing of skin, bone, and tendon. The Gamma fell to the dust.

The world went black for Cassius. Before he could fall as well, Abigail caught him. Even through the choking cloud of dust and the haze of pain, he could see the frightened gleam in her eyes.

"I felt that," he said, then squeezed her shoulder and looked around.

One by one, the vehicles from the edge of the mine braked, and the travelers jumped out, gripping their weapons. Grant rushed to the overturned truck, shaking his head and shouting orders. Cassius coughed from the dust in his lungs. He looked around, but in the swirling cloud he could no longer see the road out of the valley. *We're doomed if we fart around for long!*

"They're going to catch us!" he said, and put the silver Smith &

Wesson in her hand. "Four. Make every bullet count!"

Abigail nodded, then wrapped a handkerchief around her face. Cassius picked up his guns from the ground and hurried to Grant. For the first few steps, his legs were shaking and his spine seemed to be in a vice. Grant looked at him angrily as he gave orders.

"I bet they were after you, dadgum it…"

"Shut up!" Cassius choked out. "We've got to go, and that means now!"

"Dude, are you crazy?" Grant pointed to the overturned truck and climbed on top to see what had happened to his partner trapped in the cab. "We're not leaving anyone behind!" he shouted to the others, who spun around in fright.

Cassius had a quick look at the Mercedes; keys in the lock, doors wide open. Abigail squeezed his arm and shook her head. Her mouth formed the words silently: *Don't!*

Someone screamed.

Cassius immediately crouched down, threw his back against the overturned truck, and pulled Abigail down beside him into the cover. *Shh!* He pointed, for she would have instinctively gone to help. Her eyes glinted, but he didn't care in the least, just squeezed her as tight as he could. And then they heard the thump. The vibration running across the slick ground, the thumping of feet, in rapid succession, getting stronger and closer. *This is it!*

Grant, standing on top of the truck, was alerted to the noise, but the cloud of dust eventually enveloped him along with the others, and from then on Cassius heard only the sounds of panic. The screams were joined by the crackling of guns and grunts, and a door slammed. One of the vehicles swerved out of the way and sped past the Mercedes, then heard it hit something with a sharp thud. All hell broke loose around them. On the other side of the overturned truck, gun after gun went off, then silenced after yet another blood-curdling scream.

The buck-toothed boy was still messing with the machine gun on the roof of the Mercedes. When he finally got a shot off, a shadow instantly knocked him down and tore him apart in seconds. A skinny little boy walked out from behind the overturned truck, his face bloody, his hands cramped, but before he could cry from shock, a

Beta pounced on him.

A Beta... Oh my God, a Beta!

A grey-haired woman in a cardigan ran past them and screamed when she saw the Beta. "Sammy!" she cried, then she was also struck down.

Cassius was stunned, and as he looked for a way out, he caught sight of Megan hunched over the wheels of the Mercedes. Their eyes met, and she instinctively started to crawl towards them. He gestured for her not to move, but Megan ignored him. She just wanted to get to safety. With her hand grasping in the reddish-brown dust, she pressed down on a piece of debris and hissed loudly. Blood began to ooze from her palms, and when she straightened in pain, a menacing shadow followed.

"No!" Cassius shuddered. He hesitated to move, paralyzed by his own rules, but he saw Megan's desperate expression and couldn't deny her. He sprang to his feet and with his machete he impaled the feral that was about to pounce on her.

Abigail crawled to Megan, hunched over, and quickly bandaged the wound with her handkerchief. When Cassius returned, hand over his eyes, Abigail had already helped her to her feet.

"Which way?" Abigail asked.

"Into the Mercedes, quickly! Let's get out of here!" Cassius said, but Megan raised her hand.

"And what about the others? We can't just leave them here!"

The cloud of dust parted then, as if by magic, and the ravaged landscape revealed itself. Cassius gasped, and Megan jumped when she saw the battlefield.

Most of the travelers lay bleeding, with only a few desperate companions left to fight the overwhelming odds. The ferals moved incessantly, circling around, up and down the vehicles, getting closer and closer to their victims.

Jesus, there must be a dozen of them!

Bullets pounded the sand as some tried to pick off members of the pack, but most missed their mark and before they could right their wrongs, the ferals had jumped. The Beta pounced on a writhing, sobbing man on the ground and dragged him along. It threw his victim behind one of the trucks as if the hundred-and-eighty-pound man was just a mannequin.

A Gamma burst from the cover of the vehicle and struck a woman with its improbably long arm. She fell to her knees. The Gamma then disappeared into a cloud of dust, but the woman was shown no mercy. A Delta struck her from behind with all its might, breaking her spine and cracking her bones.

One by one, they're being picked off. They're stalking everyone!

"Get in the car!" Cassius shouted, and this time he didn't have to say it twice. When he opened the door, he saw David cowering in the back seat. "Pull yourself together! Help her!" he said and tilted his head at Megan.

David reached under his sister's arm with trembling hands and pulled her into the Mercedes like a sack. Abigail took down a Greenhorn while Cassius put three bullets into a Delta. From the sounds of it, the slaughter was in its final act, the last survivors being picked apart by the pack. *Now! Let's go!*

Cassius was about to turn back to the jeep when something stirred behind the swirling cloud of dust. An agonized scream split the air, then the outline of a towering demon broke through the mist as if born out of the billowing chaos. Cassius froze, not daring to breathe for fear of drawing attention to himself. Only his hand moved: he slowly raised his rifle, but when he realized what he was seeing, his throat tightened. He knew he wouldn't stand a chance. He could only think that all the bullets in the world wouldn't be enough.

The Alpha stuck out its shoulder and sniffed the air. Its jaw was trembling with bloodlust, its serrated teeth caked with flesh. It was looking for its next victim...

...and found it. Grant turned up at the overturned truck. He ran towards them with a disfigured face, limping and clutching his stomach. He looked back and groaned when he saw the Alpha.

Cassius turned to Abigail. Shocked by the sight, she understood the command and they got into the jeep at the same time. He revved the engine, but before he could do anything, Megan grabbed his shoulder.

"That's Grant! We have to wait for him!"

Cassius clenched his jaw and watched Grant limp towards the

jeep from the rear-view mirror. His right foot was on the accelerator, his hand on the steering wheel, and his eyes flicked between their destination – the valley exit – and the mirror.

What's taking so long?

"He's hurt," Abigail said, exasperated.

"If he's been bitten…"

Cassius didn't finish, just scowled. He waited for the Alpha to emerge, but behind Grant there was only a cloud of dust. The guy pushed his hat over his head and finally reached the flatbed of the jeep. With the last of his strength, he pulled himself up and held on, and Cassius stamped on the accelerator.

They were relieved, but it was short-lived.

The Alpha appeared in the rear-view mirror, catching up with them in two giant leaps, and a single bump was enough to send the jeep off its track and nearly toppling over.

Megan screamed, Abigail clung to the seat, but Cassius managed to keep the Mercedes upright. He accelerated again, speeding up the hill. He could still see the Alpha roaring angrily in the rear-view mirror.

5.

Shell-shock ruled inside the car as Cassius turned sharply north. Avoiding the wrecks at the Pincers, they cut across the 10 and continued on across boggy fields. For a few minutes, none of them spoke, waiting for the pressure in their throats to subside and their hearts to slow down.

Abigail peeked at Cassius, but he paid no attention. He concentrated on the road as if he had been ordered to: just forwards, hands on the wheel. His fingers were white as he gripped the steering wheel, his face set in the kind of scowl that came when he was trying to control his rage. Abigail knew: he couldn't wait to scream her head off. She was ashamed. *This was very close...*

She turned back and smiled at the two siblings. Or at least she tried to. Megan squeezed David's hand, but he didn't react, just swallowed hard and leaned his head against the window pane. Abigail tried to figure out their story. Why did they hit the road? And what could there be around Headland that was worth taking such a risk for? She surveyed them unobtrusively before turning back to the front. She saw that the woman had a heart-shaped pendant hanging from a chain around her neck, but no wedding ring; a frayed tattoo on her wrist (*Rebellious youth?*); a thin, fringed scarf around her neck (*In this heat?*). Her well-groomed face contrasted sharply with David's untidy appearance, his long hair slicked on both sides and his sweat-stained top. Their clothes were threadbare and inadequate to protect them. No equipment, no weapon even on the young man. *Did he even fire the shotgun?* She noticed the constant swearing from Grant as he tumbled around on the flatbed.

She looked out the window of the jeep and saw that they were getting farther and farther away from the 10. Her throat tightened, and she turned to Cassius in confusion.

"Where are we going?" she asked, her voice hushed with nervousness. She hoped he hadn't noticed it.

"As far away as possible! I want a detour so long they can't follow us back to the motel."

Abigail nodded in relief. *Maybe Soxy can hold out for another hour or two*, she thought, and mentally played out the tasks ahead. *The puppy needed to be fed immediately...*

"Ammo?"

...replace his water, clean out his box, and be beside him as much as possible, because the puppy craved company. She imagined how he would feel now without his mommy and his siblings.

"Abigail! Ammo?"

She flinched and blinked at him, perplexed, but subconsciously the puzzle finally came together.

"Two."

"Three and four. Damn!" Cassius drummed nervously on the steering wheel, "We've lost a lot of stuff."

"But we survived." She tried to look on the bright side, but he fell silent. He stared straight ahead into the distance, fingers thrumming against the dirty steering wheel.

The awkward silence lasted for long seconds.

"Did you see it too?" Abigail asked finally. Cassius bit his lip and nodded. "Was that what I think it was?"

"It was. An Alpha."

Meanwhile, Megan turned to the truck bed and tapped on the rear window. Only after a long pause did Grant raise his thumb.

"Shouldn't we stop to check on him?" she asked.

Cassius looked in the rear-view mirror. "No! What the hell were you thinking, traveling in this condition?

Megan clung to the two seats, her face still white with shock.

"We had no choice, we had to leave!"

Abigail leaned closer, excited.

"Leave? Where to?"

"East, to the boat-town. It was our only chance." David snorted, but Megan ignored him. "If we had stayed in Liberty, we'd either be slaughtered by the pack or starve to death, so we took our chances."

"Great!" grinned David. "None of them will starve to death anymore."

"What about the ones slaughtered in Liberty? Or do you think they died because of me?" Megan snapped. She fought back tears as she looked at her brother, who turned back to the window instead of answering. He raised his hand in surrender.

"I never said that."

"It's nobody's fault. We've never seen a pack this big before," Abigail tried to reassure them. Cassius cleared his throat, so she corrected herself. "At least not since the first years of the pandemic. And they were led by an Alpha..."

"So, it would be nice to avoid them," Cassius cut in, then turned the wheel and the jeep headed east on a wide, rambling route, but finally towards the motel. He stared at Abigail, and she could tell by the look in his eyes that the following was meant for her alone. "I think we have come far enough. Hopefully they'll lose our scent, but we cannot take any risks. We'll pack what we can and leave at dawn!"

She nodded curtly, but then remembered what Megan had said. "And what is this boat-town?" she asked, turning back. "We've never heard of it."

"It's a colony upriver, just past Headland," Megan replied. "Long way, I know, but we've talked to them on the radio. They've got plenty of water, food, and they can protect themselves from the ferals. Last year they pulled together some scrapped boats in the middle of the river, and they rarely leave them. It's safe." She turned to David. "And safety is what we need most right now."

Abigail glanced at Cassius, but he focused on the road. His face was static, not even a twitch or an eyewink.

"Did you send scouts?" she asked Megan.

"We did, but the pack slaughtered them."

Cassius grimaced.

"Now, wait a minute... you're telling me none of you have been there?"

Megan shook her head after a moment's hesitation, and Cassius laughed compulsively.

"That's the stupidest thing I've ever heard," he said, then looked meaningfully in the rear-view mirror. "And, by the way, how far along are you?"

"It's the thirty-second week."

Abigail furrowed her brows. It was one of the few topics she and Cassius hadn't discussed at all. Of course, she knew exactly why not. He didn't want to remember his past.

"What does that mean?" she finally asked.

"It means she's close," Cassius replied, then he muttered to himself: "That makes it even more stupid."

Yeah, yeah, I know the deal, Abigail thought to herself. *It's always like this, it's always amateurs, and no one with any brains,* she mimicked Cassius' voice to herself, and this time, she conceded, he might even be right. *In this state... it'd be a wonder if they made it to Headland.* And that wasn't even the worst of it. Headland was not a place you wanted to go, and definitely not in a condition like hers.

"And you?" Megan turned to Abigail. "Where are you headed to?"

"Well, not east for sure," Cassius said, not caring that he wasn't the one being asked.

"Why not?"

"We've been to several colonies," Abigail explained, softening her voice. "We've seen the same everywhere."

"Same what?"

"Same chaos," Cassius finished off.

David pulled down the window and stuck his head through it. He took a deep breath and let the cool air fill his lungs. Abigail felt sorry for him; she had stopped thinking about how pathetic the young man was being, and even felt guilty for punching him so badly in the nose.

"Are you alright?" Megan asked David. He nodded.

The oil pressure light came on and the engine gave way with a rattling, clattering surrender. Smoke leaked out of the fittings, the engine stalled, and the Mercedes lost momentum.

Cassius closed his eyes for a second, then glanced at Abigail.

"Son of a... Well, that complicates things a little," he said, looking out over the familiar terrain. He frowned and his face turned into an angry grimace.

The 285 was just about a mile from them, behind pepper trees and dry weeds. They were halfway between the warehouse and the motel. Abigail puckered her lips, remembering the puppies left behind. Much as she wanted to, they had no time to go back to the warehouse. *The aim is to survive...*

"At least we know the way," she said resignedly.

Cassius poked his head towards the back seat.

"That's the least of my worries."

6.

Cassius considered their options and realized that the situation wasn't a good one. Once again he had broken the promise he made to himself and on top of it, another harsh hike was ahead of them, this time with a pregnant woman, a milksop, and a wounded man. *Speaking of the wounded...*

Cassius took out his gun, readied it and, as he got out with a flourish, tossed to Abigail:

"Pop the hood! I'm gonna check something."

"Check what?" Abigail asked, but he didn't answer.

Cassius started back with heavy steps, while the others watched with wide eyes. He stopped beside Grant, who was crouched on the flatbed. He stayed at a safe distance and was ready to use his gun if necessary. *Good heavens*, he thought as he looked over the guy. Grant was in a bad state: blood was running from his face and he was panting for breath. No way they'd take him with them; he'd be out for sure after a ten-minute walk.

"Show me the wound!" Cassius said, tapping his thigh with his gun. Abigail appeared on the other side of the jeep, scowling.

"Calm down, dude," Grant raised one hand, but with the other he was still holding his stomach.

"Oh, I'm calm, don't you worry. Just let me see that wound!" Cassius stepped back and raised the gun. Grant grinned compulsively, then pulled up his shirt. He didn't look as if he was ashamed of being wounded... or as if he knew exactly what he was dealing with.

Cassius took a good look at the red-purple, palm-sized bruise, then put his gun away.

"It doesn't look very good," he said finally.

Grant lowered his shirt with a strained expression.

"No, it doesn't."

And that was the end of the subject.

Cassius made his way to the driver's seat, glaring at Abigail as he went. He reached under the wheel and popped the hood. Smoke billowed up, but he ignored the acrid stench and looked at the engine. Still, he was no wiser. David appeared, gently pushed him aside, and examined the engine compartment.

Cassius watched impatiently, not particularly interested in what David was doing. "Maybe I can fix it," he said finally, bored by the young man acting like a real mechanic. *There must be some junk on the flatbed to weld it with...*

David shook his head.

"No way! The crank-case is damaged. The oil leaked out and the engine had no lubrication. Kaboom! That's it, it's gone. No tools, no time."

Cassius took a deep breath.

"Who the fuck are you, the geek-squad?"

"Yes," David replied, and held out his hand to Cassius. "My name is David and this is Megan," he said, bobbing his head towards the woman who had just climbed out of the back seat.

"Good for you," Cassius grunted, then started backwards.

Grant climbed down from the flatbed with clenched teeth, and Abigail helped Megan straighten up. She gave her a grateful look. Cassius noticed that Megan turned away from Grant with an emotionless expression. *Strange...* But he had neither the time nor the inclination to find out what might be going on between the two of them, so he searched the flatbed instead and took a few things for himself. A rope, a medical kit, a pair of goggles. He didn't touch the three gallons of liquid, but he wondered about the Claymore. *That might come in handy...*

Abigail stepped closer to him. Cassius ignored her, but deep down he was furious. He quickly packed his belongings into a bag and straightened up.

"We have at least an hour's walk ahead of us."

"Two," Abigail corrected him, glancing at Megan. "I hope you're not even considering leaving them!"

"We should. And before that, they should thank us for saving them."

Silence. Abigail gave Cassius a penetrating look. He shrugged.

"All right, let's get ready to roll. We have to get back before dark."

"Where to?" asked Grant, hissing. He was having a hard time speaking, too, but he obviously didn't want to show weakness.

"To our place. We'll treat the injuries there. Bring only what's necessary."

"Radio, biodiesel," David began, but Cassius waved him off.

"None of them are important."

"For you. But we need to contact the boat-town. To let them know we're coming," he said as he put the ham radio in his bag. "Does your place have any usable vehicles?"

"I wouldn't get my hopes up, but who am I to tell a professional?"

"Oh man, how the hell did you survive the last few years on foot?" David asked, and even chuckled. Cassius stepped closer to him, which made David's grin fade.

"Look, man," he said, giving the 'man' a good squeeze. "We realized pretty soon that fuel was the biggest target on our heads, and we didn't feel much like fighting for it. You got it? We had horses, we had bikes, we walked when we had to. So, we sure can handle this little hike. What about you?"

"Okay, we're clear! You're the tough guy, I got that, all due respect and all, but you have to understand our situation." David looked at Megan. "Every mile counts for us."

Cassius threw the bag on his back and nodded.

"There's a bus. It takes us down to the port, then you can do what you want with it."

"If it's not in bad shape, we can get across the river on that much fuel," David said, walking to the flatbed. With a big puff, he took two gallons. "My own biodiesel, I made it."

"Congratulations!" Cassius stepped away from them. But Abigail didn't follow him. She lifted the last gallon off the truck.

"I'll help you."

Cassius rolled his eyes.

"Leave that!" he said to Abigail. "I'll get it."

Cassius jumped on the back of the jeep, crouched down, and started to assemble an improvised trap. The others set off. David balanced the two gallons, Grant and Megan shuffled behind him. Abigail recoiled after noticing Cassius was up to something.

"What are you doing?" she asked.

"A little surprise... just in case they do come after us."

Cassius armed one of the Claymores, hiding the other in his bag, then wiped his brow with a cloth, which he threw between the wires that encased the mine. *It'll do for bait...*

Abigail looked up at Cassius suspiciously.

"Do you think they'll follow us?"

"We'll soon find out. If they do, we're in trouble."

NEW PLAN

1.

They had to hurry to get home before dark. Cassius walked in front, a gallon of biodiesel in his hand and the Remington on his shoulder, his mind racing non-stop. He had a bad feeling, and all he could think about was that he was breaking the rules again. Two days in a row they'd just barge through the door without a thorough check of the motel and its surroundings. And such irresponsibility led to trouble.

He turned around to look at the others. At the back, Grant shuffled along, even taking off his hat during a deep breath to wipe his sweaty brow. A few steps ahead of him, David snorted and struggled to carry the remaining two gallons. His shirt was soaked in sweat, and his head was downcast. Clutching her stomach with one hand and leaning on Abigail's shoulder with the other, every step was agony for Megan. Cassius sighed. *We need to get rid of them as soon as possible!*

It was late afternoon by the time they got home. They saw nothing suspicious around the motel, but Cassius had a theory about the apparent calm. At the car-maze, he walked up to Abigail and set the gallon of biodiesel down in front of her:

"Go ahead and check the building. I'll set up some more alarms."

"We might have lost them. Right?"

"You know the rule. Pray for the sun..."

"But prepare for the storm," finished Abigail.

Cassius looked around suspiciously. He remembered the time last year when a pack of six had followed them for weeks, and they could only get rid of them in the mountains. They picked off the ferals one by one, hiding and decoying for days without campfire or rest. *The moment Rambo met Predator,* he thought, and had a good chuckle over that one.

"So, we're not going to sleep tonight either, are we?" Abigail sniffed.

"No, we're not."

She picked up the gallon and quickened her pace. Cassius turned to the three travelers and let out a long breath. He wanted to finish quickly so he had time to pack for the dawn departure. There was a lot to do before then.

"Abigail will show you where there is water and medicine," he said, tilting his head at Grant's wound. "You check that first!"

But Grant shook his head. "I feel great. I've had worse, believe me."

"As you wish."

"Is there anything we should be worried about?" Megan asked.

"Out here, always." Cassius rubbed his nose, seeing the alarmed looks on their faces. He was beginning to feel uncomfortable. "Have something to eat. We'll discuss the rest when I come back."

David and Megan nodded, but Grant just groaned. Cassius wasn't even sure if the three of them would make it to the motel, just a handful of steps away, let alone to the boat-town. *It'll be a miracle if they hold out another day out here!*

And if they were going to make even that one day, they'd have to rely on themselves, because Cassius didn't want any more risks. He just hoped Abigail would understand that.

2.

Abigail's first trip was not to the rooms or the roof, but to the cold storage. Her heart was pounding as she crossed the threshold of the kitchen and impatiently yanked open the door. She took the last few steps at a run, glancing anxiously at the rag-lined litter, but Soxy was fine. The puppy started to growl and sniffle excitedly. Abigail was gasping with relief.

"Well done, big boy, well done! You've only got a few more minutes to go, okay?"

She pulled herself up and, with her gun raised, she stepped out of the cold storage. *Okay, let's do it*, the order thundered inside her head, and she quickly checked the rooms, as precisely as Cassius had taught her. She didn't let anything distract her, though at other times she liked to wonder what kind of guests might have once lived in the cream-colored spaces. Nobody under the dusty beds. No one behind the faded curtains. In the bathrooms, only loose tiles and torn shower liners. The packed Samsonite still lay in the middle of 105; the clothes of a stocky man who fled seven years ago, leaving everything behind. *How far did he eventually get?*

When she finished, Abigail ran back to reception. David crossed the threshold the moment she arrived. He dropped the fuel and grasped his waist. Megan waited for Grant, who was well behind, and held the door open for him with her helping hand, but he pushed her aside.

"I'm fine!" Grant snorted at her, and then, clutching his hat, collapsed to the floor.

"We've got to go up to the roof, the important things are up there!" Abigail said, and though she smiled sweetly, she would have much rather pushed them up one by one, just to get them going.

The three travelers finally pulled themselves together and climbed up. Once upstairs, Abigail took a minute to chatter at them about where they would find the medical kit, water, and food and then headed for the roof hatch. She didn't want to lie to their guests, but she couldn't take the risk that they might spill her secret to Cassius.

"I've got to look around downstairs," she said. "If Cassius asks, tell him I'll be back in a minute, okay?"

Megan gave a feeble thumbs-up, David tapped his sore nose and nodded, while Grant had already retreated to one end of the roof. He threw his hat away angrily, pulling up his shirt, and Abigail caught a glimpse of the bruising that was becoming more pronounced. It looked bigger than it was. A look of fright came over the girl's face that even Megan noticed, and she turned around immediately, just in time to see the palm-sized blue-purple-green bruise.

"Jesus!" she gasped in horror.

Grant raised his head and lowered his shirt.

"I'm okay. Gimme a break."

"You sure?" Abigail asked. "It looks quite bad..."

"Yeah, sure!" Grant snapped, wiping his forehead.

"Oh, God, Grant, if you didn't exist, you should be invented." Megan shuffled over to the guy and shoved a flask into his hand. "Come on, drink up."

Abigail picked up the medical kit and handed it to her.

"There's painkillers in it. All expired, but Cassius says they're good for a few more years."

"Well, aren't you precious?" Grant muttered as he took a pill and downed it with a sip of water. He coughed and gasped for air. Megan, meanwhile, sat down in front of him and felt the bruise. Grant immediately hissed.

"Stop moving," she grinned. "I thought you were a tough guy, and here you are acting like a princess!"

Grant saw red. He tried to pull away, but Megan squeezed his wrist.

"Okay, when I'm done, you can be mad at me again, but for now, just stay still!" she shook her head. When she had a better sense of his condition, however, the teasing fell away and she looked up at him with concern. "Your heartbeat is very fast. You might have internal bleeding."

"No need to worry! Guess what, it's not my first rodeo."

Abigail's foot tapped on the rung of the ladder. All the way to the cold storage, she wondered when to tell Cassius that she had adopted a puppy. For some reason, she felt that his resistance would be easier to break right now. Here were three unfortunate poor souls who needed help anyway, no matter what he thought, and no matter how stupid his principles were. A puppy wouldn't make any difference. At most, they'd have an argument afterwards, but right now...

Right now, they had a job to do. They had a mission.

3.

Half an hour later, Soxy was stretching and whimpering contentedly on Abigail's lap, and she hoped the puppy hadn't been hurt by his half-day fast. She was worried, because she had no experience in raising a dog. *I can disassemble a Glock blindfolded but this?* Her only memory of pets was her mother's old tomcat. She had held him in her lap and sang to him when he was put to sleep.

For a second, she remembered what happened in the quarry. She remembered the shot that killed the man in the flannel shirt. Trevor. She straightened her back and tried to find strength. *I'm gonna make it up! I'm gonna make it right!* she vowed.

She gently put Soxy back in his litter.

"You're a strong little fella, aren't you? You'd better behave yourself," she said playfully to the puppy. "I'll be back soon, okay? Until then, be a good boy!"

Abigail listened carefully before stepping out of the cold storage, gathering her thoughts as she walked through the dusty restaurant. She thought carefully about what she was going to say to Cassius – *I forgot to check alarm number six* – but to her great surprise she noticed movement outside. She hurried to the reception desk. From there she could see David and Cassius standing in front of the school bus.

Cassius was watching the boy crouch under the hood of the bus as the engine clattered and revved. When Abigail reached the doorway, David pulled out from under the hood and got behind the wheel, wiping his oily hands.

"It gets on my nerves to see it in this condition. Who would neglect their four-wheeler like this?" he asked, his gaze catching on the ornament hanging on the rear-view mirror, made of human bones. David swallowed hard.

"Get to the point!" Cassius said with an unblinking expression.

"I'm not saying it's hopeless, but I've seen better." David switched off the engine, which gave in with a rattling noise. "Yes, that's what I was talking about."

"Okay, geek squad, what's the problem?

David scratched his nose, then spread his arms in a pompous gesture.

"The belt snapped."

"Uh-huh. So?"

"So? Look, it's quite a problem if we don't deal with it."

"I'm fine if it rolls down to the harbor."

"You sure are, yes, but for us it's suicide to let it go like this. The engine overheats after a while and then that's it. It might go fifteen miles or thirteen, but then it stops in the middle of nowhere. Then it's done, it's over."

"Over?"

"Finito, K.O., right? The pistons get stuck in the bore, and then there's no fixing it; even prayers won't help."

Cassius glared at Abigail, who was listening to the conversation, blinking wide eyes.

"Okay, let's assume that's our problem. What can we do?"

"What can we do? We need to change the belt." David looked thoughtfully around the maze of cars. "We should get lucky that at least one of those dingy wrecks isn't completely rotten."

"All right, you get one out. Is that it?"

"Is that it? Look, I need an exact size. Length, width, if it fits, we're good. I'll put that on, tighten it up, and it'll hold. It's an hour's work if we don't have to go through every wreck."

"Just you, no plural," Cassius said, ignoring David's angry look. "And I suggest you finish before dark; we're not using any lights."

The young man blinked in confusion, but Cassius didn't change his mind, just stood there, arms folded. David rolled his eyes.

"Okay, I'll have a look around the wreckage and then do it in the morning."

"Whatever you say, but remember, we're leaving first light for the harbor, whether you're ready or not."

"To the harbor?" Abigail asked in surprise. She had hoped she could talk to him about this, but it seemed he had decided their fate on his own.

Cassius shrugged.

"They'll drop us off there. Then we split up. They'll go on to Headland and we'll...

"We'll what?" Abigail felt her ears burn with anger.

"And we're going to do what we've planned. If we've missed something, we've missed it, I don't wanna wait any longer," he said, and started back to the motel with quick steps. Abigail hurried after him, but he raised his finger to stop her fuss. "I wanna have everything packed by tomorrow morning, so whatever your problem might be, just forget it, we have no time for that!"

"It's nice of you to be so understanding."

"If you're gonna be cheeky, I'll talk to you about your behavior today."

"Wow, my legs are shaking."

Cassius stopped. He looked around to see if they could be heard by anyone. And they could. Two heads appeared on the roof behind the barbed wire, but not side by side. Megan watched them from one corner, Grant from the other, like two sullen children separated in class by their teacher. The way David's head was tilted as he examined the engine block gave away that he was also listening. Cassius leaned closer to Abigail, lowering his voice.

"You heard what they said. Two days ago, they were attacked by the same pack in Liberty."

Abigail considered.

"The ferals must be pissed off about something."

"Or they picked up the scent. And you know what that means."

"It's only a matter of time before they find this place."

Cassius nodded.

"Let's hope that doesn't happen tonight."

4.

The moon, moving towards the western horizon, painted the sky deep blue, and the glass shards scattered in front of the entrance glistened in its dim light. The bells attached to the wires running around the motel occasionally jingled, but Abigail knew exactly what a real alarm sounded like, and when it was just the wind playing. The slight breeze carried the scent of sea.

The campfires remained dark, and they only whispered so that the slightest sniffle could be heard. In case of an emergency, they would have had a few minutes to hole up somewhere. Abigail had suggested the cold storage and volunteered to prepare the ground and Cassius hadn't objected. She would have liked to stay with Soxy all the time, but she still didn't have the courage to tell Cassius what she had done.

Grant crouched on the edge of the roof, his gun at his fingertips, watching the landscape. Megan was squirming about on a mattress and David sat next to her on the concrete, close to a flickering oil lamp. They nibbled sadly at poor sandwiches wrapped in tinfoil. The siblings seemed to be falling asleep sitting up.

Cassius was stuffing pieces of rotten wood into an empty tin can, eying the travelers in silence. When he was done, he used a Zippo to light one of the pieces of wood, which caught fire and began to smoke. Cassius gave the tin to Abigail.

"Get some sleep," he said. Her eyes burned with fatigue, but she hated it when he tried to patronize her.

"I know when I'm tired!" she said defiantly, then turned and sat down beside Megan.

The woman looked up with a smile, and Abigail set the smoking, smoldering tin down in front of them as proudly as if it had been her idea. "Against mosquitoes. Better than any of the old stuff."

"Thank you!" Megan grinned, her mouth full, and glanced at her sandwich. "Are you sure you didn't want any? We're happy to share what we have..."

"That's nice of you, but we only eat our own food." At the puzzled looks, she added: "Because of the infection. We've heard of people getting sick from eating meat from infected animals."

The siblings looked at their food at once, their faces turning pale. Abigail raised her hand.

"No, don't worry, it doesn't transform you, but Cassius says it's better safe than sorry."

"The hell with the constant yammering!" Grant grunted. "There was nothing wrong with that specimen! I shot it."

Cassius didn't even look up in the background, he growled. "Wow, we have a Bob Lee Swagger in our company."

Abigail sucked her teeth and Grant straightened up with resentment, but Cassius ignored him. He began unpacking the things in the chest alongside some torn travel bags.

"You've found yourselves a lovely place," Megan took over, sending Grant a warning glance. "Beautiful panorama, and this scent… jasmine. My favorite."

"Not bad," shrugged Abigail, "but it could be a bit more exciting."

"A little more exciting isn't always good. We could have done without it, for example." Megan felt sad as she remembered her companions, and Abigail lowered her eyes.

"That's not what I meant. If there were more of us, we could do lots of cool things, and-and-and we could protect the place. It's not a lost cause."

She glanced furtively at Cassius, who stopped packing and raised his eyes to the moonlit landscape. *Did he notice anything?* A bat flew overhead and a coyote howled in the distance. The sounds of the night rumbled around them incessantly. *Definitely a good sign...*

"What do you know about the colony?" Abigail turned back to Megan.

"We started talking to them on the radio six months ago. At first, we just shared the news. We knew about the resistance in Boston, they heard things from the Cubans."

"From the Cubans? So, there's still some news from Out there?"

"There was half a year ago, but then they went silence as well."

Abigail's face fell. Megan continued.

"We started helping each other. David told them how he had modified the vehicles, and they tried to give us tips on how to farm, but..."

"As you can see, it didn't really work," the young man finished. "So, we voted… and after a lot of nagging the majority wanted to go."

"Because we couldn't stay!" Megan snapped. "That was the only way to ensure the baby's survival! Our survival…"

David tossed aside the crumpled tinfoil, then began to grumble as he examined the parts he'd found in the car-maze.

"And do they really live on boats?" Abigail asked.

"Yes, they have a whole fleet. Their leader, Mr. Solomon, used to work on ships. Then at the beginning of the pandemic they stole one of the giants and anchored it. For the first couple of years they lived on that, but as the colony grew, they put together some houseboats. They took in everyone they could and said they'd find a job for everyone. Of course, there was a bit of chaos at first but they straightened it out and now it's back to normal."

"According to them," David interjected.

Abigail furrowed her brows.

"What do you mean, according to them?"

"He meant, sometimes you better hold your horses before you ride into a trap," Grant replied.

"Right you are," said Cassius as he sorted.

Megan angrily spread her arms.

"I still don't get it, why would they lie to us. For a long time, we didn't even mention joining them."

"Sounds logical," Abigail nodded, and the longer she kept doing it, the more she convinced herself, as well. "How many are they?"

"Mr. Solomon says at least seven hundred people live on the boats."

Abigail shuddered at what she heard. The last colony they'd been to was a shabby place in West Odessa, on the edge of nowhere, with a fence woven together from sheet metal, but that had been over a year ago. There were less than a hundred people living in such places and they were always suspicious of strangers. In some places they had to flee; in others they didn't even make it through the gates in the first place.

But the boat-town seemed different, orderly, and where so many people lived, they must really have things sewn up tight. She tried to picture what it would be like to live there, to wake up in a place where you weren't just on your own, and where it wasn't all about running away. Where you could even have friends.

"How far away are they?" Abigail asked. She couldn't suppress the excitement in her voice.

"A few days' drive, right?" Megan turned to David, who was just humming.

"Ahamm... If I can tinker with that piece of junk; otherwise we can walk."

"I know you'll do figure it out, and we'll get there safe and sound. I can feel it in my guts." She turned to Abigail and put her hand on her arm. "And I'm sure you'll also be welcome, if you do decide to join us."

"That would be great, but... Cassius has other plans."

Megan pulled a wry smile. Abigail was sure she had read between the bitter lines. *Good, at least she knows how stubborn he is.*

"Ah, the mysterious island."

"It's not mysterious, it's just that there's nothing exciting about it," she continued. "Cassius spent many summers there as a child. He thinks it's safe, and it's within the Zone, so it's not guarded. There were hardly any people there, so if anyone got infected, they've probably starved to death by now. And if not, then..."

She didn't finish, just shrugged. Megan frowned, folding the tinfoil used for packing her sandwich.

"It's hard to imagine how you'll manage there on your own."

"We've tried to gather everything we need." Abigail angled her head towards the chest. The siblings turned to the box at the same time. Megan and Cassius even exchanged looks; she gave him a friendly smile.

"Not much," David pursed his lips. He could hardly help but chuckle. "After all these years of collecting, I expected more. I don't know, so much stuff you need a moving truck. I'm worried your boat is just another rowboat."

"David."

"Jeez, I was just joking..."

"It's all right," Abigail said. "This wasn't our plan the whole time, to be honest. We were also just fleeing in the first few years. It started from Headland, then from the refugee camp in Brookings..."

"Jesus!" Megan hissed at the name. Everyone had heard of the siege back then. A couple of TV crews were waiting at the camp, and the whole country was able to watch the attack live. And of course, it was witnessed by all the leaders of the world. A few days later China and Russia announced restrictions; Europe a week after that. The Breakdown for the Outside started right there and then.

"We tried to find Cassius's family," Abigail continued. "Headland was no bed of roses even then. After surviving Brookings and the Pincers, we went all along the West Coast where some of his relatives lived. We looked at several colonies, but we couldn't find them anywhere, so we headed back. And slowly we realized that we had only ourselves to rely on..."

Before she could continue, Cassius appeared beside them with three mugs of tea, which he had been heating for a long time on a flickering stove.

"I think that's enough of the small talk for today," he said with an emotionless face, and handed out the mugs. "Hot tea, it will do you good. Get some rest, it's gonna be a long day tomorrow."

The distant howls of the coyotes ceased, and the sounds of the night fell silent.

5.

Grant listened to the undisturbed calm. His face was drenched in sweat and his fingers moved restlessly, as if he were in a constant state of numbness. In front of him on the ledge lay a spread-out map with notes: the boat-town circled, the long way signed, question marks at possible resting places. It was the same itinerary that Trevor had had.

Cassius approached with a mug of tea. Even in the dim light, he could see that Grant was in much worse shape, but there was something he wanted to know, and he wondered how he could get the man to share the information. He felt no pity for him, and he could see that the guy was also eyeing him suspiciously.

"You're welcome!" Cassius handed him the mug. Grant took it reluctantly.

"I'm touched. Who knows, we might end up being pals. We start showing each other our scars and stuff..."

"Yeah, right. How are you doing?"

"That son of a bitch hit me harder than a three-hundred-pound linebacker."

"They're hardly ever gentle."

Grant took a sip of his tea and huffed and puffed, but he finally finished it all off like it was whiskey on a cold Sunday afternoon. He dropped the empty mug on the edge of the roof and looked at Cassius.

"Well, out with it! I know you're not interested in my medical condition."

Cassius spread his arms with a self-righteous smile.

"Come on, I'm just worried that you're not aware of the situation... That you don't know what you're getting into."

"We'll manage, no need to worry about us. I'm not bragging, but I've been around, not hiding behind walls," Grant replied, gesturing towards the siblings. His face twisted in pain as he involuntarily touched his stomach.

"I don't want to be the bearer of bad news, but that wound..."

"I know, I'm not a newbie. But I promised to get them to the boat-town, and they need my help. They're suburban kids with no clue about life before the Breakdown, and they never hit the road even after. They can't do it alone, and I'm keeping my word."

Cassius nodded, considering.

"So be it, but let's get something straight. If you don't, none of them can count on us. I don't want two more around my neck."

"It's gonna be all right. Let's just get through tonight and get on the road, because if the pack have got as far as the quarry, they can follow us up here," Grant growled, then cleared his throat. "That monster... Have you ever seen anything like it?"

Cassius shook his head.

"It was an Alpha."

"Impossible! They..."

"They all died in the deformation?"

"That's what they say."

"And still, your friends are dead."

A shudder passed through Grant, and his face hardened.

"Fuck all that! Soon it won't matter. Soon we'll be so far from this place that I don't give a shit whether it's an Alpha, a Beta, or whatever. Let's just hit the road."

Cassius scratched his stubble and looked around the silvery landscape. He had a strange feeling, but he couldn't tell yet what was bothering him. In the distance, among the dark trees, there seemed to be a glimmer of an eye, but then nothing. Nothing moved and everything faded away. Strange.

He turned back and watched Megan resting on the mattress.

"Of course, such a task needs perfect cohesion. Trust, or the road will eat you alive."

Grant immediately understood what was going on and rolled his eyes. Cassius shrugged his shoulders.

"It was hard not to notice that you don't have that."

"We're good, no more, no less!"

"Fine by me. Who am I to judge?"

"Oh, right, like you're the epitome of teamwork. I saw what I saw..."

Grant stopped talking. Cassius didn't feel the need to explain himself, nor was there any reason to. He had roamed all over the Zone with Abigail, and what they had experienced together had formed an unbreakable bond between them. He knew he could always count on her.

There was a long, awkward silence, and finally Grant let out a loud sigh.

"Whatever is between us is our business... and perhaps the business of the boat-town, where they can decide whether or not to take her in, regardless."

Regardless? Cassius frowned because it was not what he had expected, but he had no time to ask.

A gruff roar rose and fell in the distance like a muffled heartbeat. An explosion. The sound wave drowned out the words. Cassius even held his breath. Abigail, who had been lying on her back gazing at the stars, jumped up and glanced at him in fright.

"What was that?" asked Megan, who was bent over and looking at Cassius in bewilderment.

"They've found us!"

6.

"We gotta be on the road in ten minutes!" Cassius thundered, then hurried to the chest. Abigail followed him, confused. Without hesitation, he immediately started packing one of the travel bags: survival cord, multitool, wool blanket, axe, survival shovel, cast iron pan, a collapsible bow and arrow, a firebox stove, a solar charger, medicines and band-aids, pencils and sharpeners, tinfoil, magnifying glasses, needles and thread. A baseball bat, as a last resort. Peanut butter, which is long lasting and filling. But most of the books had to stay. He would have liked to have read Tom Wolfe, but the informative books were more important now.

"Would somebody explain what the hell that was?" David asked.

"What don't you understand?" Grant snapped at him. "He armed one of the mines by the jeep. The explosion means the pack has tracked us."

David swallowed hard. His voice thinned out, almost like a squeak.

"Couldn't it have been just some wild animal?"

"It could, could be anything," Cassius answered. "If you want to be sure, you can wait for it, but we're leaving to the harbor."

"That's not what we agreed!" David protested.

"That was before. I told you to get a move on, but you wouldn't listen."

Megan looked around worriedly.

"How long will it take them to get here?"

"I don't know." Cassius didn't take a break in packing. "A good half hour, maybe a little more. But I'm not going to escape at the last moment."

"Even so," Megan pleaded, "we still have a little time. David, can you do something?"

"In half an hour? What am I, the Good Lord himself?"

"David!"

"I don't know, something, not much. Maybe if I can get some help."

"I'll help," Abigail volunteered, but Cassius stopped her with a single decisive gesture.

"You stay here and pack!"

She looked up at him with a defiant look, but he didn't care. Grant coughed into his hand, and tried to muster his energy. Cassius saw him grip his gun impatiently.

"Just wait a minute! How far is the harbor?"

"Fifteen minutes," Abigail said before Cassius could wave her off.

"And there's no other way there and back, right?"

"No."

Grant's face turned red. He pulled himself together and struggled to his feet, looking like he was in agony, but he gritted his teeth.

"So, we'll just drop you off there, and come back directly into the hands of the pack. That's what I call fucking gallantry!"

"It is what it is, we got you the bus. Be grateful that you can have it. I'm not going to sacrifice our safety because we might be able to fix it."

Grant's hand swung immediately, and Cassius didn't flinch. They raised their guns at the same time, pointed at each other. Megan screamed and David stepped back. Only Abigail had the presence of mind to throw herself between the two men with her hands up.

"Enough! Put the guns down and let's talk!" she shouted, but Grant just snarled and shook his head.

"That wasn't the answer I expected."

"I don't give a damn what you expected!" Cassius gripped the Glock. "It's your problem, not ours. Why should we take the risk?"

He watched Abigail with one eye, and he felt the vibe of her resistance in the air. *Here we go, same old tune again.* Cassius could feel the anger flooding through him, and he wanted to scream at her to move before she got them in trouble again.

"Okay, okay," Abigail sputtered after a moment's thought. "New plan, simple, everyone will like it. We fix the bus. We go up to Headland..."

"Bullshit!"

"I'm not finished! We'll go to Headland, where we'll look for another boat on the river. It doesn't have to be fancy, it just shouldn't sink. Then we'll come back on the water. Maybe we can even pick up the missing items on the way. What do you think?"

Abigail looked hopefully at Cassius, but he didn't respond.

"Please..."

Nothing. A muscle twitched in her cheek, and Cassius couldn't help but notice that she involuntarily put her hand on her gun. *What the hell is she doing? Is she...?* Even he didn't see that kind of madness coming, but Abigail's eyes were shining differently. He realized that this wasn't her usual defiance.

"We can't do this to them... Think of your family... Think of what if..."

"That's enough!"

"No! You have to give in now!"

"Now? How many times..."

Cassius didn't finish, he just pursed his lips. Megan's eyes flooded with tears, and Abigail tightened her grip on her gun. *This is no joke at all!* He'd never seen her so determined. And for the first time, he had a strange notion that he didn't want to see Abigail snap and do something stupid she can't redeem.

"All right," he said finally, gesturing for Grant to lower his weapon. "You've got twenty minutes to get something out of that wreck, then we're moving. If the shit hits the fan, we'll have to run and leave half the stuff behind, but we might make it."

"What about them?" Abigail asked, pointing at Megan.

"That's as much time as I can give! Take it or leave it, I don't care. But then I'm dragging you down to the port myself, got it?

Cassius took the second Claymore out of his bag and placed it in Abigail's hand.

"Before you get too deep into the repair, place this by the car-maze. An insurance policy, if you will."

The girl nodded. David breathed a sigh of relief, then put his hands on his hips.

"Twenty minutes, man?" But seeing the look on Cassius's face, he chose not to continue. "Okay, I'll do what I can." Then he went downstairs with Abigail at his back.

Cassius looked at the stumbling Megan. She clutched her stomach, turning her head in puzzlement, and finally doddered to her bag, grabbed the strap, and started for the ladder, dragging it along the ground behind her. In the background, Grant staggered and then, with a pained expression on his face, he flopped back to the ground, his back against the edge of the roof. He exhaled, but could barely breathe. He gathered what strength he had, adjusted his hat, and turned the barrel of his gun north.

"At least we know where they're attacking from."

"Don't be so sure," Cassius said and stepped back to the chest. He threw what he could into another traveling bag, and when he was done, he slung the luggage onto his back. At the ladder he turned. "I'm not the carrying-type, so shake your leg if you don't want to be left behind!"

"That'll do."

"If you see anything, don't be afraid to shout."

"I won't."

Cassius's foot was already tapping on the ladder when Grant stopped him. There were only the two of them on the roof, and Cassius guessed what the other was up to. Grant hesitated. His eyes blurred and his mouth began to quiver.

"Give this to David," he said, and tossed the folded map to Cassius. "He'd better have it."

Cassius put the map away and waited for what was to come.

The point. Grant sighed.

"Just so you know, I've got seven bullets, and I'm going to shoot them all. Six at the ferals..."

"You sure you want to do this?"

Grant nodded. "I'm not going to die in that piece of junk! If I'm going, I'd rather go here, like this, not running away like a coward."

"As you wish. Just don't let them eat you up!"

"I won't."

Grant laughed, but his voice was weak and anxious.

"One more thing. I wanted this child. God knows, I wanted it to be born and grow up... but not at any cost. Not like this!"

"What are you talking about?"

"Ask Megan, she'll tell you. Ask, but before you reach the colony. You now have the right to know the truth. And then you two can decide whether it's worth it."

7.

Abigail placed Soxy safely in the back of the bus and helped Megan with her bags. She sat her down in the front seat and turned anxiously towards the front door. No sign of Cassius yet. When she paused for a moment, her body was flooded with a feeling unlike any other: a strange mixture of fear and excitement. She felt her pulse quicken. Her fingertips tingled and her stomach clenched with excitement. She checked her gun: only two bullets left in the silver Smith & Wesson.

Impatiently she got out of the bus and tried to listen, but could hardly hear anything because of David's tapping. He cursed as he tinkered with something by the dim light of an oil lamp, his sweaty hair stuck to his forehead. Cassius was nowhere to be seen. *What's taking him so long?*

In the shadows of the motel, there was no sign of the picturesque semi-darkness they had seen from above: the distant trees and the maze of cars were shrouded in menacing gloom. Anything could be behind them. A tool clattered on the ground. Abigail clutched her head in fright and David spread his hands apologetically.

"I knew I needed more time."

His voice quivered with nerves.

"Calm down, you can do it!" Abigail said, but the gun trembled in her hand. When she looked into the darkness, the heavy curtain of nothing stared back, and in her head a panic-stricken voice intensified. *They are here, they are behind the darkness, lurking, preparing, and we have no time!*

Cassius appeared at the entrance carrying the traveling bags. He hurriedly tossed them into the bus and glanced at his watch, but he deliberately avoided Abigail's gaze. *Well, this is new! He's never ignored me before...*

"Time's up, let's go!" Cassius gave the order, grunting and puffing. David lashed out.

"I need a few more minutes!"

"You got two minutes, that's the most! Make it work, or we'll leave you guys here!"

Cassius checked his weapon, then looked up at the roof, which only showed the barrel of a rifle at the edge.

"Hey, buddy! See anything?"

"Um... nothing," Grant's voice was heard.

Cassius glanced at Abigail, stern and uncompromising, and she nodded immediately, like a student who wants to look good in the eyes of her teacher. But she didn't feel that she should make a great effort. *I was right, it was the right thing to do!*

"I'm all packed, I'm ready," she said.

"If we left now, it would be too late," Cassius growled, and David made two twists with a tool and stepped back. He wiped his hands at an easy pace.

"Well?"

"I can't work miracles. All in all, it's done. I replaced the belt and tightened the..."

The wind from the other side of the car-maze made a wistful

sound, soft at first, then more and more insistent. Abigail snapped her head up and Cassius waved David down.

"Quiet!"

The young man gawped and turned his head in the direction Cassius and Abigail were focused. Distant ringing. A muffled alarm, well over a hundred yards away. The blood drained from Abigail's face as the realization hit her brain. *They're here!*

"Get into the bus!" Cassius shouted, and they swung into action without thinking.

David jumped behind the wheel and, spotting the ornament made of human bones, tore it off and threw it to the ground. Abigail ran to the back and ignored Megan, who was spinning around frantically in panic.

"Come on, let's go!" cried Cassius. He stopped at the bottom step and pointed his gun into the darkness. Breathlessly he watched, but the night-black shroud didn't move, and the ringing had long since ceased. There was only an unearthly, resonating guttural sound.

Grant's gun blasted on the roof. He fired two shots, but it wasn't clear what he was aiming for. A second of silence, then Grant's shout:

"Good god, hurry up!"

The engine roared into life and the bus shook.

"And Grant?" Megan asked with a pale face, just realizing he wasn't limping his way towards them.

"He's covering our escape."

"What?" shouted the other three at once.

"It was his decision."

Megan struggled up, but Cassius gently pushed her back into her seat.

"We have no time. Let's go, come on!"

Another shot, the third, into the darkness and Abigail felt the ground shake in her spine. She didn't know if she was imagining it or if the rush of ferals was really going through her body. Pressing her face against the window, she caught a glimpse of a gigantic shadow breaking out of the cars and leaping almost two stories to the roof.

David stepped on the gas and the bus took off, just in the nick of time. Three shots rang out, then silence. Abigail was thrown sideways by the momentum as the bus rocked into frantic motion, and even Cassius had to hold on to keep himself from falling out of the accelerating vehicle. David cut across the grass to get around the exit ramp and up onto the 10 as quickly as possible. It was not a good idea. The bus was shaking and struggling. It slowed.

Abigail got up and looked out the window. The motel was barely visible now, but in the faint glimmer she noticed movement. Behind them, just a few yards away. *It's coming after us!*

"Faster!" she shouted, pushing herself away from the window.

"I can't," David said. "If I keep pushing, this piece of junk will fall apart."

Cassius, meanwhile, was clinging desperately to the glass, keeping a watch, but whatever he was waiting for didn't come to pass. He cried out to Abigail:

"Did you set up the Claymore?"

She shook her head in disgrace.

The bus turned onto the road and the shaking stopped. All they heard was the roar of the engine. The Blue Bird suffered, agonized, but began to accelerate. Abigail exhaled. *Maybe we've gotten away with it!*

Bang!

Something slammed into the side of the bus, almost knocking them off the road. Megan screamed and David yanked the wheel, screaming, trying to keep the Blue Bird on track. Abigail crashed onto the travel bags (*Thank goodness it wasn't Soxy's box!*) and all she could think was that it was over. She caught a glimpse of the demonic creature's bony face and sharp teeth on the other side of the window, and the image was etched into her memory.

"Gas!" she heard Cassius shout, and felt the Blue Bird finally find its balance. The bodywork stopped screaming, the wheels gripped the road, and the engine eased as it gained momentum.

The bus vanished into the darkness.

DEATH DRIVE

1.

The pack followed the tracks of the travelers, but the Alpha had picked up a new scent at the quarry. It appeared first when the jeep drove off and the Alpha instantly knew that something was different. This smell was new, thrilling, inexplicably familiar. Nothing like any other. For some reason, the rest of the pack didn't notice, but the Alpha felt the sense in every part of its body.

It pushed aside a Delta that was about to pounce on one of the poor losers. The skinny little boy was bitten on the arm, not so much sobbing from the shock as shaking like a leaf. The Alpha knew what to do. The wound would not kill the boy, and the transformation had already begun. Soon a new member would join the pack.

Among the overturned trucks, the cries and screams grew thinner. The female Beta was taking apart a woman. It tossed her shoulder bag aside before biting into her again and again.

The ferals, done with the slaughter, gathered around the Alpha. The cloud of dust settled. The sound of the jeep fleeing north was finally out of range, yet the Alpha stared into the distance, mesmerized. That smell. For some reason it had soaked into its pores, even dulled its insatiable bloodlust, and it was all the Alpha could think of.

Unable to determine what it was, the beast had to follow it. Without rest, at a frantic pace. It thought it was all in vain. The adrenaline rush was gone. The suffering and pain had returned. It wanted to rage as the darkness descended, but then the pack saw the lone jeep. And the smell picked up again, which led the feral to a new trace.

The Alpha ignored the explosion and his torn-apart companion.

Its nostrils quivered, its mouth oozed a mixture of blood and saliva. It writhed, its veins throbbed, and the drive to find that scent was ripping its body apart. The pack headed for the motel, and when they reached it, the Alpha was one step closer to having its question answered.

2.

The Alpha could hear the sound of the engine getting louder and see the lights heading east, but the crack of gunfire was coming from the roof. It jumped up and clung to one of the first-floor windows. It tore the barbed wire apart with a flick of its wrist; the Alpha didn't care that its horn-hard skin was scratched. It barely registered.

The wretch the Alpha landed beside watched it tower over him with widened eyes. The man had already raised his gun, but the Alpha was too fast. It didn't even deign to bite, it just swiped. The man's bloody hat flew off the roof. His scream, mixed with the fear of death, was replaced by a crackling, splashing sound. Blood covered everything.

The Alpha sniffed the air and opened its mouth, but that smell...

...was not what the beast was looking for.

The bus appeared in its peripheral vision, cutting through the grass and heading straight for the main road. Without thinking, the Alpha jumped immediately. Its steel muscles swung, faster than the wind, and the rest of the pack could not catch up with it. Its heart pounded in its ears, adrenaline flooded its body in waves, its strength sent it rocketing forwards. Closer and closer to the bouncing bus on the bumpy road, which was clambering up the asphalt with great difficulty, and which the driver was trying to straighten. Unsuccessfully. The vehicle swerved and lost speed.

The Alpha heard the sound of the engine. Its animal brain sensed that this was the last moment to catch the bus before it vanished into the distance. The monster was drawn by the smell, drawn by an invisible fishing line. It could sense it everywhere. The smell could only be coming from one of the people on the bus... but which one? Just a few more yards. In the darkness the passengers couldn't even see the threat behind them. If it had stretched out its arm, the Alpha could have reached the bus, but it wanted to be sure. In two giant leaps, it was beside the vehicle. It slammed a shoulder into it, trying to push the vehicle off the road, but lost its balance as the bus bounced back.

The Alpha crashed into the roadside bushes with tremendous force. By the time it regained its strength and balance, the bus was far away, and all it could see was a flickering red light in the distance. The smell faded, the adrenaline slowly died down, and the suffering returned. The pain became unbearable again.

ON THE ROCKY ROAD

1.

She knew she couldn't drag it out any longer; Abigail needed to tell Cassius what she had done.

The bus rumbled along the asphalt. Outside it was dark, and all they could see was the road lit by the Blue Bird, covered in places with debris. The noise of the engine, the wind whistling through the broken window, and the screech of the rusty bodywork drowned out the sound of the puppy whimpering in the box, and Cassius was already busy watching the roadblocks. Megan sat in the front seat, depressed, her head resting on her bag. Her shoulder shook with sobs.

Abigail touched her own forehead and hissed as she felt the bruise. Her right palm had been scraped by the shards of glass scattered across the bus floor, but she only became aware of the pain now, as the rush of adrenaline subsided. She didn't dare think about what she had picked up with her open wound from the bus floor. She hopped down on one of the seats and rummaged through her bag with trembling hands. For a split second, the demonic face flashed before her as it had unfurled out of the darkness, snarling, slamming against the window, its huge hand raking the frame, bending the bodywork...

Cassius appeared beside her. He took disinfectant, bandages, and a flask from his own bag and sat down opposite her. Neither of them spoke, avoiding each other's gaze for a moment. Abigail searched for the right words and watched with a sweaty brow as he took her hand and gently moved to disinfect her wound. She felt the nerves sting as the disinfectant penetrated to the very depths of the cut, but she clenched her teeth.

"I can see you're mad," she said when the bandage was finally ready.

"I'm not."

"Come on, say it! I defied your orders again, I was irresponsible." Her voice grew louder and more hysterical, but now it was driven by cold calculation. She had defanged him, so that he would have nothing left to bang on about. "I've forgotten my duty!"

Cassius stared at her speechlessly. Abigail could not bear the silence for long.

"Say something!"

"You were right, I was wrong."

Abigail's eyes widened, but before she could breathe a sigh of relief, Cassius shook his head in disappointment. His voice was calm, too calm, his lips pursed down in despondency, the words slowly enunciated.

"I expected too much from you. Perhaps you're not as ready as I thought you were."

"That was below the belt."

"I can't expect you to understand, but..."

"Oh, no, of course you can't!"

Cassius continued without blinking an eye.

"But you act differently when you're responsible for someone. You make different decisions, you have different thoughts. You only care about who you're responsible for. Then life is no longer about what makes you feel better. I hope you'll understand one day."

"Maybe I do now," she said with a dry smile, and stood up. Defiantly she straightened her spine. "I have a responsibility for someone."

"What are you talking about?"

Abigail took a deep breath and squatted down by the box of bags. She lifted the lid off, but left one hand on the edge as if leaning against it. She wanted to signal that whatever was squirming there was under her protection, and there was nothing Cassius could do about it now.

"That's what I'm talking about."

She saw him blink, at first in incomprehension, then rise and lean over the box with a superior expression, as if nothing could surprise him now. The sound of the engine and the grinding of the bodywork could no longer suppress Soxy's whimper. Cassius caught her gaze, his eyes wide open, seeing stars, searching for the right words.

"Are you out of your goddamn mind?"

"I found some formula at the old gas station, read what to do in one of your stupid books, and took care of him. I couldn't just leave him there, and everything turned out fine."

"Everything turned out fine?" Cassius snapped, so loudly that Megan perked up her head in the front seat. "Is that why you had no time to lay the Claymore? We could have died because of this!"

No answer. What could she have said when he was right? This irresponsibility really could have cost them their lives. She was ashamed.

"So, tell me," he continued, "what was your plan? When were you going to tell me? Hm?"

The silence grew awkward. Abigail clenched her jaw so tightly that she thought it would crumble her bones in a moment. She wanted to speak out, to say that this was again unfair. *Surviving is not the only goal!*

"All right, enough of the fighting!" Megan came up behind Cassius and turned him forcefully towards her. "You go to the front next to David! There's work to be done. Find out if we've got enough fuel, or where we're going to stop to pee, or whatever. And I'll stay here with Abigail and play tiger mom. Come on, come on!"

Cassius was about to speak, but the Blue Bird ran over something and shook, the chassis groaning as rubble scraped it from underneath. He turned his head worriedly, thinking the same thing that she was. If something happened to the bus now and they broke down, they were doomed. The pack would catch up with them.

"What's this fool doing, for God's sake?" he asked, starting forwards angrily.

2.

Abigail's mouth was still trembling with nervousness. Megan, as if everything was fine, put her hands on her hips and sat down with a big snort. She tried to make herself comfortable, but discovered it was hard to find a position that didn't make her ache in every inch of her body.

"It shows a lot of maturity the way you've cared for him," she said, gently stroking the fussy pup on the top of his head. She smiled as her fingers touched the dog's soft fur.

"It was nothing," Abigail swallowed back tears and shrugged her shoulders. "It's no big deal... it shouldn't be."

"Yeah, but even so. If I were you, I'd have done the same."

"And will you tell Cassius that, too?"

"I think you're old enough not to have to explain yourself."

"Blasphemy!" They laughed. Abigail sniffled, then wiped her nose. "Now I'm almost begging you to talk to him, to see if you can bring him to his senses."

Megan wiped a chestnut lock out of her eyes and glanced worriedly at David, who was trying to talk to Cassius while driving. They couldn't hear the conversation, but Cassius' shoulders grew tighter with each and every word the young man spoke.

"What do you think is going to happen to us now?" Megan asked.

"I know Cassius too well to worry. He plays the tough guy, but his heart always softens in the end."

"What if we reach Headland? Then what?"

"I'll convince him somehow."

"I mean, what's waiting for us there? What is it that everyone's so scared of that they want to get as far away from the place as they can? I thought the city was nothing more than rubble."

Abigail hesitated. She was searching for words because she didn't want to scare the woman. After they tried so hard to go around the city, she was starting to have a strange feeling about returning to her home. Still, she brushed those thoughts away. Headland was just a name from the past. It might not be hell, but it could be one of its pits.

"A pile of rubble, indeed, but not empty at all," Abigail said finally.

"Ferals?"

The girl shook her head.

"Remember the old posters? 'Four-legged Paradise' they called it."

Megan nodded.

"Yeah. 'The second-best place in the States to have a pet.' They had wonderful parks there, I give them that. Not exactly Liberty," she smiled sadly. "But I'm biased."

"Yeah, well... After the quarantine, things changed. Most of the animals were neglected, either because their owners had become infected or because there was nothing left to feed them. The city was full of them, and the heaps of garbage in the streets weren't enough to keep them all fed. First, they went wild, and later they too were infected by the ferals. In packs among the ruins, they hunted down everything that lived and moved, and the deformation didn't spare them either. So, Headland is now famous for two things: infected pets... and man-eaters. Believe it or not, neither of them despises the other."

Megan frowned, then her face pulled into a grimace. "You mean...?"

"Those bastards believe that by eating infected meat, the power of the animals will be transferred to them."

"Then why don't we go around it? There must be some by-pass."

"There is, but none of them are options now. Because of you."

"Because of me?" Megan asked, eyebrows raised. Abigail saw that the woman was fighting incomprehension and resentment, unable to decide whether to be offended or to simply ask for more information.

"Yeah. Going south would take days because of the swamp, and we don't have days. To the north, there are the mountains and the bandits, and we don't have enough fuel for the uphill ride nor enough ammo for the not-so-friendly parleys. Not to mention that the fields surrounding the city were mined by the army during the pandemic. So, all we can do is take a chance and hope we can cross without being seen."

Megan shuddered and squeezed her shoulder involuntarily. They listened in silence to the monotonous rattle of the bus, which slowly lulled Soxy to sleep. Abigail watched the puppy's even breathing. She envied him being able to sleep so peacefully.

In the east, the first thin streak of light appeared, and the darkness was replaced by a gloom. Megan mused as she looked at the glowing horizon slowly illuminate the landscape around them.

"After all this, I don't know how you've managed out here. For so long. Alone."

"Neither do I," Abigail said. She added, whispering with a playful smile. "I hope the boat-town is as you say it is, and then Cassius will see we have nothing to fear."

"Ah, so that's your endgame."

"What can I say? I'm not planning to grow old on an island."

Megan noticed something outside. She crept closer to the window and gaped at what she saw. In the half-light the bushes and weeds were dotted with cars that had been pushed off the road. The wrecks went on as far as she could see, the remnants of chaos stretched to the horizon.

The bus slowed as they drew closer, and Megan glanced at Abigail, puzzled. Dozens of abandoned ambulances were stranded on the road ahead, one overturned, another with its back door torn open, a third pulled over to the side of the road. The only thing they had in common was that their aluminum bodies had been ripped apart by large caliber bullets. All around them were military Humvees with roof-mounted machine guns. Their windshields were smashed, though on some the damage couldn't be seen, having been flipped over by an infernal force. They were the traces of an unimaginable battle.

The death-caravan. Twelve ambulances, on their way to the west, with infected strapped inside. They never made it to their destination.

The Blue Bird slow-danced around the vehicles, and Megan shook her head in dismay.

"I've heard of this place."

"It happened after the battle of Headland. There were soldiers everywhere, and they wouldn't let anyone move on. But people stopped waiting. Relatives of the militia members were in the ambulance vans. Their leader, Mason, wanted to take them to Atlanta in the hope that the CDC might have a cure."

They passed by the last ambulance, followed by another line of cars with horrific signs of destruction. They could barely get around a bus that had overturned and they crushed a motorbike. Abigail bowed her head as she reminisced.

"And that's nothing compared to what's waiting in Headland," she said, then turned back to Soxy.

3.

Perched beside David, Cassius watched the road. The broken-down vehicles they carefully navigated were left as static, rusting mementos of the destruction. If he had closed his eyes, he would have seen the panic of seven years before, as people jumped out of their cars one after another, clutching their children's hands or the last of their valuables. But he didn't dare close his eyes.

Instead, he thought about what might await them: where they could stop and when he would decide upon the dog's fate. He glanced out of the corner of his eye and began to watch Megan. Grant's words came back to him. *What the hell was he thinking? What's wrong with Megan?*

"Kids, huh? And women," David muttered, grinning stupidly at Cassius, who took out Grant's map and held it up to him.

"Tell me everything you know about the road!"

"Everything?" David snorted. "Aren't you asking for a bit too much? Okay, fine, I get it, straight to the point. If all goes well and we don't stop, we can reach Headland before dark. The idea was that Trevor with the Wrangler would have cleared any obstacles or traps out of our way, but so much for that. We're on our own. Grant's plan was to stay on the 10 if the overpass is still up."

"And if not?"

"In that case we take a detour on 275."

"Towards Union City?"

"Yeah, but trust me, Grant didn't want that either. The point is, we gotta get to the river somehow."

"And then what?"

"Then we find the docks... assuming you still have the same plan."

"You bet I do." Cassius nodded. "We'll get a boat and we won't stop until we reach the sea. Any danger? Were you prepared for anything?"

"Not before Headland. The only safe place seemed to be Old Mike's restaurant."

"That crappy hash house with the chewy steaks? Why that?" David howled.

"You know it, too? I dare you to tell Old Mike to his face," he winked, as if he knew something the other didn't.

Cassius froze.

"What?"

"Oh, well here's something you don't know. The old chap and Trevor used to talk on the radio regularly. He survived the Breakdown and pulled up in the restaurant. He wasn't overly talkative, but he seemed nice."

"Hold on a second!" Cassius raised his hand. "Did you talk to Cowboy Mike, who knows you're coming?"

"I wouldn't say he knows." David waited for the effect of his words. Cassius' hand clenched into a fist, so the young man swallowed and continued. "He's been quiet for a few weeks, but we weren't worried, it's happened before. The last time his radio went dead."

Cassius opened the map and looked for the restaurant someone had circled and marked with a question mark.

"When do we get there?"

"At this pace?"

"Yes, for God's sake, at this pace!" Cassius snapped. David put both hands up, oblivious to the fact that he was driving a fifteen-ton monster.

"All right, calm down! Two hours, maybe a little more. Why?"

Cassius checked the ammunition in his gun (*Three and four, two for Abigail... Not enough for anything!*), then turned back. He gestured to Abigail, who eased up to the front with her arms stretched out for balance. The bus shuddered as it crashed into something again. David stared blankly at Cassius.

"What's wrong?" the young man asked.

"You really don't understand how things work out here, do you?"

"No... well, yes... but what's that got to do with it?"

Abigail stomped her foot as she moved up beside them, and without a word, Cassius handed her the mag of his Glock with the bullets inside.

"Load them into yours!" he told her, then looked at David, who was still blinking widely. "What do you think happens out here to uninvited guests?"

Silence.

Abigail answered the question.

"Nothing good."

4.

"Stop right there!" Cassius pointed to the billboard on the top of a few degrees of slope. He tried to breathe deeply, but his chest was tight in the hot summer air. His clothes were already drenched in sweat. "Slowly, don't mess up the dust too much!"

The Blue Bird pulled off the road and stopped in the cover of the torn billboard. In the distance, floating above the mirage in the middle of nowhere, the ruined diner could be seen, the sun reflecting on its windows. Around it a few withered trees and a sea of scraggly green weeds. Downed electricity poles and ripped off wires. In the distance, the countryside was hidden behind a curtain of haze, and the sun was obscured by thin wispy clouds.

Worst case, he thought, *it's a false alarm. But if there's someone in the restaurant. Or something...*

"Keep the engine running."

"If we waste fuel like this, we won't even make it to Headland," David snorted and wiped his face, smearing a smudge of dirt across it.

"That wasn't a suggestion," Cassius said coldly, taking a pocket mirror from his bag and turning it towards the sun so that even David could understand it. "I'll signal when it's clear."

"And what if it's not clear?"

"That's why you have to keep the engine running. If you see anything suspicious, do a flip and don't stop as long as there's fuel in this piece of junk."

"Are you crazy, man? Would you send me straight back to the pack?"

Cassius tossed Grant's map into the young man's lap.

"Study it while we're gone! Make something up," he said, then jabbed a finger at the door. "Open it!"

The muggy air outside the bus hit his face and the heat reminded him how tired he was. Even adrenaline and a sense of danger couldn't dampen the fact that he hadn't slept properly in days. He would have liked to sit down and drop like a sack, but he had to hold on.

Cassius gestured to Abigail to go. The plan was simple, but by no means without risk: search Cowboy Mike's diner, with only nine bullets and some silent treatment. He decided to talk to Abigail as little as possible for a while, relying solely on instructions. *If that's the way, so be it, I can be like that! From now on we'll have new rules: I'm gonna say what we do, how we do it, and no more explanations, no more debate. When she hears the command, she will jump, salute, and execute, no questions asked.* But the very next thing that went through his mind was to tell the girl to concentrate, to spare the bullets, what to look for, and how to approach the diner. *So much for the silent treatment...*

The restaurant was about a quarter of a mile away, surrounded by a few small buildings and a gas station. Cassius wanted to approach it from the shady side, hiding in the tall grass and bushes to take advantage of the cover of the trees.

"Watch out for traps! And Abigail, be careful!"

She looked at him with an impassive face, but it was obvious even to him how hard she was holding herself and how poorly she was acting.

"I know my job!" she said, and turned defiantly away from him.

They crept to the restaurant at a reasonable distance from each other, and as they drew closer, they involuntarily slowed down. Cassius peered once more out of the cover of a ceratiola shrub. The bus was hidden by the billboard and the sound of the engine was inaudible. Everything seemed to be fine.

He turned back towards their target. Cowboy Mike's was a typical country diner with a red-and-white striped tin roof, wheat-brown walls and white plastic windows that had been boarded up from the inside at the beginning of the pandemic. The parking lot in front of the building was dusty, the American flag on the pole had been torn by the wind, and the dingy welcome sign had some funny words on it, but all these years later Cassius couldn't remember what they were. Farther away was a small gas station with four filling pumps, even farther a rickety barn and a service building that had completely collapsed.

Cassius crouched down and Abigail followed without thinking. They waited in silence, watching. Nothing moved on the shady side of the restaurant, only the rustling of the wind and the buzzing of insects could be heard. The heat brought drops of sweat to their foreheads, the back of their necks scorched by the sun. Cassius looked up at the sky, trying to somehow lower it, but it was sparkling and climbing higher.

We can't sit here still until the end of time.

He rose slowly and took a few steps, then stopped again and listened. Abigail copied him, step by step, movement by movement. One, two, three, stop. Squats. Listen. Four, five, six. Rise, start, steady steps. Balance, gun held ahead, eyes on the target.

The first wire ran thirty yards from the restaurant, but Cassius could see immediately that it was patchwork, or at least that the alarm around the house hadn't been maintained for a long time. He stepped over it and took a few more steps forwards. That's when he caught sight of the bloodstains and scorch marks in the grass. Cassius let out a soft whistle. Abigail stopped, waited, looked around, and only then started walking towards him.

He flicked a ripped human ear aside, and pinched a piece of shrapnel between two fingers. The girl stared at him in bewilderment.

"Someone blew themself up? Why?"

"I don't know. Maybe it was an accident. Maybe to avoid being eaten."

Cassius stood up and pointed to the parking lot in front of the building.

"That must be where he escaped, where he was caught. Click, safety pin out, boom. If all else fails, I'd go with the same."

"Very inspiring, but what do we do?"

"You take the back door, I'll take the front. Thirty seconds. Go!"

Abigail nodded and headed for the back of the building. Cassius, his eyes on the windows, circled the building.

Seven, eight, nine.

In front of the diner he saw three cars by the station. The SUV must have been rusting there for years, so he ignored it, but the other two looked like recent customers. The sedan was parked with the hood up and flat tires just outside the entrance, with discarded parts beside it that someone was hurriedly trying to remove. It may have been the owner of the armored pickup truck that pulled out from in front of the restaurant when it was attacked. The door was open, the barred windshield smashed in. He didn't have to think hard to figure out why it looked so familiar. The pickup had been modified in the same style as the Blue Bird: metal bars on the windows, a plow mounted on the front, and even the symbol on the side in small. The skull without the jaw. But why did they split up here? Why had the dead man-eaters left their pickup behind and not turned back to Headland?

Sixteen, seventeen, eighteen.

He did not yet know the answer, but he did notice the burned tire marks on the blacktop. They were wide, just as wide as the Blue Bird's. For some reason, the hobo and the tramp had left in a hurry. Something must have disturbed them.

Twenty-nine, thirty.

Cassius hurried to the door and opened it carefully. A thin band of light illuminated the dim interior, giving the ruins a hellish effect. Shards of glass and dust on the floor, some tables pushed aside, chairs overturned. The drop ceiling was torn down and there was a pleasant chill that made him shiver. He straightened up because he noticed the other clues.

A bloodstain on the floor, but old, too old to belong to the man-eaters. Drag marks in the dust. A long, thin, deformed footprint, shaped from blood and dust. Farther away, at the long counter, a human hand torn off. On some of the tables, there were even plates with leftover food that had rotted over the years. Cash registers had been ripped out of their places, probably when money was still worth something. *What the hell?* It didn't look like anyone lived here.

Glass clinked under Cassius' feet, but no one broke out from under the rows of tables. Dust motes swirled in the air and there was a stale, musty odor. He took a deep breath, but he couldn't smell the distinctive stench of ferals.

Behind him the kitchen was in almost total darkness. Something stirred among the dented silver-grey appliances, followed by a flickering beam of light, and Abigail emerged, breath held, gun and flashlight in hand. She glanced at the front door, then back into the darkness.

"Next time I'll come in the front."

"Fair enough. Did you find anything?"

"Nothing. They've been here and taken what they could, but there's definitely no one living here."

Cassius nodded.

"And now?" she asked.

"Something is very wrong with this place."

"You do know that you always say that, don't you?"

"Let's go!"

They stopped at the same time in the doorway, looking outside with a wry face. They were reluctant to leave the cool, pleasant interior, but they knew they had to go and stepped out into the sweltering heat. Cassius glanced first towards the bus (*In place, luckily!*), then nodded his head at the pickup and the sedan.

"One belonged to our nice old friends, the other must have arrived not long before, but for some reason it got stuck here. Seems like the man-eaters started picking out the useful parts when they were surprised by someone... or something."

"Cowboy Mike?"

"Could be. But I don't think Cowboy Mike smashed their windows."

Cassius stepped up to the armored pickup and looked inside. There were traces of blood and a severed thumb. He nodded, proudly.

"Yeah, just as I thought."

"Was a pack just passing by?"

"Just? Every time someone rolled up in front of the restaurant? And what about old Mike, the one our pain in the ass lost contact with a month ago?"

"You don't think..." Abigail didn't finish, she just kept turning back and forth as if looking for a reasonable explanation for what had happened. Blonde flyaways were stuck to her forehead, her thin face glistening with sweat.

"I don't think anything," Cassius growled. "That's the problem."

"Look!" Abigail pointed towards the sunny side of the restaurant.

Beside the building a thick steel tube protruded from the ground, topped with an air vent cover, badly damaged by an unknown force. Most of the cover was broken off, the pipe was dented, and the sides were scarred with scratch marks.

Cassius looked around, and now that he knew what he was looking for, he quickly found the shelter hatch at the end of the building. They hurried there with their weapons raised, but halfway there they could see that the double metal door had been ripped open from the outside. The metal plate was buckled, the lock fluttered despondently in place, and inside and below there was a pitch-black, putrid, stale scent.

"Can you smell it, too?" he asked as something tickled the back of his neck. She nodded. They turned at the same time towards the two-story barn, which crumbled a good hundred yards away from the restaurant, set back from the road, well surrounded by shrubs. It looked like a set built for a cheap horror movie: rusted red tin roof, wind-ripped rotten planks. The granary behind it had long since collapsed.

"Doesn't look very inviting," Abigail shuddered.

"Rarely does."

"Okay. You take the shelter, I'll take..."

"No, first thing's first! You stay here and keep watch!" Cassius said leaving no space for opposition. "I'll go and see what's downstairs."

5.

The sunshine balked at the entrance to the shelter, not daring to venture down the rotten steps. Cassius leaned against one wing of the door, switched on his flashlight, and descended into the depths.

The wooden stairs creaked under his feet, but he didn't stop. His hand tightened on the grip of his gun, and after a dozen steps he hit dusty concrete. He slowed his breathing to hear every little squeak, but the cramped, cool room was silent, with no sign of life.

The opposite wall of the shelter was covered with fiberboard, the others were uncovered brick. Beds in one corner, cupboards in another, tables and chairs pushed up against the wall. Bags and boxes everywhere, with clothes and other useless objects in them. On the table, someone had collected tools and parts from the area. There were some canned goods, mostly superfluous stuff. The bed had not been made and on one of the plates there was leftover food that had been rotting for weeks.

Cassius spoke up quietly:

"It's clear."

"Okay..."

He jogged up the stairs, back into the sun, then exchanged looks with the girl biting her lip. Slowly they started towards the barn, thinking twice about every step. To the south, thick storm clouds were gathering. The distant thunder of lightning was still faint, but he knew the storm would be here soon.

"Do you think they're there?" Abigail asked, not taking her eyes off the ruined barn. "Could they have stayed in one place for so long?"

"I don't know," Cassius answered. Sweat poured into his eyes, which he wiped away as quickly as he could. The dirty juice stung, irritating and disgusting him.

"And if..."

"Quiet!" Cassius hissed. He sensed movement behind one of the boards, but before he could do anything, his foot caught. When he regained his balance with great difficulty, he looked down and the blood drained from his face.

A putrefied human corpse lay in the grass. Even the drag marks were visible, along with thin, long, deformed footprints. Cassius raised his head and looked around in shock. *What the hell? WHAT THE HELL?*

Abigail lifted a bloody shred of cloth from the ground with a sewn name on it: MIKE. She looked at him, stunned.

"Cowboy Mike?"

Cassius nodded, but his mind was already somewhere else. His brain was racing, working furiously. He clenched his lips. His scruff tingled, sending a shiver down his spine. He couldn't move. The barn stank and the alarm that had never failed him before went off inside his skull.

"What shall we do?" Abigail asked.

"Very... slowly... start... backing away."

"What?"

"Slowly."

Cassius took a step back, but kept his eyes on the barn. Abigail followed him only after she was sure that her companion wasn't trying to be a hero or do anything stupid.

"Shall we cop out?"

"No. We just leave the battle behind."

"But it's…"

"Let's go!"

Two steps back. Three. Four. Something moved again behind the boards. Cassius heard the sound of feet on rotten wood. The soft cry of creaking slats. The crackling of a tired old beam trying to resist the enormous weight pressing down on it. The rush of something taking momentum and leaping.

His heart pounded in his ears, but he didn't stop. He prayed that nothing would happen. That they made it to the diner, where they would be far enough and the feral might not attempt to attack.

"When I tell you, you turn and run. Fifteen yards. Got it?"

Abigail nodded. It was a familiar tactic. After fifteen yards of running, you turned back to cover the other person's retreat. But they could no longer do it. Something was blocking the sun. A huge shadow appeared on top of the barn and jumped down between them.

6.

The Gamma landed with a mighty thud and pushed Cassius away. He flew several yards before hitting the ground with a loud groan. His clothes were ripped open by sharp nails, and a thick stream of blood spurted from his shoulders, covering everything around him.

Abigail spun to face their attacker, pointed her gun at the feral, and fired without thinking. She discharged two bullets from her Glock into the Gamma, which staggered from the shots, but regained its strength after a few seconds. Somewhat.

Meanwhile, Cassius tried to get up, but he was too weak and fell back into the dust. His fingers searched desperately for his shotgun, his eyes glued to the Gamma, which straightened up with a rattle and a snarl.

It took Abigail only a moment to realize that Cassius couldn't help her. She stepped back so she could fire from the proper distance, and despite the terror that gripped her throat, she held the butt of the gun firmly. Her palm was on the grip and her finger on the trigger, but...

...she noticed the strange, staggering movement of the feral. Subconsciously, she had noticed something was wrong before, but only now did she understand what she actually saw.

The Gamma gained momentum. Its right shoulder was scarred by a burn and it slumped as it tried to struggle towards Abigail. The huge leap it was capable of became a feeble shuffle. The stagger lasted barely a second; an untrained hand would have been unable to even react before the feral restored its balance. It was still a threat, except that Abigail was no rookie: she leapt aside, and the Gamma sped past her, trying to catch her with a swiping hand.

Dust swirled around its hulking, sinewy body. Its bloodthirsty grunt was mingled with a frustrated growl.

Abigail drew her machete, and when the rampaging, out-of-pace Gamma attacked again, she struck. With a powerful slash, she scarred the feral's back, causing it to lurch and howl in pain. It turned with difficulty, but Abigail was still faster. She shuddered with the thrill of success, almost floating above the ground. The Gamma just dragged its torso, no trace of the force that made it so dangerous. Abigail was sure of herself now, and sure of why the Gamma was behaving the way it was.

She was ready to end the fight. Fear was replaced with euphoria. Her panting breaths calmed, her trembling limbs steadied. She was proud of herself for having seen the signs and was eager to be praised for it. *I used my wits, and didn't just fire bullets like an idiot. And he says I'm not ready!*

But Cassius must have thought otherwise because when he stood up, he shouted angrily at her. Abigail, on the other hand, concentrated on the task at hand. She was focused on getting the Gamma to attack and finish it off with one last move. When Cassius's fingers finally found the rifle at his feet, he picked it up and fired. All his bullets entered the Gamma's body; it faltered and then collapsed.

Abigail's machete stopped in mid-air, and she glared angrily at him. Cassius limped closer, one hand clutching the wound that tore his shoulder.

"What… the… hell? Are you out of your mind?" he asked in exasperation.

"I'd have killed it! I was ready!" she snapped at him. Her ears were burning with rage.

"Bullshit, you were…"

Cassius winced and dropped his empty rifle on the ground, as if fed up with the whole thing. Abigail could only think about proving that this time she hadn't been irresponsible, so she didn't notice the blood running down his face.

"It was wounded and starving. Didn't you see? It hadn't eaten in weeks..."

She couldn't finish the sentence. Cassius fell to his knees and sat down on the ground, powerless. Abigail was there in an instant, supporting him. He looked down at his bloody palms and closed his eyes.

After her anguished cry, only the distant rumble of the storm could be heard.

7.

Cassius was angry, but restrained himself because he was finally alone with Megan. He had to be careful if he wanted to know the truth about her.

In the early afternoon the storm arrived. The wind rose and the sky darkened with ominous clouds, then the rain fell, as if trying to empty the sky in a matter of moments. David parked the bus in front of the entrance to the shelter where Cassius lay and, with Abigail's help, unpacked a few essentials for the night. Blankets, water, food. They put a tarpaulin over the door to keep the rain from soaking the basement and when they were done, they decided to stay outside. David took care of the bus and Abigail looked after Soxy. Cassius knew it was his expression that had scared them off.

Inside, on one of the tables, a single oil lamp burned, illuminating the walls with a yellowish-red light and giving the stale room a strange, gloomy shimmer. Despite a long airing out, the musty smell persisted. Next to the table-leg a box was filled with stuff they collected from the basement.

Cassius sat with his shirt off on the bed while Megan cleaned his wound. Even in a semi-dazed state, he noticed that she rolled her eyes in embarrassment, occasionally resting her gaze on his chest. When she leaned closer to wipe at the bloodstains, the air he breathed filled with the scent of chamomile from her hair, and it bothered him more than he expected. The fragrance seeped into his brain, tearing his resistance to soft shreds.

"We should've kept going," he said and rubbed his eyes. He tried to fight it, but all he wanted was to fall back onto the dirty, creaking bed. "We don't know this place, there could be anything here…"

"Stop moving! It could have been a lot worse." Megan shook her head. "On the other hand, if you don't like something, don't sulk at me, be brave and tell the girl! You were passed out and she made a decision. A good one, by the way."

When she was done, Megan threw aside the old bandage and handed him a bottle of something alcoholic.

"Here, take a gulp! Slowly, leave some for later."

From her bag she took a small medical kit with a suture needle, thread, and scissors. She meticulously laid the instruments next to each other on a clean cloth, carefully adjusting everything until it was perfectly arranged the way she preferred it.

"Yes, we could've kept going. We'd be shivering in the rain and you'd be curled up on a dirty seat. And then you could have done this yourself, because I certainly wouldn't do it that way. Would you like that? Besides, we'll be fine if we stay the night. At least we can get some rest."

Cassius handed the bottle back and Megan took a sniff before putting it away. She even sighed at the aroma of the disgusting, pungent slop, then settled back and began to stitch up the long, deep wound. Her movements were practiced, so the pain was just bearable.

"It's a pretty nasty wound. You sure you'll be all right? I don't wanna wake up in the night to find you transforming," she chattered, and when she paused in her rambling, she pursed her lips, focusing. Threads of her chestnut-brown hair kept falling into her eyes.

"I'll be fine, unless that bastard licked its claws before gouging me."

"Yeah," Megan brushed the hair out of her eyes. "Has anything else ever occurred?"

"Anything else?"

"I don't know, like someone getting scratched and transforming, or... or someone getting bitten and surviving."

Silence. She watched him out of the corner of her eye, her movements unsteady with tense anticipation.

"No, never. Ah!"

"Sorry, sorry!"

Megan paused her stitching, and when she continued after a deep breath, Cassius felt her fingers working more hesitantly. Nearby, lightning streaked through the sky and the thunder shook the walls. They both winced.

"You'd think after seven years everyone would know the rules of the game," he said in an emotionless voice. He looked at the opposite wall to distract himself from the pain. "If you get bitten, it's over, you might as well put a bullet in your skull... or someone else might do it for you if you don't have the strength. It doesn't make a difference."

Megan gritted her teeth.

"Lucky for us, you're here," she mumbled, but when their eyes met, she gave him a playful smile, as if swallowing her resentment. Her coquettish, ringing voice had almost completely returned. Almost. "I don't know what we would have done without you."

"I can guess."

Megan closed her eyes. At the next stitch, the hellish pain made him see stars, and his teeth sank into his clenched lips. She noticed.

"By the way," Megan went on, smiling with satisfaction. "Abigail found out what might have happened. At least, she has a theory."

"Really?"

"Really. The pack was camped in the barn, probably smelling

Mike. No wonder," she grimaced as she looked around. "Abigail said that the ferals are incredibly disciplined, able to watch their prey for days, if need be, and strike when it's least expected."

"Abigail isn't wrong about that."

"So, the old chap couldn't smoke them out, and they got him eventually. From what I hear, there's not much of him left. That would have been the end of the story, but for some reason the pack thought the barn would make a wonderful hiding place, so the ferals stayed and hunted down those who came later."

"The sedan."

"Probably. But they weren't always lucky."

"The man-eaters?"

"Yes. Those bastards probably killed the Gamma's companions. The two unlucky weasels you met escaped in time on the bus, but their partner blew himself up, wounding the Gamma as well. The Gamma survived, but had little strength left to hunt. It was weakened, in bad shape. Abigail said it would have died soon."

"Right… and Abigail figured that out on her own," Cassius said dubiously. He felt the woman's scathing look. Megan must have thought carefully about her answer, for it was only after long seconds that she spoke.

"You're too hard on her."

"Life is cruel."

"Oh, that's new, I've never heard that before," she scoffed.

Cassius felt his temper rising. He didn't want to talk about their problems, or about his arguments with Abigail, and not because he was unsure whether he was doing the right thing. It was simply a matter to be kept between the two of them, and he had a very good reason for that. The siblings were the best example of what happened to those who hadn't learned how to get along outside walls of false security. Walls that would come down sooner or later, without exception. Such people could only survive by the mercy of others because they were incapable of defending themselves. And Cassius didn't want that for Abigail.

"It's better if I'm strict than for a mistake to eventually cost her her life."

"She's not nearly as helpless as you think. She was pretty good while you were passed out. She scouted the area, fixed the alarms, helped David to gather up some useful stuff. She worked out that even if we left right away, we'd only be in Headland by nightfall at the earliest, and who the hell wants that? She thinks it's a bigger risk."

"Really?" He glanced towards the stairs, genuinely impressed. *Not bad.*

"So, you might as well loosen that leash before it snaps… Well, we're ready."

Megan cut the thread, gently checked the sutured wound, then put the needle and scissors away. She took a long strip of rolled bandage from her bag and wrapped it around him like a mummy. She finished in moments, then meticulously put her things away.

"I appreciate the advice, I really do," Cassius croaked, unsettled by the awkward silence. "But Abigail is my responsibility, and only mine. Our helping you won't change the situation. After Headland, we're going our separate ways, so it's best if we each mind our own business."

Megan's face blushed. She nodded, upset.

"I see," she stuttered, then stood up with a big snort. Cassius held out his hand, but she pushed him away. "I'm fine." She shuffled to the table with her bag.

Cassius moved his shoulder and was pleased to see that, despite the nasty injury, his arm still worked. She'd done a good job.

"Thank you for the care," he said, and though he wanted to explain himself, he didn't. Megan stubbornly kept her back to him, her shoulders tense as she disinfected the instruments she's used.

"The bandages need to be changed regularly and make sure you keep properly hydrated! Unless that bastard licked its claws before, you'll be fine."

Cassius couldn't help but smile. It was his weakness, appreciating it when his own cleverness was turned against him.

"That's good to know. I'm sure I'm not the first one you've tried to fix."

"You're right, and believe me, I'm pretty damn good at stitching people up. The boat-towners couldn't ask for anyone better."

"You bet they couldn't." Cassius took a break. He chewed his next words carefully. "Unless there's something to worry about."

Megan's movement froze, her head tilted to the side, but she didn't turn.

"What do you mean?"

"I mean, they don't like secrets in any colony."

She looked at Cassius, her face red, her nostrils flaring.

"What did Grant say?" she asked, and swallowed impatiently.

"He said nothing."

"Nothing?"

"Nothing, and that's exactly my problem."

"Then at least that infuriating, gossiping monkey did one thing right in his life... Let's get one thing straight: I don't care what anyone thinks, I don't care what anyone says, I'm going all the way and I'll be fine! But you know what? You were honest with me, so I'm gonna be honest with you. I'm happy to return the favor. I say fuck you all, because after Headland we're going our separate ways anyway, so it's best if we all mind our own business. Right?"

The stairs creaked and David clattered down them, balancing a box of sleeping bags. He was humming along, not caring what he'd walked into, and after dumping the sleeping bags on the table, he shook the rain off his body with a snort. He kept the empty box in his hand.

"There are still a few things here that might be useful. Seems like old Mike wasn't a complete idiot; he knew how to collect things." Megan shifted from one foot to the other, while Cassius moved his shoulders as if it would speed the healing process. David finally noticed the tension in the air. "Everything all right?"

"Of course, everything's fine," Megan said and tossed Cassius his T-shirt. He caught it with one hand, struggled to his feet, and got dressed clumsily before starting for the stairs.

"Abigail?" he asked David, who made a sloppy gesture in the vague direction of the bus.

"She's feeding the mutt."

"I wouldn't do that yet," Megan's cold voice stopped Cassius. "You don't wanna get water on that wound."

Cassius stepped over to the table, his mouth tightly shut, and looked through Mike's stuff with a sulky expression. The box contained bullets as well as tinned food. David shifted his gaze from Megan to Cassius.

"Why do I get the feeling that I'm missing something?" the young man asked with an awkward smile, but no one answered.

The rain slowly subsided, the heavy downpour turning into a softly tapping drizzle. Tired of standing around, Cassius unzipped his sleeping bag and threw it on the ground. He turned down Megan's offer to let him sleep on the creaky, dirty bed, opting instead for the hard floor. He planned to rest for fifteen minutes, but exhaustion finally seeped into his limbs, and his eyes were drawn shut, heavy with sleep. And the images started coming.

He was on the bus, but he couldn't see who was driving and he didn't know where they were going. It was a strange mixture of events that had already happened and ones that might still come to pass. They were moving, on the way to Headland. Straight into danger, into the eye of the storm. When he turned to the back of the bus, he caught sight of the children. Molly staring sadly, Nia stroking Lucas's head, and behind them, Abigail...

He was filled with anxiety, his panic fueled by the thought that nothing could happen to Abigail. She was the last one left, the last one he could save.

Then he heard her voice.

Jake.

She alone called him Jake.

He sank into the darkness.

8.

Reality and the pain throbbing in his shoulder pulled him back from his dream. Cassius woke with a gasp, lifted his head, and squinted. The shelter was quiet, the others were sleeping peacefully. Megan and David were curled up on the bed, with Abigail on the other side of the room, next to the box hiding the sniffling Soxy. He could have gone back to sleep, but anxiety wouldn't let him rest any longer, so he got up instead.

Gun in hand, he stepped through the door, shivering as the cool wind hit his face.

The August dawn slowly dried up any trace of yesterday's rain, but somewhere far away in the north the sky was still stormy. The area was completely silent, the sea of grass barely moving in the endless meadow. The wisps of clouds that drifted across the bottom of the sky seemed like a string of pearls, slowly but surely melting away against the yellow-blue horizon.

Cassius stood motionless, time slipping from his grasp, lost in his musings. He forced himself not to close his eyes and let sleep pull him back. He took a deep breath, savoring the fresh air before daytime heat drove the earthy-musty whiff of wetness from his nose. He involuntarily pressed his palm to his shoulder to soothe the throbbing pain. It helped for a second, but the torment came back.

Suddenly he heard a distant noise and recognized the pattern. The movement of a weary predator pausing to listen from the safety of tall grass. The soft rustling stopped at that point, and he could see the button eyes scanning the landscape before him. Then he heard the sad, lonely howl. It was clear, rough, yet it blended perfectly into the dawn.

Slowly, he moved forwards in silence until he found what he was looking for. He crouched down and watched patiently, doing nothing else. In the sea of grass, almost half a hundred yards away, he caught sight of a grey blob with two ears pointing skywards. The coyote gave another howl, and turned to him with the same curiosity with which Cassius had been watching it. Neither of them moved, just looked at each other with cold eyes. He felt the coyote's gaze tearing him apart, penetrating every inch of him, but he never felt a moment's fear. Only solitude.

In the distance, another animal howled and the one opposite Cassius jerked its head up at its mate's call. The coyote turned, then dove into the sea of grass with great leaps.

The distant thunder finally died down, the dull gunmetal-grey horizon turning golden yellow. It seemed as if the morning breeze had banished all their previous troubles, and the fresh air brought a strange calm. Hope.

Cassius got up and walked back towards the restaurant.

9.

He was surprised to see the Blue Bird's hood up and David fiddling around in the bus with a few rags and a bucket of water. The boy was humming Fleetwood Mac as he cleaned the dashboard, and looked up, scared, when Cassius came up beside him. It was obvious he wasn't paying attention to his surroundings, and if it had been up to him, a whole pack could have snuck up on them. Cassius remembered the first lesson he'd taught Abigail: always know your surroundings. *And she was nine.*

"The early bird gets the worm..." David spread his hands wide when he noticed Cassius's searching gaze. "I thought I'd tinker with the old girl. I don't want Megan to travel in a mess like this."

"How noble of you," said Cassius, with only slight irony. Then he picked up one of the rags and started to help the young man. They wordlessly scrubbed away the years of grime and blood, a tedious job that Cassius enjoyed immensely. To let the monotonous work absorb him; to not think, not converse, that was...

"Do you think we can get away from them?" David asked, throwing the rag into the bucket. He looked at Cassius expectantly. "The man-eaters, I mean. Do you think we can slip through Headland without being seen?"

Cassius glanced up out of the corner of his eye, but didn't stop working. He wiped dirt off one of the seats, his cloth already completely stained with red-brown grime.

"I don't know," he answered. "Either yes or no."

"Has anyone ever told you what a big help you are?"

"Yes, I still get the thank-you cards."

David snorted.

"Very funny, but we'll be there in a few hours and it would be good to know what to expect. If you've got any information that'll help... that'll reassure me..."

"Reassure you, buddy? I don't have anything on Headland to reassure you. You think this is just about man-eaters or ferals? If you do, you're wrong. At least we've heard of those, at least we can prepare for those."

"What do you mean?"

Cassius sighed and threw the rag on the floor.

"What I mean is there's a lot of talk about Headland, but there's hardly anyone who's ever got out alive. At least, we haven't met any, and we've been travelling the country for a long time. Downtown was a hell of a place before the battle, believe me, but what happened afterwards, God only knows. Anything you've heard can only be part of the horrors, and there's no one to sing the chronicle. The whole city is a blind spot. We don't know where to stop, we don't know what lies around the next corner, in the streets, in the buildings. But I can see you still don't get it, so I'll help you. What do you think people did after the army closed down the city?"

"Dunno."

"They set traps everywhere. In the streets, in their houses, and preferably ones that kill everything. Humans, ferals... and most of those traps are still there."

"Jesus, what is this? Home Alone?" David shook his head.

"You think it's funny? We'll let you go ahead. If you're careful enough, you won't step on a mine or a bear trap. But from what I've seen of you so far, it don't bode well for you."

David glared angrily at Cassius, who didn't even flinch. He narrowed his eyes and continued.

"The man-eaters could be anywhere, no news on ferals, not even on road conditions. We may run into a dead end with spikes waiting for us. There could be a pack out there, even bigger than the one we've just seen. So no. There's nothing I can do to reassure you."

David's neck twitched as he tried to swallow the lump stuck in his throat.

"What could be worse than man-eaters?"

"We'll soon find out."

Silence fell over them. David tossed aside the dirty rag, wiping his palms compulsively on his trousers.

"I think that's enough for me. It won't get any cleaner, but if I keep doing it, I'll throw up."

Cassius nodded. In less than a minute they were standing outside, staring at the sunrise. The morning breeze caressed their faces, but this time the silence didn't last long.

"I could do with a beer now," David cracked his back and glanced towards the restaurant. "And a cheeseburger, medium rare, with bacon but no pickles. I don't know what the food was like here, but I don't care for now. I'd eat whatever they gave me."

"I could also use a beer."

"Good to know. I thought you never chilled."

They laughed.

"What do you say we wake the girls?" David asked after a pause.

"The sooner we leave the better," Cassius replied, turning his head east towards Headland. *Let's get this over with...*

10.

They set off in the morning, just as the heat was becoming unbearable. In the scrappy bus they could just catch a leading wind that eased the stifling humidity.

David was humming an old country tune while driving, Abigail was feeding Soxy, and Cassius and Megan were sitting on either end of the same row with the windows down. She let the wind play with her chestnut hair, he watched the landscape. The oaks that flitted by lined verdant clearings, interspersed with the once-white wooden fences that had been used to delineate the estates of the past.

It was a familiar neighborhood. They were getting closer and closer to Headland.

After one ascent, the sharp headlights outlined the remains of the distant city on the horizon. The skeletal remains of old skyscrapers faded into ominous obscurity, but with each passing mile the picture of devastation became clearer. Obstacles multiplied along the way. Trees and fields were replaced by looted, ruined buildings.

They caught their first glimpse of graffiti in the suburbs: beneath a jawless skull, bloody letters told them where they had come. Tierra del Silbón, the sign read. Cassius knew what the words meant, and though he was reluctant to remember, he knew the story well. From first-hand experience.

"We have arrived," he said. Abigail rose from her seat beside Soxy and pressed her face to the window. Megan forgot to breathe, and David involuntarily slowed down. They watched the world outside in silence.

Tierra del Silbón. The empire of Silbón. The land of man-eaters.

TIERRA DEL SILBÓN

1.

Week eleven started out just like any other and since it was a lovely Monday morning in March, most people in Headland didn't have any particularly negative feelings about it.

One exception was Luisa Huerta.

She had been hating March now for six whole years. Of course, it wasn't really about the month; after all, no one is stupid enough to be mad at a month. Luisa Huerta's biggest problem was that the opening day of MLB was coming up and as social media manager of the Headland Blues, her over-demanding boss was making her life a misery. If things went well, she would get a day off after the first game, which Luisa, a lonely thirty-something, would celebrate with a nap and chocolate-chip ice cream.

The week, however, did not start as Luisa had expected; she began to feel the weary congestion that accompanied her physical and mental exhaustion even earlier than usual.

Well, girl, you're getting old, she thought, barely managing to get out of bed that Monday morning. True, she had been working all hours the previous week, but until now a weekend of idleness had always helped, while now the malaise had put her in a merry-go-round.

She ignored the strange wound on the back of her hand, dismissing it as a simple spider bite. Still, the two swellings, close together, did not look like spider bites at all. Nor did she think of the frightening noises in the night, as if something had been flapping its wings frantically in her room, which she chalked up to fatigue, nothing more than a silly dream.

She had a fever and a headache and could barely pick up the phone to call work. After throwing up everything she had eaten for breakfast, Luisa fed her cat and took a painkiller, hoping for a miracle that would allow her to go to work the next day. But Luisa felt somehow that this was different from any other illness. She was restless, and there was a tingling in her limbs and a dizziness that was unlike anything she had felt before.

Her body was so weak that she could not move and almost fainted, even while lying in bed. A deep, dark sleep rushed through her pounding brain, and when she awoke, panic was the first thing that flooded her thoughts. She spent long minutes in delirium, on the border between reality and imagination. Weakness was replaced by a strange anxiety. She was drenched in sweat, and when she managed to prop herself up in bed, she felt her fingers twitch. She dragged herself helplessly to the bathroom, but the glare of the lamplight caused unbearable pain, and her neck muscles tensed spasmodically. Her entire body trembled, and the sheer agony made her slam the switch so hard that it burst into pieces.

When darkness fell, she curled up in the corner of the bathroom, sobbing. Hours passed before she finally regained consciousness. She could not tell what day it was, but behind the confused, vague thoughts, it was as if nothing that tied her to her former life mattered. In a state of hazy dislocation, she watched her tense, agonized body from a distance and though somewhere deep down she was aware of her helplessness and wanted to fight against it, her spirit slowly but surely sank into the void.

And the void no longer offered a way to return.

2.

At first it was all just rumor.

A dumb story of a homeless man whom the paramedics thought might have had a run-in with a stray dog. His wounds were treated at the city hospital, he was given medicine, then released back where they thought he belonged: on the street.

A barfly who had been locked out of his home by his wife. The police had seen too many drunks to believe that a demonic creature roamed the suburban nights, attacking unsuspecting people.

A missing person, last seen in a corner shop just a few hundred yards from his workplace, ten minutes after his shift ended. He must have left because he had a fight that day with his boss, who accused him of embezzlement. Nor did they take into account the huge pool of blood found in a nearby alley and the traces of a deadly scuffle.

The events took place over the course of two days, but authorities were not overly concerned. Why would they be? These things are part of life in the big city, they said, and it never even occurred to them that there might be a connection.

And by the weekend it was already too late.

The first of the afflicted to be shot — with twelve bullets on Friday night — was a woman in her early thirties, Luisa Huerta. By midnight, fourteen people had reported to the police that they believed they had been attacked by her that day. Something must have made the poor woman go mad, most of them thought, and the authorities were keen to close the case quickly because a Venezuelan immigrant with no previous record who was suddenly shot dead seemed like a political nightmare. But there was a thing that, if even one person had considered it, might have made a difference.

Seven additional people came to the station that Saturday morning, and their attacker was not a woman but a man, a homeless man. The police decided the victims were in shock and simply mistaken. Clearly, they only thought that the woman covered in blood and dirt, acting so aggressively, was a man. Luisa Huerta was a lone perpetrator, and despite the spontaneous protests that followed the police crackdown, the reaction of the uniformed officers was justified and proportionate. Period. At the end of an eventful couple of days, it didn't even make the news that one of the wounded had attacked her nurse in the hospital and escaped during the turmoil. The nurse was treated, then wished well and allowed to go home to rest.

On Sunday, around the time Luisa's brother, Rafael Huerta arrived at her shuttered, brick-fronted house on Palmer Avenue to collect his sister's belongings, a conscientious coroner and two detectives had a clue as to what might be behind the horrific events.

Luisa was bitten by a rabid bat in her home, thus causing the aggressive behavior. They made a round of phone calls to contact the people Luisa had injured and discussed the details of the case over lunch. Not an everyday case, they thought, maybe even worthy of a study.

Then they pushed the body of a second "rabid" into the autopsy room, with seventeen bullets in it. Then a third.

3.

On the last peaceful Sunday afternoon, Rafael Huerta parked his maroon Silverado in front of his sister's home. When he saw the candles and flowers on the porch, he remembered the promise he had made to their mother back home in Venezuela. He knew he had failed by not taking care of his little sister. Fifteen years ago, everyone in the family had wanted to dissuade them from taking their big trip, especially since it fell on a Tuesday and the thirteenth, but they were adamant, a twenty-year-old man just scraping by after compulsory conscription and his teenage sister. They were chasing the American dream, and neither the family nor superstition could stop them.

Rafael sighed, stroked his black crewcut and graying goatee, then set off on feet that felt heavy as lead. He wanted to spend as little time in the house as possible, yet sunset caught him unawares, lying curled up on the floor in the middle of the living room with a bottle of beer in his hand. Luisa had always kept one in the fridge especially for him just in case he finally did drop by. The beer was almost gone, and it was warming up in his hand.

After a while, he got tired of brooding. He fed his sister's cat, cleaned up the mess left in the bathroom to get rid of the bad vibes, then took out the trash. He fell asleep on the couch, lost in a dreamless vacuum.

In the morning, every channel was covering the weekend attacks. Rafael was shocked to see the atrocities illustrated with a picture of his ever-smiling sister, and horrified to see the rumor on social media that the infection must have been brought in from Venezuela. He would have preferred to respond to the racist pigs one by one, but there was no time: they were banging on the door.

The police and the public health department had him out in no time, and no explanation was given as to why he had to leave the house. No matter how much he threatened, no matter how much he begged, he could not take his sister's belongings with him, he even had to leave her cat behind. The police watched him impassively and waited patiently for him to disappear.

"You killed my little sister, you bastards! You think you can get away with it?" he shouted at them, to no avail.

He drove to his workplace, face red, frantic, almost wishing someone would mention the incident to him, that they would ask him about his sister, or just give him a bad look at The Home Depot. More than anything, he wanted to vent his anger, but his colleagues showed nothing but understanding. Rafael had calmed down by the afternoon and drove home with a haggard look on his face. He thought that the country they had suffered so much to reach and fought so hard for had suddenly betrayed them. He wanted the police officers to pay for what they had done. A murderous desire raged inside him, and he wanted to be free of it. Then something happened...

The CCTV footage from the corner shop across the street from the incident was leaked at sunset, and in shock, he watched his sister's last moments on earth. The unbridled devastation she had wrought. Rafael had never imagined that Luisa could be capable of such power and cruelty. A woman who hated gym class and couldn't throw a baseball straight had moved like a lioness, and the police could only stop her with a desperate hail of crossfire. Even then Luisa seriously wounded two of them before she died. The footage clearly showed the despairing struggles of her last victim and the horror of the wounded policemen.

The images shocked the whole country. Even the protests died down, and as more and more footage of the night in Headland came to light, everyone realized what was happening: Luisa Huerta was the first of the infected, but not the only one. Smartphone footage came in non-stop, frantic screams in the streets multiplied throughout the night, and emergency rooms were flooded with bitten and wounded victims. People cried out and shook their heads, but it was the events of the next weekend that led to the real panic.

That Friday afternoon, a maintenance team discovered the bodies of nineteen homeless people in an old wagon in a closed subway tunnel. However, judging by the blood and footprints, there may have been more victims, and some might even have managed to escape. The marks suggested people had dragged themselves to the surface, into an alley, and yet there was no trace of the bodies. Even experienced investigators could not explain the incident. The next day, participants in a suburban kids' tournament were attacked by eight rabid humans. More than fifty people were wounded, including two dozen children. It was clear that there was a serious epidemic raging in Headland, but the patients weren't huddled up coughing in hospital corridors.

The mayor called for calm, the CDC was working at full speed, the internet exploded, and every half hour there were more reports that the police had been confronted with rabid people. On Sunday, the President made a speech about hope and solidarity, about the American people overcoming this difficulty as well. Social media was abuzz, and no one wanted to miss the trend: it was #UnitedWeCan… or alone we fail. New profile pictures emerged, thoughts and prayers were sent. The stars sang "One Day Like This" from Elbow, and some TV channels started using the term "affected person" instead of "rabid." In San Francisco, they held a community candle-lighting ceremony and believed that all was and would be well. People were confident that the government would solve the crisis.

Then on Monday, the entire city of Headland was quarantined.

4.

Those lucky enough got out on the 10 or over the bridge in time, but there were still almost a million people trapped in the city, which was completely overwhelmed with panic by early afternoon. Shops were looted, gas stations were emptied to the last drop, but the traffic jams meant that few people made it home before sunset. There were stretches of road where ferals allegedly dragged people out of their cars, so many travelers abandoned their vehicles and fled home on foot. Others camped on the exit roads and waited for a miracle, hoping that the government would change their mind and lift the blockade. If any supplies did arrive, they could not get into Headland, as panicked crowds stormed any point of escape. Smoke grenades and tear gas were used to disperse the crowds in the afternoon, and rubber bullets were used in the evening.

Rafael was one of the first to leave downtown, moving to his sister's shuttered, brick-fronted house on Palmer Avenue to be as far away from chaos and as close to the city boundaries as possible. He was lucky because his colleague, a Home Depot delivery man, was texting him when he spotted the soldiers on the 10 at dawn. It was too late to escape, but at least he could prepare for the worst and get to the stores before the big rush. Rafael did his shopping, he refueled, and then, to the ire of the local neighborhood watch, he forced open the locked front door. After a thorough search of the attic, he sat out on the porch with a bottle of beer in his hand to think about what was coming.

By then, the news was all about the Lower Mississippi rabies strain. CDC researchers discovered that the pathogen had mutated in bats, and humans were a dead-end host, spreading the disease to their own kind through bites. The incubation period for the infection was extremely rapid, so isolation seemed to be the only solution until a cure could be found.

Rafael guessed what that meant: no hospital could quarantine so many dangerous patients and no staff would be willing to take on the task. So sooner or later guns would be fired, starting in the place where the most cases were — the downtown area — and people would be fighting each other to survive. He turned off the TV, opened another beer, and sat back on the porch on the sunny side of Palmer Avenue.

As he watched the 10 behind the houses opposite and listened to the sound of the horns, the shouting, he noticed children walking home from school, young and old, with backpacks. Since school buses were also stuck, they were allowed to walk home under the supervision of a single teacher, who was nervously talking on the phone and barely paying attention. The children chatted happily, unaware of what was happening and waving goodbye to those who had been left behind. The parents of those who made it home were waiting for their children with luggage in their cars. They immediately grabbed arms and backpack straps to hurry them on their way, hoping for luck to escape the city.

Rafael knew, and time proved him right: they had no luck.

Arriving in front of the shuttered, brick-fronted house, one of the children — a girl with long, blonde hair — stopped and waved to Rafael with a broad smile as if they had known each other for ages. She had a cheeky twinkle in her eye, clear even from that distance, and she was talking non-stop, bouncing around the others. He had an idea of who she was: the daughter of the Spencers next door, whom Luisa used to look after when her parents went out. Rafael waved back and lifted an imaginary hat from his head as if to bow, even gesturing broadly with his hands like a knight would do to a fairy-tale princess. The little blonde girl giggled and then ran home with great leaps.

When the street was silent, Rafael sat back and closed his eyes. He remembered Luisa, a memory from decades earlier, when he had walked his sister to school after their father's death. She must have been about the same age then as the Spencers's daughter was now, and she never let go of his hand for a single step. The tiny fingers dug hard into his palm, and she looked up at every other move, as if afraid her brother would disappear from her sight. And when their eyes met, she would smile, overjoyed.

Thinking of the old days, he dozed off and started awake as something clattered on the steps leading up to the porch. He opened his eyes slightly, to see if it was all a dream and, half squinting, he caught sight of the blonde girl standing in front of him, eyes wide and sparkling, wearing a mischievous grin on her face and holding a large glass, which she gripped with both hands to keep from falling.

"Lemonade; I made it!" she chattered, handing the glass to Rafael, who received it without a word and took a sip. "It's real lemon, not powder. And sugar, but not much. My mom says you shouldn't put too much in it because it causes cavities. Have you ever had a cavity?"

Rafael was confused and did not know what to say.

"Yes, I have," he finally croaked.

"And the lemonade? You didn't say if you liked it."

Because I didn't have time...

"It's delicious. Thank you very much! And I can taste that it's made from real lemons; it tastes like real lemons."

"See?" Pause. The girl's eyes sparkled even more. "Are you Luisa's brother? We love Luisa very much, and miss her very much."

Rafael handed back the empty glass.

"Me too, and I'm pretty sure she would be very happy to hear that. But tell me, what's your name, little urchin?"

"Abigail," she said and put her hands on her hips. "And I'm not an urchin!"

5.

People thought that the first week would be the worst, but there was still enough food in the fridges, fuel in the cars, and some order on the streets. In fact, as the handful of survivors later discovered, this was the last moment when it seemed that things might return to normal.

When the people of Headland realized that the quarantine was not going to be lifted soon, the crowd went home and locked themselves in to tough it out in the comfort of their respective houses. The city watched with bated breath, the streets were frozen, and the nightly screams seemed to have subsided.

Below the surface, of course, the tension grew hour after hour, like magma bubbling beneath a volcano, waiting to erupt with devastating force. The alleyways smelled of death and the sewers emitted a strange murmur after sunset, as if something demonic was about to happen, but when their locks clicked and their shutters closed, people still believed that help was on the way.

The message from Washington was clear: there was no room for discrimination in the search for the infected, and the press watched any excesses with a wary eye. The police were in an intolerable situation. Rafael was right again: guns were fired over the weekend, and the uniformed officers had a problem not only with the infected but also with vigilantes. Tasers and handcuffs were useless against the ferals. When the situation became untenable, the frontline police and nurses resigned one by one, and the supply system began to collapse. At first, the shops opened only in the early morning hours; at the beginning of the second week they closed for good. The government sent aid, but no one was prepared to feed a million people in a war zone.

On the fourteenth week of the year the ferals that had been lashed down in overloaded hospitals had escaped and word spread that the police had been ordered to fire on anyone who had been attacked. They denied it, but the wounded who were bitten feared the authorities and avoided reporting their injuries. The chaos grew even worse, and the virus spread unstoppably in dark alleys and musty basements. By then, people were shooting at anything that moved in the dark.

With power and internet still accessible, news of a last glimmer of hope reached everyone: the National Guard had set up special forces to liberate the city building by building using only dart guns. The population was prepared: experts analyzed what was going to happen and repeated the message around the clock that no one should be outside on the day of the operation. On the TV channels, huge numerals displayed the countdown, which reached zero at six o'clock on Saturday morning. In Headland, sirens went off and the sky was painted red with beacons.

Operation Daybreak became the most-watched broadcast of all time, but after the connection was lost with three different platoons around noon, the livestream was shut down. The operation was canceled completely at seven that evening, and although it was said that they would return the next day with the remaining soldiers, it never happened.

By Sunday the people of Headland knew they were on their own, and on Monday they took control and formed armed groups to search for potential infected. An ex-soldier organized a militia, which anyone who wanted to fight could join – mainly against the ferals, but with so much discontent, no one ruled out the possibility that the militants would eventually turn against the government. The members of Mason's Army were not interested in Washington politicians, and the hundreds of eligible candidates began training at Smallwood High despite protests from the press. Even Rafael was contacted, but he slammed the door on William Mason without a second thought. No matter what promises they made him, he had vowed back in Venezuela to put an end to soldiering for good and not waste to his time on agitated civilians.

Instead, he had a plan of his own, and he felt that the time had come to carry it out.

6.

The Spencers wished to throw him out, but politeness kept them from doing so. *Old habits die hard*, Rafael thought, but he had a hunch those customs wouldn't last much longer. Every day more and more of civilization rotted away.

He tried, of course, to make a good impression: he had shaved and put on clean clothes — his favorite short-sleeved shirt — yet he was not offered coffee, tea, or even a glass of water. He did not resent the aloofness, but simply noted to himself that in a few more days people wouldn't even let their neighbors in.

One more reason to convince the Spencers of his plan as soon as possible.

The mother was wringing her hands, her gaze darting to the window again and again as she sat on the sofa in front of him, and the father stood at the door, stooping but ready for anything if Rafael's intentions were not friendly. The children were ordered up to their rooms, but early in the conversation he had noticed Abigail listening at the top of the stairs, clinging to the banister.

Rafael turned back to the father, Benjamin Spencer. He straightened up, cleared his throat, and tried to wrap his opinion as neatly as possible around the stupidity of what the other man was planning.

"Patriotism is a fine thing, Mr. Spencer, but I still don't think you've thought this through."

"I'm not waiting for the government to do something about it. Mason has reassured us that we have a chance."

“Mason only says what people want to hear, but folks like you are usually used as bait because it’s worth throwing a freshman in there for a few ferals.”

“This is nonsense!” the father snapped, nervously adjusting the neck of his expensive cashmere sweater.

“You’re a clever man, Mr. Spencer, but your reputation doesn’t count for anything, and what matters even less is the fact that you sometimes play neighborhood watch. This is war, not a climate protest.”

“And why should I listen to you?”

“Because I served two years in the army back home, and unlike Mason, I was trained in guerrilla warfare by Colonel Benavides himself. Believe me, you’re just cannon fodder to them.”

Benjamin swallowed hard and looked at the mother, whose eyes were glistening with tears. She was about to cry.

“I can’t just sit and do nothing.”

“You don’t have to. The best thing to do is to dig in. Prepare for the worst. Booby traps, guards. Fortunately, Palmer Avenue is a good place to set up a perimeter. Of course, that means convincing everyone in the area and getting everyone on board. If you could talk to them, it would help.”

Silence. Benjamin looked at Rafael expectantly, and pressed his lips together so tightly that they were paper-thin.

“Is that all? And how much better is this than Mason’s plan?”

“This you might survive. “

“Or we die of boredom when we could be doing something. More than waiting for the rescue squad.”

“You’re living in a dream world, Mr. Spencer. I guarantee you won’t have time to be bored.”

They looked at him wide-eyed and puzzled. Rafael took a deep breath and continued.

“In case you hadn’t noticed, looting has already started downtown, and the suburbs will be next. And you have a nice big house with an expensive car in the driveway; all you need is a target on the door. And maybe a month ago the pacos would have rushed to help with sirens flashing, but now they won’t give a shit.”

“Benjamin!” Mrs. Spencer begged her husband, but he shushed her.

"Seven of my staff at the foundation have already enlisted in the militia. A lot of people count on me. I can't let them down. What would they think if I..." He bit off the sentence and looked at his wife. "What kind of example would I set for my son?"

"You belong with your family. If Mason and the other idiots want to take control, chévere, let them do it, they might even manage to clean up the city. The question is, how long will it take?"

"We have enough food, and the locks were changed last year, so there's nothing to worry about. Mason has promised to look after the area and I believe him!"

Rafael had seen enough to know when it was pointless to make any more effort, so he got up, made sure her parents didn't notice when he winked at Abigail, who was cowering on the stairs, and went home. He opened the last bottle of Corona and, staring at the news, thought he might be able to persuade the neighbors separately, without the help of Spencer, but finally gave up. He knew that as soon as the news got around, most of the fathers would follow Benjamin into the militia, and he had no intention of teaching self-defense to housewives who had one eye watering for the children and the other crying for a husband.

He was not surprised that the TV coverage of Headland was tapering off, and that the world outside the quarantined area was slowly getting used to what had happened. The interest of people for a singular tragedy had limits, and their city had already gotten more than just fifteen minutes of fame. The talk shows that used to run all day had been replaced by repetitive reruns, and Rafael was confident that in a few weeks Headland would be no more than an ongoing headline, like the weather or the stock market.

He was brought out of his slumber by a clinking of glass followed by screaming. The noise of a scuffle was coming from the Spencers's, and when he ran out of the house with his Beretta in his hands, Rafael could hear their desperate voices clearly. Crying and pleading. One after another, the lights were turned on in the houses in the neighborhood, but no one helped. Neighbors watched from their windows to see what was happening.

There were three burglars, dressed all in black and armed with crowbars. The first one pushed Mrs. Spencer to the floor of the living room, the second led the children to their mother, and the third pointed a gun at the father, who was holding up his hands. Even in the darkness, Abigail's eyes were wide open and gleaming with fear. The little urchin desperately grabbed her brother's hand as the burglars gave orders.

Rafael immediately spotted an opportunity, like a pair of scissors slowly closing. He had to act within moments, while the burglars were focusing on keeping the family in line. For a second, the thought flashed through his mind that he could make up for his sin; he couldn't save his sister, but maybe he could save the Spencers. He might be able to save little Abigail...

It was dark in the living room, and the sound of the scuffle drowned out the click of the back door's lock. The burglars did not notice. They weren't expecting a neighbor to play the hero. A few moments later, Rafael was inside, reckoning he would only have to use his gun once. The rest would be taken care of by the shock and the deafening sound of a 9mm bullet in the living room.

He took a deep breath and stepped out of the shadows. His finger tightened on the trigger, muzzle flash flared in the semi-darkness, and the screaming reached its peak. And Rafael was right.

7.

The ad hoc neighborhood meeting didn't even last half an hour, and by the afternoon everyone was working on fortifying the area. Rafael had surveyed the possible entry points days earlier and classified them according to the level of risk. The most dangerous were the western entrance on Ronnie Road and the woodland to the south. The access road was barricaded, entrances and windows were reinforced, and tripwires and alarms made of paracord and noisy household appliances were installed around the houses, but Rafael still had a serious problem. He knew these would not do much against a seasoned crew, so he went all out to make it look like Palmer Avenue was home to ruthless professionals.

They sprayed graffiti on the walls of the houses, as if they were home to a bloodthirsty gang. Rafael painted a terrifying figure on his garage door, a lanky grotesque man wearing a wide-brimmed hat and carrying a bag of human bones. The words TIERRA DEL SILBÓN were scrawled in red underneath.

"Silbón? What the hell is Silbón?" Benjamin asked, his lips pursed, but Rafael just shrugged his shoulders.

"A silly story people used to scare each other with back home," he said.

He convinced them that the pretentious, politically correct world was over. The body of the burglar that was shot and didn't have a chance to flee like his accomplices was simply hung at the crossing for everyone to see. Anything to deter looters and avoid hand-to-hand combat.

"Either we get tough, or we're going to be swinging from one of these lamp posts," was the wisdom of the time.

They found a bunch of old CCTV cameras in a neighbor's garage and put them up in visible places, but didn't bother plugging them in. Barbed wire was strung across the fences, and trenches were dug so that those trying to get through in the dark would break their ankles.

Rafael even used an old trick he had learned in Venezuela during his military service: he used PVC pipes, bullets, and nails to install a makeshift mine in the forest. Then they designated the guard posts and prepared the duty roster. There were not many weapons, just enough to beat back an amateur gang, but Rafael figured that solving this would be a problem for the next few days. He also planned to gather up some dogs; one of his colleagues, for example, had two Anatolian shepherds, and he was determined to put them to good use.

They collected fuel from cars that had broken down in the area, got a generator, stocked up on drinking water, and even took a police scanner from one of the abandoned patrol vehicles. There was no longer much activity on the protected channels, but they did get some important information. Rafael warned the others that public services could be shut down at any minute. The internet and phone lines were soon cut off, as if those responsible did not want the scary news to leak out of Headland. The photos circulating on social media had already caused enough trouble. Television broadcasts revealed that, although the government said the outbreak had been stopped at the limits of Headland, suspicious cases were being reported in several US cities. It was only a matter of time before the virus got out and the infection spread elsewhere.

There were eighteen houses on the street, fifteen of which were still inhabited by almost forty people. Half of them were children, most of whom, fortunately, were teenagers. Rafael was convinced that the kids would have as much trouble with all this as they did with school, so he was surprised that they were the ones who enjoyed soldiering the most. At first, of course, the parents were reluctant, but eventually the voices of concern were silenced and the dozen or so teenagers realized that a night of standing guard or a foray spree was more exciting than sitting in front of a game console. They volunteered for what seemed like fun tasks, and after the second day, they swore an oath to each other and even painted their faces to look more determined and scarier. Their leader was Jason, a tall blond guy with a smug smile on his freckled face. When Rafael was not with them, he was in charge, keeping order and giving commands, which the others eagerly followed.

"Come on, little birdies! Faster, harder, or you'll end up being feral food!" The words came from Jason's back garden, where the youngsters were practicing most of the day. They quickly established a hierarchy among themselves. They even used punishment to motivate each other, and Jason was not joking when it came to retribution.

Kids, thought Rafael, smiling at their enthusiasm. He felt most sorry for them but then he remembered how spoiled and wimpy this generation was; they had had everything but appreciated nothing. He believed that once this craziness was over, these kids could start their lives over as better people. Because they would have learned something that neither their parents nor their school had taught them before.

It was only later that he understood that the boys had got a taste for blood that had yet to be spilled. But by then it was too late.

8.

They started the mornings with training and a briefing and were lucky in the first week because the nights were relatively quiet and peaceful. Although they had heard screams and gunfire from the far end of Ronnie Road over the last two days, the guys on watch said the chaos was at a safe distance from them. By mid-April, the soldiers of Mason's Army were using the protected channels, so Rafael learned that there was a complete curfew around the downtown area, but the militia still couldn't handle the ferals.

The 10 was silent, with only a few people spotted wandering among the abandoned cars, still hoping to get through the checkpoints. At first, they could be seen trudging back, but later only the sound of gunfire or the explosion of a mine could be heard.

"National Guard seems to have toughened up," Rafael told those who were discouraged. If anyone wondered why they were not trying to find a way out, the sound of guns and mines finally gave a blood-curdling answer to that unspoken question.

Rafael calculated that the greatest danger would come from outside, so he ignored the internal problems. The first sign he really should have heeded was on a Monday night.

Palmer Avenue was rattled by gunshots and shouting and by the time the adults got to the intersection at Ronnie Road, the clash was over. Four bodies lay bloody on the tarmac; all four were ferals, their skin covered in filth, their clothes were torn, and they stank like drowned corpses. The young men on guard duty surrounded them, led by Jason, the blond boy. The initial shock had worn off, replaced by pride and coolness. One of them, a pimply-faced boy, took pictures of the ferals with his phone and laughed as he showed them to the others.

"What the hell happened?" Rafael asked, slowing down as he approached the group. He froze when he saw the ferals. Their faces were human, but the infection had given them a demonic grimace, their mouths frozen in a bloodshot snarl, and the glassy eyes still glinted with beastly fire. Their bodies emitted an uncanny stench that stung his nose.

Cristo, they've broken through the first defense line. He did not want to think what would have happened if the ferals had broken into one of the houses.

"The bastards thought they could outsmart us, but we were ready for them," Jason grinned as he looked around in satisfaction. Rafael felt a pang of discomfort as he caught a glimpse of the boy's smug face and cold steel eyes in the still flickering streetlight. "We've shown them that Palmer Avenue is going to cost them, huh?"

His companions cheerfully agreed in the background.

Mrs. Spencer caught Abigail as she ran out of their house and covered the little girl's eyes, while the teenagers' parents looked at the slaughtered ferals with their hands over their mouths. One of them had enough strength to drag his child — the pimply-faced boy taking pictures with his phone — off home, though he protested desperately in embarrassment.

"And what about that one?" Rafael pointed to the fourth body, lying face down with a samurai sword sticking out of its back.

Jason shrugged and brushed a bloody blond lock of hair from his face.

"He was still alive, so I took care of him."

"How the hell did you get a samurai sword?"

"Heirloom. My mom and dad let me keep it. And I finally got a chance to use it."

A proud, wide grin spread over the boy's face. His parents whispered in concern.

Rafael closed his eyes for a moment and shook his head. The mothers' patience was on the edge as they hugged their children, but something else was bothering him: the attack had come at the worst possible time, as they had planned to go on a foray the next day. Bad omen, and if that was not enough, he found it hard to trust the youngsters, who had tasted something that intoxicates many people. Rafael had seen it before, back home, and he knew it rarely had a happy ending.

"All right," he took a deep breath. "We'll reinforce the guard, me and Benjamin will stay with the boys. The rest of you go home."

"What about the bodies?" asked one of the mothers.

"We'll hang them all over Ronnie Road before we leave tomorrow. Let everyone know we're not messing around."

The kids erupted into cheers and shook their fists in vicious contentment.

9.

"Sure this is a good idea?" Benjamin Spencer asked, looking around the car with concern. Rafael didn't answer, and the others in the back of the SUV were all just humming. There were six people in the Grand Wagoneer, four of them with guns, the others only with crowbars they had taken from the burglars a few days ago.

The foray proved to be a complete failure. The shops had been looted and the little food they found was enough for a few days at most, but only if they tightened their belts even more.

They had to do something, but it made Rafael sick to his stomach to think about it. *Survival has no smell,* one of his drill sergeants used to say, but he was beginning to doubt it. He had known this moment would come and had prepared himself for it, but that didn't make him feel any better. He only went along with it because the situation was so dire.

Rafael turned back and glanced at their bald, bespectacled neighbor, the smell of his sour sweat filling the air.

"Tell me the details again!"

"We brought the old man home a week ago," the bespectacled man pointed to the nursing home on the other side of the suburban crossing. His hands were shaking and his palms were clammy with sweat. "He said the nurses had long since left, and most of the residents had been taken away by relatives. There's only a few left, most of them unable to look after themselves. Who knows, maybe they're already dead, poor folks..."

"And the storeroom? I wanna know about the storeroom."

"It's supposed to be half full, filled up a few days before the quarantine was announced. Canned food, frozen goods..."

"Meat?" someone asked in the back. It was Jason's father, who had the same sneaky look as his son, his neck almost disappearing between his broad shoulders and behemoth head.

"And vegetables," nodded the one with glasses.

"And your old man doesn't mind what we're up to?" Rafael asked.

"He doesn't give a shit about it, he hated the place, so even if he knew, he'd probably be cheering us on from the front row."

"Then let's go ahead and do it!" Rafael opened the door of the SUV and stomped his right foot down onto the concrete. He quickly counted to three and followed with his left foot. It was a boyhood superstition, something he had picked up in the army because he believed it brought good luck.

All six of them got out and blinked anxiously towards the nursing home. The brick and timber-framed building was lined with tiny flower gardens and shrubs, the idyll disturbed only by a few broken windows, a messy lawn, and a rough tire track that had ploughed up the grass. Thick brick pillars led up to the main entrance, a gray-roofed porch with whitewashed edges shaded the entrance. There was no movement behind the dark glass doors. The area was quiet; only one of the nearby detached houses had a car parked in front, and even that had its door ajar. There was no one around. The ferals were now prowling the downtown area.

Rafael glanced at his team and felt like laughing. He was looking at a bunch of random jerks. Benjamin wore bright chino pants for the action, with matching sailing shoes. Jason's father's broad shoulders danced just like a peacock in front of the gym mirror wall, eager for something to happen. The guy with glasses wiped his nose, not caring where he aimed the barrel of his handgun. One of their stocky companions dropped a crowbar in the background, which clanged loudly on the concrete sidewalk.

Benjamin looked toward the Pacifica behind the Grand Wagoneer, in which two mothers sat with Jason and his gang. Though tired from the night watch, the boys stretched their necks impatiently, waiting for orders.

"What do we do with them?" Benjamin asked.

"They stay here," Rafael replied dryly.

Jason's father snorted.

"Then why the hell did we bring them with us? As an escort?"

"Exactly. Let them stay right here, at our fingertips," Rafael said, then sighed. "Now, let's get this over with!"

He checked his gun and headed for the nursing home. They crept to the back door, which they pushed open. As quietly as they could, they stepped into the dim, empty hallway. A stale smell wafted along the beige walls, and a lamp flickered at the far end of the corridor.

"The kitchen and the storeroom are on the right," stammered the bespectacled neighbor. Jason's father, meanwhile, pointed his gun down the dim hallway.

"Do you think the ferals have a taste for old meat?"

"Shut up!"

Rafael crept towards the kitchen, raised his hand in warning and listened, but heard nothing. The kitchen was dimly lit and the storeroom was in complete darkness, but even by the glow of the flashlight they could see that their friend was right, and that there was more than they had hoped for. The shelves were packed to the rafters, the freezers half full. Rafael was now mostly concerned about time and logistics, but the fact that the nursing home seemed to be completely empty filled him with an unearthly calm.

"We need more hands for this," Benjamin said as he carried his flashlight along the shelves. Rafael nodded.

"Tell the boys, but no shenanigans! Quietly, intelligently, and no side-quests, comprende?"

Jason's father grinned and turned on his heel. Rafael closed his eyes and smiled. They could hold out with this hoard until the government or the Masons sorted out the problem; he didn't even want to consider what would happen to them if the world failed.

The boys were worn down from the night watch, so they loaded up the cars stolidly and silently. Rafael ignored them after the second round, instead opening a paleo-friendly granola bar and grimacing as he wondered whose idea it was to feed the poor elders such tasteless sawdust. The Grand Wagoneer and the Pacifica were almost full when he noticed that Jason and his companions were missing.

10.

The noises came from upstairs, fighting and shouting, banging and breaking glass, then desperate wails. Rafael ran up the stairs as fast as he could, the beam of his flashlight dancing on the walls. The sound of the scuffle grew louder.

"You think you're tough, old fucker? Huh?" he heard the voice, probably Jason's, closer and closer.

He found the boys in the upstairs lounge, and they were not alone. One of them was kneeling and rubbing his head where someone had hit him, and Jason was standing over an old man who lay on the floor bleeding and moaning, with a shattered wall mirror beside him. At the far end of the lounge, in the dim corner, skinny figures huddled.

Rafael leapt over and shoved Jason back. The boy was still on an adrenaline rush, spittle spurting from his mouth, his fists shaking menacingly.

"That's enough!"

Jason's father and Benjamin emerged from the stairs. Rafael had to raise his hands to prevent the two pale, deadly men, gasping for air, from accidentally shooting them. "Step down!" he called to them, then crouched down to the old man on the ground and quickly checked his wounds.

"What the hell happened?" asked Jason's father.

"Nothing!" Jason shouted, shaking himself. "We were just looking around. Seeing if there was anything else. And they came at us."

The elders, huddled in the corner, got up and shuffled over to their companion on the floor. The shards of broken mirror crunched under their feet. When Rafael saw that the old man was going to survive, he leapt to his feet and promptly pinned Jason against the wall. The boy couldn't breathe, his body making a loud thud. His father cried out, but Rafael didn't give him a second thought. He pushed his Beretta under Jason's jaw and cocked the gun.

Everyone around him started screaming.

"Hey, hey! What are you doing, man?"

"What the f..."

"Jesus Christ!"

Rafael, however, paid no attention to anyone or anything, concentrating on one thing and holding the gun to the boy's face tighter and tighter. He could see Jason's haughty eyes clouded with fear, his mouth curled and his body twitching. He would have even started to beg if the tight grip hadn't squeezed all the air from his lungs.

"Who the fuck you think you are, huh?" Rafael reprimanded him. "You think this is a fucking video game?"

Jason shook his head, but the vice-like grip did not slacken.

"You do this one more time and I'll hang you on Ronnie Road myself, you son of a bitch! You got that?"

The answer was a vigorous nod.

Rafael let go of Jason and the boy fell to the ground. No one moved for a few seconds. Even the wounded old man stopped moaning and looked around in concern. Jason's father gasped and was about to step forward, but Rafael was ahead of him.

"Discipline your son, or I will! And if you don't like it, you can hide out in your penthouse downtown, maybe you'll learn a lesson there. Have I made myself clear?"

"All clear, mate," Jason's dad spread his hands wide, his eyes never leaving the barrel of Rafael's Beretta. "Clear as day."

Jason got up, pushed his father's hand aside, and headed downstairs. Instead of regret and shame, his eyes burned with vengeance.

11.

As much as the residents of the nursing home grumbled, the storeroom was almost completely emptied, leaving only a few days' supply. Rafael took care of the old man's injuries, then politely apologized for the inconvenience and collected the shards of mirror before leaving. When Benjamin asked if they should take the elders with them, Rafael shook his head in silence. He did not dismiss the possibility, but he wanted to reconsider, under calm circumstances, and eventually blessed his wits for not getting weak. The news that night was that the outbreak had already hit some of the big cities on the East Coast.

The government was desperately fighting, but the world had woken up and no one wanted to risk the pandemic crossing the ocean. European and South American countries closed their borders and China quarantined all travelers, regardless of where they came from.

Rafael knew that Headland was hopeless, and help was now certain not to come. Whatever the government's plan was, the G-men would now focus on Baltimore and Miami, and they would be lucky if they didn't get a bomb dropped on them. Their survival depended on how wisely they allocated their resources. Therefore they decided to leave the old folks in the nursing home.

After Jason's trouble, the kids were no longer at Rafael's beck and call. They locked themselves in one of the empty houses, a gray family home with five bedrooms and didn't stick their heads out, no matter how much their parents pleaded with them. The music was loud during the day and at night it was suspiciously quiet around the building. Rafael realized only later that after dark the kids were organizing their own operations — more for the adventure than for the resources, but they were doing something right. They got cars, fuel, and weapons. Benjamin saw Jason and his mates unloading serious electronic equipment from a van one morning. The parents desperately implored Rafael to do something, but he shrugged.

"What can I do? Beg them not to be stupid?"

"You might be able to influence them," the others said. "They won't listen to us anymore."

"I'm pretty sure I'm not gonna be the one to convince them."

"Please, Rafael! They'll get themselves killed if they go on like this."

"Or they'll hang me if I say something wrong," he said, but no one responded. Of course, he knew he had to think of something, because this could not go on, but he didn't want to rush things. The parents were not pleased with his hesitation, and the tight-knit community of Palmer Avenue fell apart in a matter of days. From then on, people were left to mind their own business, and apart from Benjamin and a few conscientious neighbors, they didn't give a damn about having to work for their safety.

Nor did they care when news came over the police scanner that the Masons had changed strategy and it became clear that the situation downtown was critical. They were up to something, but the cryptic messages did not say what. And at the other end of Ronnie Road, the residents of two different family homes were slaughtered during a single night.

Rafael knew what he had to do, but he tried to delay visiting Jason at the gray house that the boys had appropriated. *Damn kids,* he thought, and remembered why he had never wanted children, especially in that day and age. After all, they were all the same spoiled, entitled, narcissistic brats who thought they were the center of the universe. Nothing was ever enough for them; you gave your whole life in vain. *And to hell with their parents, as well,* who chose the easy way for the sake of their own comfort.

After knocking on the door for the umpteenth time, the pimply-faced boy finally opened it. His face twitched as he caught sight of Rafael, and then he yelled back.

"Jason, they're here to see you!"

He turned without saying goodbye, leaving Rafael alone. Jason emerged from the direction of the living room, wiping his hands, and approached as slowly as one who has all the time in the world. Beneath his stubble, the long dimple that crossed his chin had disappeared, but the glint of his cold steel eyes had not changed.

"Hey, hoss," the boy drawled with a great deal of irony.

Rafael looked around the house and clicked his tongue in satisfaction.

"I see you've been busy."

"You know how it is. We try to do something for the community. To give back what we've been given. If there's anything you need, let us know. We'll work it out."

"Yeah."

In the background, a girl stripped to her panties walked by with a joint in her hand, humming some saccharine pop song. No matter how hard he tried, Rafael could not recognize either her or the song.

"Expanding the gene pool, eh?"

Jason glanced around and snorted as a thick smell of pot hit his nose.

"Yeah, taking in the fallen."

Awkward silence, an imbecilic grin, and an eye-roll. Rafael noticed the guy was seconds away from slamming the door on him.

"Your parents are worried about you, Jason."

"I thought they would be happy that we're so independent. Isn't that what they wanted?"

"Don't pretend like you don't know what I mean."

"I get it. I'm not stupid. You think we're just snot-nosed kids you can control, and then if you don't like what we do, we're gonna get a smack."

"That's not true. You're part of the team."

"We don't give a shit about the team, in case you hadn't noticed! And we don't give a shit about your old asses! Look around, Rafael, and tell me what you see. In one week, we've done more than you have because we didn't fuck around."

"It don't give you no balls if you do it for fun."

"The world is in ruins and you're worried about what's right and what's wrong? And you're worried about coffin dodgers?" Jason bit off what he was going to say, then grinned to himself. Proud, content, while hiding his right hand behind his back. "But don't you worry anymore. We've chosen a real Nobel Peace Prize-winning solution."

"What are you talking about?"

"I'm talking about them not suffering any more. Believe it or not, they even thanked us for our generosity, not in words, of course, but with a grateful gleam in their eyes. And the things you foolishly left behind, we took them, so they wouldn't rot in the empty nursing home."

Rafael's face paled, his lips quivered. Anger was about to burst out of him, but Jason pulled his right hand from behind his back and Rafael saw that he was holding a gun.

"So, say thank you and get the fuck outta here while I'm still in a good mood."

12.

He had no one else to rely on, and he didn't regret it in the least. The only one always hanging around was Abigail, the little girl from next door, who preferred to spend her time outside, unlike the other children who were cowering in their houses. When Rafael checked the traps and alarms, she would follow, almost breathless as she rattled off the hundred or so questions that came to her mind there and then; when he fried his share of the meat from the nursing home, she would eat her grilled mac and cheese sandwich and tell him about the summer camps she wanted to go to.

She was with Rafael during one of the afternoon watches, too, on a sunny Saturday in early May. Somehow the distant sound of gunshots died away, and for a while they watched in silence as white clouds rolled across the blue sky, Phillips Tower with its tuning fork-like radio towers peeking out from behind the trees.

"Are the boys being punished now?" Abigail asked, pointing at the gray house with her thin fingers. "Mom said they were bad. Is that true?"

"True, but they're not being punished. They moved away of their own free will."

"Why? Don't they like living at home?"

Rafael smiled and had to choose his words carefully.

"It happens at this age. When you get older, you'll understand."

The little girl wondered.

"Strange... but I think it's stupid."

"It is."

They noticed movement on the 10. Rafael raised his binoculars to his eyes and watched two men as they headed towards the checkpoint from downtown. They had guns on their shoulders, white armbands on their right arms, the distinctive mark of Mason's Army. They smoked cigarettes and talked, dodging stalled cars.

"Hm," Rafael muttered to himself.

The Masons had not ventured into the suburbs before, but this was the second day Rafael had seen them lurking around. He followed them with his binoculars and watched as they pulled up a few hundred yards away, moving from cover to cover as they approached the first checkpoint.

"What the hell," Rafael grumbled. For a moment he forgot Abigail was there with him.

"Are those men trying to escape too?"

"Yes, but they won't make it. The soldiers did a thorough job."

"What will happen then? Will they go back?"

"If they have any sense, they will."

"But Mom says bad things are happening downtown and we shouldn't go. Did you know I used to take my dance classes downtown? We used to go there a lot."

"No, I didn't."

"If downtown is really so dangerous, why don't we help the people who live there?"

"Because we can't help everyone who's in trouble. Then we'd end up getting in trouble too."

Abigail wondered.

"That's not what Mom said."

"Your mom is wrong."

"Hm, maybe. I'll tell her you said that."

Normally, Rafael would have been worried that he was about to find himself face to face with Mrs. Spencer, but this was not even close to a normal situation. Just before sundown another detachment, this time a five-man squad, arrived from downtown. The militiamen held a map in their hands and gestured broadly around, as if in a tactical meeting. The next day, more and more came, smaller drones swept overhead, and in the evening a man claiming to be a commander appeared, looking for Benjamin Spencer on Mason's behalf.

The tall, broad-shouldered man with grayish hair and deep-set green eyes refused to say what they were up to, but asked for clear passage for an operation that was due to take place over the weekend. A 'special operation,' as the commander described it.

Rafael had a bad feeling and wanted to say no, but the others didn't want to antagonize Mason.

"It'll be over in a day, no more," the commander assured them as he left, then took a chocolate bar from his bag and handed it to Abigail, who was huddled at the top of the stairs, eavesdropping on the conversation. He looked around at the people who were standing there uncertainly. "We're the good guys, and we're gonna sort this problem out. However, if you can, don't be out there that day. It won't be safe..."

On the day of the operation, most people were up at dawn out of excitement or fear, so they could see the members of Mason's Army slowly marching up to the checkpoint. The majority suspected they were witnessing a historic moment, feeling how people must have felt at the New York Stock Exchange on Black Thursday, or standing on West Street in New York City on that particular September day.

Rafael was sure that the Masons had had enough of the fiddling and wanted to take full control. By breaking out. And if they could not do it with kind words or pleas over the radio, they would try it with force.

However, news of the operation had spread, and a small crowd began to gather around Ronnie Road at dawn on Saturday, filled with those who wanted to take the first opportunity to get away. Families, young couples, all were weighed down with bags and hoping for the best.

The National Guard must have been preparing for the action, because as the sun rose, a thick cloud of smoke appeared over the distant checkpoint, and after six o'clock the guns started firing. Rafael watched anxiously, but his attention was focused on the crowd gathering at Ronnie Road, eager to see how the battle would unfold and whether Mason's Army would breach the quarantine and escape Headland. Even Abigail turned up outside the Spencers' house, watching the excitement from the cover of a bush.

At seven in the morning, the youngsters appeared at the door of the gray house, armed to the teeth and — it soon became clear — ready to join the fray on the side of the Masons. The parents, already upset by their children's behavior, exploded. Rafael felt caught between two fires and knew that he had no trump card in his hand. The kids would not listen to him, but still he had to try to dissuade them from fighting.

"You don't go to war against your own people," Rafael said, but Jason evaded him. He held an AR-15 in his hand and was adjusting his flak jacket.

"I don't give a shit what you think, old man," Jason snarled, then turned to the others. "Get a move on, little birdies! The party can't wait!"

Rafael wouldn't let it go.

"You better listen to me, because this could all be a distraction.

And the main attraction could be happening somewhere else."

Jason paused.

"What are you talking about?"

"Isn't it obvious?" Rafael pointed in the direction of Route 10, where armed men in camouflage uniforms and white armbands were marching toward the checkpoint. "You might not see it yet, but I do. They are all amateurs, most of them your age, because Mason is smart enough not to send his best soldiers into battle on the first wave. Don't be stupid! Only idiots volunteer for the slaughter."

"Bullshit!"

"A smart soldier waits. Just an hour or two, then we'll see how things are going. We can listen to them on the radio, and we'll know exactly what's happening."

Jason thought about it, then signaled to the others.

"We wait until nine, not a minute longer."

A far-off scream ended the conversation. They all turned their heads and watched as the crowd on Ronnie Road began to move. Something was happening in the distance and the panic spread like a gigantic wave. Then they heard shouts, first farther away, then closer and closer:

"Ferals!"

13.

"Everyone! Get inside!" Rafael shouted. People began to scream and run, and in moments the chaos broke their ranks. The refugees from downtown pushed each other forward, at first begging to be let in, but a few seconds later they were threatening to shoot. A standoff broke out between them and the residents of Palmer Avenue.

Rafael didn't hesitate, nor was he considerate. Shoving his way forward, he ran up to the porch of the shuttered, brick-fronted house, raised his gun, and pointed it at the family closest to him.

"You, inside! Come on!" he shouted, and then took aim at those further away, who, spotting those rushing towards the house, started to move too. Rafael knew it was too risky to wait for them. "No one else! No one else!"

The family of four pushed into the building with their luggage, and Rafael stepped to the door, about to close it when he saw the Spencers. Benjamin frantically tried to dissuade the crowds heading for his house, while Mrs. Spencer clutched her son's hand and spun around, calling Abigail's name.

A pickup truck came from the 10 and braked in front of the crowd. Four militiamen jumped out of the truck, one of them the commander seen earlier, who began shouting orders.

"The door! Come on, close the door!" he heard from behind him, but Rafael waited. Worrying for the girl overrode his instincts. His eyes were searching for Abigail, and he was about to go to help find her, despite the increasingly loud screams and the growing crowd, when he spotted the first feral. Someone fired a gun, one car crashed into another, and the shrieks were joined by bloodcurdling screeches. Rafael was unable to look away.

The feral jumped on top of one of the cars and threw itself several yards onto a pregnant woman. Like a wild beast, it sank its teeth into its desperate victim. Another feral dashed across the lawn of the house across the street, and despite the escapees shutting the door in its face, the monster leapt and forced its way into the building. Rafael pulled himself together and looked around once more, but Abigail was nowhere to be seen.

Then the lock clicked. A wardrobe was pushed in front of the door, and Rafael stepped to the boarded-up window, watching through the cracks to see what was happening outside. He heard the wailing of the family behind him.

"Silence! Not a peep!"

Outside the Spencers' house, the crowd started to disperse and Rafael immediately realized why. There were at least a hundred ferals; no one had ever seen a horde so enormous, and they were attacking everything. One after another they burst into the houses.

"To the back door, hurry!" Rafael shouted.

They ran out, not stopping until all of them were far away from the screams.

14.

Six adults, ten youths, and five children survived the attack; everyone else was torn to pieces. Benjamin's remains lay on the porch. Mrs. Spencer and her son lay in the driveway. The woman was already transformed, but her death was caused not by bites but by bullet wounds. *Who killed her?* Abigail was gone, there was no trace of her, and Rafael searched until dark, all in vain.

Following the crowd, the ferals later attacked the checkpoint, and the soldiers were able to repel them only at great cost. Those who reached the ruins of the roadblock were not fired upon, and the National Guard organized the transportation of the survivors under the media's suspicious gaze. News of this spread like wildfire. The next day, tens of thousands more set off for the checkpoint, and the government realized that change was needed. Quarantine was lifted and all hell broke loose as people fled from Headland. Some immediately set off to the south, while others headed for the Florida Keys, hoping to leave the country on one of the yachts anchoring there.

A refugee camp was set up in Brookings and people were examined there, but the crowds were becoming increasingly difficult to restrain. Mason tried to get twelve infected people, family and friends, out of the city in ambulances, but the National Guard would not allow it and resorted to the most violent methods possible to stop the caravan.

Images of the battle and the devastation went around the country and people saw for the first time what would happen if the problem was not eradicated. Infections appeared one after another in nearby small towns, and a horde eventually attacked the camp at Brookings.

Rafael, of course, was unconcerned for a while, and spent the next few days searching the area for any sign of Abigail, but his efforts proved futile. The girl was nowhere to be found, and when he gave up all hope, Luisa came to his mind again. As much as he wanted to, he could not save either of them; he had failed.

The last street meeting on Palmer Avenue was attended by seven adults and only one youngster, Jason. The question that no one wanted to ask, but that was on everyone's mind, was what next. Should they go or stay?

"I know the first instinct would be to go, but I don't recommend it, at least not for now," Rafael began. "Out there we will be prey, one among thousands of refugees, but here we can be safe. So I wouldn't go with the crowd, not for a while."

But the six other survivors did not listen, and were about to vote him down when Jason spoke.

"Go where you want, but we're staying! This is our home, and we're not gonna just leave it!" he said, and walked away without a second thought. Before he stepped out the door, Rafael nodded towards him, but there was a menacing fire in Jason's eyes, the kind that made him shiver.

The parents could do nothing, not wanting to leave their children behind; reluctantly they decided to stay. Palmer Avenue was permanently torn in two. There were no longer enough adults to rebuild the old system, and most of them were discouraged from pretending that nothing had happened. The kids once again locked themselves in the gray house and communicated with them even less than before.

For the first few nights they heard ferals prowling around, but on the fourth day they noticed the kids hunting down the infected one by one in the dark. More and more bodies appeared on the lampposts of Ronnie Road, and Rafael could see that they were no longer driven by the desire to survive, but by the pleasure of killing.

In the second week they took over the other empty houses and began to organize their own defense. They drew a jawless skull on the wall of the gray house, got uniforms, and kept a few unfortunates as slaves in exchange for food. They ignored the adults, and even gave them orders after a while. Rafael began to suspect that it was the end of the story when one of the parents said:

"What can we do? Better to adapt. If they protect us, I won't resist."

Rafael found it hard to accept, but he knew what was happening in the world. Before the power went out, they had seen the ferals' attack on the intersection of 10 and 285 on TV, and they saw the fall of Miami. Some lucky ones had separated themselves in Key West, but most of them dismissed the thought of staying. Seeing the wave of migration, the world had closed its doors to North America and

Rafael realized they had nowhere to run. They might as well stay; it made no difference.

"It's okay," Jason snapped once. "We're having a good time here. And if there's something you don't like, just fuck off."

Rafael tried in vain to open up to them and make suggestions to teach them further, especially the new arrivals who were picked up from other parts of the city, but Jason turned him down relentlessly. They did not need him, and if he had been honest with himself, he would have accepted earlier that he didn't need anyone either. Except that the shuttered, brick-fronted house was haunted by the ghost of his sister, and Rafael felt it would be bad luck to leave the home that Luisa, the ever-smiling Luisa, had worked so hard to create. He felt he owed it to his mother and his sister.

The situation only got worse after the battle of Headland. The youngsters were away more and more, and when they came back, they threw raucous parties, caring for no one and nothing. The ferals, of course, were no longer to be feared, for most of them had left Headland, and those that remained were hunted down by Jason and his boys. Even when there was no party, strange noises came from the gray house at night.

More and more travelers showed up on the 10, and some of them said the pandemic was also unstoppable in the big cities on the East Coast. Most of them were headed south, hoping to somehow make it through to Mexico.

Rafael was less and less concerned. *Why should I care? It's over!* The only thing that still bothered him was the sound coming from the gray house at night. One day, when the kids went on their usual foray, he decided to take a look around. He didn't know why; perhaps he was just bored. He crept in through the back door and looked around the rooms, finding nothing but stinking, stale emanations and piles of trash. Empty bags, used condoms, cigarette butts. Then he heard rustling from the garage.

Rafael held up his gun and snuck to the door, opening it carefully. The stench, which surpassed anything he had ever smelled before, immediately hit his nose. It was dim inside, but he noticed the ropes stretched out to hold a kneeling, limply writhing figure. Without thinking, he approached, but when he reached it, he recoiled in horror at the sight. The bound figure was a feral, with brutal wounds, cuts, and burns on its body. It had been tortured.

Rafael did not turn around as he fled the house.

15.

He was a spoiled brat, just like Rafael when he was a child. Legend had it that his parents gave him everything he ever wanted, yet the boy grew demanding and short-tempered over time. He believed that the world revolved around him and if he wanted something, he had to have it; there was no forgiveness or understanding.

Whenever little Rafael did some mischief, his father would always tell him the story of the pampered boy, and lie that his spirit would come for him if he didn't behave. Rafael had heard the story so many times that he knew all the twists and turns by heart.

In the story, one day, the boy wanted to eat deer meat, but his father wandered the endless lands in vain, and he came home empty-handed. The boy became furious and in his infinite conceit he killed his father. He cut out his heart and liver, and ordered his unsuspecting mother to cook the entrails for him. But his mother became suspicious, and when she found out what her son had done, she cursed him for all eternity. With the help of his grandfather, he was captured, tied up, and brutally flogged. Aguardiente was poured over his wounded back and two hungry, rabid dogs were unleashed to devour him as he writhed in terrible agony.

His ghost had haunted ever since, and travelers across the vast grassland plain of the Llanos often see him carrying his victim's bones in a huge sack across the desert, whistling an ominous tune. He had become a lost, vengeful soul that superstitious people named El Silbón. The Whistler.

Rafael thought of it when, on a sunny June afternoon in the twenty-third week, the youngsters caught him and dragged him out to Ronnie Road. The man just smiled to himself and stood there, silent as he was beaten. When Jason asked what was so amusing about such a fateful moment, Rafael told them the story of El Silbón.

"That's a good one," Jason grinned. "I'll remember that."

Then he himself pulled Rafael up onto a lamppost on Ronnie Road.

A PIT OF HELL

1.

David automatically slowed down when they set eyes on the first buildings in the suburbs. Abigail pressed her face to the dirty window, her eyes wandering as she watched the world outside. Her heart pounded in her throat, her stomach clenched, and for long seconds she didn't even notice that she was holding her breath. *Home sweet home,* she thought, and twisted her lips into a bittersweet smile as she turned back to the others.

Megan sat silently in the front row, staring ahead with slumped shoulders. David's body tensed behind the wheel, his head tilting left and right, looking for potential threats. Only Cassius seemed calm, though Abigail knew him well enough to spot the tell-tale signs. He moved purposefully to the front of the bus to give orders, no emotion reflected in his face, but his lips were pursed and his fingers drummed on his gun.

The ruined city was still. The wrecks multiplied around them, and after a ramshackle welcome sign they reached the old military checkpoint, of which only a few Humvees and trucks remained on display. Farther away, containers rusted in the fields, with stop signs and boom barriers tossed aside nearby, along with torn sandbags and an overturned SUV that had been blown apart by a large-caliber rifle.

The 10 turned before the long stretch of straight road leading into the city center. Behind the dense crown of trees, the roof of Phillips Tower appeared, with its huge radio antenna that resembled a tuning fork. The old world, doomed to decay, was in chaos: green and yellow foliage had encroached into the gaps and crawled up every building, the fragmented asphalt was covered with dunes of dust. On the side of a church, a worn mural proclaimed the last glimmer of hope: GOD ABOVE.

Megan climbed up to get a better view, but she had to hold on as the bus struggled to maneuver around the wrecks.

"Where could the man-eaters hide?" she asked anxiously as she spotted another graffiti. A jawless skull, drawn in blood. The neighborhood was full of them.

"No idea," Abigail replied. "And I've got a feeling that no one alive knows except them."

"I don't wanna be the one who finds out," David cut in. He cleared his throat and brushed back his sweaty hair. "We can still go up north. Just say the word."

Abigail glanced furtively at Cassius, then shook her head. She got neither permission nor prohibition, so she answered.

"It's no better in the mountains, and I don't think we have enough fuel to get around."

David stared speechlessly ahead for a while. "Damn it, I'll manage if I have to! I'll drive economically, and downhill we'll be fine. The momentum swings us along."

"What if you're wrong?"

"Then it's a walk... but at least not in Headland. That's something."

"For you, my dear brother. As for me, I'm finding it difficult to walk!" Megan snapped, but held on tight as the Blue Bird crashed into another wreck.

"Panic in silence, and keep your eyes open!" Cassius hushed them. He ignored the ice-cold stares, instead pointing to the grassy section running alongside the two-lane road. "Drive into the field!"

David winced.

"And the mines?"

"Those are further away. Look, if I have to explain everything I ask, we'll never get out of here. So do as I say."

The air around them was frozen solid.

"Ooookay, man..."

The bus slowed down. The debris crunched under its wheels as it left the asphalt, and the chassis groaned on the uneven ground.

Cassius turned back, his eyes searching for Abigail. She nodded as if in answer to an unspoken question, her eyes saying sadly, *I'm fine, I'm home...* Then she turned back to the dirty window to see if she could finally find what she was looking for.

Behind the alley that lined the road, a familiar landscape emerged: a suburban street with once-elegant houses was now a wild space. The weedy lawns were covered in trash, the windows of the buildings were broken, and the facades had become rusty.

When Abigail found what she had been searching for, her fingers tightened on the leatherette seat. Their old home sat lazily in the midday sun, right next to the shuttered, brick-red house where her favorite neighbor, the ever-smiling, ever-fooling Luisa Huerta, had lived, and where Abigail had met her brother Rafael, the one man who she never drove crazy with her questions. *What could have happened to him? Did he survive the battle of Headland?* Memories flooded back into her mind. The screams, the blood...

...the time spent under the car...

...and the rattle that she did not understand back then. *Mommy...*

The shaking of the bus brought her back to reality. Palmer Avenue disappeared into the canopy of the trees, but the past would not creep back into the darkness. It stayed with her.

Abigail went over to Soxy's box. Through the back window, she tossed one last glance at her receding home, then smiled encouragingly at the fidgeting puppy. She picked up the box and carefully placed it on the seat beside her. She stroked Soxy's soft, fluffy noggin, watching the landscape outside dance in the sweltering heat. Her throat was tight from the acrid air, her pixie blonde hair was even more tangled than usual, and thick drops of sweat appeared on her forehead. The hellish dryness made swallowing an active effort. She wanted to curl up on the floor, in the shade of the seats, but then she remembered the dirt and blood, the rusty junk, and the grease. She shuddered as she pictured the filth she had recently dug her hands into.

They passed a crumbled, concrete-gray parking garage, and she noticed something: a black pipe sticking out of one of the windows, looking toward the 10. She jumped up, as if pushed out by a spring, but when the bus got closer to the parking garage, she realized that what she thought was a gun was in fact just a metal rod. False alarm.

Abigail muttered a curse under her breath, then sat back down. She glanced at Soxy and wondered how difficult it would be to protect the puppy in a dangerous situation. She dismissed the idea that they would be safest on the island, but Cassius' words came back to her. *You behave differently when you're responsible for someone. You make different decisions...*

Inconspicuously, she looked forward, in the direction of the man still standing beside David. *Pff, he can't be right.* The words echoed in her head, but she felt ashamed. Selfishly, she had forgotten how he must feel returning home to Headland, where so many terrible things had happened to him as well. *What could be going on in his head?* Was he remembering his family? His wife and his son... Or was he stubbornly shutting out all distractions and concentrating on his task, as he had been taught?

She turned back to the landscape outside and tried to think of something else. Of the boat-town, of the people who might live there, but then she scolded herself for being so distracted.

After the bend, David steered the bus up onto the road, but the Blue Bird still had to maneuver around the cars. In some areas the space was so narrow that the chassis cried out again and again as they scraped through wrecks. Ahead of them, a pedestrian overpass had been bombed. Behind that the light-colored cladding of the Phillips Tower and its still-intact, bright-green glass was clearly visible, a dazzling contrast with the darker tones of the surrounding structures. Abigail glanced around. The noise barrier wall had been breached in several places, and downed wires dangled from the street. On the only signpost still standing, faded letters announced to go straight on to the Garibaldi Park overpass, the only clearway through downtown. A wind chime made of human bones waved next to the sign.

They slowed down to dodge a car with a tiny corpse in the back seat, still strapped into a child seat. From the front, a female figure was trying to reach back for it, and the windshield was riddled with bullets. Abigail turned her head. *You make different decisions, you think differently.*

As the sun streaked across the zenith and the wind blew every cloud from the light blue sky, the heat was at its peak. She wiped her forehead in vain, sticky sweat dripping into her eyes. She leaned her head forward and closed her eyes to get some rest. Only a few minutes of calm before they reached the once-busy downtown, but then someone tapped her shoulder.

Abigail snapped her head up. Cassius towered over her, his hand on his gun, his fingers still. They weren't drumming now. The bus was already in front of Phillips Tower, once a landmark for travelers.

"Get ready!" he said with face like stone. "We're here."

They had reached downtown.

2.

"Back down!" Cassius said and readied his gun. But the roar of the engine and the noise of the road must have drowned out his voice, because David looked up, puzzled and frowning.

"What?"

"You're driving too fast."

"The hell I'm driving too fast! I wanna get out of here as soon as possible, so I'm not going to fuck around until we're found."

Cassius gritted his teeth, but repressed his anger. He continued as if talking to a five-year-old.

"Remember what I said about traps and watching eyes?"

"Yes, I do."

"If you drive like a madman, we won't notice either. So do what I tell you."

David took his foot off the accelerator. The bus began to slow down, the whirring of the wheels becoming softer. Cassius nodded in contentment.

"Are we even going the right way?" David asked. "If there's something I need to know, don't wait until the last minute, okay?"

"Don't worry, we're going the right way! The Garibaldi Park overpass is another two miles. Let's hope the road is passable, because then we'll just roll over downtown."

"And if it isn't?"

"Then we are doing it off the cuff."

He had already thought through the variations, and of all the bad options, this one seemed the least scary. The overpass and the stack interchange running from the park to the industrial district would save them from having to go through downtown or Union City, where they had no idea of the dangers they might face.

Cassius turned to Abigail. "Go back and stand guard! No catching flies, no looking after the dog, but standing guard! If you see anything, you call out immediately. Have I made myself clear?"

"Yes." Abigail rolled her eyes, then spun around. Her clenched fist slammed into every seat on her way backwards.

Cassius glanced at Megan.

"You lie down on the seat and whatever happens, don't get up. It would be best if you just kept yourself quiet."

Megan nodded at first, but her eyelashes fluttered at the last sentence and she smiled wryly.

"Any other orders? Or duct tape over my mouth so I don't speak?"

"I know it sounds funny, but it's not."

"All right, I'm gonna lie down now, nice and quiet, so I don't disturb you," she said, adjusting her bag meticulously before leaning her head on it.

David looked up expectantly.

"And me?"

"You drive and pray!"

"Great. It's always the driver who's screwed."

Cassius waited for Abigail and Megan to be settled, then turned forward again. He stared at the seemingly endless strip of asphalt on the road, trying not to think about the splitting pain. He squeezed his injured shoulder with his right hand and glanced carelessly at a familiar building, the bottle-like Moulmein Pagoda. He and his wife had spent their honeymoon in one of their suites.

Concentrate! He straightened up, his face becoming stern.

"What if they've all died in the meantime?" David asked. "Or maybe the hobo and the tramp were the last ones. There are no others left alive, and they're gone. Maybe... who knows..."

"I don't think so."

The bus swerved around an overturned truck and as they rolled past the Moulmein Pagoda, they noticed a fresh pool of blood on the ground outside the hotel entrance. Next to the stain were drag marks, and a red palm print was clearly visible on the asphalt from where its owner had desperately tried to save himself. Unsuccessfully.

"So much for your theory," Cassius growled.

David began to accelerate involuntarily.

"Damn!"

At the next crossroads, blocked by closely packed cars, a large animal ran across and vanished into the shadows. Cassius caught a glimpse of gray fur passing among the wrecks. *Hopefully it was just a stray dog that got spooked by us*, he thought, but he was convinced that two glowing eyes were following them from the shadows. Something in the window of one of the buildings moved, as if the wind had been playing with a curtain, but Cassius didn't have time to observe.

"I told you to slow down!" he angrily snapped at David. "And try to stay in the middle of the road; keep an equal distance with both sides."

David nodded, but his hands were slow to obey.

Cassius closed his eyes and squeezed them shut. In addition to the pain, he was tortured by the heat, the world swirling around him, reality dissolving and blurring. He leaned against the plastic panel, feeling his knees wanting to let him down. He could hear Megan's breathing and see her legs dangling from the seat, swaying back and forth. At the back, Abigail watched the right side of the road, motionless.

"Anything interesting?" he asked, and she flinched.

"Nothing."

Silence. They listened in vain; the wind muffled all other noise.

"Keep listening... on both sides!"

The answer was a sulky mumble, but Cassius was already looking at the road. Something was bugging him, and though the familiar alarm had not yet sounded in his head, he felt his subconscious trying to signal him. With his left hand, he gripped the steering wheel and with a subtle gesture navigated the bus to the middle. David, of course, looked up angrily out of the corner of his eye, but Cassius' mind was elsewhere.

"Tell me, how are your instincts?"

"My instincts?" David asked. "Why? Is something wrong?"

"I'm trying to find out."

"I have no idea. I never pay attention to them. But I'm supposed to bring good luck. That's what my mother said."

"Good to know, because I've haven't noticed it yet."

"Haha... Very funny," David shook his head and turned away. He bit his bottom lip. "Now that you mention it, man, something's giving me the creeps. I don't know what it is, maybe it's just in my head. My mom said I was a little hypochondriac when I was a kid, but then I guess I grew out of it."

Another long, awkward silence.

"It's all right, it was just a routine question." Cassius patted the young man on the shoulder, then pointed ahead to where the middle of the road was covered with debris. "Dodge it on the right, at a steady speed!"

On that side of the road was a vacant, weedy lot, but across the street was a tall, tiered office building from which they could easily have been ambushed if they got too close. The trees in front of the building had branches weaving in and out of the windows, and it was impossible to tell if anyone was hiding in the shady levels.

The seconds slowed.

Cassius was prepared for anything, but nothing happened.

After the mountain of debris, the Blue Bird slid back into the middle and Cassius puffed. But he could not overcome his anxiety. He saw that Megan's legs had stopped swinging; she crouched quietly, hissing softly as she listened. Abigail slowly rose and leaned closer to the window, her mouth agape, her eyes tracing something interesting outside.

"What is it?" Cassius asked. She looked at him worriedly. She hesitated to say what she thought.

"The side streets... It's as if they've been deliberately blocked off."

Megan looked up; her face snow white with fright.

"Oh, my God!"

The puzzle pieces finally came together in Cassius' mind. The tightly packed cars barricaded the side streets. The bus could only go straight on, towards the Garibaldi Park overpass, which cut through the downtown area at a height of thirty feet for miles, trapping anyone who ever drove on it.

"We should turn back, shouldn't we?" Abigail asked, glancing furtively towards Soxy's box. Cassius gestured for Megan to stumble back.

"At ease. Maybe that's what they want."

David growled.

"Or the whole thing could be a hallucination. Because if they were really here, they'd have attacked us by now. That's what I'd do..."

Cassius did not answer, and Abigail also turned back to the window. He had seen too much to believe they could get away with it so easily. *I should have stuck to the original plan,* he thought, but then he grimaced angrily. Never mind, they are here now.

David's croak brought him out of his brooding.

"Fasten your seat belts!" he said anxiously. "We'll soon arrive at the first stop on our tour of Headland."

At the end of the long, straight stretch of the 10, they glimpsed the oaks of Garibaldi Park and the caramel-colored facade of the Plaza on the left side of the road. Behind them rose the on-ramp to the overpass in the distance. The wind whistled along the 10, kicking up dust on the road, the tiny particles knocking against the windshield.

"We're in no hurry," Cassius reassured David. "If you can, go even slower."

They drove through the last intersection, which, like the others, was blocked by wrecks and debris from both directions. With bated breath, they watched the remaining hundred and fifty yards, and finally the overpass emerged from the cover of the Plaza, turning sharply left after the long ascent to leave Headland to the north-north-east. All alongside it were trees, wires and skyscrapers. Below them were roads, canals, and a skate rink, and in the distance a few factory towers and colorless industrial buildings. The overpass seemed untouched, with no sign of serious damage.

Abigail inched forward while Megan huddled in the cover of the front seat, only her forehead and gleaming eyes visible, like a timid but curious cat.

Cassius looked for tell-tale signs. The place was deserted and silent. Then every muscle in his face tensed.

"Stop!"

"Why?" David asked, already turning the wheel to roll to the curb. But Cassius was gripping the wheel.

"Stay in the middle of the road!"

The Blue Bird came to a halt, the engine coughed on at idle. Without a headwind, the stifling air stuck inside the bus, their noses filling with the sour vapor of fear. Abigail swallowed hard and looked at Cassius.

"What is it? Did you see something?"

"It's a trap."

3.

The long ascent was like the outstretched tongue of a monster, leading unsuspecting travelers into the belly of the beast. Cassius, however, would not let the overpass distract him like a red cloth unknowingly luring a bull straight into a trap. He knew that the bus would be a target in the middle of the road, so he gave himself ten seconds to decide. *Where to go next?*

He looked around. To the right were neat brick buildings reminiscent of the old town: bars, offices, shops. To the left, the once-modern Plaza, which looked naked and orphaned without the crowds, and beyond the mall, the wide paths and oaks, the rotting benches and decaying kiosks of Garibaldi Park.

There were no vehicles visible on the ascent, the overpass had been meticulously cleared, but farther on, dozens of cars were lined up like a wall. The Blue Bird would have had trouble passing between the wrecks, and if they had slowed down, it would have been easy to ambush them from one of the cars.

"A trap?" Abigail asked, lowering her voice. She was whispering at the end. "Are you sure?"

Cassius took out the binoculars and just hummed as he scanned the obstacle from wreck to wreck. At first nothing moved among the rusting vehicles, the end-of-the-world stillness seemed undisturbed. Then he noticed something even he had not expected.

"Now I am."

Abigail grabbed the Vortex out of his hand and raised it to her eyes, but Cassius had to make a casual gesture to point it in the right direction.

"I don't see anyth..."

She bit off the sentence so abruptly that Megan and David raised their eyebrows at the same time. Abigail withdrew the binoculars, unblinking.

"Don't you even think of making a fuss!"

"Damn it, Cassius!" snapped Abigail. "We should at least reconsider, look around..."

Megan pushed herself up from her seat and shuffled over to them, then with a forceful gesture took the binoculars. Cassius pointed her in the same direction. Her half-open mouth slowly closed in recognition.

"Gosh!" she turned pale.

"I'll make things easier for us. Trap or no trap, we're not going up there!"

"Fine by me," David shrugged, and without hesitation put the bus in reverse. "I don't even want to know what the hell is up there, we'll just turn around and be on our way..."

Cassius stopped him, his hands on the steering wheel again, his eyes scanning the surrounding buildings.

"Don't move," he said. "They're probably watching us."

When he looked behind, something seemed to flash in one of the buildings, but it happened so fast that he could only see the puff of dust that had been stirred up. It could have been anything, even hurried footsteps.

"Okay, now I'm curious," David said, and asked for the binoculars, but he got no help from anyone. He searched through the wrecks for long seconds before finally catching sight of what was freaking the others out.

Cassius turned back towards the overpass. A red-haired woman cowered on the ground among the wrecked, lined up cars, her hands chained to one of them, her clothes torn. She was waving desperately towards them, and through the binoculars she could be seen clearly, writhing and sobbing.

Cassius bit his lip. It was a textbook trap, yet that was not what worried him. Rather, it was that those who set this trap ignored the details and the fact that their scheme might be seen through. They didn't care.

They want to hit us when we least expect it...

...and if we're not careful, we'll drive straight into the belly of the beast!

4.

As much as she wanted to help, the situation was clear to Abigail: whoever had chained the woman to the car must be nearby, waiting for them to make a mistake.

And a mistake could exact a heavy price: Megan and Soxy were unable to protect themselves, and they couldn't count on David either if the situation heated up. But even then, they couldn't just turn away. They had to at least try, they had to at least consider it, so they could say they did what they could.

"What if we split up? David and Megan stay in the bus, we'll move closer. There could be two or three of them at the wrecks. We can handle that. We'll free the woman, David will catch up, then we'll drive off east."

Cassius scratched his stubble.

"There's no what if, because we're not even trying."

She sighed and involuntarily glanced back towards Soxy's box. *If it is a trap, this is the only way*, she kept repeating to herself. *You think differently, you behave differently...*

"I thought so. We turn around and disappear. A heroic plan, I'm sure it'll make us feel good, but..."

"We're not turning back."

Three puzzled looks stared at Cassius.

"Why not?" David asked, aghast.

"Because if I'm guessing right, and I usually am, that's what they're expecting. They're waiting at the crossroads... waiting for us to turn around."

The eyes drifted from Cassius to the crossroads a hundred-and-fifty yards away.

"They expect us to go slowly, looking for an escape route," he continued. "Then they'll surround us, shoot the wheels, and cook us for dinner."

Megan sniffed and wiped her nose.

"Correct me if I'm wrong, but none of us want that."

"Well, I certainly don't."

"So what?" David posed the million-dollar question. "Neither ahead, nor back. I have a gut feeling we gotta go somewhere; we can't just hang around here all day."

Abigail was struck by an old memory: the day she and her father had spent an entire morning at the Plaza and then had hot dogs in the park. The kiosk, where she could ask the justifiably famous Monsieur Butter King for as many caramelized onions as she wanted on her bun, was crumbling beside a wide path of wild trees and bushes.

"What if we cut through the park?" she asked. "Then out onto Greenwood Avenue. We could even bypass Union City. We'd fly down the old main road, then back up to the 10 after the overpass."

David raised an eyebrow and glanced toward the seemingly impenetrable, overgrown park.

"It's gonna be a bit uncomfortable... and slow."

"But when they see what we're up to, we'll have to hurry, no matter what," Abigail looked at Cassius. "I see no other option."

He nodded, his face emotionless, but his eyes sparkled again. It might have been contentment.

"Good idea, let's do it."

Abigail proudly straightened her back, and Megan sat back in her seat, hunched forward with her hands on her knees, her eyes fixed on the overpass. David put the bus into gear, but before he could slide his foot on the accelerator, Cassius leaned closer and lowered his voice.

"Slowly pull away as if you were heading for the overpass. Let them think we've taken the bait."

"And then what?"

"When you get to the entrance of the park, a sudden turn and then hit it. Can you do that?"

David mumbled something under his breath and toed the throttle. Abigail noticed the young man's hand shaking nervously on the steering wheel, his free foot drumming rhythmically. Cassius raised his binoculars to his eyes and watched the waving red-haired woman, and Abigail felt it was time to take control.

"Wait," she said to David, raising her hand, which stopped in the air like a warning sign. Cassius noticed that she was playing conductor.

"Not so theatrically. Only the blind can't see what we're up to."

"It's all the same now," Abigail replied, and when the Blue Bird was in line with the gravel path, she lowered her hand. "Now! Move!"

David stepped on the gas and turned the wheel with all his might. The bus shuddered, the engine roared, and they had to brace themselves to keep from crashing from the sudden shift in direction.

Cassius leaned against the dashboard, clenching his binoculars as he balanced. A shadow crossed his face and his mouth curled into a bitter smile. Abigail knew the gesture well.

"Got you, bastard!" he hissed, then turned to David. "Step on it as hard as you can! They've just revealed themselves."

5.

He could clearly see the movement. When the bus ran off the road with screeching wheels and a sharp bend, someone seemed to lift his head in one of the wrecks. The bus skidded up onto the sidewalk, hitting the curb, causing Cassius to lose his balance. By the time he had recovered, two other figures were standing among the wreckage next to the red-haired woman. They watched the fleeing bus, then swung simultaneously towards one of the junk cars.

"Bingo!" Cassius said, lowering his binoculars.

"What did you see?" Abigail asked impatiently.

"That we gotta hurry."

The engine roared with effort. The Blue Bird aimed for the weedy path, and branches snapped, leaves flew, rubble crunched under the wheels.

"We're being followed," Cassius continued. "We've got to be on the other side of the river by sundown, or we'll be in trouble!"

Megan groaned softly and slumped in her seat. Abigail ran to the back of the bus, and Cassius held onto the railing. Even without the Vortex, he could see the man-eaters' jalopy speed towards the exit and disappear into the cover of the trees.

The bus suffered on the winding path. Its wheels were constantly swerving off the gravel and the back swayed like a pendulum from David's desperate steering. Barely able to see the tree branches hitting the windshield and the leaves covering everything, Cassius dictated their path to the young man from memory.

"Right!"

David hit the brakes. *Too fast*, Cassius thought; he glanced back, worried. They might buy some time in the park, but not at this speed. Ahead of them the path forked in two.

"Left!"

"Everybody hold on!"

David slammed on the brake and turned the wheel. The bus swerved, its tires scraping and scattering hundreds of pebbles, its rear end drifting towards the outside curve of the bend. In vain the young man steered against it, and the bus crashed through a lamp. Cassius fell against the door, Abigail sat down hard on her backside.

"I told you it would be rough," said David after he straightened the bus with great effort. The engine revved again, and the Blue Bird roared up the trail.

"Step on it, and less talk!" Cassius balanced himself, adjusting his injured shoulder. Pain flooded through his body. "We're almost out!"

David leaned on the steering wheel, his foot on the gas pedal, almost pushing himself forward, but the bus accelerated with difficulty. Abigail jumped up to the back window. She glanced anxiously in the direction of the 10, which was now obscured by thick vegetation.

"See anything?" Cassius tried to shout over the roaring engine.

"Maybe... I don't know."

Abigail snatched up the Browning, ready to fire at anything coming up behind them. David cried out.

"Cassius!"

He turned back to the young man. In front of the bus, the last of the oak's craggy branches split open, revealing the park's exit. The once ornate metal gate had fallen down, but the two columns of stone were so close together that they looked like the clamping jaws of a vise. The Blue Bird dashed between them without braking. The bodywork caught in the iron straps and plowed up the side of the bus with an unearthly screech. The wheels then bounced on the curb and the bus rose into the air.

David frantically applied the brakes, but the vehicle barely reacted. The building opposite was approaching them at breakneck speed. The wheels finally stuck on the dusty, slippery asphalt. At the last moment, the bus came to a halt in front of the art deco tower block, only inches from the thick concrete front. But they could not rest.

"Come on, let's go," Cassius ordered. David nodded mechanically and turned the wheel, his legs barely obeying as he fought through his shock. Cassius squeezed the young man's shoulder, both encouraging and warning him. "Step on it if you want to live!"

The Blue Bird started up again and dove into the shadows of the overpass, into a benign twilight. Cassius murmured a prayer for a few more calm seconds, just enough time for them to disappear between the buildings, but the prayer didn't help.

Abigail screamed. He spun and caught sight of one of their pursuers. Out of the park leapt a car, a modified pickup truck fortified with bars, heading toward them at a frantic pace. The bus sped under the overpass and, coming out of the shadows, the bright light blinded the passengers for a moment. However, the pickup persisted, swerving and slamming its front end aggressively into the side of the Blue Bird.

Bang! Megan screamed as objects rose into the air around them.

"Abigail!"

She understood the command coming from Cassius. Through the broken window, she aimed at the pickup driver, trying to balance herself. All she could see were outlines, but that was enough. She took a deep breath and pulled the trigger. The first one missed. Abigail closed her eyes for a moment, then after another deep breath, tried again. The gun fired.

The pickup veered off the trail, then rolled over, flipped several times around its axis, and landed in the window of an old store.

Abigail snorted. She looked at Cassius.

"Tell me that was the car you saw."

Cassius shook his head. He faced David, and pointed to the crossroads ahead.

"Left, over there! Then follow the overpass."

David seemed to relax, the Blue Bird's movements slowly becoming steady under his hand. Cassius glanced at Megan crouched behind the seat.

"You all right?"

She nodded, but was still breathing heavily. Abigail stepped over to Soxy's box to check on the puppy.

"Let's not relax just yet," Cassius said, "The danger hasn't passed."

"Did she get them? Are you sure?"

"If you're in doubt, you can go back and check it out. Alone, and on your own two feet."

"Okay, I believe you, but this piece of crap can't take another maneuver like that."

Cassius didn't even dignify that with a response. His gaze was already on another mountain of debris, and this time the alarm in his head sounded loud and clear. He peered over David's shoulder, watching the overpass, nestled now under the cover of the skyscrapers. Nothing moved. All around them was apocalyptic chaos. Broken windows, graffitied or crumbled plaster, piled up wreckage.

There was no one behind them.

The mountain of debris was getting closer, its outline becoming clearer. Another pile of rubble, this one in the geometrical center of the road, as if it had been meticulously planned and painstakingly carried there. But this barrier was different in some ways from the previous one: not only was it high, but its edges reached right up to the sidewalk.

"Slow down!"

"You're driving me crazy, man!"

"I guess I'm going to succeed eventually."

"We'll get around it, just like the last one. That wasn't so bad, was it?" He looked up at Cassius, waiting for confirmation.

"We'll make a detour. I don't want to take any risks," Cassius said after a moment's thought, and in his head he was already visualizing a map of the area. If they did it right, they might lose their pursuers for good.

But the bus lurched forward, bringing Cassius back to reality. David stepped on the accelerator, and the Blue Bird went into a frenzy.

"What are you doing?"

"I'm not gonna fuck around! We're breaking through," David replied. Before Cassius could object, the bus was speeding past the last crossing.

"Are you crazy, David?" Megan shrieked, but he didn't react; he was focused on the target.

Cassius saw there was no turning back.

"You'll get us all killed, you idiot! At least hit the brakes, or we'll roll over!"

David switched gears at the last moment. When he reached the mountain of rubble, he slammed on the brakes and steered the bus onto the sidewalk. The Blue Bird wobbled over the obstacle and squealed as if it was going to fall apart. After they rocketed up the curb, they mowed down an old trash can and a flower bed at a frantic pace, the roof taking off the neon sign of a pub. It looked like they were going to make it; David slid across the pavement with perfect flair, but before they could catch their breath, Cassius spotted the trap the man-eaters had set.

"Brake!" he shouted.

Beyond the mountain of rubble, a spike strip lay on the ground. David pushed on the brakes, but the bus couldn't stop. With screeching wheels, they ran straight across the spikes that snagged the Blue Bird. The tires nearly exploded as they drove over the barrier. The bus shuddered and derailed like a train, skidding out of control into the opposite lane. They slid on the asphalt almost to the next intersection, throwing sparks, but then finally stopped. The cloud of dust slowly dispersed around them, some of it drifting into the bus. The smell of burning rubber permeated everything.

David coughed and gripped the steering wheel. Megan got up,

her face white as a sheet, snorting heavily, and Abigail also appeared in the back, holding Soxy.

Cassius felt like he was about to explode with rage, but he finally tamped down his anger. He glanced at David, who was scratching his eyes and spitting dust.

“What did you say earlier about walking?”

6.

They listened but heard only the buzzing of insects. Cassius opened the door and stepped onto the asphalt with his gun raised. He waited and counted, his eyes fixed on the surrounding buildings. Abigail stood directly behind him on the steps, watching him impatiently. Megan blinked widely; David hunched behind the driver’s seat.

It was quiet. Outside, only the heat raged, sunbeams scorching the broken, dusty asphalt amid the musty, tired scent of death.

Abigail was sick of the waiting game.

“We should get going. The sooner we get out of here, the better.”

Cassius nodded.

“Get your gear. Only what you can carry, everything else stays. Move it!”

Abigail turned and started back with quick steps. She was aware of her task, her hands working in automatic mode. Megan and David, on the other hand, looked at each other perplexed, their faces quivering, and finally, reluctantly, began to pack. When Abigail appeared beside them, her bag slung over her shoulder, Soxy’s box in her hand, the siblings were still trying to organize their belongings. Cassius glanced impatiently over, his mind counting down without stopping. *Ten more seconds...*

“The fuel and the radio stay!” he snapped at David. Abigail took the radio out of the young man’s hand and threw it onto the seat, but David refused to let go of the last half-full gallon of biodiesel.

“If we can find a usable vehicle somewhere, it might come in handy.”

Cassius pointed towards Megan. “You’ll have plenty to carry, don’t worry.”

"I'm pregnant, not disabled," Megan said with arms akimbo, but he waved her off. David angrily dropped the gallon on the bus floor.

Abigail scrambled forward and took Cassius' place on guard duty. He watched her with piercing eyes as she carefully placed the box containing the whimpering puppy next to the Blue Bird's wheels.

"Both eyes open," he told the girl, then climbed back into the bus. He grabbed his bag and just as he felt the strap tighten on his shoulder, he knew the whole plan was over. What they had fought so hard for, and sacrificed so much for, was now lying in the back of the rickety Blue Bird; boxes piled on top of each other, their belongings scattered. It would have taken them at least an hour to unload everything from the bus and put it somewhere safe. It made absolutely no difference what he took with him.

His fists clenched in helplessness.

Cassius turned, dodged the blinking Megan, and stumbled down the stairs. He walked past Abigail and, to her utter dismay, without a second thought, started for the intersection.

"Let's roll!" he thundered.

Abigail picked Soxy up off the ground and tried to catch up with him.

"What's wrong?" she asked.

Cassius watched the windows and alleys, then turned back towards David and Megan. They followed with stuttering footsteps.

"It won't work."

"We'll come back for the stuff later. If we get some kind of a car, we'll..."

"I don't mean the stuff," he lowered his voice, "I mean them. It was a goddamn stupid thing to do."

"So, what's your call?"

No reply. Abigail continued in an angry whisper.

"I know you won't do it. You didn't leave them at the quarry or the motel, and you're not going to do it now... are you?"

"This is different. This is unfamiliar territory."

"It's very familiar to me," Abigail glanced at a nearby building that had once housed a restaurant called the Milkshake Factory. Every kid in Headland wished they could celebrate their birthday there; Cassius remembered the butter-colored walls and the sweet, milky smell.

"We know nothing about this place anymore. Where's safe to stay."

She stopped and looked back, alarmed.

"Do you hear that?"

Cassius raised his head and listened. The sound of an engine intensified in the distance. It was coming towards them.

7.

"We got two minutes! Hurry up!"

Cassius put his bag in David's hand, then grabbed Megan's stuff and headed for the intersection. The siblings followed reluctantly, Abigail at the back, glancing into the distance incessantly. The road behind them was still clear. But the sound of the engine grew louder every second.

Fat drops of sweat appeared on her forehead, and the heat made it hard to think straight. She knew where they were, remembering the birthdays she had celebrated at the Milkshake Factory, but she could not decide which building would be safest. *Who knows where there could be traps waiting for us...*

They turned the corner and started to run. The wide street was lined with closely spaced brick buildings, there were tram tracks with a stop in the middle, and taller, brown-painted apartment blocks in the distance.

Megan could manage ten steps, then groaned and hunched over. When Abigail caught up with her, she tried to help, but with Soxy's box in her hand, it was no easy task.

"Cassius!"

He turned around. He was clearly elsewhere, his eyes darting around looking for an escape route. Abigail remembered what he had taught her: you can escape anywhere, even to the first building that comes your way, but you will only survive if you know how to get out. Cassius came to his senses. He stepped back angrily and took over supporting Megan. She blinked apologetically.

"I'm sorry... but I can't!"

"It's fine, it's not your fault," Abigail said, looking at Cassius without contradiction. “We must find shelter. We can’t go on like this.”

From beyond the crossroads, from the direction of the mountain of rubble, the engines of multiple vehicles roared. Based on their sound, they must have been ferocious machines, monsters of the underworld.

“Over there, quickly.” Cassius pointed to one of the three-story buildings, which had once housed a popular, trendy café. “We’ll slip out the back door. Get in!”

He did not have to say it twice. Abigail ran in first, Glock drawn in her right hand, the box in her left. Cassius and David followed with Megan groaning loudly.

“Move it!” Cassius shouted at David, who had stopped to gasp for air. The monstrous vehicles were just around the corner. Abigail could see in her head as the battered but reinforced cars slowed down by the mountain of rubble. The roar died away and they could hear rough male voices shouting instructions, followed by excited cries and running feet.

Cassius navigated the siblings towards the back door of the old café. David’s legs buckled, but he gritted his teeth and made it there. Abigail put Soxy on the floor and ran to the front entrance. From a safe distance, she watched the crossing from the shadows, but no-one turned the corner. All she heard were voices.

She started to back up. She thought about the next logical outcome, just as Cassius had taught her. In a few minutes, the man-eaters would realize their prey was no longer on the bus. They would split up and start searching for them. It would be impossible to go through all the buildings, but they would scout the streets, looking for traces. And that is all the time the four of them would have to vanish into the void. If they stayed, they would eventually be found.

Abigail looked at Soxy. *Just hang in there, big boy... and as quietly as possible*, she thought. Last fall, their deaths had been a matter of seconds away when they had merged with a family of six, and a pack turned up in the neighborhood at night. The family’s baby had cried out at the worst possible moment, and they lost so many bullets they had been suffering ever since. The surviving members of the family eventually moved on south. *Lucky for us*, Cassius added later.

"Abigail!"

She winced at his voice and turned around. Cassius touched his fingers to the butt of the gun, his lips pursed. Abigail knew immediately that something was wrong. David was panting in the background, and Megan was sitting on an overturned shelf, completely exhausted.

"What is it?"

"The back door is blocked. We can't get out that way."

They went to the front door at the same time. The shouts intensified; from the sound of it, the man-eaters were already on their way to the crossroads. It meant that the café was the only safe place, and that they couldn't go back out on the street.

"Upstairs," Cassius ordered.

They headed for the stairs at the back of the café, Cassius and David helping Megan up. The stairs creaked and a cloud of dust swirled around them as they climbed.

"Quickly!"

On the first floor they laid Megan down on a leather sofa and threw their bags on the floor. The spacious room was filled with dusty chairs and tables, lamps and lanterns hung from above, curtains, ornamental cases, and mirrors everywhere. The café's late owner had tried to make the upstairs nostalgic, and it was a surreal journey back in time. Seven years after the end of the world, it felt like being in a scene from the middle of the nineteenth century.

Cassius shoved the silver Smith & Wesson into David's hand and pushed him towards the stairs.

"Nobody comes up here alive, okay? The gun is loaded, ten rounds. Make it count! Nod if you understand."

David nodded, but not very convincingly. Abigail anxiously watched the young man and the woman lying on the couch with Soxy's box at her feet. *It's just the two of us against who knows how many man-eaters... We have no chance. We can't protect them...* She thought about giving Megan the baseball bat they had brought with them, just in case she needed to protect herself, but eventually dismissed the idea. With the condition Megan was in, it would have made no sense.

She stepped to the window and, peering cautiously out, she finally caught sight of the enemy.

There were six of them at the crossroads. They were all wearing torn, ragged jeans, their naked torsos covered by elbow and shoulder pads, their faces hidden from prying eyes by helmets with facemasks. Beneath the hockey gear, their bodies were painted black, cut in places by white hatch marks that looked like tribal symbols. Each held a weapon: carbine submachine guns armed with bayonets, crossbows or axes with nails.

After a brief debate, they split into three. Two went straight ahead, two to the left, and the last two came towards them. A lanky one with white shoulder pads and a shorter, stocky figure with a red smiley on his arm.

They walked in perfect unison, at a specific distance from each other, their eyes scrutinizing every building. When the short, stocky figure looked up at the window where they stood, Abigail could almost feel the fire of his murderous gaze in her veins. She held her breath and glanced anxiously at Cassius.

"What is it? What's happening?" David asked quietly from the background. Cassius waved him off.

Abigail raised her gun and pointed with her chin at the approaching man-eaters. Cassius understood the question. He shook his head and gestured for them to wait.

For what? Of course, Abigail knew their situation was not easy. If they opened fire now, they might surprise the two men, but who knew how many would follow them and how many would besiege the building. However, if the two man-eaters were not taken down, they might find them eventually, which would mean hand-to-hand combat.

Maybe they won't see us. Perhaps they'll move on.

But they did not.

The man-eater with the white shoulder pads paused and pointed at the dust on the asphalt. Abigail knew exactly what the men were looking at. Their tracks, especially the groove they had left as they dragged Megan, leading straight to their hiding place.

The two figures snapped their heads up at the same time. In a flash, they started towards the building and disappeared into the cover. Cassius and Abigail backed away from the window.

"Damnit!" she hissed. "What do we do now?"

They had one minute to think of something if they were to survive the day. The rubble crunched downstairs as the man-eaters entered the café, but the sound of footsteps soon died away and only the rustle of clothes could be heard. *They communicate with hand signals. They are now deciding what to do...* The man-eaters' radio crackled with static as their companions checked in from the distance.

"This is Scorpio! Clear!"

An unnerving hum ripped through the ether, the message echoing and broken.

"Diesel, clear!"

One of the chairs creaked as it was moved, then silence, little later another static.

"Python, do you copy?"

The muffled reply came from below. "Standby!"

Abigail took a deep breath to calm herself. Her heart was pounding and refused to slow down, the vein in her neck throbbed. She glanced at Cassius, helpless. He gestured for David to hide, then helped Megan up and guided her behind the sofa with Soxy's box. Just as he finished, the staircase squeaked. *They're coming...*

Cassius rushed over to Abigail.

"You have the element of surprise; I have the brute force. Use a knife!" he whispered, and pushed her towards the curtain by the stairs. The heavy yellow shroud seemed the perfect hiding place.

Abigail slipped noiselessly behind the curtain and pulled the knife from her belt. From her cover she could see everything: Megan, biting her hand as she snuggled into the cover of the sofa; David behind one of the cupboards, eyes closed; and Cassius turning one of the large mirrors in the exact direction he had intended to hide.

What the hell is he doing? Is he using himself as bait?

Their eyes met once more. He gave the signal — *not a word!* — and she readied her knife. They both knew they could not make a sound. The kill had to be silent, or all the man-eaters would be on their trail. *And then it would all be for nothing...*

The last step creaked softly. Abigail dared not move. She could hear a wheezing breath and smell the sour odor of sweat mingled with the tang of gun oil. Her body shuddered as she felt the presence of the man-eaters. The air filled with tension. Then it seemed as if the sound was cut off.

Abigail held her breath. Every fiber of her being protested against it, but she peered cautiously out from behind the curtain and caught sight of the two man-eaters, barely an arm's length away. They were both looking at the mirror, which Cassius had cunningly adjusted, and in which his figure was clearly visible.

The two man-eaters raised their weapons and took a careless step forward. Unable to contain themselves, they burst out laughing.

"Found ya," the one in white shoulder pads chuckled. His short companion lowered his gun, letting the other take the glory.

"Now, come on out..."

That was the signal, and Abigail did not hesitate.

She dashed out of her hiding place, lunged at the short man-eater, and plunged her knife mercilessly into the man's neck. With her free hand she held his head, then kicked his leg out, and the blood-choked, gurgling man collapsed like a sack.

His white-shouldered companion, unable to control his instincts, spun carelessly, and that was his fatal mistake. Cassius sprang to his feet and immediately attacked, but the bulky man deflected the first blow with his weapon. The knife sliced through his side, and the man-eater cried out in pain. *Damn!* Without thinking, Abigail leapt at his neck, her hand covering his mouth, and Cassius pulped his liver with three lightning-quick stabs. As the man-eater's body tensed in shock, Cassius and Abigail simultaneously caught at the gun-wielding hand, but were too late.

The rifle went off, the bullet scraping the decayed wooden floor.

"Oh, no!"

Megan screamed; David threw himself to the ground. The man-eater collapsed, helpless. Cassius and Abigail looked at each other, not daring to move, as if they could undo what had happened. After a few seconds of silence, the walkie-talkie sounded, crackling on the short man-eater's side.

"What the hell was that, Python? Can you hear me?"

8.

There were eight of them, and they approached from the crossroads at a brisk pace. They wore the same silly outfits as the two already lying on the floor covered in blood, but one of them, the man at the head of the procession, stood out. His face was covered by a black military helmet and he wore an ultra-modern tactical vest and olive-green trousers. He was tall and wiry, towering almost half a head above the others, who followed respectfully. His light movements showed confidence.

He must be their leader, Abigail thought. She turned to Cassius, scanning his face to see if she could read his intentions. His expression was unchanged, his stubbled features showing no emotion.

"Do you think they saw their companions come into this building?"

"We'll soon find out."

The man-eater hanging at the back, a frail, gas-masked figure, paused and broke away from the group. Her long red hair peeked out from under the mask. She headed for the alley opposite. She had noticed something, but her companions were not the least bit interested.

The leader raised his walkie, and when he pressed the call button, the transmitter of the short man on the floor buzzed and sounded static. The noise lasted barely a second. Cassius swung immediately, but didn't get there in time. The raspy voice seemed to speak to them from another world, impatient, commanding.

"Python, can you h…?"

Cassius switched off the walkie, but in the dead silence the short crackling sound of the reception gave them away.

The man-eaters turned at the same time towards the upstairs window from which Abigail was peering. They stood motionless for a few seconds, then readied their guns and moved away from each other. There was only one goal in front of them: besiege the hideout.

The leader looked at his companions contentedly, and said something else into the walkie, but Abigail could no longer hear it. The tall man repeated the message, and when he got no response this time, he raised his receiver in a casual gesture, indicating that he wanted to talk to them.

Abigail glared at Cassius.

"What if they want to negotiate?" she asked quietly.

"Negotiate? About what to flavor us with?"

"At least it would buy us some time."

Cassius reluctantly turned the walkie-talkie back on, then pressed the transmit button, but for the moment he said nothing. The signal lasted a single second, and Abigail saw the leader nod before he raised his receiver to his mouth again.

"Good, my birdies, it's good to know you're not slipping through our fingers," he said in a raspy voice, then removed his helmet. He raised his freckled face to the sky, cupped his jaw, and spread his hands theatrically. His companions watched in silence.

Abigail had a strange feeling when the scarred, arrogant face turned towards them. The cold, steely blue eyes, the long dimple that sliced his chin, and the shock of blond hair belonged to someone she had thought would forever be in her past.

The leader of the man-eaters continued as he gestured with his hands in a spectacular manner.

"I don't hold out much hope for you, but at the same time, I don't want any bloodshed. If I read the situation correctly, you have put an end to our two companions... No need to answer, silence means assent."

Cassius and Abigail were silent. Assent.

"Well then, let's make a deal. My men told me there are four of you, so an eye for an eye and a tooth for a tooth. I'll take two of you, and I promise the rest can go. That's the best deal I can offer you, and it's good for about a minute."

Abigail looked at the siblings, who were shaking like jelly and blinking in alarm.

"Calm down," she whispered to them. She waited for Cassius to say something promising, but he didn't respond. "They're lying, aren't they?"

"Of course they are," he hissed.

Abigail turned back to the window. After a brief pause, the leader croaked.

"Well, what's the decision? The clock is ticking."

His companions lowered their weapons with a grunt, one even lighting a cigarette.

Abigail then had a flash of inspiration and snatched the walkie from the unsuspecting Cassius' hand. As soon as she pressed the button, she said it, with a mixture of a wide grin and disgust on her face.

"I see you haven't changed a bit, Jason. You're just as stupid as ever."

The man-eaters fell silent and looked at their leader in shock. The smoldering cigarette fell to the asphalt.

An angry, defiant shadow crossed Jason's face. His upper lip curled back, he bared his teeth, and he raised the walkie close to his mouth.

"Who the hell are you?"

Cassius' features tightened, but before he could snatch the receiver from Abigail's hand, she nimbly stepped away.

"Don't you remember your old neighbor? You disappoint me."

"I don't know which of those idiots you are, but if you think this will..."

"Of course I don't, silly boy." Abigail's smile grew wider and wider, and she began to enjoy the game more and more. She ignored Cassius' signals. "I remember you well. If you had something on your mind, you had a hard time letting it go. Tell me, do your friends know that you used to wet your bed when you were in high school? Your mom laughed and told my parents all the details. Stress because of the game days, my ass; you were just piss-a-bed boy."

The man-eaters couldn't help themselves: they laughed out loud, but Jason shushed them after a few gasps. Then he shook his head in disbelief.

"Abigail?"

"Bingo, dumbass. Have you stopped biting your nails?"

Jason's face contorted. Cassius took the receiver from her and gave her an angry look.

"We were supposed to be buying time. You're just going to piss him off."

Abigail shrugged self-consciously.

"Never mind. I'll be all the happier to pop a cap in that brat."

Cassius froze in shock, but had no time to react. Outside, Jason gave the order to his men and the man-eaters headed for the building.

"Now, be tough." Cassius sloppily tossed the walkie back to the girl and stepped to the window, ready to take down as many of the attackers as he could.

A shout came from the alley. The man-eaters froze and turned in the direction of the sound.

The gas-masked, red-haired figure came running, waving frantically at her companions. She stopped, gasping for breath, and took off the gas mask. It was the red-haired woman who, not long ago, they had believed was a victim of the man-eaters. Cassius was right again. Abigail pursed her lips, trying not to think about what would have happened if they had taken the bait and driven up the overpass.

The red-haired woman said something to the men gathered around her, who all at once snapped their heads up and glanced toward the alley. Jason pushed them aside and headed to the rusting dumpster the woman had indicated. As he approached, his footsteps became more and more restless.

When he got there, he froze, and for a moment he stood still, watching the mysterious thing lying on the ground behind the dumpster. Even from their position above it was clear to see that his limbs were heavy, and his back was hunched. Then he turned and walked out of the alley, back into the street. He did not run, he did not hurry, but Abigail noticed that his gait was firmer now than before, while he was looking nervously around.

David jumped up, his face stretched with astonishment.

"Does anyone understand what's going on?"

Abigail silently shook her head no.

Jason gave a whistle and motioned for the others to go back to the intersection. The man-eaters followed in quick, panicked strides, their eyes on the surrounding buildings. They disappeared so quickly it was as if they had never been there.

"What the hell?" whispered Cassius. He looked at Abigail in disbelief. They were both thinking the same thing.

"What were they scared of?"

The walkie-talkie crackled to life in her hand. It was Jason. He was shouting to drown out the engine noise.

"My apologies for the early goodbye, but there are some things we don't fuck around with. Good luck, my little birdies!"

9.

They stood in the doorway of the old café for long minutes, none of them wanting to move. The sound of the vehicles driving off had finally died away, and outside there was only the rustle of dust stirred up by the wind. They were alone, yet they hesitated. Abigail hung the walkie onto her belt and glanced at Cassius.

"Do you think it's a trap?" she asked, knowing that he was wondering the same thing. His gray-green eyes darting back and forth told her he was considering their options. He scratched his dusty stubble with his fingers.

"They could have fired on us if they wanted to. It'd be nice to know why they didn't."

"Shall we go and see?"

"Yeah."

Yet for a few seconds, neither of them moved. Finally, Cassius decided to go first: he sighed and stepped out into the bright light. After a brief pause, Abigail followed, but stealthily watched the intersection where the man-eaters had disappeared only a few minutes before. Her face was scorched by the sun within a few moments, the heat clutching her chest like a vice.

"You take the alley!" Cassius said. Abigail nodded.

They split off from each other. He crept to the crossroads, she to the alley. When each had reached their destination, they both ducked against the wall. Abigail held up her index finger to signal to him and, after a moment's hesitation, he peeked around the corner. She watched curiously as his stiff shoulders eased and his tense posture relaxed. Cassius scratched his nose, waited a moment, then strode at an easy pace towards the girl, down the alley.

"Are they gone?" Abigail asked.

"Yes."

"Then let's see what's upset them."

They walked to the container slowly, as if more afraid of the answer than of the man-eaters themselves. Abigail could not imagine what could have been such a frightening discovery that they would run away without thinking, but whatever it was, they had to take it seriously.

The only sound they heard was the buzzing of flies.

Abigail was the first to arrive, and she winced when she saw the coagulated blood, fur, and bone, the remains of some animal. The slaughter had been brutal. Whatever had devoured the animal, it killed swiftly and ruthlessly. The smell of decay hovered in the air, insects buzzed around them, and a feeling of fear like no other permeated their pores.

Cassius crouched down by the remains.

"Judging by the amount of blood, it must have been a deer," he concluded.

"And what attacked it?"

"I don't know, but the tracks suggest it was recent, maybe dawn. And we're in the attacker's hunting ground."

"Ferals?"

"Or worse," Cassius pointed a few yards away. There were bloody footprints on the tarmac, the imprint of huge paws. Like a dog's, yet larger, frighteningly deformed.

"Rabid animals?"

Cassius nodded.

"We gotta get out of here."

10.

"Get out? Where to?"

David stared at Cassius with his arms outstretched, and pointed at Megan on the sofa as if he couldn't imagine what was not understandable about their situation. The young man continued hysterically, his arms going in wide circles during the rant. "In this condition we won't make it to the next block, let alone the river. We need to get a vehicle or we're screwed."

Cassius didn't flinch, he remained perfectly calm.

"I see you've missed the point. After sundown, this place will be crawling with rabid animals. We have to go!"

"But like how? Carry Megan in my arms to the city limits?"

Before Cassius could answer, Abigail waved him off. The girl looked at the siblings with a serene smile.

"We'll figure out something!" she said, pulling Cassius aside. She forced herself to be firm. "We have enough problems; stop playing the stern daddy!"

He raised an eyebrow.

"Looking forward to your suggestions, mommy!" he said, and put his hands on his hips.

"I'm thinking."

"Then think fast, because time is running out."

Abigail smiled cynically, half saluted, and hurried to the window. She glanced down the silent, empty street, but saw no sign of an intact vehicle; anything usable had long since disappeared from the streets of Headland.

Think, come on! She tried to kick start the gears in her brain which were spinning at a snail's pace, but the heat drained all her energy. *Assess the situation*, she heard Cassius' voice in her head, *and use all your senses...* Her face twisted into an angry grimace. As if it was so easy, but then she blushed. She felt ashamed. *Think! What is there? Ah, yeah... Control your fear, don't panic! Plan your next move before you make any unnecessary effort. Improvise, be creative...* She snorted so loudly that even David snapped his head towards her in the background. *Creative... How am I supposed to be creative? Just like magic?* She thought anyone else in her position would be looking for a car, but maybe there were other options.

She noticed something on the side of the building across the street. The old, four-story brick house had been renovated before the epidemic, and its industrial metal-framed windows still looked strong. She could imagine the young people strolling into the trendy café after a hard day's work, chatting and having a drink. Cassius had told her about it, and it was one of the most exciting things he had ever said to her. Friends, together, free, doing what they wanted.

"I have an idea."

"And I'm listening."

She pointed to the building opposite. There was a bike rack fixed to the sidewalk at the entrance. Alongside the bikes, with long-deflated wheels, someone had parked a kick scooter before the Breakdown. Cassius immediately understood what she meant and nodded.

"If you can ride it, it's fine. Otherwise, we're no better off."

"I envy your optimism," she scoffed.

Cassius took the bullets from the dead man-eaters, then slung his bag over his shoulder and waved to the others.

"Let's go for it!"

He left her no time to think. Within a minute they were clattering down the stairs, and another minute later Abigail was examining the scooter. It was old, telescopic, but still in good condition. The kind of thing that would make a terrible gift, but perfectly fit for their current purpose. *Whose was it? What could the person have been doing for a living?*

"Abigail! Is it usable?"

She shuddered. She held up her thumb, then started back to the others. Megan, still panting and clutching her belly, gave a thin smile out of the corner of her mouth when she saw the girl pushing the scooter towards her. If she had had the strength, she might have laughed. Abigail and David helped her on, placing the smaller bags at her feet.

"I gotta check something," Cassius said. "One minute!"

Abigail nodded. She could guess what he was up to. While Megan tried the scooter, Cassius jogged to the bus to check on their stuff. The man-eaters had ransacked their belongings, taking anything they thought would be useful. Cassius took only one thing — the book filled with his notes about their plan — then he returned to the others.

"Maybe we can start over," he said to the girl, who simply shrugged.

Cassius took a deep breath, and looked around. They were about five miles from the Headland Bridge. Even Abigail knew that first they had to go down Greenwood Avenue, then left onto Hickory, then back onto the 10.

When they were ready to go, Cassius straightened his back.

"No talking, only hand signals. We're going against the wind, so we might have a chance." He glanced at David, who was standing beside Megan, helping her push the scooter. "And we're in no hurry. Move slowly, thoughtfully, and avoid any sudden movements. Let's try to glide along the road without even the wind noticing we were here. Is that clear?"

All three of them nodded. A minute later, they were heading northeast on Greenwood, and five minutes later Abigail and Cassius looked at each other. They both heard it, they both felt it. Something was watching them. Something was following them.

11.

Abigail tried to keep the pace Cassius had set. Her gaze drifted away from the buildings she was supposed to be watching, and she just squinted in the blazing sunlight. Her thoughts wandered, and she found herself trying to recall, if only for a few seconds, how the street used to look, the names of the shops, the memories associated with them. When she realized her own inattention, she shuddered. *Eyes up!*

David and Megan whizzed past her without much effort; the young man only had to push the scooter occasionally on the flat terrain. If it hadn't been seven years after the apocalypse, fleeing disfigured ferals and rabid savages, it might have seemed like a peaceful Sunday excursion.

But the silence roaring from the skeletal buildings was sobering.

Abigail quickened her pace and caught up with Cassius. Their eyes met.

"Eleven o'clock," he said quietly. He was careful not to let the siblings hear anything of their conversation.

"I can see it too."

Something stirred deep inside an old car showroom ahead, just enough for them to sense its presence. They moved involuntarily to the right side of the road. Cassius motioned for David to roll closer to them. The young man obeyed and then, unsuspectingly, continued to stare at the nearby buildings.

"Maybe it's just some harmless animal," Abigail squinted. "It might be more scared of us than we are of it.

"Maybe."

Their fingers tightened on their triggers and they braced themselves for the worst, but when they passed the car showroom, nothing happened. There was only a faint thud in the dim light, as if something had carelessly knocked an object to the ground. It could have been the wind. Cassius looked meaningfully at Abigail.

"You take the right side, I'll take the left. Signal at the first suspicion. Let's try to reach the next intersection, the Monroe Building."

"The gray one on the left?"

Cassius nodded.

The gray skyscraper was a good hundred yards away. They were on the edge of downtown, where in the late eighties a series of former industrial buildings had been renovated into lofts and studios and occupied by artists and posh playboys. But now the gleam of the fancy neighborhood had worn off. Most of the fire escapes had collapsed, and the advertisements painted on the firewalls had faded, with fallen bricks making some completely illegible. The Monroe Building stood on the next corner; a soulless monstrosity of a twenty-five-story concrete-gray building, the windows of its gently curved facade reflecting the sky in a turquoise blue that dazzled Abigail.

"If all else fails, we'll run in there," said Cassius. "I know the way. The stairwell has a strong, fireproof door, and we'll be safe behind it."

They moved away from each other, their bodies tense with concentration, their guns scanning the area, and eventually Megan noticed their anxiety, as well.

"What is it? Did you see something?"

"Don't panic just yet," Cassius said. "Nice and easy; we are walking like pigeons."

Just before the crossroads, more white and brown brick buildings appeared, enclosing them in a cauldron and shading them, but leaving no means of escape. Chunks of plaster fell from one of the buildings, yet when they turned their heads, they saw nothing but the swirling dust. It could have been coincidence.

Too many coincidences, Abigail thought. She turned her bag over and carefully tucked Soxy and the box into the bottom, then padded it out.

"There, I'll hide you a bit now," she smiled at the puppy, "but just to keep you safe."

Cassius glanced at the frightened siblings.

"We're almost there," he whispered to them. He tried to calm himself. The back of his neck was tingling, and his arms were getting goosebumps.

At that moment, the rubble behind them crunched. All at once they turned back and saw the monster standing thirty yards away. Terrified and shocked, they were unable to scream. Megan's lungs whistled and David groaned as the air rushed out of him. His feet hit the ground and the scooter came to a jolting halt.

Cassius and Abigail took aim at the demonic creature, but did not yet fire. They waited, pale-faced and wide-eyed, stunned by the sight.

The rabid beast must once have been an AmStaff, with pointed ears and short, dirty-brown fur. Its bull-like head was swollen gigantic by the virus, its huge mouth protruding claw-sized teeth, its tongue dripping saliva onto the asphalt. Its muscles ripped under its hairless skin, and its sides were covered with gangrenous scars like burn marks. The infection had made its body twice as large as it had been, and now it stood before them like Cerberus, whose two heads had been cut off and whose body had been scorched in hellfire. Its black pupils mesmerized them. The rabid AmStaff lowered its head, bared its teeth at them, and snarled.

"No sudden movements," Cassius said, slowly articulating the words. He straightened up, bulging his chest. "Nice and slowly we start backing away. If anyone turns around, we're all dead!"

Abigail kept eye contact until it occurred to her that they could be attacked from the side. She snapped her head to the right in fright, but there was no sign of any other beast yet.

"I'm sure it's not alone," Cassius answered her unspoken question. Abigail brushed aside the blonde strands of hair that clung to her forehead, thinking that they could not retreat into infinity.

"We must do something," she said to Cassius. He nodded.

"Megan and David, head for the Monroe Building!"

There was a rusty "What?" from Megan, who had a petrified look on her face, her tongue flicking with the fear of death.

"The scooter stays. No stopping, no trying to be heroes. The stairwell is just past the reception desk on the right, by the elevators. If we don't get there in time, barricade yourselves in."

David carefully laid the scooter on the ground, and with Megan, they stumbled towards the tower block. That was when the rabid AmStaff launched an attack. Cassius fired, the sound of the shot echoing off the surrounding buildings. The thunder was deafening, but it hit. The bullet struck the animal's shoulder, and the AmStaff howled and rolled sideways. Then it stood up and shook itself. Its bare, wrinkled face was furious. The shot seemed like just a scratch to it, but it unnerved the animal.

Cassius took a quick look at Megan and David. The siblings were now far enough from them.

"Run when I tell you!" he ordered Abigail. She hesitated.

"I'll cover you from the entrance."

He gave a wry smile.

"I was hoping you wouldn't forget it."

They looked at each other. Cassius's smile melted off his face and Abigail bit her lip.

"Meet you there!"

She started to back away, remembering what he had taught her: don't show fear, don't run, don't turn your back on your opponent. Despite all that, they were about to do the stupidest thing, but she did not object, for Soxy's and Megan's sakes. All that mattered was getting them to safety.

She swept her gun across the surrounding buildings, and that's when she spotted the second beast. She staggered.

"Cassius! Three o'clock."

He flinched and turned his head slowly, very slowly. A distorted, blood-red Akita stepped through the fallen door of the brick building, oblivious to the crunching debris beneath its feet. It was as big as a wolf, its bushy, elongated head barely showing its deep-set button eyes. Its once-friendly muzzle was bloated beyond recognition, the hair along its spine was ruffled, and its long, disgustingly spotted tongue dripped sticky saliva onto the ground.

"And now?" she asked.

"Back away! Don't stop!"

Abigail looked back and saw that the road to the Monroe Building was still clear. Megan and David had reached the crossroads. The siblings watched them in horror, then David yanked open the double glass door and pushed Megan into the spacious lobby.

An echoing roar intensified from the worst possible direction. From behind Abigail and Cassius. *Oh, no!* Something else appeared in the alley opposite the Monroe Building – a slow-moving shadow, a jet-black specter. Abigail's blood ran cold.

"Cassius, look!"

The Rottweiler that emerged from the alley was the size of a bear, its forelegs like hydrants. A Roman legionary's shield would have fit in between its shoulders. It approached menacingly, and they saw that the beast would soon block their path to the building. With each step they drew nearer and nearer to being surrounded by the savage animals. If they waited any longer, they would have nowhere to run.

Megan cried out in the lobby of the building.

"Now!" Cassius thundered.

Abigail fired three bullets into the Akita, then ran. Cassius charged the AmStaff and tried to keep pace with the girl. The rabid beasts fell, wincing in pain.

The Rottweiler remained. The black beast's nostrils quivered, adrenaline gushing through its body at the sight of its prey on the run. Its muscles tensed and it swung towards Abigail. She stopped, aimed, and fired. Just once.

The .308 Winchester bullet burst from the Browning's hammer-forged, fluted barrel and tore through the chest of the leaping beast at the speed of nearly three thousand feet per second, coating the concrete with sticky brown blood. The Rottweiler slammed into the dirt of the road, its tongue twisted out of its mouth.

She smiled proudly. The bullet had gone right through the animal's heart.

"Bull's eye!"

"Get in the building, come on!" Cassius shouted, turning back to see what had happened to the other two beasts.

The AmStaff and the Akita slowly struggled to their feet, then with ponderous movements, they set off after their prey. Cassius and Abigail had a head start of fifty, perhaps sixty yards.

Abigail pushed against the door, which yielded to the pressure and opened. She fell to her knees and smashed her palm into rubble. She hissed, pain mingling with disgust on her face. Cassius caught up with her, and pulled her to her feet.

"Go on!" he pushed her towards the reception area. He called out to David. "Get to the door, come on!"

Abigail found her balance, then took off running. Cassius did not follow. He crouched down, and fired without hesitation. The bullet struck the Amstaff in the skull and the animal fell back without a sound. The Akita remained, trying to attack from the side, but it could not outwit him. Aim, fire, miss, and then again: aim, fire...

The Akita was only a few yards away when the bullet hit its rump, and the animal collapsed, paralyzed and unable to move anything but its head. Cassius spat on the floor.

"Stay," he gasped, and got to his feet.

David pushed his sister towards the stairwell door, but Megan had a hard time moving. She huffed and laid her forehead on her brother's shoulder. Abigail gestured for them to continue.

Cassius wiped his sweaty brow and walked over to Abigail, who was staggering around the reception desk. Before they could say anything to each other, the noise outside grew louder. The echoes of crunching debris, followed by grunting and howling, filtered in from the street.

One by one, the rest of the pack emerged from the neighboring houses, almost a dozen of them. The beasts approached with relentless snarls and demonic eyes. They surrounded the building and headed straight for them.

"We don't have that many bullets," Cassius groaned. It looked like a hopeless situation. The rabid beasts galloped towards them at a terrifying speed. "Run!"

Cassius and Abigail headed for the stairwell, towards Megan and David, who were standing dumbfounded.

"Quick!" she called to them.

David shoved Megan into the dark stairwell, then braced himself against the heavy fire door, but he spotted the beasts rushing into the hall, exploding through the glass without slowing down. His face turned pale and he started to back away. He let go of the heavy door.

"Wait, you idiot!" shouted Cassius.

But David kept retreating as if he hadn't heard. Abigail gathered all her strength and accelerated. She knew that if the door closed on them, they wouldn't have time to open it again before the beasts were on them. Every second counted. David's mouth twitched, but he finally came to his senses. He threw the door open, gave them one last desperate look, and disappeared down the stairwell.

"Motherfu..."

Cassius fired a short round into the approaching beasts, just in case, but he never stopped to count how many bullets hit. He just made sure Abigail was in front of him. The empty lobby echoed with the barking of the savages and the crunching of debris, the hellish paws stirring the dust, the ground shaking. The animals had eaten into their head start. Only yards separated the beasts from them.

"No..."

They arrived at the stairwell just in time. Cassius grabbed the closing door and pushed Abigail into the stairwell, then threw himself after her. At the last moment the lock clicked. The ferocious beast behind them slammed with elemental force against the fire door and bounced off it. There was a whimper and a disappointed howl, followed by silence.

They stood motionless in the darkness for a while, then Abigail took out her flashlight and Cassius turned angrily towards the others.

"Up you go, don't just stand there," he shouted.

The door banged again. Another, much fiercer beast must have run at it, and after that impact they didn't hear a howl but a persistent growl. The hinges bent, the lock cracked, and light leaked into the dark stairwell through a thin rupture.

"They're gonna break it down!" Abigail moaned.

"Come on! Up!" Cassius yelled.

They started to run, but Megan found it hard to manage even a few steps on her own. With Cassius and David under her arms, Abigail covered them, ready for the worst. At the next bang, the metal door buckled, one of the hinges snapped out of place, and they could clearly hear the growing, excited yelps from the hallway.

Abigail glanced at Cassius with a desperate look. They were still only on the third floor. *We'll never make it up there like this!*

Cassius put his hand on her shoulder.

"Take my place! I'll cover you."

Abigail angrily shook off his hand. *This is suicide!*

"No!"

There must be some other way!

There was a metallic clang from downstairs, the impact of an object far heavier than a hinge falling to the ground. As one they looked down into the darkness, which was broken by a sharp light, revealing the horror. The door burst open, and the rabid beasts trampled over each other as they started upstairs. Their demonic barking echoed off the walls, and the sound followed like a destructive tide as the animals ran, leaping over railings and banging into walls.

Cassius nudged Abigail and began to fire. He took a few steps back to cover the others. She looked up in despair at the terrified siblings. Her brain began to twitch, but fear paralyzed her. *Think, think, think...*

Then something occurred to her. She put her bag on the floor, reached in, and gently pushed Soxy aside. She could hear the thundering steps, closer and closer; not even the sporadic hail of bullets could drown them out. Cassius fired as sparingly and accurately as he could, but the fight was hopeless. Every beast he shot was replaced by even more.

Abigail pulled a shirt from her bag. It was her favorite, the one that said CHEER UP, and she quickly wrapped it around the baseball bat. Then she kept digging through the bag, calling out to David.

"Cover Cassius!" She tossed her Glock to him. David caught it and clumsily aimed it at one of the beasts. But he chose the wrong target.

A Doberman, jumping over its dead companion, threw itself at Cassius. It had a head like Anubis', an underworldly muzzle stretched by the forces of hell, its teeth rattling and its eyes gloved with fire. Cassius wrestled the beast to the floor, falling on his wounded shoulder. He held on, his fierce grip trying to hold the savage's head so that it couldn't bite him. He screamed as the hulking body pressed his spine against the stairs. The hold he had on the animal with his bare hands was superhuman, still it kicked and clawed, scrabbling for a better position.

David fired with his eyes shut. The next beast tumbled backwards from the bullets. Abigail had three seconds to save Cassius. *Come on...*

She finally found what she was looking for: wound disinfectant and a lighter. She used the antiseptic to soak the cloth wrapped around the baseball bat, then lit it with the lighter. The alcohol-soaked T-shirt caught fire and burst into a bluish-yellow glow. Abigail immediately swept towards the Doberman, which jumped aside at the sight of the fire.

The beasts began to back away from the blazing fire, snarling and howling. Abigail yelled backwards with the makeshift torch in one hand and the other outstretched towards Cassius.

"Don't wait for us, just run!" she shouted to the siblings, helping the man to his feet.

David put his arms around Megan and they began to drag themselves upstairs, step by step, inch by inch. Cassius scrambled to his feet, recovering his gun and firing towards the retreating savages. Just in case, he reached into his bag and pulled out a piece of cloth. He lit it with the makeshift torch and threw it into the deep, pushing the animals further back towards the first floor.

The girl's upraised hand shook with the fatigue and shock that hit her at that moment. Cassius took over the torch so Abigail could rest. He gave her a wink.

"Well done!"

Despite her exhaustion, Abigail smiled with a huge sigh. She was giddy and her expression was practical gleeful.

"I know."

Just then the man-eaters' walkie-talkie crackled in her belt, and through the static they could clearly hear Jason's raspy voice.

"Are you still there, my little birdies? If you are, well done staying alive. For now."

Abigail grabbed the radio and, in a furious gesture, threw it into the deep after the rabid beasts.

12.

Even Cassius admitted that the fire was a brilliant idea, but they could not sit and relax, for they could clearly hear the wild animals lurking downstairs, just waiting for the right moment.

After taking a deep breath, Cassius bandaged Abigail's hands, then the two of them searched the fifth floor, where they would camp for the night. In one of the offices, Cassius found an old mahogany desk, a bottle of Jameson in a drawer, and company papers, so they finally had tinder and firewood. Abigail returned with a first-aid kit and liquid soap she had found in a janitor's closet. They couldn't remember the last time they had properly cleaned themselves, and not just scrubbed in a rush with cold water.

They used the mahogany desk to make two fires in the stairwell; one on the fifth floor, the other on the landing a half floor below. This was a way of keeping the rabid beasts at bay while preventing the light from being seen from outside. On the fourth floor, they built a barricade of chairs and tables to act as both a barrier and an alarm. The plan was that if the beasts somehow broke through, they would lock the doors and hole up in an office.

Abigail took the first watch. She brought Soxy to her side, fed him, and tidied up the litter, then sat down in the stairwell's propped-up doorway with her back against the door frame. When the puppy had dozed off, she took from her bag one of the magazines she had brought with her. The fire, crackling cozily, gave enough light for her to read.

At Cassius's instruction, she lit a large stack of papers every ten or fifteen minutes and threw it into the deep. The burning, falling lantern illuminated the stairwell, and when it landed, the animals sniffing below leapt aside, growling and whimpering. Only indistinct sounds could be heard.

Cassius made a bivouac for Megan, and David opened some cans and passed them around. They put their bags down in one of the smaller office spaces.

After calmly spooning up his dinner, Cassius settled himself by the window where he could keep an eye on everything and everyone. He blinked at the dusky landscape outside. From the north-facing window he had a perfect view of the city. The overpass ran a few hundred yards away, the red-yellow twilight sky to the left painted Phillips Tower and Moulmein Pagoda into a post-apocalyptic postcard. To the right, to the east, the end of the overpass was visible, and beyond it the A-frame pylons of the Headland Bridge dominated the horizon.

Beside the table in front of him, he noticed a box full of all sorts of things. He pulled it closer and looked inside to find the belongings of someone who had worked here long before. A birthday card signed by colleagues, a family photo, perfume, cutlery, and post-it notes. He sniffed the perfume, and set the notes aside politely at first, but temptation got the better of him and he read the flirtatious messages the mysterious worker was exchanging with someone in the office.

He smiled when he reached the end of the messages. Meanwhile, it was getting dark outside. Abigail was still sitting by the door to the stairwell, but she had put the newspaper aside and was massaging her aching hand, her gaze lost in the distance.

Cassius leaned his head back and took a deep breath. He was thinking about how they could collect the things they had left on the bus, or eventually replace them, when he noticed Megan and David, who were whispering, lying side by side on their makeshift beds in the far corner.

"You're not mad at me, are you?"

"Why should I be?" David asked, but did not return the look.

"For forcing you to make this trip."

"It doesn't matter now, does it?"

Beat. Megan queried David with her eyes. He finally continued.

"We don't know what would have happened if we had stayed. Let's forget the whole thing."

"Maybe we should have gone with Nelson. South."

"Maybe. Although I definitely think the old man would have freaked out when he realized he couldn't get rid of us."

They laughed together, but their happiness was brief.

"Do you think he's all right?"

David shrugged.

"I'm sure. Nelson is indestructible, he'll outlive us. We'll long be feral feces while he's still wandering around somewhere in Patagonia. He won't rest until he's produced his own smoke, then he'll sit in that stinking armchair and puff away all day long."

Megan smiled.

"That's good to hear."

They both fell silent.

Cassius closed his eyes. Sleep rushed down his tired body like a tidal wave breaking through a dam. His imagination did not take him far; it kept him in Headland. He saw Abigail cowering under the car. He heard the demonic grunts coming from her mother, whose body was struggling against the transformation and about to lose...

...and then everything changed. He was on a rusty boat, the world swirling around him, and strangers were talking to him. He was looking for Abigail, but she was nowhere to be seen. He was spinning around desperately, but the crowds were closing in.

Then he heard his wife's voice.

"Jake!"

He awoke with a jolt. Cassius sat up. Upstairs was silent, moonlight streamed in from outside. The twilight made the world around him dreamlike. He took a deep breath. His heart rate slowed down.

In the far corner, David breathed softly, and Abigail, sitting in the stairwell doorway, dozed off. Her head tilted to one side, her mouth half open, the firelight dancing on her cheeks.

Cassius was on the point of waking her when he heard a rustling from the direction of the bags. He rose cautiously, and crept over with his gun in his hand. His internal alarm system was silent, and somehow, he felt no danger either.

Squatting over the bags, Megan sorted through the leftover food. She took out a can and squinted as she read the handwritten label.

"Chicken and vegetable stew... hmmm..." she whispered to herself, smiling like a proud hunter.

Megan raised her head to look around, and she noticed Cassius leaning against the wall. She shuddered, then gave a soft squeak, her hands clutching her chest. She giggled like a child caught in the act.

"I got hungry," she said, blushing.

Cassius stepped closer, gently took the can from her hand, and with a firm movement popped the lid. He handed it back to Megan. She took it with a relieved grin, sniffed it, and closed her eyes in pleasure.

After the first bite, she held up her index finger.

"Wait a sec... I've got something for you," she said with a hint of a smile. She turned and shuffled to her bunk. She rummaged in her bag for a moment, then ambled back to Cassius with the surprise in her hand. When she reached him, she handed him a book.

"I found it in a drawer. I thought you might like it."

Cassius took the book and nodded gratefully.

"Thank you."

Megan crouched down, meticulously adjusted the place around her, and began to eat the chicken and vegetable stew. Cassius kept himself from grimacing at the stale, artificial smell coming from the can. He sat down beside her and glanced towards Abigail, who was still snoozing.

"You're not going to wake her up and scold her, are you?" Megan asked.

Cassius shook his head.

"Good," she said with mock severity. Megan must've noticed the smirk on his face because she grinned shyly. "What is it?"

"Don't get me wrong, but... you remind me of my wife. Whenever she had something on her mind, she could never hide it. Those dancing little wrinkles, they give you away."

"Busted." Megan took a bite of chicken stew and carried on while gesturing with her spoon, as if conducting a symphony. "If you knew me, you would know that if there was something I wanted to say, I would definitely say it."

Cassius knitted his brows.

"Then let's not go round in circles, it's getting late. You think I'm too strict with her, but I think children need discipline. Since I'm responsible for her, I won this round."

Megan stopped with her spoon in the air, a carrot balanced on it. She could barely get a word out past her aggravation.

"Wow."

"Look around! The world is a brutal place, life is full of cruelty, and it doesn't matter how nice you are. If you're running from monsters, and you want to survive, you have to be a monster, too! And Abigail is not."

"This world needs kind people, more than ever."

"Uh-hmm. Yet all the good souls are dead, one by one, and I'm pretty sure they all regret their last moments. Abigail needs to learn that she can't save everyone." Cassius felt himself getting more and more involved. He shook his head in disappointment. "There will come a time when I can't be there for her, and she has to be ready. Then she can't think the way she does now, then she'll have to... toughen up. The sooner she does, the better off she'll be."

Silence.

Megan put the empty can down and pulled her blanket tighter around herself. She shuddered.

"When I stitch people up, I don't just look at the wounds. I listen to them, and after a while I know what they need. Don't laugh, I can imagine how funny that sounds, but now I know what your problem is. And I'll tell you."

"I was beginning to worry you'd keep it to yourself."

"Your problem is you don't have a real goal."

"Well, you couldn't be more wrong."

"Don't make me laugh! Forget the island and the gardening. Forget Abigail, she's not some baby bird anymore who's testing her wings. Your goal is not to run away, but to stay and help others. Pass on your knowledge. Maybe that's why you feel lonely, because there's no one to listen to all the wisdom your head is stuffed with."

Cassius snorted.

"So, I'm a gym teacher without students."

Megan shrugged.

"After all, it suits you, with your whistle and all," she said with a flirtatious smile, then turned back to her softly breathing brother. "Like here's David. Do you think that's what he wanted? For everyone to think he was some loser? You think he didn't want to learn how to defend himself? And now you're acting like you can't wait for him to piss off."

"Maybe it's because..."

"Blah-blah-blah-blah, stop right there!" she interrupted sharply. "Talking through that tough guy mask again!"

"Whoa, you know me that well?"

"I'm a good judge of character. I may have told you that."

"Maybe."

Cassius glanced at David, who turned around huffing in his sleep.

"It must've been tough for him to be treated like a loser. From what you told me, I thought your colony was a cut above the rest."

"Because it was. Not perfect, but we loved living there. Nelson was a good man, but a bad leader, and Grant was a good boss, but a lousy man. They had one thing in common. They were both terrible teachers. And neither of them was a soldier like you, so..."

Cassius raised an eyebrow.

"Why, who said I was a soldier?"

Megan stared at him, puzzled.

"Weren't you?"

"No. I spent most of my life as a trucker. I had a beautiful wife who I didn't treat as well as she deserved, a seven-year-old son, a real rascal... and a daughter on the way to us."

She patted her stomach as the realization hit her consciousness. He went on impassively.

"I had no intention of joining the army, and they don't take stubborn idiots like me anyway."

"But I thought you were..."

Cassius closed his eyes and reminisced.

"It all started when the epidemic broke out. I immediately sent my wife… Susan down to her parents' place. Somehow, I felt this was different, this was going to be trouble. I stayed on to work, but I wish I hadn't, because the city was locked down and I was stuck there, alone. The first week was the worst, the total uncertainty, the contradictory news, the lies. We talked on the phone and I promised Susan I would get out, but I just had more and more stupid ideas. The last one was the worst bullshit of all. I got all my money together and hired a coyote to get me out, but he scammed me and ran off with the money. There I was, penniless, trapped in a zombie town. That's when I first heard about the militia. People started to organize themselves to solve the problem, not long after Operation Daybreak. They called themselves Mason's Army. They offered food and shelter, so I joined. The first week was training. Mason taught us everything he could. He promised we wouldn't give in, and we started walking the streets like some kind of stupid vigilantes. I shot my first feral on the tenth day, and the rest went like clockwork. I never thought of them as humans again."

"And Abigail?"

Cassius looked at the girl. He remembered everything clearly, even after all these years, but recalling it was harder than he thought.

"Abigail... Palmer Avenue... It seems like yesterday. Before the battle of Headland, Mason had been upbeat, always telling us that we were ready, that we had the right to do this. To attack our own compatriots... We felt bad, of course, but the gears were turning and there was no stopping it. Before the operation, a few of us went around the streets and warned the residents. That was the first time I met Abigail; her father was one of the leaders of the area where they lived. Then on the day of the uprising, all hell broke loose. People knew what we were up to and gathered around the checkpoint so that if we finally succeeded, they could get out as well. That's when the ferals showed up. The destruction was brutal. Abigail's parents were attacked; her father and brother were torn apart immediately, but her mother managed to hide. Unfortunately, it was only after she was bitten. I found the girl in the driveway, sheltering under their car. Her mother was transforming. If I hadn't helped, she would have attacked Abigail too, so... I helped."

"And the battle?"

"I have no idea what happened, because Abigail and I hid while the ferals were lurking outside. I was supposed to give her to one of the neighbors if it was safe, but I couldn't find anyone alive. When I asked her if she had any relatives, she mentioned a man named Rafael, but the guy's house was also ransacked. I didn't want to leave her there on her own, so I took her with me. We headed to the west, since the other route, Florida and the archipelago, seemed to be the stupidest thing."

"Did none of her relatives survive?"

"I was hoping to find someone in the Brookings camp who knew her, but before I could ask around, the ferals hit us. And then the same thing happened at the Pincers, during the great attack. It was the worst thirty hours of our lives, and I wouldn't have bet dollars to donuts that we'd survive. I still don't know how we did it, but the longer we were together and the more I tried to get rid of her, the more she stuck with me. Since she was a drag on me, I taught her everything I could. So that she wouldn't get me killed before I found my family."

"But you never found them, did you?"

"No, I didn't. We went to every possible place they could have gone, all for nothing, so... it's time to sing a different tune."

"And that's it? You're leaving for the island because there's no hope?"

"I told you; survival is all that matters. This place is lost, this world is over. And my goal could not be clearer: to sit on the beach under a palm tree without having to look over my shoulder."

Megan mused quietly, biting her lip. Cassius watched her silently as she shook her head.

"I think there is hope. I think it's worth a try."

"Worth a try? We did try, and we failed. What do you think I've been doing all these years? Since we were constantly on the move, we learned what most hide-and-seek players didn't. Which you guys don't have the faintest idea about. Those hiding out for months, years, before they finally decided to hit the road, weren't prepared for what's out here. Whenever those people found us, they begged us to help. Some we abandoned. Some we didn't."

"And how did you decide?"

"The principle was relatively simple. If I looked at the person and didn't want to punch them in the face, they could stay. Otherwise, goodbye. If there was even the slightest chance of a situation going badly, I turned my back, or worse, I blew a couple of holes in the person. The trouble was, Abigail was letting me do that less and less."

Megan giggled, but then put her hand over her mouth as if in shame. Only after a few long seconds did she look him in the eye.

"And what happened to the people you helped?"

"Always the same." Cassius looked out the window at the moonlit city, hoping that the outlines would help him remember. "There was this boy, maybe twelve years old, three months after the Breakdown. His name was Jimmie, and he'd been with us for two months after his mother had gotten so stoned, she didn't even wake up when four ferals were skinning her body. He was a smart kid, really, but a cheeky little rascal at the same time. He never listened to me, and one day a feral bit his finger clean off. You know what happens when a wound doesn't hit an artery, right? It can take days until you transform. He was the first and the last that I ever watched go through that. Never again."

Megan's eyes shone in horror. She waited for what would come next.

"Then there was Patrick and Sarah. Father and daughter. Sometimes you just gotta run and only worry about yourselves. We were faster. Joe and Linda. That was the first time I watched someone die rather than lose someone else. Christopher. Appendicitis. Jess. She finally grabbed a rope when she couldn't take it anymore and hanged herself from a tree. Can you imagine? You survive all this shit, but then you turn the lights out. Because at least then it's your own decision, not someone else's. Not some monster's. And then the kids we found in an orphanage. Lucas, Nia, and Molly. You think I didn't try? That for the last seven years we've been wandering around alone and I haven't even tried?"

No answer, and Cassius was suddenly in no mood for anything. He got up and straightened his back.

"Sometimes I feel like I don't have the space for all the faces in my brain. Dying is nothing. Losing someone who's important to you is different." He paused, then flicked the book. "Thanks for the gift. Now, let's get some sleep. We've got a tough day tomorrow."

Cassius turned, but Megan's soft voice stopped him.

"Sometimes you don't need more space."

He halted. She smiled at him, her eyes twinkling sadly, and then she pulled a necklace from under her scarf and unclasped the heart-shaped pendant dangling from the end of the chain. Inside the pendant was a photograph. It was of a four-year-old boy. Cassius understood right away.

"See, I tried again, because that's what we do. And whatever happens, I'm going to do it all over again. It's my destiny."

Silence. She looked up, her sky-blue eyes reaching into his soul.

"Can I trust you? Do you want to know the truth?"

"Of course."

Megan pulled her scarf off her shoulders. She did so cautiously, as if she were still deciding whether this was a good idea. At first, in the dim light, Cassius couldn't see what she was showing him. Megan tilted her head to the side, and he could make out a scar on the back of her neck.

"We were working in the fields; nothing had happened for a long time then. And you know how it is. We'd become complacent, almost forgetting what it was like to live in constant terror. Fortunately, there were only three in the pack, hungry and weak. The surviving watchman finally took them down, but..."

"But?"

"Too late. The last feral found me."

Cassius fell behind. "It bit you?"

Megan nodded, timidly, as if ashamed of what had happened to her. Cassius stepped closer, wanting to touch the bite mark, but he got control of himself. He shook his head in disbelief.

"And?"

"As you can see, I haven't transformed."

"Maybe they weren't even ferals, maybe..."

"Oh, believe me, they were; I'm not that green. They were ferals, very much so."

Cassius crouched down and stared in silence. He was stunned, and for a time he couldn't speak.

"That's amazing. I've never heard of anyone who survived a bite. Maybe you're not the first, maybe there are others who are protected." He thought about it, then finally just waved his hand. "Not that it matters. It's not like there's some lab that can make a vaccine… But what freaked out the colony?

She hesitated.

"The fact that I was four months pregnant. And the colony thought it was because of the baby, that she was sucking up the infection. And that I was going to give birth to a monster."

13.

Cassius was awake when the fire went out, and the embers that followed were not enough to hold back the beasts. The animals started to build up. The sun was just tumbling over the eastern horizon when they heard scratching from downstairs, followed by hungry, excited growls. Impatient, unworldly whimpers.

He shot two more animals as they galloped up the stairwell, then closed and barricaded the fire door. He used the heavier desks and cabinets that they had prepared the night before.

Abigail moved Megan, David, and Soxy to safety in one of the smaller offices. She checked the silver Smith & Wesson, gave it back to David, and explained what to do if the animals broke through the door. She put Soxy in Megan's hand and garbled care instructions just in case something happened to her. She gave the puppy one last look, then turned and hurried to Cassius.

They pushed the heaviest cabinet into place together. When they were done, they stepped back and looked at each other. Cassius wiped his brow.

"Are we happy?"

Abigail tightened her jaw and nodded silently.

"Good, 'cause you look a bit worried."

Abigail's stern eyes didn't blink, her shoulders stiffened, and her mouth quivered. They glanced resolutely at the door. They didn't have to wait long.

The door shook with a tremendous rattle, the bolts groaned, the screws loosened. The metal bent and seemed to yield to the demonic force.

"Ammo?"

"Not enough."

At best, they had a few minutes. *This is the moment! This is it!* Cassius watched Abigail choke back a cry, but at the next rumble, adrenaline took control of their bodies. She screamed defiantly, and it also did him good. It fired him up. It helped him forget that they were about to fight the last battle of their lives.

David appeared beside them.

"I want to help," he said. He held the gun awkwardly, like a child.

Cassius shrugged. He could have sent him back to the room, but it no longer mattered. And a man should be on his feet when the time came, not huddled in the corner. He adjusted the silver revolver in the young man's hand.

"H-H-How do I do it?" David asked.

"Keep your eyes on the target and only the target. Take a few deep breaths and hold. Pull the trigger firmly. Be prepared for the sound of the round discharging. It will be loud and the gun will recoil. Then repeat. As long as it takes. Or as long as you can."

"And what if I run out?"

"Then it's over, buddy. Then it's over."

David nodded in confusion, almost certain that only some of the information had gotten through. *That should be enough*, Cassius thought. David tightened his grip on the gun and pointed it at the door.

"Like this?"

"Perfect, buddy." Cassius smiled encouragingly at him. The young man stared white-faced at the door, which was about to burst open.

The barricade still held, but the rabid beasts were trying to claw their way through the gap. All three could smell the stink; the air filled with the stench of carrion.

"Oh, my God!" exclaimed David. He stepped back involuntarily.

"Don't panic now! We'll fire as soon as they break through. Is that clear?"

Abigail stood still. David trembled silently beside them.

"Get ready!" Cassius shouted.

The door burst wide open, the cabinets and desks shattered, the way cleared. Cassius fired without hesitation, three bullets at the first beast, which had just leapt over the fallen cabinet and was already falling to the floor, whimpering. A smaller specimen. *Of course it was a small one. They always send the smallest first.* Abigail laid the next one down. That animal twitched a few more times before it died. David fired at anything that moved, but no more than one bullet found its mark. Cassius, on the other hand, had no time for advice. The best was yet to come. Megan screamed and David kept muttering something under his breath.

The third attacker was a gigantic specimen, a German shepherd with thick fur. The beast leapt to its feet, and in one graceful movement it dodged the bullets that were raining down. Cassius wasn't thinking, he had only one goal in mind: to put as many rounds as he could into the monster. David followed suit and then the Smith & Wesson barked and clicked.

"I'm out!" he shouted.

Then it's over, buddy!

A strange sound came from the hallway. Whimpering and yowling intensified, and then, to their dismay, the animals waiting outside began to run upstairs. At lightning speed, as if their bodies were being tortured by an unknown force.

"What the..."

One by one the frightened animals, tails between their legs, disappeared. It was still not clear what was happening. Stunned, Cassius and his companions lowered their weapons. When the last beast, a huge Siberian husky, appeared, crashing into the doorframe and falling off, they were unable to react.

The animal ignored them. It was running away from something. Desperately, it jumped up, but the unknown force held it back, preventing it from fleeing after its companions. The husky galloped straight towards Cassius instead. He leapt aside, his gun raised, but he did not have to fire. Without changing direction or slowing down, the rabid beast sped past him, straight at the window.

Jesus, Cassius thought as a sudden possibility flashed through his mind. *Is it going to jump? Why?*

The husky sped up, with its tail between its legs and its head bobbing back and forth, whimpering constantly. Its body shook, tormented by an invisible force. It sped up, bending its back forcefully, its hind limbs thrust forward. And then it happened, what Cassius had been waiting for. Without slowing down, the beast ran at the window, the glass shattered, and the animal dashed out. Its body was temporarily suspended in the open air, before disappearing from sight.

David was taken aback. Abigail glanced at Cassius, who blinked for a few seconds. His gun hand was still. The hallway was silent.

"What was that?" she asked.

He shook his head.

A strange energy filled the air, as if electricity was vibrating around them. Footsteps approached; they raised their weapons at the same time.

Two hands appeared in the doorway, side by side, palms open, and then they heard a voice.

"Don't shoot, I'm a friend!"

They were so shocked they couldn't have pulled a trigger if they'd wanted to. A few seconds later, the two hands were followed by a body. Standing in the doorway, in the dimness of the hallway, was a middle-aged man. He wore thick-rimmed glasses, a gray beard covered his round face, and his worn shirt didn't match either his vest or his corduroy trousers. Cassius would sooner have thought him a widowed high school teacher than a formidable figure to be feared.

But when he stepped in with both hands raised, they noticed something on his right arm like nothing they'd ever seen. It was some sort of electrical gadget, a glove with cables, a display, and coils. A tiny LED on it flashed green.

The mysterious stranger took a deep breath and looked around theatrically. No one spoke, they could clearly hear the screeching of the beasts fleeing on the upper floors. Then that, too, died away.

"My goodness, I see I made it just in time." The man with the glasses lowered his hands and put them on his hips. "How fortunate! You might have been in quite some trouble."

Stunned silence. Megan peered cautiously out from the doorway of the far office. Noticing the mysterious stranger, she stepped forward. The bespectacled man nodded and gave them a broad smile.

"Oh, what a rude bloke I am, I forgot to introduce myself. My name is Norton, and I'm pleased to meet you. Well, let's not stand around here, let's get ourselves to a safer place," he said, holding up his right hand with the strange gadget on it. "Even my little dog whistle won't keep them away forever."

DOG EAT DOG

1.

Jason was sitting on the twelfth floor of the Moulmein Pagoda, in the semi-darkness of the presidential suite, in front of a window that spanned an entire wall. The beige splendor of the room was faded and the air was fusty, but Jason didn't care in the least. He indulged himself in the comfort of the armchair and, with a bored expression on his face, watched the city wake up to a new day. He gazed out over his domain like a weary monarch over an empire that stretched to the horizon.

The city lay largely still in the warm light of the sunrise. A cloud of dust swirled between the buildings and the wind blew the morning clouds from the sky.

Jason raised the walkie-talkie he held in his right hand, pressed the push-to-talk button, and spoke:

"You still there, princess? Hope you had a good sleep."

No answer. Jason smiled to himself.

"Believe it or not, I was rooting for you a little. On the one hand, you were a sympathetic little shit, and on the other, I wanted to catch you myself. To squeeze your soft, warm arm until it turned white. To see your pupils dilate, to smell the terror on your skin. And guess what, I have a special surprise for you. I can barely keep it to myself."

Silence.

"Say something, my princess. I wouldn't even wish it on you to be torn to pieces by a rabid beast; there's nothing more horrible... Well, maybe there is, but I swore I wouldn't spoil the surprise yet."

The only answer was static. Jason smirked.

"Please don't punish me with your silence! Let's make a deal. Visit us and I promise to tell you what happened to Rafael. It's an instructive story, I'm still touched by it. And believe me, you'd better turn back, because I wouldn't cross that bridge if I were you... Hey-hey, princess!"

The lock clicked and the door creaked. From the dim corridor, the red-haired woman entered, a gun in her hand, a look of concern on her face. Jason quickly lowered the radio, biting his lip, furious at being interrupted. He looked up impatiently.

"What happened?"

"Scorpio hasn't checked in."

Jason changed the channel, the forced theatricality of his voice and the playful glint in his eyes fading, both quickly replaced by anger.

"Scorpio, where the hell are you?"

The redhead rolled her eyes and spread her hands.

"You think I didn't try that?"

"Sure, but my voice is deeper. Where are those idiots standing guard?"

"In the underground garage. They were supposed to check in a while ago. They've got two hours before the shift change."

"And no one was checking on them? I mean, before you shuffled up here to bother me?"

"No one is better than you, boss."

There was irony in the redhead's voice, but it only made the urge to throw her on the bed and rip all the clothes off her slim, muscular body even more irresistible. He noticed that she was still panting from climbing the stairs. His gaze strayed to the drop of sweat running down her neck and stopped on her undulating chest beneath the delicately knit, tight top.

Then he shook his head. He stood up angrily and headed for the door. Before the redhead could follow him, he turned to her:

"Make yourself comfortable. When I come back, you won't be wearing that top!"

Jason laughed again. He liked his own jokes and was sure the others appreciated his sense of humor.

2.

They had to carry a torch to see in the pitch darkness of the underground garage. It was one of the reasons Jason hated the place, and on the rare occasions he had to go downstairs, he approached it from the street outside rather than from the stairwell. He would trudge through the hotel lobby, out onto the dusty, stifling street, around the corner, past the barbed wire barriers, and finally down the driveway. Straight into the dark, into the cool.

Someone always accompanied him. This time it was a guy who had the odd whim of smearing himself with the blood of his victims, then not washing it off until the next unfortunate, be it human or animal. The others called him the Madcap.

Jason did not like to be in the Madcap's company. He recognized his nauseating smell from afar. Nothing improved his opinion of the man, whether he spoke or worked quietly with his lips pursed. There was just no trace of sophistication in the man's work that Jason could respect. And when the prey was so scarce and the excitement so little, one was apt to regard the hunt as a sublime activity. Back in the old days, when they had more fun, it was sport. Now, it had become art.

They dodged the level crossing gate, and as they entered the darkness, Madcap shouted his way toward the pitch-black bowels of the underground garage.

"Hey, you idiots, like what the..."

"Shut the fuck up!" Jason interrupted sharply. He quickened his pace, and, as he passed, looked into the guardroom at the end of the driveway, where his men usually holed up, from there they could keep a safe watch on the street front, in case anyone or anything unauthorized should surprise them.

The room was empty except for the smell of body odor. The first thing Jason looked for was blood or signs of a struggle, but when he saw nothing suspicious, he concluded that his men had probably drunk themselves into a stupor and gone to sleep in one of the cars. It was easy to get lost down here: the team stored food, ammunition, and vehicles in the cool underground garage. Sometimes the sentries got lazy from doing nothing and started drinking, playing cards, and smoking cigars. Even he admitted that it was not the most exciting job in the world.

To keep the rabid beasts away, they had installed metal wind chimes in the surrounding streets to make noise, rubber was regularly burnt to make the area smell unpleasant, bear traps were set, and barbed wire was put up everywhere. Most of the ferals skirted the city, and the majority of the packs preferred to hunt in the countryside, where they had a better chance of finding food.

"Do you think they're lying around in one of the cars?" Madcap whispered. Jason shrugged.

"If they are, I swear I'll cut off their booze for the rest of the month. Worthless, no-good gang..."

Something clanged in the darkness, like a piece of metal falling on concrete. Or an empty bottle. They snapped their heads up and turned towards the sound. Jason raised the torch high, but nothing moved on the border between darkness and light. There was only the outline of concrete pillars and cars, with a gloomy glow around them.

Madcap shuddered, and involuntarily took a step back.

"What was that?"

Jason spread his arms wide and shook his head as if he could not believe the other was panicking. Then he shouted into the darkness.

"Wake up, my little birdies, rise and shine! Get your asses out 'cause rack-time is tickin' away!"

No answer. Jason's nose was then stung by something: the nauseating smell of swamp, the stench of decay, growing fleshier and stronger. He hissed, scrunched his nose and turned his face away in disgust, but the smell did not disperse. He waited and listened.

Madcap swallowed hard and blinked nervously up at Jason.

"M-maybe..."

"Maybe what?" Jason asked, but he didn't wait for the answer. Instead, he moved briskly towards the source of the sound. He was going to put these men through hell. He realized that he had been too lenient with them. *But now! Times they are a changing...*

Something moved behind him and he heard a muffled groan, then a thud. When he turned, there was no sign of Madcap. Jason lowered the torch and, though panic raged in his head for a few seconds, his sangfroid finally overcame the anxiety that was in every part of him. In the darkness he could hear quickening footsteps.

"Did you run away, you cowardly dog? You're all idiots, the whole lot of you..."

The shuffling came from the side this time. Jason jerked his head around in fright, yet saw nothing. Only now the swamp smell was stronger, as if the stinking thing was right next to him.

"Holy fucking shit..."

He turned around to see if he could discover the source of the stench, and he caught a glimpse of something among the wrecked cars. It was as if a figure had rushed past him in the twilight. Jason's movements froze as he listened intently to the black silence around him, but all he heard was the faint crackle of the torch.

Then he caught the echo of sniffles. The sound of crusty skin scraping on concrete, which grew louder, and footsteps following each other more and more rapidly. He got the jitters, his chest was tight with fear, and by the time he realized what was happening, it was too late. He felt the air move.

Jason was attacked from behind; an infernal force picked him up and slammed him against a pillar. He slipped to the ground, gasping for breath as a throbbing, paralyzing pain spread through his body. His limbs were helpless, he couldn't move, and his brain was clenched in shock. He struggled to roll over onto his back so that he could at least see what was happening.

The torch landed on the ground a few yards away from him. The flame had died down, barely illuminating the underground garage. Even so, he could see the shadows darting behind it. He heard the thumping of feet and a hungry growl.

"Fuckin' hell…"

In a haze of pain, he was flooded with the realization that his men were not drunk, nor were they dozing in one of the cars. They were very likely dead. At that moment, all he could think about was survival, that he could not die. This was not the death he had imagined for himself. In fact, he had never imagined any death at all.

A sinewy, elongated leg stumbled beside him. Its skin was dirty and bloody, with steel muscles and long toes. With his last strength, Jason looked up at the demon towering over him.

He had never seen anything like it, though he and his men had fought quite a few ferals. The demon stared down at him from a height of eight feet, saliva dripping from its huge jaws onto its chin as its long, killing claws did a slow tango. It leaned in closer, and Jason could have sworn the Alpha smiled before striking down at him.

The pain lasted only a few seconds before his scream was swallowed in a sea of blood. Then everything went black.

3.

The Alpha stood in front of the Moulmein Pagoda, waiting impatiently for the rest of the pack to finally return from their hunt. The last screams had died down a few minutes earlier, and all that could be heard from the building was the rattle and thunder as the ferals scoured the hallways, searching for hiding people.

Then there was silence.

One by one, the pack members emerged. The last was the female, the Beta. Their mouths were bloody, their teeth bared, with flesh stuck in between them. They were still panting, but there was contentment on their faces, a demonic happiness. The adrenaline coursing through their bodies soothed the pain, and the success of the hunt was like a reward to their brains, easing the agony, even if only for a short time.

The Alpha turned towards the long stretch of road, dancing in the scorching heat. It could still smell the stench of the neighborhood, however faintly. Burnt rubber, oil, and that familiar aroma it still could not explain. Which had driven it from the motel at the crossroads all the way to Headland. It did not care about exhaustion, for its mind was snared by an inexplicable desire to search for that thrilling scent.

It took a deep breath and closed its eyes. The smell led it northeast, towards the bridge. It knew that the answer to its questions was waiting out there.

COTTAGE IN THE WOODS

1.

They were unable to take their eyes off Norton's mysterious gadget. It still glowed green, data flashing and sine waves dancing on its tiny display. As they left the Monroe Building, they could still hear the rabid beasts yowling on the upper floors. During the escape, Abigail threw quick looks at Norton in the stairwell. She could see Cassius eyeing their rescuer suspiciously as well, but neither said anything. They concentrated on the task at hand: getting out of the building as quickly as possible.

The stairwell was full of the bodies of animals that had been shot. On one landing, the pile was so high they couldn't get around them and had to crawl over the stinking stack. In the lobby, the destruction was immense: overturned furniture, metal railings torn and twisted out of place, paw prints in the thin layer of dust. The animal that had fallen from the fifth floor lay outside in a pool of blood, shards of broken glass all around it.

Before she stepped out into the street, Abigail looked back once more. Something moved in the stairwell, and a shuffling noise grew louder in the darkness. Dread ran through her as she gripped the butt of her gun tightly with sweaty palms. She braced herself for the worst. But the rabid beasts did not attack. Norton's bracelet still glowed green.

A gray Ford Mustang Mach-E was parked across the street, dented on the front but in good overall condition, as if it had been kept in a garage for the past few years, perhaps even washed regularly. The trunk was open and a bundle of ropes and a hand truck had been left next to the dead Akita, which was the closest body to the car. In the middle of the intersection, a box resembling a generator rumbled by; on its side they saw a display screen similar to the one on the glove. Cassius and Abigail looked at each other. *What is all this? Who is this guy?*

The air outside was still. There was no fresh morning breeze, and they could already feel the scorching August sun on their faces.

Norton jogged forward, stopped in the middle of the intersection, and checked the four-way junction. When he was done, he gave a thumbs-up to the group waiting at the entrance to the Monroe Building. Cassius helped Megan through the debris that had gathered around the doorway, then turned back to Abigail, who was covering their backs. For the first time in her life, she saw uncertainty in his eyes.

"What do we do?" she asked in a whisper, watching the stairwell out of the corner of her eye. As Norton moved away from them, the scratching and yelping grew louder in the darkness. The invisible force that had been holding back the rabid beasts diminished with the mysterious man's departure.

"You know the drill!" Cassius replied, and glanced towards Norton. Their unexpected companion was re-tying his shoelaces but had to start over repeatedly when the string kept slipping through his fingers because of the glove.

Yeah, trust no one! Abigail snapped.

"I know the rule, but that wasn't the question! If we stay here, it's over! We're not going to outrun those savages."

Cassius pursed his lips. He hesitated. She was losing patience when he finally spoke.

"Keep your eyes open! At the first opportunity, we're bailing." Abigail nodded and started to walk away, but Cassius's voice stopped her. "And we're not making friends! We just want a ride, not more company."

Abigail shrugged her shoulders. When she reached the car, Norton and David were making Megan comfortable in the back seat. Norton fastened her seat belt, then wiped his brow in a theatrical gesture. The back of his greasy hand left a long smudge of dirt and his un-ironed shirt protruded from his trousers.

"There we go!" he announced and cracked his lower back like an old man waking from an afternoon nap.

David sat down beside his sister, fastened his seatbelt in a flash, and prepared to lock the back door, but first he looked up at Abigail with sincere enthusiasm.

"You won't believe what he's developed! A beast repellent to keep out the infected."

"That's great!" Abigail replied, before she turned back to Norton. "Do you live around here?"

"Oh, no, I've got a little cottage in the hills."

Abigail gave a satisfied sigh.

"That's great. We're also heading east."

"This meeting was destined," Norton snapped his fingers, then pointed to the Akita carcass. "My only regret is that I must leave this beast behind. It would have been an excellent specimen for my experiments, but *c'est la vie*, right?"

"What experiments?" David's eyes lit up. Cassius, who had just arrived, waved him off.

"We'll have time for small talk later! Now let's get out of here!"

"Don't you worry! As long as my gadgets work, we're safe," Norton said.

Debris crunched in the lobby of the Monroe Building, shadows ran across the furniture in the dim light, and something roared up from deep inside the skyscraper. The rabid beasts gathered impatiently in the hall, waiting for their chance. One of the animals, with its back ruffled and drool dripping from its mouth, could no longer control its instincts and tried to rush out of the building, but its body shook as it reached the door, shaken by the invisible force of the beast repellent. The creature yowled and slumped away. Norton proudly spread his arms.

"See? I told you!" He smiled and started for the roaring machine that stood in the middle of the intersection.

Cassius glanced towards Abigail, who understood the silent order. *Yes, I'll keep my eyes open, just as we agreed!* She slid her hands to her hips, close to her gun, ready for anything, and kept her eyes on the rabid beasts cruising the hall. Cassius followed Norton and, with the help of the hand truck, they hauled the bigger beast repellent to the Mach-E and loaded the machine into the trunk.

"I think something's wrong," Abigail gulped, and pointed towards the building. "The battery's running low, or, I don't know..."

The beasts left the hall one after another, but again they didn't get far; they stopped at the edge of the sidewalk and snarled at the cluster of prey just beyond their reach. Abigail opened the passenger door so she could get into the car at any time. Even in the heat of the moment, Norton's face remained smug.

"Calm down, they're only testing the big gun... Of course, when I turn it off things might get hairy, but there's no need to panic!" He raised the hand encased in the glove of cables and coils. "The little brother will protect us too, just with a slightly shorter range."

"How much shorter?" Cassius asked anxiously.

"A few yards... um... quite a few yards. Is everyone ready?"

Abigail nodded and got into the front-right. When the strange machine was finally in place, Norton pressed a large red button on it, and the buzzing of the huge beast repellent machine stopped, its vibrations ceased, and the girl felt a strange sense of release, as if a humming in her head that she hadn't noticed until then had subsided. The trunk door closed. Cassius sat directly behind the driver's seat, in the best possible position to keep their rescuer under control. However, Norton didn't seem to mind.

"Ready to go?" he asked after hopping behind the wheel. He looked with almost childlike excitement at the others, who turned anxiously towards the Monroe Building, where one after another the rabid beasts were shaking, as if casting off their impalpable chains. The animals howled and clawed at the concrete with their paws, their heads down.

"It's about time," Cassius said. "I hope you know what you're doing."

Norton started the car, which beeped to life. The service sound was strange in the ruined city, and Abigail couldn't remember the last time she'd heard something like it.

The rabid beasts that were lined up in front of the skyscraper started after them. In larger and larger leaps, they galloped, bloodthirsty, towards the car, until they stopped ten or fifteen yards back, as if something still held them at a distance. Another invisible wall, which for a moment seemed to hold. Then, after a few seconds, the distance began to dissolve: the animals tottered and snarled, and with lead-heavy feet they rose against the unseeable tide. The fur stood on their backs, their demonic eyes blazing with murderous lust, and inch by inch they stole the yards between them and their prey.

Abigail felt her heart pounding in her throat at the sight. She involuntarily slid up in the seat. Megan screamed, squeezing David's hand so hard he moaned.

Before Cassius could yell at him, Norton quickly twisted the beast repellent gadget. The device buzzed, hissing as the man held out his hand towards the beasts. The glove's diode began to flicker green, and the animals' bodies tensed as if electrocuted. They tried to struggle but failed and backed away. Then one after another they raised their heads like obedient dogs waiting for orders.

Norton pointed his index finger in the direction of downtown. The animals gave a yelp of pain, tucked their tails, and started running — in the direction Norton's upraised fingers had commanded. After a few seconds, there was no sign of them; they had all disappeared into the cover of the surrounding buildings.

Megan let go of David's arm. The young man turned and watched through the back window as the last of the beasts galloped off towards downtown without looking back, leaving only stirred up dust behind them. Norton grinned in satisfaction.

"As I've said, this little fellow is versatile," he said, and flexed his gloved fingers. Meanwhile, the beast repellent gadget was silent, the green vibrations had softened, and Abigail's body was once again filled with a strange sense of release.

The Mach-E took off, gliding noiselessly along the road. The car covered the distance without the slightest effort. Megan and David sighed in relief, and Abigail sat back and tried to slow her still pounding heart. Only Cassius did not relax. He was watching Norton through the rear-view mirror, and Abigail could see that he had his gun in his lap the whole time, his finger resting on its side. *I hope he's not up to anything stupid! This weird guy is our only hope...*

The car reached the end of the overpass at the edge of downtown, which had been a silent memento running alongside them overhead. No matter how hard they watched, they saw no movement behind the railings, no sign of man-eaters or ferals. After the half-collapsed off-ramp, they turned onto the 10, which took them straight towards the Headland bridge.

"How the hell did you manage to maintain an electric car?" Cassius asked after a long silence.

Norton shrugged and adjusted his misaligned glasses.

"That's a boring story, and I don't want to brag."

"Be brave, don't hold it back."

"Well, if you insist. I'm an engineer myself, so tinkering for me is a curse I'm glad to have, ha-ha, and luckily there were enough electric cars left in Headland for me to cannibalize for spare parts. I told you. A boring story."

Cassius nodded. Abigail knew he believed in simple, precise answers.

"And what about the beast repellent?"

"Oh, that's a bit more complicated. I'll save that story for a special occasion, like a lunch. If you are not in a hurry, I'd be happy to host the four of you in my humble abode. It's safe, I guarantee you."

"How far away is it?"

Norton nodded towards the Headland bridge looming on the horizon.

"Across the bridge, then north through the hills," he said, and chuckled. "It's a quiet little place, away from the hustle and bustle of the end of the world."

Abigail snapped her head up and immediately began to babble. "We're headed for the boat-town. Do you know the place?"

"Of course I do. They've done a fine job of fixing up the wrecks. I'm planning to visit them some day."

"Really? Would it be a big favor..."

Cassius interrupted her.

"We'll go together for a while then," he said with a raised hand and a grim look at Abigail. "Then we'll see."

Typical! She swallowed back her anger and glared defiantly at the road. She remembered Soxy, who must have been scared to death during their escape from the tower. Abigail took the pup out of his box and gently placed the furball on her lap. After a good stretch, Soxy seemed to sense something because he turned his head towards Norton and growled. Their rescuer blinked in confusion, then laughed theatrically.

"Isn't it cute? You have one hell of a watchdog!"

"Yes," Abigail said, and she gave him a faint smile. Exhaustion ran through her body, and her thoughts were gripped in a vise of dullness.

The car reached the next neighborhood, where soulless industrial buildings replaced apartment blocks and shops. In the distance, the slowly crumbling stadium of the Headland Blades could be seen. Cassius had visited every match day, at first with his friends and later with his son. Abigail had never been to this part of town before and, knowing her parents, they didn't often come here either. As her hand rested on Soxy's back, her eyes were glued to the window, but after a while the monotonous landscape outside blurred before her. She thought to herself that they had been seconds away from death again, and that they would run out of luck sooner or later. *Maybe Cassius was right? Maybe there was another way?*

First to get on the boat and drop the stuff off on the island, then to take the siblings up the river...

...or simply to turn north and try to reach the boat-town through the mountains...

It doesn't really matter. *The point is not to take any risks ... Stay away from Headland, listen to Cassius...*

Abigail turned back. She saw David stick his head out of the rolled-down window. The adrenaline had long since evaporated from him, replaced by paralyzing shock. Megan's body was drenched in sweat, her face was snow-white, and she was breathing hard. Her hand rested on her round belly, but her fingers were clenched. *Perhaps they would be better off without us, too. David would have instinctively avoided the danger, maybe they wouldn't even have stopped on the way... He would have chosen the mountains and tried to save on fuel; after all, you can roll downhill...*

She shook her head, trying to shake away the silly thoughts. She glanced at Cassius and remembered what she had heard the night before. He must have thought she was asleep, that's why he'd said such things to Megan about her, but she had heard everything clearly and felt betrayed. *He shouldn't talk about me to anyone else!* Her anger eased when she looked at Soxy. She forced a smile on her face and playfully scratched the puppy's head. *Nothing will happen to you, big boy! I won't let it.*

Abigail sighed heavily and lifted her weary head to the road ahead. The Mach-E accelerated around a bend and they finally came face to face with the Headland bridge. The slowly rising sun sat on top of the bridge's concrete-gray, A-frame pylons, its fan-like cables frayed but still holding. *I wonder what awaits us on the other side of the bridge?*

2.

After the Headland bridge, they turned north. The road ran through scrubby hills, with less and less wreckage to either side. They were in a place where not many people had been before the pandemic and which was certainly not on the itinerary of those fleeing the Breakdown. Most headed south back then, the gamblers moving toward Florida.

At nine in the morning, they passed the last old restaurant and gas station that even Cassius knew. OMG Wings & Chicken Fingers, with the most crispy and delicious fast food in the area. Soon after the ruined building, the road began to wind upward and the hills and woodland on the east bank of the river embraced them.

Cassius studied his map and wondered where they would go when they said goodbye to Norton. When he looked up, he sought Abigail's gaze, but she glanced aside. She was wrinkling her droopy nose furiously as she watched the road. He knew she was angry about something, but instead of wondering why, he turned back to the map. He was no longer the least bit interested in the cavalcade of topographical landmarks and roads. His thoughts were far away. In his mind he was back on the fifth floor of the Monroe Building, and his brain was coiled on the same thought, like a snake.

It was a matter of seconds and we would've checked out...

Norton's arrival was sheer luck, and luck was something you couldn't control, you couldn't prepare for. Cassius hated the idea that their survival had depended on such a small thing, on chance, and he couldn't shake the overwhelming feeling that there would be more of it in the future. But now, for the first time, it occurred to him that he might have been wrong.

What if we're always in danger because I can't trust anyone? Not even people we don't need to be afraid of... He thought of Molly, Lucas, and Nia, and remembered them chatting happily that particular morning as they left the safety of the farmhouse where they'd been holed up for a few days.

"We're gonna leave without you if you don't get moving, Lucas!"

"No, Molly! I don't want to go! Why can't we stay here, Nia?"

"Just because, that's all. You know the rules."

"Stupid rules..."

He smiled as he remembered Lucas's voice. If they hadn't left, if he'd trusted the old couple who'd taken them in for the night, the kids might still be alive. He glanced sideways at the siblings. *I won't be able to protect them alone. I just can't...*

The car ran over something and brought Cassius back to reality. Norton slowed, then turned down a bumpy dirt road.

"If you'll allow me a word of advice, you'll have it easier at the top of the hill. The road curves with the river, so you'd have to take quite a detour. But from the top, the old tourist trail will take you down to the other side, and from there it's a day or two's walk to the boat-town."

Megan raised her head and looked desperately at David.

"A day or two? Jesus, how are we going to make it?"

"We'll manage," Cassius growled, and glanced at Norton. "When do we get to your cabin?"

"Ten minutes. The view from up there is spectacular, and that alone is worth it." Norton winked at them, and stepped on the gas.

The dirt road ran steeply uphill and deep into the woods. Potholes occasionally bounced the car, but Norton didn't slow down, driving almost blindly. Maples, cypresses and willows lined the road, and when they passed a clearing, they caught a glimpse of the city in the distance, lazily basking in the mid-morning sun. After a few curves and some unpleasant bounces, they reached the top of the hill.

"Here we are," Norton said after a long, quiet stretch, pointing ahead.

The car drove between two metal poles topped with homemade DIY gadgets, most of which had green diodes flickering on them. No fences or barriers. At the end of the dirt road, at the edge of a clearing in the dense forest, a two-story farmhouse appeared with outbuildings and metal towers around it. Cassius squirmed to get a better view of where they were going.

"You live here?" he asked. *This is a security nightmare.*

"Oh, there's more than meets the eye."

The Mach-E swerved in front of the building and stopped on the gravel road. Norton killed the engine. Cassius's fingers returned to the butt of his gun, and he looked around as far as he could from the cover of the back seat. A larger garage, built sometime after the main structure, stood next to the whitewashed, porch-fronted farmhouse. The white paint had weathered away, the ornamental plants running around the base of the house had been overrun with weeds, and the damaged roof had been repaired with elements of inappropriate color and shape, but apart from aesthetics the building was in good condition. Cassius couldn't imagine how anyone could have survived the last few years here. Even if it was deep in the woods, the house should have been a pile of rubble this close to the city.

Norton wiped his glasses with a cloth and got out of the car. David followed first, then Abigail, who was still managing to avoid Cassius's gaze, and finally Megan, who straightened up, gasping for breath, with her knees buckling. Cassius could see that she was struggling for balance, barely holding on. Norton stretched out his limbs and, with one eye on Cassius, who was turning suspiciously, helped unload their belongings from the car.

"I'd say you are most welcome, but I can see you want to go. Should you change your mind, there's food, drink, medicine, and hot water inside."

"Hot water?" Abigail's eyes lit up. Even Megan giggled powerlessly beside her and then cuddled into her, not only in delight, but because she needed help to stay standing.

“Yes,” Norton winked. “There are some things I can’t let go from the comfort of the old world. And I’m not alone in that, am I?”

Abigail nodded with a broad smile, but when she glanced at Cassius the cheery look faded from her face. She swallowed hard. “What now? We need to refill our supplies.”

Cassius hesitated, trying not to think that it was all too good to be true. David showed up beside him. He put his arm around Megan.

“We won’t make it three feet like this.”

Cassius had the same concern, but was reluctant to show Norton how much trouble they were in. He knew the tricks, that seemingly selfless help could end in an unpleasant bargain.

“What do you want in return?” he asked distrustfully.

“Nothing,” Norton replied.

“Nothing?” Cassius raised his eyebrows.

“Can’t a man simply help the needy?” Norton spread his arms wide, but then thought for a moment. He put his finger on his chin like a bad actor. “Yet it’s true, nothing in this world is free. Let the payment be your company! I can’t remember the last time I had a good conversation with someone; a guest is a rare treasure around here. And besides, I’ve got everything I need.”

Norton proudly showed them around. Behind the farmhouse were cultivated fields, and from the porch there was an unrivaled view of Headland melting into the horizon. A tower with antennas and wires rose in the distance. In addition, there were solar panels on the roof, a small wind turbine in the clearing, rainwater collecting barrels at the base, and cameras and searchlights monitoring all of the farmhouse’s surroundings. The whole thing had a strange, repulsive, suffocating feeling, yet the area seemed tidy and orderly.

Cassius turned to Norton.

“You sure it’s safe?”

“Safe?” he snorted. “The house is protected by alarms, and they don’t just shriek if they detect an intruder. The ferals are far away, and since our last encounter, the man-eaters are not stupid enough to mess with me. So, yes, it’s definitely safe. I’ve been pretty comfortable here for the last seven years.”

"You just go to Headland every now and then to collect rabid animals."

"What can I say? I'm curious, I'm a researcher. I'm trying to understand what's going on around me, but so far I have little good news." Norton stopped abruptly when it seemed he had a great deal more to say, then swallowed. "You know what? Come on in, let's have lunch, and I'll tell you everything! It'll be informative, I promise, and at least you'll get some rest. And when the car's charged, I'll take you to the boat-town. Is that a deal?"

Cassius nodded. Megan and David headed for the house, relieved. The pebbles crunched beneath their feet, then were drowned out by their light-hearted conversation and laughter. Norton rushed forward to open the door for the siblings, performing the role of a gracious host by bowing and leading the way.

When the others were inside, Cassius caught Abigail's arm. She turned back angrily.

"What's wrong with you?" he asked her. "And don't take me for an idiot, 'cause I know you well!"

She pointed her sharp, stubborn chin towards him.

"I'm fine!"

"Let's skip ahead in time to the point where you stop fooling around and tell me what's wrong!"

Abigail bit her lip. She pulled up the shoulder strap of her bag and tightened her grip on Soxy's box as if about to walk away, but instead she opened up.

"I heard everything you said to Megan last night."

Cassius shook his head in puzzlement.

"And?"

"You think I'm just a lame duck. Who's not ready for anything, who's too stupid to understand your orders. Who couldn't be left alone for a minute."

"I don't recall saying that."

"That was the point, don't deny it."

"I guess I still do..."

"But it's okay. I hear you. It's time to grow up, right?"

Cassius answered her slowly, calmly, but his nose was already quivering with irritation. "Look, Abigail, I'm not gonna go explaining myself! I stick to what I said."

"Good to know," she murmured, then turned and walked towards the farmhouse. Cassius was left alone. He looked around. *I hope we made the right decision...*

3.

Cassius stepped up onto the porch and ran his gaze over the dry rotten wooden floor and the cracked, chipped railing. Two armchairs stood to the right of the front door, one of them worn, its seat cushion frayed and frazzled. The other was covered in dust. A wind chime had been hung from the ceiling, the plants had long since dried up in the flowerpots, and a formless spotlight had been fixed in place of the lamp by the door in sharp contrast to the rustic farmhouse atmosphere. Security cameras on the roof and around the building monitored the surroundings, and a router-like device was mounted above the front door which, like the other gadgets, glowed green.

By the time he entered the farmhouse, the others were already unloading their belongings in the hallway, and he caught sight of Abigail's Browning. Of course there was no sign of Soxy's box; she must have taken it with her. After a brief assessment of the situation, Cassius decided to keep everything with him and only put things down where he could keep an eye on them all the time. Meanwhile he did some quick calculation: no matter how much ammunition they had packed up at Mike's, only five bullets were left in the Remington; the Glock half empty.

Abigail, Megan and David stood awkwardly in the vast living room, Norton hustling excitedly around them, trying to tidy up as if he really wasn't expecting guests. He didn't stand much of a chance: a long table dominated the center of the room, with stacks of papers, books, dismantled electronic devices and wires, and a few walkie-talkies; clothes sat in piles on the chairs; and magnetic boards pushed up against the walls, covered with formulas the likes of which Cassius had never seen. The room was full of plants, ferns and runners hung from the ceiling, fruit tree saplings stretched along the edges, and flowers in clay pots were placed on the steps leading up. The staircase also served as a tasteful partition. Behind it was a spacious kitchen and dining area with antique furniture, a retro fridge, and leftovers sitting out on the table. Further on was a window niche with comfortable seating and in front of it, close to the sooty fireplace, a coffee table, sofa, and armchairs where cozy reading evenings could be held in the world that used to be.

Norton gave a puzzled ahem and gestured round. He was no longer wearing his beast repellent glove; the gadget lay on the table, on top of one of the stacks of papers.

"Welcome to my humble abode!" He raised his index finger and hurried to the kitchen, returning with a glass of water for each and a tray of snacks, which he passed around with immense pride. "Go ahead, go ahead! Both the bread and the cheese are homemade. I learned how to make them from YouTube when I still had internet. Good ol' times, huh?"

Abigail and the siblings immediately took a glass each and some snacks. Cassius was the only one to shake his head, and despite his meaningful glance at Abigail, she quickly downed the glass of water and then avidly took a bite of bread and a large piece of cheese.

Seeing that Norton was drinking with them, Cassius finally grabbed the last glass, but took a slow, hesitant sip. The pleasantly cool, clear water had no taste at all, but still he shivered at the comforting sensation. Abigail looked around with a broad, satisfied grin, Megan slumped wearily on the sofa, and David grinned as he stood at the light switch, turning it on, then off, then on again, as if he couldn't believe what he was seeing.

"There really is electricity," the young man muttered to himself. After he recovered from the amazement, he picked up Norton's beast repellent glove from the table and studied its every detail with genuine admiration. "You made this all by yourself?"

Norton nodded, but the smile that had been on his face since they met faded at that moment; his eyes clouded.

"Let's say so. I've tried a lot of things over the years. It would have been a luxury to stick to engineering. Sometimes a little farming, then a little forestry. I even immersed myself a little in genetic research through my wife. We had plenty of time, so there was no distraction, right?"

Abigail raised an eyebrow and turned her head inquiringly to see if she could find Mrs. Norton hiding somewhere.

"And your wife? Where is she?"

Norton's piercing green eyes flashed. He swallowed and started fiddling with his wedding ring. Cassius coughed politely in Abigail's direction, but she didn't take the hint, her curious eyes still fixated on Norton, who, embarrassed, picked up a sprinkler and sprayed water on one of the plants.

"Well, the pandemic didn't spare us either, even though we withdrew from society."

"I'm sorry," Abigail said, bowing her head.

Norton smiled and put the sprayer back in its place.

"Oh, no need to be, my dear! Life is like that. Fortunately, I have enough books, so I can do everything in-house." Norton picked up a tomato from the kitchen counter and held it up. "I've got my own vegetables, fruit, dairy... Except for meat. That I don't eat any more. So, I've got everything except the company. I'm a bit worried that you'll get too used to all this good stuff, and I won't be able to get rid of you."

Norton forced himself to give a wry laugh and the others, except Cassius, followed his example. Megan and Abigail giggled happily as they snuggled on the sofa, while David seemed a little confused by their host's words and blinked around in bewilderment. Cassius watched Norton with an emotionless expression as he slapped his thigh.

"Well, what are you waiting for? Eat, drink, rest! *Mi casa, su casa*... I hope I'm saying it right, my Spanish is getting a bit rusty."

The tension finally eased and they all dispersed. Norton escorted Megan and David to the kitchen, where he promised them a special dinner, and Abigail inquired about the bathroom. She was gone shortly afterwards for the hot bath she'd been longing for.

A minute later, Cassius was alone in the middle of the living room. He adjusted his belt, then asked where the guest room was so he could get cleaned up. Secretly, he hoped he could look around, and Norton seemed not to mind. Their host pointed him towards the rickety stairs, which Cassius climbed with weary steps. He looked around the upstairs hallway and found one of the guest rooms. The knob almost fell apart as he closed the door behind him; he had to use his fingernails to turn the loose screws back into place.

When silence finally fell around him, he threw his bag on the floor and leaned the Remington against it, but kept his handgun and knife with him. He walked to the window and looked out.

From that height, Cassius could observe Norton's empire. He could see the windmill the scientist had set up beside the farmhouse, the fields beyond the building, partially surrounded by the forest. The view was spoiled only by the wires that ran up and down the estate and the electronic waste piled up beside the run-down shed.

Cassius sighed deeply, trying to resist the fatigue forcing his eyes to close. He massaged his face, then washed and changed clothes in the bathroom attached to the puritanically furnished guest room. He didn't have the strength left to shave and he carelessly folded his laundry into his bag. Only then did he notice the closet at the other end of the room. There were women's clothes and boxes inside. The boxes were filled with old stuff, and on top of one was a laptop in good condition.

Cassius plugged the laptop charger into the outlet, then flipped open the top and waited, drumming his fingers on the aluminum case. A few seconds after pressing the power button, the device came to life and he couldn't believe his eyes. It had been many years since he had seen a working computer, and although the device crackled loudly, its ancient fan suffering, it worked. It would serve his purpose.

His throat tightened as he remembered something. From his bag, he pulled out the flat metal box wrapped in a striped cloth that held the fragments of his past. He opened the lid and rummaged through the bits and pieces, then took a flash drive from the pile. Cassius plugged the drive into the laptop and waited as the device recognized it. He hesitated before he finally opened the folder that contained the memories of his old life. He didn't need to search through the photos; he clicked on one instinctively.

It took a few seconds for the machine to open the file, but finally the photo, taken before their last Thanksgiving together, appeared on the screen. He focused only on the faces. His wife's proud smile as she rested her hand contentedly on her baby bump in the armchair in front of the TV. His son frolicking on the couch with black paint under his eyes like a football player, his father's watch on his wrist, his knee pads still on his legs. Barefoot, because he hated socks so much.

Cassius stared hungrily at the images on the flash drive and soon forgot where he was, what was happening around him. He no longer cared about danger, questions, uncertainty. He simply collapsed onto the bed and closed his eyes for a moment.

It turned into long hours.

4.

Abigail stepped out of the downstairs bathroom, drying her wet hair and wearing clean clothes. Her body was still tingling from the hot water and she could smell the soap in her nose. A mist was billowing from the room, which she watched with fascination at first, having not seen anything like it for some time. She rubbed her hair once more and spread the wet towel on one of the chairs.

The living room was silent, except for the sound of Megan breathing on the sofa. The others were nowhere to be seen; even Norton was gone. Abigail shuffled comfortably to the table where Soxy was waiting for her excitedly in his box. Hearing the footsteps, Megan turned to the other side, huffing loudly to find the most comfortable position, and watched the girl with the puppy.

"I fed him while you were bathing," she said in a sleepy voice. Abigail nodded gratefully.

"Are you feeling alright?"

"Sure," Megan said, but her answer wasn't convincing. She slid her hand gently over her stomach. "It's just that since we've been here, the baby hasn't moved."

"It's gonna be okay," Abigail tried to reassure her. "Believe me: once we get there, you won't be able to keep that big boy inside."

"Or big girl."

They laughed at the same time. Meanwhile, Abigail took Soxy out of his box and set the squirming furball on the floor to play freely.

Watching the puppy find his feet, she thought of how little she could be with him, just when he needed it most.

"And you?" Megan asked after a beat of silence. "I can see something's bothering you, too."

Abigail shrugged, but she worried that she'd done it too quickly and had given herself away. She couldn't take her eyes off Soxy, however, whose paws were drumming on the wooden floor. In her mind she kept thinking that maybe she had done something stupid to the puppy. *What if he had a father? Maybe he was hunting, or who knows where he was, and on his way back to his pups.* And she'd taken Soxy away from his family.

"Everything's cool." She wanted to choke back the rest of her fears, but eventually the rush of honesty won. "I used to think we could save everyone if we just wanted to, but I'm afraid we won't be able to this time."

"Nonsense!" Megan said after some hesitation. "We're very close; nothing can stop us now! You heard Norton, he's taking us to the boat-town tomorrow, and then we can forget all this horror. Sounds like a good plan, doesn't it?"

"Like a great plan."

Megan struggled to her feet and, with her hands around her waist, headed for the bathroom. She tried to keep her upper body balanced, but she wobbled and stumbled.

"I think it's time to take a shower. In the meantime, I'm only going to think about positive things. And maybe I'll finally be inspired to give her a name, because Belle seems like a lousy idea at the moment."

When she reached the bathroom door, she stopped and turned back to Abigail.

"I'm grateful to you for saving us, though. And whatever happens to me, if my child is born and healthy, it will all have made sense."

After the bathroom door closed behind Megan, Abigail turned back to Soxy, who was playing with a sheet of paper. She tried to believe what she was hearing, that even the smallest success, even the saving of a single soul, mattered in this world. Soxy, of course, was not bothered by Abigail's internal struggle. He was happily chewing on the fully typed paper that had fallen from the table.

"Hey, stop that!" she said, picking the puppy up off the floor. Only then did she notice what was written on the paper: NEW WORLD MANIFESTO, with Norton's name underneath as the author.

Strange, she thought, but considered it inappropriate to continue reading the text of the eccentric man.

5.

When Cassius woke up, it was late afternoon. The lights outside were dimmed, the laptop was in sleep mode, and there was no noise filtering in from the hallway. He took a deep breath and cracked his joints. He chided himself for his irresponsibility, and after a few seconds of listening, he stood up and walked downstairs, his bag in his hand and his gun slung over his shoulder.

Downstairs he found David sitting in the kitchen alone with a mug of tea in his hand. Through the window he could see Abigail playing with Soxy on the porch and the sound of running water was filtering in from the bathroom. Megan was probably splashing around.

"I can't recall the last time we had more than three hours' peace," the young man sighed as he caught sight of Cassius, whose head almost scraped the lower ceiling of the kitchen, "and now I'm sitting here with a hot cup of tea in my hand, and if all goes well, we can sleep tonight in a soft bed with clean blankets."

Cassius glanced anxiously back towards the living room.

"Let's not get too carried away, and that's not a suggestion! Anything could have happened."

"Fortunately, nothing did."

"Yes, fortunately." Cassius shook his head, walked to the kitchen window, and looked out. He didn't see any movement at the back; everything seemed quiet between the farmhouse and the woods. "Where is our host, by the way?"

David shrugged.

"In the cellar, which he turned into a lab. He said he still had some work to do, but he'd be happy to show us what he's been working on this evening."

"It's fascinating."

"Believe me, it is. While you were asleep, the guy took me on a tour and showed me everything."

Everything? I doubt it. Cassius scratched his nose. Something was bothering him, and although he couldn't explain why, he felt that the house had an oppressive atmosphere. The more time he spent within its walls, the more the strange feeling soaked into him.

"This place is a gold mine," David went on. "Even in the boat-town they don't have stuff like this. I don't see why they haven't come begging from this guy yet. I mean, I could restart the whole of civilization with half of these inventions. If I could take them all, I'd make myself president in five years and lead the attack on the ferals from the newly rebuilt White House."

David sighed and sipped his tea. Cassius went to the cupboard, found a mug, sniffed into the bottle of tea leaves, and then boiled himself some water. He made sure not to say anything, but David was not at all embarrassed by his lack of reaction, and didn't let up.

"Get this. The dude has a hydroponic smart greenhouse. You can control the crops with a freakin' cell phone, and you can shape the microenvironment of the greenhouse however you want. It's like a glass cabinet. You could just make as many as you want for as many people as need it."

"I'm impressed."

"You better be, man. With the motion-sensor security system, you don't need as many guards. Thanks to the beast repellent, you can say goodbye to constant dread. And who knows, we might even find a cure. Oh, and I saved the best for last! The next gadget the dude is working on will not only control or keep the ferals at bay, but will also be able to attract them from up to a hundred miles away. Like a magnet... Can you imagine what that means?"

"I'm trying to..."

"You could gather all the ferals in the area and isolate them. And then we could tell the outside world that there's hope, and ask them to send help. Just thinking about it gives me goosebumps."

"I bet it's the only thing the outside world is waiting for."

The water boiled and Cassius filled the mug and let the tea leaves soak. He sighed.

"Don't get too excited, Mr. President! We have to reach the boat-town first."

David let go of the mug and leaned back in his chair.

"Yeah, yeah… Has anyone ever told you you're a killjoy?"

"Yes, and I still have the thank-you cards."

6.

At dusk, they met in the living room, rested and fresh. They could have done with more sleep, but they were well enough for the circumstances. By the time the sun dipped over the dim and hilly horizon, they had forgotten that just hours earlier the four of them had been staring death in the face. David and Megan sat on the couch, Abigail in one of the armchairs, and Cassius alone by the window seat where he could see every corner of the room and where his back was protected. He studied the nearby bookshelf, which, to his surprise, was lined not only with scientific books but also with political and philosophical ones. *The Basic Laws of Human Stupidity... Radical Curiosity... The Quest for Cosmic Justice... The Dawn of Everything...* However, Cassius didn't attribute much significance to which books were present, as he himself was trying to read everything he could find. *Seven years after the Breakdown, you can't be picky!*

By the time they all settled down, Norton had arrived from the kitchen with a familiar smile on his face. The tray in his hand held one orange drink and four red ones. He wore brown corduroys and a shirt of a color that did not match, a scarf around his neck, and wool-lined slippers instead of shoes. Balancing the tray as he reached his guests, Norton handed them their drinks, his mouth clenched to make sure that not a drop spilled from the glasses. The orange refreshment was passed to Megan, who looked around in disappointment and enviously watched the others.

"Here we go!" the scientist said. "Non-alcoholic for the mother-to-be, and a homemade surprise for the rest of us. I am extremely proud of it."

Abigail took the glass with a broad grin, but didn't drink

immediately. David knocked back the red liquor without thinking after a toast in the air.

"Ahhhh," Norton clicked his tongue, closing his eyes. "That was good!"

"Cheers!" Abigail said, somewhat embarrassed, and despite Cassius' stern look, guzzled the second alcoholic drink of her life. He could see her gasping for breath and tears welling in her eyes, but he was determined not to say a word this time. *Maybe I really should loosen the reins,* he thought, and leaned against the window frame. He held the glass in one hand and put the other on his hip, close to his pistol, trying to convince himself that they might be safe. *After all, what evil motives could a foolish scientist have?* He took another look around the living room, searching for signs that might tell him Norton's true intentions, but saw nothing suspicious.

"Here's to dear old Boston!" came the reply from a satisfied David, and even Megan pretended that the yellow juice was some cardiotonic. Cassius was the last to go, and he eyed his glass distrustfully for a few seconds more before slowly taking a sip. It was a strong, luscious drink, a fruit spirit of some kind, and he felt the heat draining down his throat finally dissolve into his body, and calmness flood every part of him.

After they'd finished clearing their throats, Megan grabbed David's empty glass and took a sniff, but after a few drags she felt ashamed. Norton collected the glasses and shuffled out with them into the kitchen, bustling about like a maniac housewife. On the way back, he straightened something on a shelf, then wiped the wet stain David's glass had left on the coffee table with a cloth. When he had finished cleaning, he sat down in the armchair in front of the fireplace and looked around with crossed fingers.

"How long you been living here?" Cassius broke the awkward silence.

"Almost twenty years. First with my wife, and now... now alone," Norton answered, fiddling with his wedding ring.

"Didn't the people in the boat-town ask for your help?" Abigail soothed her throat with more of the fruity drink.

"Why would they? If they've made it this long, they certainly have their own resources. And as for me, I am well off here. I was fine before, when civilization hadn't, how shall I say, sped up and driven into the abyss like a madman. No, I never cared for the glamour of society, the hustle and bustle of the big city. My wife and I only ever went to Headland for work at the most, because the real life is here. Away from all distractions."

"I hear you, buddy," Cassius said. Abigail glared at him sternly.

"But at least I understand why you don't want to live in the boat-town," David glanced around. "Even I would love to have a place like this, with all this stuff. I don't want any competition, but I could grow a helluva Mary Jane here."

"I'll take that as a compliment," Norton winked. "Don't get me wrong, they seem like nice people down there, though we rarely talk on the radio. If we have new information, we share it, but apart from that we don't seek each other's company. Why would I force it? My place is here, with my research, as difficult as it is alone. Because I firmly believe that you don't just leave it at the first obstacle, you face it head on and try to make the world a better place. Small at first, and who knows, maybe one day I can dream bigger."

"Amen, my man," David said bitterly. Megan slid her hand down his leg and squeezed his thigh. David hissed and looked angrily at his sister. Seeing the strict look on her face, Norton raised his hand in a conciliatory gesture, his voice softening.

"But I do acknowledge that an unborn child needs a safe environment, and there are nurses in the boat-town. Perfect place for you, perfect choice."

Megan nodded, and their host continued. Norton was relishing the opportunity to perform; his face flushed with excitement, gesticulating wider and wider as he monologued.

"I've got nothing against those who live in a colony, it's just I don't understand this fitful adherence to the old things. Trying to recreate society, huh? For what? It was chaos before. At best we didn't eat each other. No wonder Nature eventually stirred the pot."

"I beg your pardon?" David said. Norton just smiled at the stunned looks on the faces of his guests.

"Come on, you know exactly what I mean. Why have we gone this far in the first place. Eight billion people, a selfish, self-serving, back-stabbing lot, all trying to get by, and not giving a shit about the consequences. There is not enough food, not enough water, not enough resources, but we need more and more of everything, we need to harp on endlessly. What happened was completely necessary."

Abigail turned her head away; she was not prepared for what had started out as a light conversation to take such a turn. Cassius felt his body tense, but he couldn't tell what was bothering him. Megan was the first to react. She brushed a chestnut lock of hair out of her eyes and gave Norton a level stare, like a teacher reprimanding a student.

"That's not a nice thing to say! What happened was terrible..."

"It's beside the point! It was heavenly for the virus that infected us. For us humans, it was just a stage in the never-ending process of evolution."

"A stage?" Cassius scratched his forehead. For some reason, the effects of the alcohol refused to subside; his ears were on fire and his throat was burning hot. What he had heard set off an alarm in his head, which for some reason his conscience quickly shuffled off. A strange, pleasant numbness flooded his body. His normally alert mind was wandering, but he didn't notice it at first. He blamed it on the long journey and the torture of the past few days. *And when was the last time I drank? Who knows, maybe...*

A shudder passed over him. *Concentrate!*

"Exactly, a stage," Norton kept going with his parable. "After all, that is what evolution is all about. The strong survive, the weak perish. Selection works, and rightly so, for only the strong should survive."

"That sounds a bit cruel," Megan said. Her voice was thin and unsteady by then. She broke out of her strict teacher role and sank into the sofa. Norton was emboldened and continued, spectacularly apologetic.

"Oh, don't worry, darling, it's just my opinion. I'm sure you're all sorry for what's happened, but I don't see any change. One violent world has been replaced by another, just like it happened so many times in our history. The Neanderthal was eventually defeated by Homo sapiens sapiens, and evolution did not stop then, nor will it stop now!"

Norton leaned forward and lifted a long chestnut hair from the coffee table with the tip of his index finger.

"Just think about it! Due to climate change, the genetic mutations responsible for ginger hair may slowly disappear, wisdom teeth may no longer be needed, and we may soon have no little toes. It's all just a stage, a fact of life, so no need to be scared."

"How the hell can you compare a devastating virus to redheads?" Megan blurted out, but she slurred her words in the middle of the question, and she even giggled at the end. It was obvious that she didn't understand this behavior. She clasped her hands shyly over her mouth, her eyes downcast, and blushed.

David gave a tense look at his sister, but Norton was not offended, and with a light movement he swept the long hair to the ground. He shrugged.

"How can I compare? Nature doesn't care what we think, the world still changes and we change with it. Your pretty little chin is just another proof of the constant mutation. As our jaws have got smaller, our brains have grown, tools have been made, languages have been created, science has been developed, and sensations have been made. Thousands of years ago, we built pyramids and pantheons, and we looked at the stars without telescopes. We have become superior, but also conceited and arrogant. We believed that the world revolved around us. And Nature... or God, the great Gaia, call it what you will, realized that it was all a big mistake. A top predator that eats up its resources and exploits others is destined for destruction. And evolution is always a correction, my friends. Homo... sapiens... ferox, if I want to be so stylish."

"I sort of feel like you're supporting the ferals," Cassius remarked. He put his right hand to the handle of his knife, but was careful not to be too conspicuous.

"I'm just a neutral observer... a realist, if you like, nothing more!" Norton excused himself and looked at Cassius with a penetrating gaze. An inexplicable thrill crept up his spine. His forehead was sweating, his breathing was getting heavier, yet he did not panic. Somehow, his ever-fluttering brain now seeming to be on vacation. Although he was determined to be cautious, he would have liked to sit down, even to lie down on the sofa.

Abigail, too, was more quiet than usual. She tucked her legs under herself and tilted her head back, only her eyes fluttering occasionally. Megan took a deep breath. David suppressed a yawn and shook his head. Slowly, all four of them slipped into a strange, languid state.

Norton glanced at his watch, then got up, strolled to his flowers, and sprayed water on one of the plants with his sprinkler.

"At first, I also believed that there was hope, but I soon realized that the Silent Zone would sooner or later break down the barriers, and generations later there would be nothing we could do about it. That is the law of the Universe. From civilized naivety back to the instinct of the beast. Back to where we started. Isn't that poetic?" he asked, and laughed, but only silence answered. Abigail sniffed and scratched her nose. She wore the expression of someone who after a moment of confusion was trying to handle the whole thing like a casual conversation, where friends contemplate the matters of the world over a campfire and some Bud Light.

"I don't know about you, but I'd rather die than be rabid," she said in a peevish, sleepy voice.

"That's nonsense, my dear! Living is always better than dying."

"Yuck!" Abigail shuddered. She formed the words slowly, watching her host with sleepy eyes. "I don't even want to imagine living as a feral."

"My beloved wife always said it was like being stupid," Norton smiled, and for a moment he pondered. "You don't know about it; you just exist, and that's all. You wouldn't believe the strange things I've observed in the ferals over the years... Strange, yet uplifting things. There's more of their old selves in them than you could imagine. I have seen some holding on tenaciously to the things of their lost life, a ring, a dress..."

"That's bullshit!" Cassius snorted. His body felt like lead, but he was still trying to fight it. "It could be a coincidence..."

"Why would it be? It may seem odd, I know, but the ferals may be more than mindless beasts, and perhaps we need not fear that one day we'll be transformed. That is the world order!"

Megan, who had been resting her head on David's shoulder, slowly leaned into his lap, her hair hanging in her face, before she fell asleep.

"Why don't we think of a way to reverse all this?" David asked. "Maybe we can, can't we? There must be a cure!"

Norton shook his head and looked at the young man as if he was a kindergartener who had just asked why there wasn't always a weekend and why every day couldn't be his birthday.

"There is no reversing it and no cure. Once that virus enters your body, it's over, you might as well shoot yourself in the head. But why destroy them, I ask?"

"Maybe because nobody wants to live like this!" Cassius muttered. Instead of thundering words, his voice was weak, his torso bent forward, and his hand had long since slipped from the hilt of his knife.

"You only think that way until you transform," Norton replied. Through the gloom of his languor, Cassius could still see their host's smile turn into a bizarre snarl, and his teeth flash. "As strong as you think you are, you'll only focus on survival."

"But it's... but it's... it's still... cruel... it can't... be," David gasped, his eyelids slowly giving up the fight. He swallowed hard, then his head jerked back up. Norton didn't mind the apparent inattentiveness.

"Life is cruel, and those who have resisted so far have perished, just like everyone else. We can fight to the last hour, but it's useless." He indulged in a long pause, holding up his index finger. "Or we can help Nature achieve what it wants. We can even be its allies at last, instead of the enemies we have always been."

Norton smiled to see Megan and David unconscious, then glanced at Abigail, who was staring ahead as if stoned. The girl was swaying back and forth with her mouth half open, and in less than a minute she passed out.

Cassius's knees buckled and he strained like hell to regain his balance. A shuddering thrill overcame him as his mind was flooded with a clear moment of realization. As his body struggled to stay awake, he looked up with a vengeful glance at Norton, who wiped his glasses and spread his hands.

"Well, I'd like to offer you another drink, but I'm afraid we've run out of time," he said with a sigh. Cassius held out his hand to the man, but he had no strength left to reach him, to reach any of his long-fought goals; his fingers gripped the air.

"You drugged... us, you bastard!"

Norton crouched down beside him, their faces so close that Cassius could see the madness in the scientist's poison-green eyes.

"As I said, life is cruel."

That was the last thing Cassius remembered, then he began to plummet towards the endless darkness.

7.

The root cellar was musty and dark; Cassius could barely see. It took a few minutes for him to regain full consciousness, to get used to the dimness, and for his mind to clear after the long stupor. He felt the rope tighten on his wrist and his nose filled with a moldy, stale smell that reminded him of the time when, as a child, they had wandered into Fraser's barn and found old guns in a hideout under the floor. Then the memory faded, replaced by a haunting reality. He soon realized, from the metallic screech and the pain that split his shoulder, that he had been hung from a drainpipe.

Cassius raised his head to look around. He was in a spacious but low room that had once been used as a pantry, but was now packed with boxes and gadgets, both large and small. The only source of light was a bulb that hung from the ceiling, shining down on a wide white table with scattered electronics and notepads with a narrow aisle around it, surrounded by junk stacked waist-high. The Remington leaned against the table and his bag was on a nearby chair, unzipped. The cellar wall was made of ashlar, the floor of concrete slabs, and the far edges of the room were completely dark; the light bulb illuminated only their immediate surroundings. There was no escape route.

Cassius moved his limbs to make sure everything was working properly. His legs were free, but his back and head were in excruciating pain. He dared not imagine how they had been dragged from the living room; their host had probably not been gentle with them.

The first sound he heard was David's voice; his indistinct whimpering was followed by Megan's panting, but nothing more. Cassius turned his head in fright, and it was many long seconds later that he noticed Abigail, still unconscious. All four of them were bound and hung by their hands, except Abigail who was not in line with them. She dangled on a hook a bit farther, next to the table.

"What happened? Where are we?" David murmured, as Megan cried out beside him. She was in a terrible state, her face contorted in agony, her forehead beaded with sweat.

"We were drugged by that bastard. He put something in our drinks," Cassius groaned, watching Megan anxiously. "You okay?"

She moaned and hunched over, shaking her head only when the pain eased a little. She tried to free her hand to touch her stomach, but the rope wouldn't let her move that far.

"What the hell does he want from us?" David turned his head in desperation.

"I don't know," Cassius said, then he hissed towards Abigail, who had finally come around. "Hey! Nod if you're all right!"

Abigail squinted, her eyes hurt by the light, but finally nodded. It occurred to Cassius for the first time that she might be separated from them for a reason. He was overwhelmed with horror, and looked up in despair at the rope restraining his hands, which was looped through a rusty metal pipe. The pipe ran across the ceiling, barely supporting the weight of the three of them. It bent and moved, and the concrete wall crumbled around it, but he couldn't tell if he would have the time or strength to free them.

Cassius cursed himself for his carelessness. *That's why we trust no one*, then his angry thoughts were replaced by pleading as he jerked on the drainpipe running above them. *Please...* to no use. The loose metal pipe shuddered, but held, despite his and David's futile attempts.

From a far corner of the cellar, they heard a rustling sound. Cassius snapped his head up and yelled into the darkness, his face contorted. "Are you there, you bastard?"

Nothing. At first only the echo answered, followed by a strange wheezing. David stopped tugging at the metal pipe and froze. Megan began to cry.

"It's gonna be all right!" Cassius reassured her. "The most important thing now is to..."

The sound of approaching footsteps interrupted his words. In a white cloak, Norton emerged from the edge of light and darkness. He walked slowly and thoughtfully to the table, like some demonic apparition. In his left hand he held Soxy's box. In the other he wore a beast repellent, similar to the one he had worn before, but smaller and more modern. Clearly an upgraded version.

Norton looked them up and down. A sinister smile played on the edge of his mouth, which vanished in a moment, replaced by a condescending grimace. Abigail cried out in despair when she saw the box in Norton's hand.

"Don't you dare touch him, you hear me?"

"Hey, what the hell do you want from us?" Cassius demanded, cutting her off.

Norton didn't respond, only moved his lips as if talking to himself. He placed the box carefully on the table, then picked up a voice recorder from the top of a stack of papers and pressed the RECORD button. His deep, resonant voice echoed off the cellar walls.

"Radio Frequency Motivator, Test Eighteen. Participants: four travelers I found in Headland. Two male, two female. One pregnant. Condition of the subjects: satisfactory. Bonus: a puppy, perhaps a month old, mixed breed."

Norton touched Soxy on the head, but something happened that he hadn't expected. The puppy growled and snapped at Norton's finger.

"Huh, what a beast." He snatched his hand away and just chuckled. "I'd better watch out, or it might bite me. I hope it's not rabid..."

"Please, let us go!" Megan whimpered.

Norton pressed the STOP button on the voice recorder. The smile returned to his face, but it expressed no grace: the grin was more threatening than empathetic.

"Oh, don't you worry, darling, I will let all of you go, but I have work to do first. A mission, if you will, and what I do, I do in order to heal the world."

"Heal? How?" David asked. "You said there was no cure."

"None that you'd desire!" Norton stepped closer to Abigail. "There are a thousand ways and means of healing. And if Nature wills it so, I shall bring salvation to a world that has hungered for it so long."

Abigail glanced defiantly at Norton. Cassius tugged at the rope that bound his hands.

"Leave her alone!" he hissed, trying to free himself. The loose metal pipe was still holding, so he put his full weight on the pipe as hard as he could.

Norton, meanwhile, made a few twists on the beast repellent and offhandedly commented, "If you'll take my advice, save your strength, you'll need it! You're not the first to hang there."

After the final adjustment, the beast repellent glove began to hum softly, its diode flashing green, and a strange creaking in the far, dark corner of the cellar followed the fine-tuning of the device. Cassius turned his head towards the sound in fright, and by then he felt in every part of his being that something worse was about to happen than he had previously expected.

"Don't do anything stupid!" he shouted, hoping to get Norton's attention, but the man didn't move from the table, just shook his head.

"Stupid? I'm not going to do anything stupid... I've got it all planned out!"

"Damned bastard!" Abigail's face contorted into an angry grimace, and Norton turned to her with a menacing glare, raised his gloved hand, and flexed his fingers, signaling that he was ready.

Shit, Cassius thought.

"Hey, hey, buddy! You can still let us go, I promise we won't hurt you!" He tried to distract the scientist. "I'm sure you don't really want to hurt us. Don't do this!"

"Of course I don't want to hurt you. Still, I must," Norton said. He was silent for a moment, but he couldn't resist the temptation. He walked around the table, stepped over to them, and continued. "I know what you're thinking. You think I'm evil, killing innocent people just for fun, but I'm just a messenger for the new world. The time of mankind is over. Of that, I'm sure."

"You're crazy!" sputtered David, then spat into the scientist's eyes. Norton wiped his face with a monogrammed handkerchief, and when he finished, disgust was replaced by a mocking smile. He clenched his fist and punched David. Megan screamed, and Cassius tugged on the metal pipe again. He could feel that his efforts had already had an impact. He could swear that he was getting close, that the pipe was coming loose.

"All right, let me tell you a secret, but don't tell anyone," Norton said and tucked the handkerchief in his pockets so carelessly that the corner of the textile stuck out. "There is no redemption, there is no cure, because we are suffering for a reason."

Thick beads of sweat rolled down David's forehead and the veins in his neck bulged as Norton leaned closer. "What the hell are you talking about, you idiot?"

"What am I talking about? Nature has decided to push us back into the twilight from whence we came. Where we really belong."

Megan shook her head, pleading. "You could save others. Why don't you help them?"

"We tried long ago, as God is my witness, we tried! We started all this," Norton said, waving his gloved hand around, "to undo the horrors, but I realized I'd gone astray. The virus should not be destroyed, but given a way to spread freely and return the peace to the Earth we ourselves have driven away! The thinking, selfish man... destroyer of his own world..."

The blood ran from Cassius' face.

"You want to deliberately spread the virus!"

Norton turned his head to the ceiling and burst out laughing with pride.

"Indeed, I do, and I've never been so certain of anything in my life! I'm so excited I can't even tell you!" Norton punched the air with uncontainable enthusiasm. When he calmed down, he gave Cassius a disparaging look. "You'll be a Delta at best before you die of permanent deformity, but the girl... the girl might even become a Beta. And the unborn child, an Alpha... Do you know what I'm talking about? An Alpha, in my army..."

Megan sobbed. Cassius closed his eyes in disbelief.

"What army?

"Soon there will be enough of us to attack the man-eaters, and when Headland is mine and my pack is even stronger, then the boat-town is next. I will lead mankind into a new era where we can live in harmony with Nature once more." Norton paused briefly, and tears appeared in his eyes. "Where there is no politics, no war, no exploitation."

Norton gave another twist on the beast repellent, which amplified the muttering from the corner and the wheezing was replaced with an animal growl.

"I know how you feel!" Cassius gabbled, trying to buy some time.

"I felt the same after losing my family. But revenge is not the answer. Your wife wouldn't want you to!"

"Keep my wife out of this!" Norton shouted, squeezing Cassius's throat with his left hand as hard as he could. Cassius felt the fingers pressing in on his windpipe, felt nausea and shortness of breath blurring the world around him, but he could still hear Megan and Abigail's desperate screams clearly.

"It's not too late. You could still make it right!" Megan pleaded with Norton. "There is hope, believe me!"

"Darling, you still don't understand?" Norton let go of Cassius's throat and stepped in front of Megan. The ominous sounds intensified in the corner. "I am working to make everything right! You look like someone who fought against the system as a youngster, so I use the lingo you understand. I'm gonna save the planet… just not the way you wanted."

He stroked her cheek tenderly, but Megan defiantly pulled back her head, and the sudden movement made her dress slip aside. She tried to cover her neck, but Norton forcibly grabbed her chin and turned her around so that the bite mark was visible. A wound that, though healed, still showed the perfect outline of a feral's jaw.

"Hey, leave her alone!" David kicked, but Norton ignored him. His face went white at the recognition.

"You've been bitten... How is that possible?"

Cassius took another pull on the pipe. Norton gave a low chuckle.

"Well, that's new even to me, but beggars can't be choosers!" After a moment's hesitation, Norton picked up a knife from the table and cut Megan's rope. She would have collapsed if the crazy scientist hadn't caught her and dragged her to the table.

"Hey, what are you doing?" Cassius shouted at the top of his lungs, but Norton didn't stop, even when Megan tried to bite him. She screamed and struggled, but she was so weak that she had no chance to get away.

"Stop it!" Norton snapped at her. When they got to the table, he gently but firmly pushed her down into a chair and slapped her across the face. Megan raised her hand to her cheek, looking up at him with bloodshot eyes.

"You'll rot in the deepest pit of hell for this!"

"Oh, what elegant language! But don't deceive yourself that you're important to me, darling! There are still a few slaps where that came from, and my experiments don't need you to be conscious! So sit tight, and enjoy the show!" Norton looked at Abigail with his hands on his hips, clicking his fingers in satisfaction.

""Where was I? Ah, yes... You'll make a wonderful Beta, I'm sure! A strong specimen who can survive anything," he said and started to back away. The diode of the beast repellent flickered and the cellar virtually exploded with clamorous sound from the dark corner, the demonic roar from the depths mingling with the clatter of metal. Their faces flushed with horror, and Norton's smile turned into a sneer.

"And since you asked about my wife," he winked playfully before switching on another light, "don't you want to meet her?"

They all groaned at the same time as the shadows were illuminated by a glimmering light. Beside the stairs leading up to the surface, in a metal cage set tightly against the wall, a female Delta raged, ready to attack.

8.

Abigail tensed every muscle in her body as she realized she was to be the Delta's first target. She turned her gaze to the table, where Soxy was whimpering in his box, but she knew that if she didn't concentrate now, it would be over for her. She took a deep breath and tried to come up with a hasty plan, anything that would give her at least some chance of survival, but her mind kept racing back and forth. *Come on!*

She looked at Cassius, who was watching her and the frenzied Delta, tugging harder and harder at the metal pipe that squeaked above him, releasing concrete dust as the only proof his efforts were having an impact. Norton didn't mind in the least. The smile returned to the crazy scientist's face, but the female Delta apparently didn't feel the same for him, for when Norton went near the cage, the feral immediately latched onto the bars and tried to grab him. Norton recoiled at the sight of the claws and quickly pressed something on the beast repellent. The female Delta screamed and threw itself onto the concrete floor. From there, it looked at them all in confusion.

"There's still some adjustments to be made, but that's what the test phase is for, isn't it?" he excused himself. *So much for the ferals and their clinging to their past.* Abigail glanced up at the hook in the ceiling from which she had been hung and saw that the stoutly woven rope could not be torn and the metal peg in the wall would not budge.

The lock clicked and the metal door creaked as Norton carefully opened the cage. Abigail screamed, but the Delta had not yet attacked. The beast repellent wouldn't let her. The feral crawled out of her cage, seemingly still searching for strength as it snapped its jaws at Norton and Abigail.

The crazy scientist raised his hand and looked at the desperately swaying girl.

"You needn't worry, my dear! I promise it won't hurt, it's just a bite. We'll be done in no time." Then he winked like a pediatrician at his little patient. "You really are lucky! The last device didn't work nearly so well, and my beloved wife had almost torn everyone to pieces before I could stop her."

Norton gave a signal and pointed to Abigail with his gloved hand. The Delta threw herself at the girl, who reacted just in time. She grabbed the rope and pulled herself up, then kicked her attacker with her foot as hard as she could. The weakened feral was expecting easy prey, so the kick took it by surprise and the momentum sent it flying straight at Norton. They both slammed into the opposite wall, then slid down it. The feral yowled from the proximity of the repellent and threw herself against the cage to get as far away from the misery-inducing gadget as possible.

Norton didn't delay either. He fumbled his way to the table, cursing, but he could barely stand up. His face was a mixture of incomprehension and horror, his whole body shaking.

"Damn it..."

Once he got up, it was time for the next surprise. Megan yelled a battle cry from her nearby chair and stamped on Norton's ankle, which crumbled under the blow. The bone cracked, and a painful scream echoed through the room.

Cassius's veins froze at the sight, but the shock lasted only a few seconds. Gathering all his strength, he gave another yank on the metal pipe, which finally gave way, dropping him and David to their knees. The falling pipe clattered to the floor, stirring the dust that had gathered there. David was the first to break free and though his hands were still tied he ran to Megan, just in time. The feral cowering beside the metal cage had regained its strength and attacked. It dodged Norton, who was screeching in fear as he cowered behind the repellent, and threw itself straight at Megan.

But David intervened. He overturned the table and threw his shoulders against the Delta. Together they fell into one of the larger piles of boxes, scattering the contents everywhere. Cassius finally freed his hands. Without a second thought, he jumped to the table, picked up the Remington, aimed it at the Delta, and pulled the trigger. He fired a hail of bullets at the feral as Norton cried out in despair. Cassius finally turned the gun on the scientist, but he pulled the trigger in vain: it clicked empty. His face contorted, he trembled with rage; he had acted on instinct, unaware that he had discharged the entire magazine into the feral.

When the realization dawned on him, he struck Norton with the gunstock, and the scientist collapsed unconscious to the cellar floor. Cassius dropped the Remington, grabbed the knife from the table, and freed Abigail. She jumped into his arms, but the joy didn't last long.

They turned as they heard Megan's wail. She was helping David up, but could no longer hold on and fell to her knees. Cassius and Abigail were there in an instant. He reached under her arm, but he could see in Megan's eyes that something was terribly wrong.

She was holding her stomach with both hands and shaking all over. "I think my water just broke!"

The stunned silence lasted for long seconds.

"Let's get out of here!" Cassius said. Still supporting Megan, he grabbed his bag, waiting for Abigail to get Soxy to safety, then motioned with his head. *Up,* out of this dungeon.

9.

After struggling up the concrete stairs of the narrow passage, they fell out of the door and glanced back towards the dim cellar, terrified and gasping for breath. No one followed them. Cassius quickly slammed the heavy wooden door shut and pushed a cabinet in front of it, but the makeshift solution didn't seem very sturdy. *I should have crushed the life out of the bastard,* he thought, but it would be insane to go back and correct the mistake.

"Get your stuff!" he ordered.

Abigail led Megan to the backpacks in the hallway. David grabbed a walkie-talkie from the table, but tripped over something and fell to his knees. He retched and shook silently before finally rousing himself and getting to his feet. He tried to straighten his back and, seeing the looks of concern, he rallied and put on a carefree face, while showing them the walkie he had just snatched.

"We've gotta warn the boat-town that we're coming. I don't want to be an uninvited guest," David said to Cassius.

In less than a minute, they were on their way. Abigail tucked Soxy into the bottom of her bag and decided to carry the siblings' belongings so that David would only have to deal with his sister. Cassius found the key fob to the Mach-E, then hurried forward before either of them could touch the door knob.

"Wait," he said to Abigail, and peered cautiously out the front window. The moon illuminated the area in front of the farmhouse, but the woods were in total darkness; a pack of ferals might be waiting for them in the trees.

"What is it?" Abigail asked anxiously.

"The bastard said he would soon have enough soldiers."

Abigail's eyes widened at the realization.

"Ferals? But he said the house was protected by a security system."

"Yeah, and he would never have lied," Cassius replied sarcastically. He checked his gun. The Glock was half empty, and Abigail couldn't have much ammo left either. If they couldn't get the car to work, they would have neither the strength, the time, nor the bullets to fight their way to the boat-town.

Megan groaned and clutched her stomach.

"Okay, so what can we do?" David snapped, seeming to find it harder and harder to hold the collapsing woman. "We can't just hang about here forever!"

Cassius looked around once more, then waved a finger at them to be quiet.

"Don't get distracted, don't make any noise! Abigail and I will cover you; go straight to the car! Ready?"

The answer was a sharp nod. Cassius turned the door handle and stepped out into the silent night. Abigail followed the siblings. She watched the dark forest with her breath held, listening to the trees whispering in the soft wind. She paused for a moment to peer into the black mass of night, which then fell silent, as if the vastness itself were preparing for one final battle.

Cassius shook away the haunting thrill of the trees stretching skyward before his eyes, obscuring the twinkling moon and stars, cutting them off from the outside world.

David staggered with Megan to where the car was parked in the open garage. Cassius kept his eyes on the trees the whole time, but helped them the last few yards. *You're seeing things... You can do it, come on!* The young man opened the door and pushed his sister in. She accidentally touched his right arm as she clambered onto the seat.

David hissed and pulled his hand away, his eyes flashing, though it was unclear whether it was from pain or sudden rage. After realizing his mistake, he tried to act as if nothing had happened, but by then three wide-open pairs of eyes were staring at him in shock. The young man took a hesitant step backwards, but Cassius immediately grabbed him.

"Did you get bitten?"

"No."

"Show me."

David shook his head. Cassius squeezed the young man's right hand, twisting it towards himself. David cried out, while the others were horrified to see the hasty bandage wrapped around his wrist and the bleeding bite underneath. Megan groaned, tears welling in her eyes as the realization hit her, and Abigail promptly looked at Cassius as if she knew exactly what he was up to. After seconds of shock, David pulled his hand away.

"I'm fine! I don't feel anything," he fulminated. He involuntarily hid his injured, trembling arm behind him. "Perhaps nothing's gonna happen to me either. Maybe I'm immune like you. Right, Megan?"

She sniffled as she got out of the car, but Cassius stopped her and softly pushed her back into her seat.

"We don't have time for this!" he growled, then turned to David, who had backed up a few steps. Every muscle in Cassius' face tensed, and his hand on his gun rose. "And you..."

"I said I'm fine! I really am."

"Cassius!" Abigail warned. "We've gotta go!"

"You know the rules! No waiting for the..."

The sharp siren of an alarm interrupted the discussion, an ear-piercing sound coming from the farmhouse, followed by a strange resonance from deep in the forest. It was similar to what they had felt near Norton's gadget, only much stronger, harsher, like when the gentle roar of a finely tuned engine turns into a coughing, clattering wreck. *What the hell?* Before they could react, something shrieked among the trees. Whatever it was, it suffered from the defense system being activated; the howl eventually turned into a gurgle and then died away.

Abigail's face went white, but her reflexes were activated. She turned towards the sound with her gun raised, yet the dark forest obscured everything. Only her eyes worked, darting from one tree to another in fear.

"Norton's ferals?"

Cassius left David in the cold and, without looking back, threw his bag into the Mach-E. He knew they had to keep moving until the ferals lurking in the trees were disoriented.

"Get in the car!" he shouted to Abigail, and with a single push of a button he started the vehicle.

Abigail got into the passenger seat and David, after some hesitation, sat next to Megan. She was still crying and gently touched his brother's cheek. He squeezed his sister's arm with his unhurt hand.

"Everything's going to be fine, okay?" the young man whispered.

Cassius looked back through the rearview mirror, and when all the doors were closed, he stepped on the gas.

The Mach-E swerved, but he leveled it easily, and without slowing down, aimed for the two poles that marked the property line. The car cut through the trees, the wheels kicking up dust, the farmhouse plunging into the darkness behind them. Everyone in the car watched for an attack from the ferals stalking the area, but nothing happened.

Cassius slowed down just enough to spot the potholes on the bumpy road. The car shook and squealed with each jolt, jerking them up and down and pressing them into their seats. Megan slumped in the back and David fastened his seatbelt and gripped the safety handle with his left hand.

For the first few minutes, none of them spoke, holding their breath and turning their heads nervously, terrified that at any moment they might be struck down. But the feral whose voice they had heard seemed to have been alone.

"Do you think he's dead?" Abigail asked.

"Norton?" Cassius laughed, but it was a false and short one, a laugh of uneasiness without even the sparks of happiness. "I don't think so, but if we're lucky he won't come round for a while."

"That's good..."

"Anyway, we've learnt another lesson. And it seems that luck is still with us."

"Spare me." Abigail turned away, a clear sign that she didn't want to hear his latest parable. But Cassius's pride wouldn't let him give it a rest. The desire to deliver a self-righteous zinger nearly blew his mind. *Why am I always right?*

"I wasn't kidding!"

"Awesome, 'cause neither was I."

Boom!

A gigantic body slammed into the car, which nearly flipped over from the force of the impact. The window next to Abigail shattered, the bodywork buckled, and panic broke out inside. The B pillar was gripped from the outside by bloody, filthy claws, but their momentum finally swept the attacker off the vehicle.

Cassius maneuvered them back onto the dirt road at the last moment. Before the car had gained speed, they could clearly hear beastly grunts and the pounding of feet on dry ground. Now they were certain: the feral was not alone.

"They're here!" Abigail groaned, eyes wide open. Megan and David screamed incessantly. Cassius somehow kept the Mach-E straight and throttled up, while Abigail braced for another encounter, turning her gun towards the window.

The next roar sounded far behind them, way far away. *We might have lost them...*

Cassius was by this time not in the least concerned about the dangers of the bumpy road. He wanted to get out onto the main road as quickly as possible, to lose the ferals on the flat ground away from the trees that were currently only at arm's length. But the forest didn't make it any easier. The glow from the floodlights reflected off the dark trees and only illuminated a scant half a hundred yards of dirt road. It was impossible to tell where they were.

The thudding of the ferals pursuing them seemed to have subsided. All that could be heard in the car was the angry wind buffeting against the vehicle and the panting of the siblings.

"Hold on!" Cassius' order echoed as he caught sight of the asphalt road ahead, running perpendicular to their current path.

He slammed on the brakes and turned the wheel sharply. The car spun, then came to a halt with a screech of tires. Except that it was facing the wrong direction, towards Headland.

The dust and smoke slowly cleared, and they heaved a sigh. Cassius's hands were on the steering wheel. He was ready to turn, but something appeared on the boundary of light and darkness. From behind the pitch-black curtain, a huge shadow emerged, like a villain stepping onto a stage from the unknown.

In the pale glow of the flood lights, its sturdy body tensed, its figure that of an unthinkable monster, its shoulders rising and falling as it gasped for breath.

It was about to attack.

"The Alpha." Abigail paled and pointed straight ahead.

Cassius put the car in reverse and stomped on the gas. The Mach-E accelerated and so did the Alpha, which almost flew with each leap. Abigail leaned out of the window and without waiting for the order, she fired. The beast didn't even notice. Without slowing down or changing direction, it ate up the yards, getting faster and faster.

"It's gonna get us!" Megan yelped. David almost climbed up the door, holding on to the grab handle. They both closed their eyes and tried to curl up as small as possible.

The distance between the Alpha and the car was getting shorter and shorter. Abigail cried out frantically to Cassius as he finally spun the steering wheel and swerved the car in the right direction. The Alpha disappeared from sight. Cassius pressed the accelerator, and the car rocketed out.

On the long, straight stretch of road, there was nothing to restrain the Mach-E, which finally had its wheels resting comfortably on the smooth asphalt.

Abigail turned back and waited with a blank expression for their attacker to reappear. Cassius had his eyes glued to the mirror. For a moment, the glare of the rear lights was unbroken. The girl sighed in relief just as the Alpha burst out of the darkness and charged against the car, sending it skidding and crashing into the guard rail.

Cassius's injured shoulder slammed into the B pillar. He saw stars and his brain tried in vain to warn him of the impending danger, but he couldn't move from the crippling pain.

There was no time to catch his breath; the Alpha was already snapping its gigantic jaws beside Abigail. Its steely claws clamped on the door as it tried to rip the metal apart. She fired immediately. She didn't dawdle, didn't aim, simply pointed her gun at the feral and pulled the trigger three times with a battle cry.

Two bullets struck, and the Alpha staggered backwards with a howl of pain. Blood and chunks of skin burst from its right eye, and its hands immediately clutched at its snout. Half-conscious, Cassius knew that those few seconds were their only chance to escape from the grip of the Alpha and the rest of the pack.

He tried to control his movements through a haze of pain. His fingers tightened around the steering wheel, his right foot sought the throttle, but every action felt like it took hours, as if he were watching the last moments of his life on earth from the farthest reaches of his mind. When the Mach-E started to move, Abigail helped keep the wheel steady. The car finally accelerated, heading straight north.

10.

"Did we get away?" David asked in a voice distorted by fear.

Cassius and Abigail exchanged meaningful glances, but neither replied. *For now, we did*, Cassius thought, and moved his injured shoulder, but the pain would not ease. Abigail carefully took Soxy into her lap and leaned closer to him.

"How the hell did they follow us here? They should have lost our scent a long ways back!"

"I don't know, but if they haven't stopped so far, they won't now," Cassius said quietly.

"What if they didn't come after us, but... Couldn't they have just..."

"Just what?"

"I don't know. Maybe they're looking for new hunting ground," she shrugged.

"I bet my bottom dollar they've been following this pair since Liberty, non-stop," Cassius huffed, watching the two siblings through the rearview mirror. "But I have no clue why. If their friends were still alive, I could understand, but now..."

Silence.

He noticed the bruises on her face.

"You all right?"

Abigail nodded in silence.

"We have to warn the boat-town!" She finally blew out a loud breath and turned back to the siblings. David stared ahead of him, his face white as a sheet, and it was long seconds before he noticed Abigail watching him. With trembling hands, he took the walkie-talkie hooked to his belt and switched it on.

"When do we get there?" Megan asked.

"Soon," Cassius replied. *I hope...*

He involuntarily sped up, his gaze scanning the northern horizon for the lights of the boat-town. He muttered a prayer to himself, but when he couldn't see anything around the next bend, he was already cursing inside. Out of the corner of his eye, he looked at Abigail, who held Soxy in one hand and her Glock in the other, staring silently ahead. The only sounds in the car were David's fiddling and the static from the walkie.

"Blackbeard One, Blackbeard One, this is Papa Hotel Five, over..."

No reply came from the boat-town. Abigail swiveled her head restlessly, her eyes fixed on David and the distant landscape.

"Maybe they're asleep, huh?"

David shook his head.

"A dozen watchmen patrol even at night, and there's always someone by the radio."

The Mach-E cruised along without engine noise. Through the dented, half-ripped door, a pleasant summer night breeze blew in, but Abigail and Megan still shivered. The woman was in a terrible state, panting, her hands clutching her stomach, her face dripping with sweat and her top drenched.

Cassius barely made the next turn; it was only then that he realized he was speeding like a madman. He slowed down and began to control his breathing, counting to himself. Three seconds in, three seconds out. He forced himself into a natural rhythm, without gasping. He was still thinking about the pack, and he felt that they'd witnessed something very bad, and that something even worse was about to occur. He had learned that nothing happened by accident and that things, especially bad things, have an outcome. They rarely just ended without closure.

He could overhear Megan panting harder and harder, her breaths becoming more and more interspersed with painful moans. *Hang in there, woman!*

The only sound coming from the radio was a stiff crackle. Abigail turned back impatiently. David nodded intensely.

"They're there. I know it!"

The silence that followed, however, lasted for long minutes and was finally broken only by Megan's pained scream.

"It's okay, we're almost there," Abigail tried to reassure her after she noticed that David was focused only on the walkie-talkie as he pressed his injured hand to his armpit.

The road took another curve, then climbed a hill, followed by a long, straight descent. The moon illuminated the valley ahead, its light reflecting off the slender S-shaped river, its silvery glow spilling over the trees in the hills.

"There! Look!" Cassius pointed into the distance. Ten miles away, in the middle of the river, dots of light appeared close together. The trees lining the road sometimes hid them, but as they drew nearer it became more and more certain that it was not only the moonlight dazzling their eyes.

"The boat-town!" Abigail smiled.

Cassius sighed in relief and took another glance in the mirror at Megan, who was almost delirious with pain and probably didn't realize how close they were to their final destination. *You just gotta hold out a little longer*, Cassius thought, giving David a nervous look.

"Got anything?"

The radio crackled a different tune; the reception was getting better. David raised his head and grinned broadly to acknowledge that something was happening, something good.

"This… the boat....n... can y... ear us...?"

"Yes!" the young man exclaimed, raising the walkie.

With a glint in her eye, Abigail looked at Cassius, who tapped the steering wheel in contentment. Every yard brought them closer to their destination.

But the joy lasted only a moment.

The Mach-E began to slow, and Cassius turned his head in puzzlement. He kept pushing harder on the accelerator, but in vain. The car lost speed, and after a few yards the pace they were traveling at seemed like a walk in the park.

"What are you doing?" Abigail asked.

"Nothing." He shook his head. "That's the problem."

"Why are we slowing down?" Megan stood up, but Cassius immediately hushed her.

"There's nothing wrong, just lie back and relax. We're almost there!"

"That's good... that's good," she panted, and fell back like a rag doll.

The car got slower and slower, but before it came to a complete halt next to a huge billboard at the bottom of the slope, the steering wheel spun itself, the Mach-E made a smooth turn and started up the hill. Back towards Headland.

"What the hell?" David pushed himself between the two front seats and noticed that Cassius was trying to turn the steering wheel, but it was holding steady.

The Mach-E did not respond. Cassius was no longer in control.

"This can't be," Abigail moaned, still not understanding what was happening. Cassius had a hunch, and when he exchanged looks with David, he realized the young man was thinking the same.

"Looks like our host is finally awake," David said as the Mach-E began to accelerate.

Back, right into the clutches of Norton and the pack.

11.

"I knew I should have beaten the hell out of him!" Cassius snarled, slamming angrily on the steering wheel.

His foot trampled uselessly on the brake with all his might as the Mach-E hurtled up the hill and its passengers looked at each other with growing despair. They were helpless. Megan summoned all the strength she had, turned back, and clung to the seat, watching the lights of the receding boat-town. David gripped the walkie-talkie, mouth agape and motionless, trying to process what had happened. Slowly coming to, he scanned the interior of the car for answers, but so far nothing had caught his eye.

"How the hell is he doing this?" Abigail asked, pressing the buttons on the dashboard. It didn't help.

"He must have modified the car so he can control it remotely," David noted. Cassius shook his head angrily.

"And is there nothing we can do about it?"

David opened his mouth to speak, but then something must have occurred to him. His gaze lost focus as the fingers of his free hand danced like an air guitarist's.

"Whatever you're thinking about, don't take too long," Cassius warned.

Abigail did some quick mental math. It was a good thirty minutes since they had left the dirt road to Norton's house, but even at that seemingly insane speed they had only covered thirty or forty miles. If they didn't figure something out soon, they'd be chauffeured straight to their doom.

"I've got an idea!" David said, and this time he didn't wait for the usual questions. He lowered the window, which fortunately Norton hadn't blocked, and to the astonishment of the others, he pushed himself out through it, his body almost bending in the wind as he tried to reach the roof.

"Jesus, David, what are you doing?" cried Megan, then grabbed him with both hands and wrapped her arms around his legs. David, however, had no intention of jumping out. The rhythmic movement of his body indicated that he was doing something on the roof, but the others couldn't figure out what it was.

When the young man climbed back into the car with a loud huff, he was holding the radio antenna that he had torn off the roof of the Mach-E. At the same moment the car jerked, the dashboard lights went out, and the vehicle began to slow down.

Megan's eyes lit up with joy as David sat back down beside her and she hugged her brother tightly. Abigail glanced hopefully at Cassius, who knew that it was too soon to celebrate, and it didn't take long for the others to realize it, too.

The car had slowed, yet Cassius still couldn't control it.

The Mach-E finally ground to a halt at the top of the hill. The whirring of the wheels ceased, and all that could be heard was the faint rustling of trees and the chirping of cicadas. Everything around them was almost dark, with only the moonlit river running down to the right and the starry sky above.

All at once, questioning eyes turned to David. Abigail was the first to speak.

"What just happened?"

"Er... I don't know what happened."

"We stopped, that's what happened," Cassius grumbled.

David blinked a few times, then leaned over Cassius and pressed the START button, but the car wouldn't respond. They had broken down for good. The boat-town was still several hours' walk away, an almost impossible distance to carry Megan.

"Most probably the whole system was connected to the farmhouse," David muttered.

"And now what?"

Instead of answering, David held up the torn antenna. Abigail closed her eyes, Megan groaned.

"Would anyone else like to press the button and see if the car will start?" Cassius asked ironically, and when no one answered, he looked out the window. He searched for signs and danger, but there was no movement outside. He sucked on his teeth, opened the door, and got out. "Let's go!"

He reached into his bag, tucked his notebook behind his back in his belt, put a few things in his pocket, and threw the bag back on the seat. "Bring only what's important."

Megan's face went white.

"You want to walk?"

"It's either this or the ferals. Your call!"

David was the first to follow. He got out and climbed on top of the Mach-E, made himself comfortable, and raised the walkie-talkie to his mouth.

"Blackbeard One, this is Papa Hotel Five... This is David, damn it! Do you read me?"

The radio crackled.

"This is the boat…n... Hello..."

"Hello, hello," David's eyes lit up as he tried to hold the radio even higher. "This is David from the Liberty Colony, we've spoken before!"

A high-pitched male voice answered.

"This is Blackbeard One! We thought something happened to you on the road. Where's Trevor? It's been a long time since we've heard the lunkhead's voice."

Cassius helped Megan out of the car, and Abigail quickly sorted out the things she needed from her bag. She handed the Browning to Cassius. Holding her Glock in one hand and Soxy's box in the other, she took a few steps away from them and observed the distant landscape. Megan sat down on the ground, clutched her belly, leaned her back against the car, and snorted so hard that Cassius thought she was going to give birth right there.

David, meanwhile, shook his right arm, as if to relieve the pain.

"Unfortunately, Trevor didn't make it," the young man said. He didn't rush the answer, he seemed to be searching for words. "Er... I guess we would need a little help from you. We're on our way there, but we've got a problem."

"What problem exactly?"

"We're really close to you, we can see the lights, but we've been ambushed by a pack. We'll need transport and firepower."

Silence.

David was drumming nervously on top of the Mach-E. He glanced at Cassius, who was pointing his finger at him that he'd better hurry. David spread his hands helplessly before raising the radio to his mouth again.

"Can you hear me?"

Cassius looked around, but there was still no sign of the pack. *Maybe we'll have enough time*, he figured. *We'll make it*, he thought, but then he remembered his aversion to another unfamiliar place. If it had been just him and Abigail, they would be running, at worst fleeing across the river, but he knew they had to try the boat-town for Megan's sake.

After what seemed like endless seconds, the high-pitched male voice rang out again.

"It won't work, David! You know we can't risk it."

"No, you can't do this..."

"I'm sorry, but that's the order I was given. And one more thing..."

Another pause. They all had a feeling that worse news was about to come.

"We'd hate to see you lead that pack straight back here. It would be best if you didn't come at all... In fact, the watchmen have orders to shoot if they see you. I'm really sorry... It's what we have to do for the majority."

"What?" David's eyes widened. He slammed his fist on the top of the car, then yelled. Cassius lost his patience. He leaned the Browning against the Mach-E, snatched the walkie-talkie out of David's hand, then stepped aside and spoke forcefully into the radio.

"Listen up, you idiots, because I'm only gonna say this once! We have information that I'd be curious to know if I were you, assuming you want to live to see Christmas this year. Suffice it to say, it contains a mad scientist you already know and a secret plan that affects all of you. So, get your asses over here and help! Is that a good enough reason to change that order?"

There was a long silence.

Megan groaned in pain again, and Abigail hissed at him.

"Let's go, Cassius! You hear me?"

Cassius waited three seconds, then nodded. He put down the walkie-talkie and was about to pick Megan up when the radio crackled, but this time someone else was on.

It was a gruff, thick male voice.

"Who is this?"

Cassius mumbled a quick curse before answering.

"I promise to introduce myself when I see you! But you'd better take my words seriously!"

The gruff male voice didn't wait long. Cassius already knew he was talking to the boss. Or at least someone with influence.

"Let's meet in the valley, mysterious stranger, at the big billboard! You've got twenty minutes." A pause for effect. "And it better be a great story, or you'll rot in the belly of a ship! Is that clear?"

"Loud and clear."

Static followed, and the conversation was over. Cassius hung the walkie-talkie on his belt, slung the Browning over his shoulder, and helped Megan up, all the while keeping his eyes on the road to Headland. He winced as he realized that the ferals could be hiding in the woods even ten or twenty yards from the road, in their immediate vicinity.

Abigail happily cuddled Soxy's box.

"Come on then!" she said, relieved.

Megan cried with joy and clung to her brother. She was about to leave, but David stopped her. She turned back, stunned.

"I think my journey ends here," the young man said.

"What?" Megan asked, her eyes wide.

The others looked puzzled as David raised his injured arm and showed them. The black streak indicating infection was already starting to run up under his skin, and as Cassius stepped closer, he saw the yellow spots in the young man's eyes. David shrugged, resigned, his face reflecting acquiescence.

"That's life, right?"

Without thinking, Megan threw herself into her brother's arms.

"No..."

David hugged her tightly.

"You gotta go!"

She just sobbed, digging her fingers into his shirt and pulling him towards her. Abigail closed her eyes. Cassius waited a few seconds before trying to pull her away.

Then, in the distance, a feral let out a guttural scream. Still far, but not far enough. They were now certain of what they had only suspected: the pack was closing in on them. Who knew how much time they had?

David gently pushed Megan away.

"You must go!" he said. Ignoring Megan's sobs, he looked at Cassius. "Please take care of her!"

Cassius picked her up and nodded towards David.

"It was nice to meet you, geek squad!"

David laughed, but his face was contorted with pain.

"Oh fuck, come on! Just go!"

With tears in her eyes, Abigail approached him and shook his hand.

"Goodbye!"

Then they turned and started running. The bottom of the slope was about a mile away. The big billboard was not yet visible in the darkness, but the three of them knew it was there. They just had to hurry. It was all up to them. *Let's hope so*, he thought, ignoring the fact that the boat-towners might change their minds.

"Abigail!" Cassius tried to whisper and shout at the same time, but all he could do was grunt. "Go ahead! Take cover in case we need it!"

She quickened her pace.

Cassius was determined to run as fast as he could and not look back, no matter how tempting it was. He managed for a while, but eventually broke the promise he had made to himself.

He saw David standing beside the car, straightening up and reaching into his pocket. The young man pulled out a Savarette, then climbed comfortably back on top of the Mach-E and lit the joint. He didn't sit down. He didn't move. He just watched them get farther and farther away from him. The end of the cigarette glowed in his mouth. Its smoke embraced him, like a halo in the silvery light of the moon.

Cassius could still hear David softly singing some old pop song. The young man's voice faded, yet he carried on. *You gotta be on your feet when the time comes.*

David was on his feet. And the time had come.

12.

The cool night air, which he used to love so much, didn't make breathing any easier. Megan got heavier and heavier; Cassius's body was almost cracking under her weight, his injured shoulder in a vice of pain. *You can't give up*, was all he could think. He was close to collapsing, even though they were still hundreds of yards away from the bottom of the long slope and the billboard hiding in the darkness.

Meanwhile Megan's body had gone limp in his arms. Cassius couldn't stop to check whether she was all right. After a while, he felt his slowing footsteps become a shuffle, and in his vain attempts to hold her, she slipped further and further out of his grasp. *Two hundred more yards*, he thought, and pursed his lips.

"We're almost there!" Abigail called from ahead of them.

A shout sounded in the distance. It came from the high ground; it was David.

"I can see them! Hurry up!" he cried out as loudly as he could. "Jesus..."

Abigail slowed and turned, looking up the hill where the car was barely visible.

"Don't stop, just run!" Cassius shouted at her.

His eyes were fixed on the billboard at the bottom of the slope.

The valley ahead of them curved away with the river, just enough to obscure the continuation of the road so that it was hidden by the trees and the hillside. He only hoped that the colony's armed men would arrive soon, otherwise it would be over for them; they couldn't face the pack by themselves with no place to hide, and they would have neither the strength nor the time to reach the boat-town itself.

Fighting off the fatigue, he staggered the last steps, hugging Megan even tighter. *We made it*. The thrill of victory crossed his mind, but he knew it was only the first half of the task.

The best was yet to come.

Gasping and staggering, Cassius stopped at the billboard, but no matter how hard he watched and listened, he saw and heard no approaching cars. Hesitantly, he turned around and put his finger to his mouth to keep everyone quiet. Desperation slowly overcame exhaustion.

Where are you?

He thought he heard engines revving in the distance, but from so far away that he wasn't sure if it was just his imagination playing tricks on him.

"Did you hear that?" he asked Abigail, but she was busy with Soxy, so she looked up, puzzled.

"I don't know," she answered uncertainly.

At the top of a distant rise, David shouted again, but this time it wasn't a warning for them. It lasted only a few seconds, then silence. Dead silence.

"Oh God, no!" sobbed Megan.

Cassius spun around, his mind working frantically. Ahead of them was the long ascent, to the left a steep hill with its dense forest; to the right the grassy, bushy bank led to the river, and behind them the road curved away past the billboard. There was nowhere to run, nowhere to hide.

The next roar was not from David. A beastly, guttural sound came from the trees only a few hundred yards away, calling its companions to feast and destroy.

The ground shook and they felt the ghostly resonance in every part of their bodies as panic overcame them. Cassius gently set Megan down and, with a protective gesture, pushed her behind him.

They looked up at the same time, yet saw nothing. A few bats flew overhead, then one by one the cicadas fell silent. The wind died down, the trees stopped dancing, and Cassius was again seized by the strange sensation of the vast canopy reaching higher and higher past them, the branches of the trees creeping over and suffocating them.

Their whole bodies trembled with fear and the resonance grew stronger as the pack rushed down in the darkness.

Abigail pointed ahead, but could only whisper.

"Th-there..."

And that was when in the light of the moon showed Cassius what had horrified her. At the side of the road, among the dark trees, figures were moving, coming towards them with lightning speed. Branches bent and broke in their path.

"They'll soon be here." Megan shivered and looked desperately up at Cassius. "What's gonna happen to us?"

"The boat-towners are coming, don't worry," Cassius assured her, and looked back towards the colony. *Come on!*

He desperately searched for a way out. It seemed that there was nowhere to run.

"We have to get moving! We can't wait for them here," Cassius said to Abigail. "We must try..."

Abigail couldn't say a word, she just backed away slowly, clutching Soxy's box tighter and tighter. They raised their guns at the same time and aimed at the midnight-black curtain, which the ferals might break through at any moment.

The pounding footsteps came closer and closer, growing progressively louder.

How many could there be? How many were left? Whatever the answer, they couldn't take that many. *Ammo? Who cares...*

Cassius looked back. He was sure now that he had heard something. *An engine sound! That's it!* He cried out, but help came too late.

The first feral jumped down from the top of a small embankment right beside them, dragging branches and leaves with it. Megan screamed and the guns barked loudly. Abigail and Cassius fired instinctively, but none of the bullets hit. The Gamma landed unharmed and was turning to throw itself at them. Megan fell to her knees, burying her face in her palms.

The hail of bullets didn't ease up for a moment. Cassius saw that he couldn't retreat without leaving the woman cowering on the asphalt, so he took a step forward, not caring how many bullets he fired into the airborne Gamma. *It's all the same now anyway!*

The feral collapsed lifeless a few feet away from them. *Maybe three bullets left in the Glock...*

The pounding of feet grew louder and more intense, the noise in the trees increasing. The ferals were so close they could be heard clearly: the underbrush crunched beneath footsteps and the bushes were crushed to bits by muscular feet.

When a second feral emerged from the trees, it was illuminated by light as bright as daylight as three cars cut out of the bend. Their floodlights covered the area, and what had been hidden by the darkness of night was now visible.

On the hillside, the ferals appeared one by one from the trees, ready to attack. Cassius knew there was a good chance the pack would have heard the cars before they did, so he prepared himself that the rescue mission wouldn't be as easy as they had hoped.

Three armored jeeps slowed behind them, and the machine guns mounted on their flatbeds exploded to life one after the other, firing relentlessly at the ferals among the trees. Cassius crouched down, dragging Abigail with him; the dusty asphalt was their only shelter. Megan covered her ears at the deafening noise. He could hear Soxy yelping painfully in the box.

The machine guns, however, gave no pause, leaving no free prey for Cassius, who had raised his pistol. The rain of bullets took down everything approaching, chopping branches and bushes.

Just then the Beta burst from the trees and immediately lunged at the jeep nearest to the hillside, knocking it aside in one movement. Before it could throw itself at the next car, however, the other machine guns exposed it to cross-fire and brought it down in a long volley.

The bullets smashed asphalt, broke trees in two, and created a choking cloud of dust, but the chaos was over as quickly as it had begun.

"Hold your fire!" they heard a gruff man's voice trying to drown out the infernal noise.

The machine guns fell silent.

The air was filled with the stench of swamp, scorched earth, shattered concrete, and gunpowder.

“Clear?” someone asked from a jeep, and another one answered:

“Clear. For now.”

Then a third one:

“Watch the woods! I bet it’s not over yet.”

Abigail and Megan lowered their hands from their ears. Cassius raised his head slowly. The glare of the floodlights blinded him, so he could only focus on the sounds. The door of one of the jeeps opened, and a heavyset, grim man stepped up to them. They could only see his silhouette, but he was as tall as Cassius.

“Rise and shine, lazy bones! Let’s go, because this was only the first wave!”

Cassius helped Megan up. *The boat-town is awaiting us!*

FOR THE GREATER GOOD

1.

The woman with raven black hair and the elderly man with broken glasses sat silently in the cabin where they had been sent to be safe during the uprising. The gunfire had been silent for an hour. Some of the rebels had been killed, the rest captured, and George Solomon wanted to make his own decision about their fate.

The only thing the two remaining members of the Council governing the boat-town could do was wait. Though they did not support the rebels, the raven-haired woman and the old man with the broken glasses knew exactly why Solomon no longer trusted them. After all, it was the very people he had thought he could count on who had fueled the discontent in his absence.

There were six chairs around the table in the center of the cabin, but only the two of them were there in the candlelit room. The three companions who had started the rebellion were captured, and after sunset the last of the fighting units surrendered. The coup ended in blood.

Two years after the pandemic broke out, when most of the world had already given up on America and its people, they were about to prove that the outside world setting up the quarantine were right, and that they could not unite even in the most difficult moments. However, the boat-towners believed that they would not repeat the childish failures the others had, that they were destined for better than the unfortunates who had eventually turned against each other, or those who were killed by the ferals in a careless moment. And here they were!

The raven-haired woman shook her head, then rose and walked to the cabin window. It was dark outside and she could barely see anything except the river glistening in the moonlight.

"We should go outside. See what's happening," she said. There was impatience in her soft voice.

The old man with the glasses winced.

"Solomon said not to leave the cabin until he returns."

"And from now on he's going to order us around as if we were his subordinates?"

"That's the way it was before," the old man shrugged. "All we did was pretend it was different. We all looked the other way, even you sometimes."

"Then it has to end now!"

"And how do we do that? Most of the men with guns don't take orders from me anymore, they always run to Solomon when I request something. But you know what? I don't give a damn! The point is, he's looking out for us. We've got food, we're safe..."

"Oh, just shut up, will you?" the raven-haired woman gestured at him angrily. She pushed her chair out of the way and headed for the exit. But before she could put her hand on the knob, the metal door creaked open.

From the dim, silent hallway, a grim, heavyset man entered the room. He had to keep his head down to avoid hitting the frame. He had a round, bald head and a stern face with a few days' stubble. From under his dirty white linen shirt, the tattoos covering his torso showed. They had to have been done before the Breakdown, some most likely in prison. His hooded eyes flashed menacingly as he folded his hands across his chest and stood in the doorway.

The raven-haired woman staggered back, but then swallowed her fright.

"John... Thanks for finally dropping by," she panted. "We'd like to know what's going on out there!"

"Mr. Solomon will be here soon," John replied. He had a thick, gruff voice and pronounced his words with assertive emphasis.

An awkward silence fell over the room. The raven-haired woman glanced at the elderly man with the glasses, but he closed his eyes and said nothing. After a few seconds of hovering, the woman sat back in her seat, crossed her legs, and turned her head towards the cabin window in protest.

The candle in the middle of the table flickered. The sound of footsteps came from outside, growing louder and louder. John stepped aside, and a menacing shadow appeared in the doorway, waiting outside for a moment, then, after a deep breath, the figure stepped into the light.

The old man with the broken glasses straightened up.

"George," he said respectfully, and rose to his feet, but the newcomer signaled him to sit back down. He was a black man with a scar on his cheek from ear to neck, his hair gray, his body robust. His full chin showed determination and a will to act. He wore a long coat, a gray turtleneck, and black trousers with knee pads. His heavy, stamped boots sounded like hammer strikes and he held a lighter between his sausage-like fingers. On his belt was a .44 Magnum, a knife, and a flashlight.

Solomon entered the cabin with his hands behind his back and sat down on one of the chairs opposite the two remaining members of the Council. John closed the door and stood behind Solomon. The raven-haired woman glanced at them, puzzled, then peered at the heavyset man.

"Is he staying as well?"

Solomon nodded. He slowly adjusted his coat, which was sweeping the floor, then put his right hand on the table and looked at the others as he fiddled with his lighter. The woman with the raven-black hair and the old man with the broken glasses leaned back and hunched at the same time.

"I know how difficult the last few days have been for you," Solomon said, then tapped the lighter on the table, followed by an unbroken silence. He continued after a long pause. "I appreciate your perseverance, and your loyalty. Your resistance to temptation."

The raven-haired woman snorted and the old man looked at her with a frightened expression. Solomon continued, ignoring them.

"But now our ordeal is over, things can return to normal tomorrow. I can't promise that everything will be the same, but..."

"Back to normal?" the raven-haired woman snapped. "How?"

John's face turned angry in the background. Solomon's eyes

flickered and his lighter stopped in his hand. Nobody spoke for a long moment, but the look on their leader's face showed that he was thinking carefully about what to say.

"What have I told you since the first day I set up the Council? Either of you remember what my condition was?"

The old man with the broken glasses nodded vigorously, while she remained silent.

"I said that there could be no tribalism in the boat-town. I said that, as a last resort, and only as a last resort, I would have the final say, but that we were all equal here. I said that all anyone had to do was speak up, anyone who wanted something, anyone who had an opinion. Because the consequences of not talking to each other would cause conflict. Was I right or not?"

"You were right, George," the old man nodded.

"And people have died in the meantime. My people, whichever side they chose, but they were all my people."

"Are we your people too, George? Yours?" the raven-haired woman asked with a scowl.

"Is it so terrible to have someone to lead you? Here's the living proof of what happens when I leave for a week, because while we were out there risking our lives, you were conspiring against the system we built together."

"We didn't stand by them, George, you know that," the old man appealed. His forehead beaded with sweat, and his eyes were fixed on either the raven-haired woman or Solomon.

"And I believe you, so you will not be harmed."

"What about the others?" the raven-haired woman asked. "Tell me you didn't hurt them either!"

Silence. A mocking smile curved the corner of John's mouth, but Solomon just stared at the woman and the old man.

"Those who laid down their weapons were not harmed. Those who were wounded were treated. And the dead will be buried with dignity."

The raven-haired woman pushed back her chair and stood up with a furious look on her face.

"What have you done to them?" she bellowed, pointing with her head at the empty chairs.

John stepped over to force her back into her seat, but Solomon stopped him with a single wave. Seeing John's contorted, blood-red face, it was the right thing to do. She took a startled step back and raised her chin defiantly as the heavyset man recoiled in obedience to the command.

Solomon took a deep breath and stood up. The old man with the broken glasses submissively followed, trying to straighten his back, but succeeding only as far as his old bones would allow. John opened the cabin door and stepped out of the way.

"What have you done to them?" she asked again, this time more quietly, almost pleadingly.

"Let's take a walk!" Solomon replied bluntly.

2.

The boat was anchored in a long, straight stretch of the river, fifty yards from the shore, and there was almost complete darkness and silence on board. Only a few torches were lit on the three-story river cruise ship, and no movement was visible in the gloomy glow, but armed guards stood at every corner. Cigarettes occasionally lit up in the darkness, and even less often the wind brought whispers. A hundred yards away, in the middle of the river, a tugboat and a barge could be seen on the silvery surface of the water. The only light was on the bridge of the tugboat. The barge had been towed in before Solomon's departure, but its connection to the main vessel had been interrupted by the sudden riot.

Solomon led the procession towards the stern with his flashlight, the old man and the raven-haired woman stumbling behind him, and John trailed them carrying a storm lantern. None of them spoke until they reached the deck. But seeing the swarming gunmen, the woman scrambled forward to Solomon's side.

"Nothing's lost yet, George," she said to the man, who didn't turn back. "Be empathetic with them, and don't pretend you don't know why they did what they did."

"You think I'm not empathetic?" Solomon asked. He slowed

and pointed with his free hand to the window they had just passed. Two armed men stood inside, the door open behind them and light filtering in only from the hallway.

She leaned closer, and only then did she notice that in front of the armed men, people were kneeling with their hands tied behind their backs, their heads bowed, motionless.

"If I wasn't empathetic, they'd all be resting at the bottom of the river with a bullet in their skulls, so keep your opinions to yourself!"

"Is that what it is from now on? You're gonna make all the decisions on your own? Because if you are, feel free to push me in with the others, kick me out if you want to, but I'm not getting involved."

Solomon stopped. His piercing, sadly glittering eyes were deep in the raven-haired woman's gaze.

"I know you've suffered a lot, Becky, a lot more than we have. And now you must think life is cruel, and everyone else is, but it's not like that. You have to believe me when I tell you that I work for the greater good, for the colony, and I don't do what I do because I'm a tyrant. Am I right, John?"

"You're right, Mr. Solomon," said the heavyset man in his gruff voice, but she huffed angrily.

"Keep my past out of this, because it's got nothing to do with it! It's all about you, and your power mania. And I told you not to call me that!"

Solomon impassively shrugged his shoulders.

"As you wish, Rebecca! But before you do anything stupid, think of the orphans who count only on you," he said, then turned and walked away. "We're almost there, so let's not waste any time!"

3.

Four silent boat-towners stood on the stern of the cruise ship, weapons slung over their shoulders, torches burning in their hands, their light casting ominous shadows on the metal surfaces. The air was faint with a strange, nauseating smell, just enough to make you wonder what it was. It reminded Rebecca of death.

Solomon slowed his steps and paused at the railing, watching the silvery stream flowing south. The old man with the broken glasses stopped, suspecting something ominous, but no one wanted to hurt him. John side-stepped him, pushing him away with his shoulder, which made the old man cry out, but in the end he said nothing and did not complain. Rebecca leaned over the railing, terrified of seeing something horrible in the water.

But there was nothing in the waves crashing over the stern, only the dark depths beneath the white foam.

"Where are our companions, Solomon?" she asked one final time. Solomon cocked his head at the superstructure. Rebecca and the old man turned at the same time to look up at the three-story rear facade.

They went pale seeing the three bloody bodies hanged and stretched out on the second-floor railing. The lifeless corpses of three of their companions. Rebecca cried out and turned towards Solomon, but before she could do anything, the men with the torches surrounded her menacingly, encircling her as she was about to attack.

"What have you done, you madman? What have you done?" she shouted. The torch-wielding men were not enough to restrain her and John had to hold her down. She burst into tears.

The old man with the broken glasses stumbled around in the background with a trembling mouth, trying to shrink himself as small as he could. No one paid any attention to him.

Solomon stepped closer to Rebecca.

"Tomorrow morning, everyone will see what happens to those who defy me and incite rebellion against me. And they will get the message, I have no doubt. Those who obey will have a roof over their heads and food on their plates. Those who don't will be dragged up where your companions are without a second thought."

"How could you do this?" Rebecca asked, tearing herself from John's grasp.

"I did it for the greater good. Maybe one day you will understand! But if you don't..."

Solomon didn't finish the sentence, and he didn't need to. His tone said it all. He bit his lip and walked away without looking back. John watched them in silence for a while.

"You can cut the bodies down in the morning if you like, but till then they'll stay there!" he said in his gruff voice. After that he, too, disappeared into the darkness.

The old man with the broken glasses followed him a minute later.

Rebecca was left alone with the speechless, motionless torchmen. No matter how much she wished to escape from the horrible sight and hide in the depths of one of the cabins, her legs would not obey. She glanced desperately up at the corpses, but it was not until the first light of dawn that she dragged herself back to her own cabin, sobbing and trembling.

She took a knife, rope, and tarp to cut the bodies from the railing, and looked for volunteers, knowing she could not manage alone. But no one dared to help. By morning, everyone knew what would happen to anyone who defied Solomon's will, and none of them wanted to share the fate of their companions.

WELCOME!

1.

After a quarter of an hour's drive, the two undamaged jeeps reached the shimmering boat-town, anchored opposite a ferry terminal in the middle of a wide stream. The austere pier was reached by a dirt path off the main road, which was regularly maintained so that no deep ruts formed. The woods running along the shore were thinned out to prevent enemies from taking cover close to the banks. A rusty sign on the pier proclaimed the name of the old business: GREAT RIVER FERRY. Oil drum fires lit the surroundings and revealed a watchman standing at the rail of the rickety-looking metal structure.

The jeeps pulled in beside other vehicles lined up along the riverbank — reinforced pick-ups, construction trucks, and a tower-crane — and a moment later a gunman jumped out of each car to secure the area. They were organized and kept a safe distance. On the way to the boat-town, only the heavyset, gruff-voiced man had spoken to them; he had introduced himself as John. Before they turned off the main road, he was the one who had told them what to do when they arrived at the riverbank. His words had an uncontestable tone, and Cassius was convinced that John was not new to the job of commander.

The two gunmen who had been the first to disembark took up positions halfway between the pier and the jeeps, then signaled that the position was clear. John granted them permission. Cassius and Abigail helped Megan out of the back of the jeep and, supporting her, they headed for the pier. Cassius held his gun in his free hand

and Abigail balanced Soxy's box in hers. The line was rounded off by John, who, leaving the cover of the jeeps, turned back once more and surveyed the dark landscape with his shotgun raised.

But there was no sign of any ferals. The night was still.

They all trudged across the dirt, hoisted themselves onto the unsteady pier, then boarded a waiting motorboat to cross over to the colony of a dozen broken-down vessels. Cassius, Abigail, and Megan were seated in the middle of the motorboat. The gunmen, along with John, surrounded them. No one spoke a word; they just stared ahead as the engine revved and the boat moved off with a jolt.

Cassius took stock of their situation and considered their chances. The shore was receding, and the gunmen were squirming nervously. In the face of such an overwhelming force, he could only hope that the inhabitants of the boat-town were hospitable people, not driven by distrust. *But if things did take a negative turn...*

He looked around stealthily. The man sitting opposite him had long, shaggy hair that could be grabbed in close combat. The lad with the high and tight haircut cowering beside him wore clothes one size larger, easy to get caught in. The stocky guy behind them had massive boots that could inflict serious injuries. *Better watch out for that!* Further back, a woman who could have been a weightlifter scratched her nose. She was apple-cheeked, unprepared for a fight, and not paying attention to them like the others. The gunman piloting the motorboat had no face or eye protection; his eyes, nose, ears, and throat were vulnerable. The middle-aged, bearded man sitting next to John, on the other hand, held his weapon like a seasoned veteran.

"You've got a pretty little home, kudos!" Cassius said, trying to keep up communication and get a reaction out of the gunmen.

He got no response.

Just relax, he thought, but the expressionless faces made him doubt. He watched anxiously as the men eyed Abigail with wistful eyes. Two even murmured to each other and laughed sardonically.

Cassius turned to John.

"Once we have her safe, we have to talk!" he said, wanting to get this over with as quickly as possible. *We'll get a doctor for Megan, wait for the baby to be born, then get out of here as fast as we can. I hope*

Abigail won't come up with anything stupid this time...

John, however, cooled things down.

"I'm not the man you're looking for, my friend. That's Mr. Solomon. And you better have something exciting to say, because you've cost us people and gear."

Cassius swallowed hard, then nodded silently.

The first light of dawn appeared on the western horizon. As they approached, he finally got a closer look at the boat-town, which was comprised of cruise ships, tugs, barges, and scows. Spotlights and lamps dotted the boats, torches and campfires burned here and there. Apart from the low rumble of engines, the colony was silent, but the lights in the cabins were coming on one by one as morning approached.

The motorboat moored alongside one of the tugs, where two torch-bearing figures waited for them on board. They were both black teenagers, a slender boy with a curly faux hawk and a girl with a Halle Berry hairstyle. The relieved smiles on their excited faces were in sharp contrast to the sternness of the gunmen huddled around, their eyes gleaming as they reflected the torchlight.

The teens caught the rope thrown towards them and pulled the motorboat tight to the tug. John clambered over first, then stopped a distance across the tug and continued to watch them from there. The shaggy-haired gunman helped Cassius lift Megan from the motorboat. She was barely conscious and once they were on deck, Cassius lifted her into his arms and thrust his chin impatiently forwards.

"Get a doctor immediately!" he snarled at the shaggy-haired gunman, who refused to move. Cassius looked around angrily. "Which way?"

"Not so fast!" John held up his hands. "We have to examine you first. And the mutt, as well." He pointed towards Soxy.

"You can check us once we get her to safety," Cassius snapped. "Unless you want her to have her baby right here!"

After a moment's hesitation, John waved his hand and stepped back. The shaggy-haired man understood the order and ran off, while the slender boy sprang to lead the way towards the colony's center, a huge cruise ship.

"This way," he said, grinning at Abigail like an excited schoolboy. The girl with the Halle Berry hairstyle took their belongings from them, chattering so much that for a moment Cassius thought it was Abigail speaking.

"We heard over the radio what happened. We thought you weren't going to get to the billboard on time, some even had bets on it, but we said you would make it. And you did! Unbelievable! My name is Maya, by the way, and this is my brother Shaun. Wait, we can't go that way, we'll just turn in here..."

They walked across the deck of the tugboat, around the metal stairs to the bridge, and through one of the open double doors. Maya made her way forward, using her torch to point the way ahead. Inside, only a few storm lanterns were lit. The musty, oil-scented hallway was empty, the place more like a warehouse. After a short walk, they emerged on the other side of the tugboat, then proceeded over a metal duckboard onto a barge with an open cargo hold full of boxes and bags.

The ships rubbed against each other, playing a squeaking adagio beneath them, while the metal floor chimed and echoed with each of their steps. The flame of the torches flickered in the gentle night breeze, and a full-bodied smell of smoke wafted through the air.

"Are we going much further?" Cassius asked, huffing loudly and looking back with caution. John and the high and tight lad followed them, stern-faced, palms pressed against their gunstocks.

"We're almost there," Maya replied, jumping over a thick metal cable. "Be careful, don't trip! It would be terrible if something bad happened right now, wouldn't it?"

And she laughed, followed by a snort from Shaun.

"Don't be stupid, sis! Show us the way!" he waved, before turning to Abigail. "You didn't get bitten, did you?"

"No," Abigail shook her head. "We're all clean."

"All right, we'll check you out anyway, just in case," the slender boy winked.

"Whatever you need to do!"

They hurried across the barge and onto the next boat. As best he could, Cassius tried to observe the colony on the way. A drunken, muttering figure was curled up at the base of one of the fire pits. John kicked him as they went by and ordered him into his cabin. In one corner, suspicious men were talking and quickly turned away when they saw the strange procession. Only then could Cassius see their insidiously flashing eyes. There were tables and chairs in a large open area, some overturned, and an aproned figure seemed to be mopping up blood on the deck. On one of the ships, workers were welding something, and he noticed that there were guards, watching not only the outside world with wary eyes, but the colony grounds as well.

After reading the many signs pinned to the sides of the vessels, he was sure the community had its own PR department. OUR HOMETOWN, RESPECT YOUR RATION, WORK BUILDS OUR FUTURE, and NO FERALS, the texts proclaimed.

After crossing over to another barge, they finally arrived at the cruise ship. Just in time: Megan groaned in pain in Cassius' arms. He struggled to hold her; she nearly slipped out of his grasp with every step. As the colony came to life with the dawn, they began to realize how gigantic it was: everywhere they looked they saw ships tied together, creating the impression of a huge labyrinth. More and more people appeared on board, watching them with curiosity.

Abigail glanced at Cassius. He motioned with his head for her to stay close behind him. This was not, by any means, a place where he would want to lose sight of her even for a second.

Maya slowed in front of a door, slid her torch into a holder attached to the railing, then unhooked a flickering storm lantern from the wall. Shaun did the same.

"Tell me we're there!" Cassius groaned.

"We're here." Maya grinned proudly.

They stepped inside a once-modern, now run-down cruise ship. The cream-colored walls were stained with dirt, the blue and white geometric patterned carpeting was trampled, and the gold banisters were peeling. Fortunately, they only had to walk a few steps. Maya opened the door of a nearby room, lit with only a flickering candle, and pointed to the double bed.

"Put her there! The midwife will be with you shortly."

Cassius gently laid Megan down on the folded mattress and looked quickly around. It was a cramped room with a large cabin window and a navy-blue sofa. At least the bedding looked clean and the pillow was a good height, so Megan could rest comfortably. Abigail hurried over to help. She adjusted Megan's legs while the pregnant woman blinked back to consciousness. Her gaze was unfocussed, her hand only clutching the air as she reached out for Cassius.

"Have we arrived?" she asked. Her words sounded like a low whimper. Cassius nodded, wiping her sweaty brow with a cloth.

"We have. We've made it!"

Megan's face immediately tightened with pain.

"That's good, because I can hardly keep this big girl inside..."

Maya and Shaun watched them with concerned looks while the high and tight lad stood in the doorway. There was no sign of John.

"Shoo, shoo, make way!" someone called from the corridor, and the high and tight lad jumped aside. A stout woman in her fifties appeared in the doorway. She had irregular red marks on her face, and her graying hair was held up with a scarf. She wore an apron over her knitted sweater and thick-rimmed glasses on her nose and carried a tattered book in her hand entitled *A Practical Manual to Labor and Delivery*.

The midwife adjusted her glasses and with a wave of her hand she pushed Cassius aside to reach the woman in labor. Sitting on the edge of the bed, she put the back of her hand to Megan's forehead and gently squeezed her wrist. A look of unease came over her face, which even Cassius noticed. Megan cried out; the contractions followed one after the other with increasing frequency.

"She'll be all right, won't she?" Cassius asked the midwife.

"Of course, but she needs to rest now, so get out," she ordered. Maya and Shaun obeyed without a second thought, and after some faltering, Abigail followed. Only Cassius's legs refused to move. The midwife noticed this. "She's in good hands, I promise. But you're not going to help her if you keep stumbling around, so get out! Once we're done, you'll be the first to know."

Cassius took a deep breath, then with hesitant steps he left the room. Maya closed the door after him with a pompous gesture and grinned encouragingly at him.

"It's all right now," she said in a high-pitched voice. "Josie has already delivered a dozen or so babies, and most of them survived."

Abigail looked up at Cassius, blinking widely. He forced himself to say nothing in reply, instead glancing at the high and tight lad.

"Have you shot them all? The ferals? Tell me there are none left!"

The answer was a single confident nod.

"The Alpha too?"

The high and tight lad's eyes then widened.

"What Alpha?"

"The pack was led by an Alpha."

"Wow!" Shaun opened his mouth, which he forgot to close for several seconds, while looking at his sister. "We've never seen an Alpha before."

The lad swallowed, then straightened his back.

"That too... We don't make mistakes."

Yeah, sure! Cassius didn't believe him, but the best he could do was to trust the seemingly perfect defense system of the boat-town. *We may be safe in the middle of the river, but I still have to tell them about Norton!*

Shaun stepped closer to Abigail and put his hand on her shoulder.

"How about if we find you a room? And some breakfast."

Cassius examined the boy with piercing eyes, then he searched for Abigail's gaze, but she ignored him. Instead, she smiled broadly in response to Shaun.

"That would be awesome!"

2.

The first sunbeams crept over the distant hills, forming a golden bridge between the bank and the awakening boat-town. It was a promising morning: mist stretched over the dark green trees, the gray-blue water flowed gently south, and the bottom of the sky was bathed in a cheerful pastel glow. The wind blended the smell of fish with the scent of trees blossoming on the waterside, spiced with gasoline and the aroma of breakfast sizzling in the kitchen of a nearby ship. There was a faint buzz of insects and splashes of fish could be heard.

Abigail stood at the railing and turned her face to the rising sun, her eyes closed for a long moment. The box with the softly snoring Soxy was in her hand. Cassius was trying to talk to John in the hallway. When she left them, they were arguing about where the boat-towners would put them up until Megan's baby was born. *Until the baby is born...*

Her face twisted into an angry grimace. It was quite obvious that Cassius still hadn't given up on his plan and wanted to bust out of the boat-town as soon as possible. As she looked out over the slowly waking colony, Abigail was more and more sure of herself. *We did the right thing, and we could be safe here. Why the hell would we need a goddamn island?*

Then she thought of David and how happy he would have been to see what she was seeing now. The boats basking in the sunshine, rocking gently, and the people walking around her fearlessly, happy. She hoped the young man hadn't suffered much and that he had found peace in at least one thing in his last moment of consciousness: Megan and her baby would find a home in the colony.

Watching the armed men in the towers of the ships, Abigail felt that here, at last, they had found the rule and order that Cassius had missed elsewhere. The decks were clean, life was organized. Women washed clothes on one houseboat, men chopped firewood on another, and on a third one, older men sorted through the items collected on foraging trips. A guy in a sweatshirt baked bread, perhaps from the very flour for which wheat was grown in the fields nearby, and a huge metal structure smoked the fish caught at the upriver fishing farm. On a distant ship, small children hurried along with books in their hands. *Are they going to class? Then there really is a school in the boat-town, just as Megan said...*

Abigail grinned like a Cheshire cat and ignored Cassius, who was grumbling incessantly in her head, warning her that she shouldn't daydream just yet, that she should concentrate.

Damn it all! This is the place we've always been looking for! Where we can stop running, where we don't have to watch our backs!

As far as she was concerned, everything was perfect. Even the things that would horrify Cassius.

Most of the ships were shabby, dingy white. Only one houseboat stood out from the crowd, anchored on the edge of the boat-town, on the northern side of the colony. Once grey, it was now painted a hundred colors. The three-story houseboat most resembled a pyramid with its roof cut off, defiantly standing amidst the currents that the river pounded it with. On the open top deck, movement could be seen beneath the rainbow-colored tarpaulins, and she could hardly believe her eyes when she spotted someone playing guitar on the balcony. If she listened closely, she could even hear the tune.

Who could be living there? How nice it would be to look around...

The sunlight caressing her face was obscured by a shadow. Maya and Shaun appeared beside her. Abigail straightened up and Maya held out a hand to greet her in the way of someone who wasn't used to new people as an everyday occurrence.

"Abigail, right?" Maya asked cheerfully. "That's your name, isn't it?"

"Yes. Abigail."

"Cool. And tell us, Abigail, how long are you planning to stay? My brother was supposed to ask that question, but he's still playing the hard man."

Shaun went pale.

"Maya... Are you crazy?"

Maya, on the other hand, just shook her head.

"Relax, bro, only the blind can't see, right?" She winked at Abigail, who blushed considerably. "So?"

"I don't know yet," Abigail replied. "But I'd love to stay as long as possible, even forever. I hope Cassius can come to an agreement with your companions."

"If you're not troublemakers, I'm sure he will." Shaun stepped closer, his chest now swelling with confidence. "There's plenty of room and food and things to do... At least that's what they always tell us when we feel like complaining."

"That sounds great."

"Yes, it is!" Maya took back control of the conversation, then pointed with her head towards the multicolored houseboat. "If you stay, we'd be happy to show you the home of our gang. And who knows, maybe Shaun will even find the courage to show you around." Maya chuckled and nudged the boy playfully with her shoulder. "It's a pretty big colony, so a tour would take a long time, wouldn't it, bro?"

"You guys live there?" Abigail asked, eyes wide open, glancing at the multicolored houseboat with longing.

"That's right. The wonder of the whole colony."

Shaun rolled his eyes.

"Yeah, sure…"

"Well, not the whole colony, but we like it. And the rest of them, the daft old bastards, can go fuck themselves."

Abigail gave Maya a quizzical look. Someone cleared a throat behind their backs, and the three youngsters turned around at the same time. Cassius approached them with a stern face. He slowed down and turned sideways so the teens could leave without him blocking their way. The siblings understood his intention and stepped back.

"See you around," Maya chattered, and with that the teens disappeared down the hallway to the bottom of the cruise ship. Cassius watched them for a moment, then looked back to Abigail. His stiff posture finally relaxed.

But not Abigail's. Her face hardened as they looked at each other. Her fingers gripped the railing.

"What now?" she asked.

"We've been given a room where we can stay until the baby is born."

Abigail shook her head.

"And then?" She restrained herself from launching into a long monologue about how he was being silly again and it was completely pointless for them to move. And dangerous, too, if part of the pack were still lurking outside.

Cassius raised his eyebrows.

"We're moving on. We've done what we had to do, more than we promised, so there's no reason to stay."

"That it looks safe, isn't that a good reason?"

"Safe? It might be for a while. Until the same thing happens that always does. A little stabbing here, a little shooting there, some palace revolt... this place isn't for us, you can see that."

"That's not how I see it. I think it's worth looking around."

"Go on, then, you've got a few hours."

Abigail stamped her foot angrily before she turned and started walking. She didn't know where she was going, she just wanted to leave him before saying something she would regret. But Cassius's voice stopped her, and his emotionless tone made it even worse.

"But don't roam too far, we're leaving in the morning!"

Abigail stopped. She felt her ears begin to burn. *I can't believe we're going down the same road again! And besides... Why shouldn't I say something I'll regret?*

She turned back and looked defiantly at him.

"So, tell me, what's the plan? Your super big plan? Are we going to start collecting like stupid cavemen again?"

"Maybe. For now I just want to get as far away from this place and Norton as possible. We can deal with the rest afterwards."

Tense silence. Abigail gathered her strength. She pulled away, her face reddening.

"What if I don't want to leave?"

"It always starts like this, you know that! At first it's all very exciting and they're nice to you, but then it turns out they're also just humans. You saw the way those men were looking at you."

"I can protect myself. And besides, there are other women here. What makes you think they're so interested in me?"

Cassius exhaled a lungful of air.

"We're not staying, period. The discussion is over!"

"It's over?" Abigail erupted. "I'm not a child, don't tell me what to do! I'll stay here if I want to!"

She furiously turned, but he didn't let it go; Cassius grabbed her arm and spun her towards him.

"How many times in the last few days have we nearly died because of you, huh? Only because you wouldn't listen to me. I told you we're better off alone!"

Abigail tore her hand from the grip.

"You're better off alone!" she snapped at Cassius, who was taken aback. "You! But not me anymore..."

Abigail clenched her jaw tightly and, after a moment's hesitation, raised her eyes to the sky and left him alone. And Cassius didn't try again to stop her. *Good, now think about it!*

3.

Cassius packed his things in the musty cabin they had been assigned, then sat down on the bed and closed his eyes. He felt dead tired, but for some reason he couldn't sleep. His mind was racing and Abigail's words echoed in his head. *She should know by now that no one could be trusted in a place like this! Why should these people be any different from anywhere else?*

He had no idea how much time had passed while he had been sitting on the bed, motionless, but when something hit the open door, his eyelids popped up. Seeing a rubber ball bouncing on the floor, he shook his head in annoyance. From further down the hall, he heard a woman scream.

"What did I tell you, cheeky little rascals? No playing in here!"

Cassius rubbed his eyes before getting up. A sharp, bright light streamed in through the cabin window, and the noise outside intensified. It was rush hour in the colony.

He massaged his injured shoulder and picked up the plaything from the floor. It was a ribbed purple ball, a shape and color he'd seen somewhere before, and it took him only a moment to figure out where...

The tip-tap of tiny footsteps drew close from the corridor. A little boy appeared in the doorway and flinched in fright when he saw Cassius holding the ball.

"I'm sorry, mister!" the startled little boy said. "Can I have my ball?"

Cassius smiled and handed it to him. The little boy took it and was about to run off to play, but then he must have remembered something because he turned back.

"I haven't seen you here before, mister. Are you new?" he asked, blinking widely for an answer.

"I am new. We came last night, the three of us..."

Soon four, Cassius added, but only in his thoughts. When he spoke to children, he was careful not to say anything he would have to explain later.

"What's your name?" Cassius asked instead, covering the gun

resting in its holster with his right hand, blocking the spot where the little boy's curious gaze was fixed.

"Bobby."

And he didn't lie. The other kids were chanting Bobby's name from a distant point in the hallway, wondering where he was. Cassius smiled, feeling better.

"You know, Bobby, I once knew someone with a ball just like that."

"You did?"

"That's right. Now, wait a minute, I got something for you."

Cassius took out the matchbox car with the worn-off number plate from his flat metal box. Bobby watched open-mouthed, his surprise only amplifying as the man handed him the toy. A rare gift in a place like this.

"Here you go, Bobby! It's so you don't get bored if you really can't play in the hallway."

The little boy took the toy and looked up at him with happy eyes.

"Thank you very much, mister!"

After a happy giggle, he took off in a great leap, leaving Cassius alone in the musty room, which at that moment seemed more cramped and uninviting than ever. The sounds from the corridor were distant and muffled.

After closing the lid of the flat metal box, he stepped over to the cabin window and peered out. Life on board the ships was a hive of loud arguments and bouncing instructions. The tower-crane on the riverbank was moving large metal boards onto the boat-town. On the last barge downstream, a funeral was being held, and a body wrapped in a tarp was being lowered into the river, where it was immediately swept southward by the current. A small vessel headed north. *Probably to the fish farm*, he thought. *I'd surely take a look at that, and if it's not bad, I'd even stay for some angling…*

He shrugged, closed the door behind him, and started back to the level where Megan's room was located.

4.

It was almost noon when the door creaked open softly, and the midwife poked her head through the crack, her face worried and tired. Cassius was sitting with his back against the wall and immediately jumped to his feet. Josie, leaning against the door jamb, summoned him with a wrinkled forefinger.

When Cassius reached the cabin door, he tried to peep into the room, but the midwife blocked his way. Megan lay motionless on the bed, her chest slowly heaving. Cassius looked at Josie, who leaned closer, almost whispering.

"The baby girl is fine."

He sighed in relief.

"That's very good."

Yet the midwife was not happy with him, and even raised her hand when Cassius tried to squeeze past her. She fidgeted with her apron, as if reluctant to tell him what she knew.

"But the woman is not going to make it. She's only got a couple of hours at most."

The blood drained from his face. For a moment, he didn't know what to say, just stared blankly at the midwife, who finally stepped away from him so he could enter the cabin.

"You can still try to talk to her," she said. "I'm sorry! I really am."

Cassius pulled himself together and staggered into the room while the midwife stepped out into the hallway and closed the door, leaving them alone in the airless space.

Megan was all drenched in sweat, and at first she didn't even notice that he had arrived. She lay with her eyes half closed and her head turned to the side. Beside the bed was a mustard yellow bassinet on white legs with the newborn baby inside, whimpering softly somewhere under the covers. Cassius nervously stepped closer and glanced into the bassinet, only to sigh in relief.

The baby looked healthy, and there was no sign that the bite on her mother had affected her. She was a beautiful little girl, with downy hairs on her shoulders and ears. She was just giving a big yawn when he peered down at her.

Megan mumbled softly and moved her head. Cassius hesitated about what to do and finally sat down on one of the chairs and took her white, clammy hand in his. He felt the heavy air crushing his lungs; a silk cord wrapped around his heart, squeezing it tighter and tighter. Megan turned to him and gave him a sweet smile. She made a gentle gesture as she tried to touch Cassius's cheek, but her hand fell back onto the blanket.

"You've been through quite a lot, haven't you?" she whispered, and the wrinkles dancing at the corners of her lips gave her away again. "You don't get enough rest these days, do you?"

Cassius closed his eyes. Megan wanted to say something more, but she had a hard time speaking. He understood what she wanted and gently took the baby out of the bassinet and laid her next to her mother.

"Congratulations... it's a girl."

She stroked the baby.

"Hello, Hope!"

"Hope?" Cassius raised an eyebrow.

"Yes. Hope. Because that's what she brought into our lives. And I'm going to watch her grow up and become a strong woman!"

Cassius turned his head away.

"But if I don't," Megan continued, "I want you to look after her. Just like you did with Abigail."

"I'm… not…"

"Please! Promise me... Teach her everything you know... Tell her how happy I was when I first saw her... and that I have no regrets whatsoever." Megan broke out in tears. "I'm sorry so many people died because of me. I'm so sorry..."

"It's all right," Cassius comforted her. "We're here now, and all that matters is that the baby is healthy."

"Do you really think so?"

"I really do."

She wiped her eyes, then took off the heart-shaped pendant around her neck and handed it to him.

"You know what to do with it..."

Cassius nodded.

"I will give it to her. And I will tell her all about you."

"That's good... that's good..."

Megan smiled, and Cassius squeezed her hand. As gently as he could, yet firmly enough to make sure she knew she wasn't alone, not for a moment. Not even when she leveled her glassy gaze at him for the last time.

Cassius felt the slender fingers slacken. The light was gone from her eyes, her face had gone stiff. The candle on the table flickered.

Then only the soft whimpering of the baby remained. He cupped his hands around his mouth and cried.

Less than an hour later, Cassius stepped out into the hallway, holding Hope, and waited for the midwife with his back against the wall. When Josie finally appeared, he let her take the baby from him and feed it. After that, he was absorbed in loneliness. He placed his hand on the cabin door once more and checked that it was closed properly.

He didn't have much time to think, because John appeared beside him.

"Come with me! Our leader is ready to see you."

5.

The procession was led by John, with two armed men following behind Cassius. They walked in silence, but that didn't bother him. Not only did he not have the strength to talk, he could barely put one foot in front of the other. After a while he realized that he was not watching where they were going, which was a stupid thing to do. He kept staring at the floor, his legs without strength, his head filled with crazy thoughts. *What is the point of all this?*

He didn't know where Abigail was, he had no idea when or how he could next speak to her... And his despair grew even greater when he thought of Hope. *What the hell was I thinking? How could I possibly protect a newborn baby? We can't stay here, but we can't take her with us...*

What worried him most was that whatever was going on in his

head, he couldn't and wouldn't break his promise. He had taken a burden on himself that no sane person in this world would do, especially at the request of a complete stranger.

Not a stranger! No, echoed in his head.

With great difficulty, he raised his head to at least see where they were. They had left the cruise ship and crossed two barges being used to store barrels marked FLAMMABLE. Cassius could already see that they were heading for the old-fashioned yacht on the edge of the boat-town, nearest the middle of the river. The hundred-and-thirty-foot-long yacht must have been built in the nineties and its whitewashed sides were scuffed with the letters that spelled out its name: PURA VIDA. Several watchmen stood on its deck, and it was well out of the way of the boat-town's inhabitants. This was clearly headquarters.

John, who had been walking briskly, slowed down at the plank leading to the yacht and waved his head towards the watchmen. He glanced back only once to check on the others, then continued, as determined as before. At the stairs to the bridge, the gunmen who had been escorting them stopped; John and Cassius reached the top alone.

There was only one man on the open-air bridge, protected by a blue tarpaulin: a black man with a scar on his cheek from ear to neck, wearing dark trousers, a gray sweater, and heavy boots. He had a half-burnt cigar in his mouth, a lighter between his sausage-like fingers, and a .44 Magnum in his belt. When he saw Cassius, he blew out a cloud of full-bodied smoke and rose from the brown sponge-covered chair.

Instead of reaching out his hand, he took a thorough look at their guest.

"I'm George Solomon, head of the colony. I'm sorry for your loss. It is sad that this great sacrifice was in vain."

"Her sacrifice was not in vain," Cassius said after a long silence. He could see Solomon was expecting some sort of introduction.

"I'm glad you think so. I like that attitude," Solomon scratched his head, searching John's gaze. "Tell me, where are you from? You and the girl."

"We met Megan and David about halfway. That's when we decided to help them."

Solomon took a big puff on his cigar. Cassius suspected that this was not the answer they were looking for, but he had learnt that in such a case he should say as little as possible if he wanted to avoid inconvenience.

"I see," the head of the colony cleared his throat. "Don't worry about your past, no matter how much some people here may fear that you've brought some infections with you, or that you'll rob us in our sleep... Because that's not true, is it?"

Awkward silence.

"No," Cassius replied.

Solomon gave him a penetrating look, and only after another sniff did he throw a broad, confiding smile behind the cloud of full-bodied smoke.

"Of course not! It would be nonsense to try such a thing anyway, and I hear you guys are clean... I personally welcome all busy hands and anyone willing to do something for the boat-town."

"I'm flattered, but I don't think we'll be here long. Nothing personal," Cassius explained. "We prefer to go our own way."

"And what way is that?"

"A peaceful one. We don't bother anyone if we're not bothered." Cassius glanced sideways at John. "And we usually leave unnoticed, as if we weren't even there."

"I see... but I wonder if that's what the girl thinks."

Cassius looked at him, startled.

"Abigail? Our business is our business, it's none of yours!"

Solomon stepped threateningly closer. John put his hands on his hips, his fingers drumming on the butt of the gun resting in his belt.

"Everything that happens here is my business," the head of the colony said and, after a pause for effect, gave Cassius' shoulder an overfriendly pat. A false grin spread across his face. "You were probably unaware of that, so forget about it. Let's get to what you wanted to talk to me about. I'm dying to know what information you have that I don't!"

"It's about the scientist who lives up in the mountains," Cassius began, but Solomon just waved.

"Ah, of course, good ol' Norton. I should have guessed! He's an innocent chap, he hasn't rocked the boat much so far."

"I wouldn't bet on it, though! The bastard drugged us, locked us in his cellar, and spilled his guts. If half of what he said is true, you've got something to worry about."

"Aha," Solomon gestured towards John. His look told him he didn't know whether to laugh or not. "Are you sure we are talking about the same person? The absent-minded, looney professor?"

"I didn't do a DNA test, buddy."

"More respect, my friend!" John nudged Cassius, but Solomon shushed him.

"Relax, there's no need to get tough yet. Of course, what goes around comes around, but right now I'm more interested in the details. So?" The head of the colony looked at Cassius with a piercing glance.

"Norton has developed a beast repellent to control the ferals, and he's determined to gather an army of them. If he's strong enough, he'll attack the boat-town."

Solomon was the first to snort.

"Wow, just wow! We don't hear stories like that every day, right?"

"Right, Mr. Solomon," John laughed.

Cassius frowned nervously.

"I have a hunch you're not taking what I said seriously."

"Because it's not so easy! But let's toy with the idea that you're telling the truth. What do you think we should do? Should we gather an army as well and attack first? Lay siege to the place?"

"Not a bad idea, but that's your business. Mine was only to warn you of the danger. And that the house is heavily secured."

"Is that so?"

"It is, damn it!"

"All right, don't get so worked up. Tell me, if this guy is so dangerous, how did you escape?"

Cassius was silent. He would have liked to have answered immediately, but he knew that in situations like this it was unwise to pat himself on the back. He might even end up being seen as a threat.

"We were lucky."

"Ah, well, we're also lucky here in the boat-town. Lucky, for instance, that we're so far from the riverbank and lucky that so many armed men are protecting our sleep. Devoted people, prepared for anything."

"You know best..." Cassius shrugged.

Solomon bit his lip, then stubbed the end of his cigar.

"I appreciate your rushing here to warn us, but we can defend ourselves. This place is an impregnable fortress, we're loaded with ammunition, and we've got a few tricks up our sleeves that even my people don't know about."

John chuckled, a sound that came from the confidence that he knew more than others. But Solomon's face remained frozen.

"So thank you for your concern, and I promise we won't let our guard down... but I'm not going to risk any more men and resources because you think an absent-minded professor is plotting in the mountains. Just let him come and give it a try, and he'll see who he's messing with! Have I made myself clear?"

Cassius nodded. John tapped him on the shoulder, indicating that it was time to go. Solomon sat back in his seat and touched his mouth with the cigar.

"One more thing, Mr. Cassius!"

He turned back, surprised.

"Till you and the girl have settled your business, don't wander off too much alone! If you're going to be a guest, you might as well behave like one."

Then Solomon was enfolded in the full-bodied smoke of his cigar.

6.

Abigail was given an apple, then Maya pushed her assertively onto the multicolored houseboat. The busy teenagers on board looked up at their arrival and stopped what they were doing. All eyes were focused on the girl.

"Come on, we'll introduce you to the others!" Maya said, keeping her palm on Abigail's back the whole time. If Abigail hesitated for a moment, she gave her a firm shove.

Abigail blushed up to her ears at the stares she received and shook hands with the youths one after the other. Some hugged her tightly, others just winked warmly. One little girl clapped her hands happily and gently took Soxy's box, placing it on the floor. The smaller ones immediately gathered around the box to pet the puppy. Abigail watched them with a worried expression, and again Cassius' words came back to her. *You behave differently when you're responsible for someone.*

"Be gentle!" Maya raised her hand at the sight of her increasingly excited mates. "You don't need to eat the poor thing. And the puppy either," she laughed, and whispered in Abigail's ear. "Don't stop, or you're dead! Right, left, come on, up the stairs!"

Maya made her way forward and Shaun covered their backs as they walked along the handrail to the stairs to the upper levels. Abigail didn't know which way to turn, trying to say a kind word to each person and feeling she'd expressed at least a hundred times how glad she was to be here, clutching the apple tightly in her hand. Fortunately, the rush subsided when they reached the middle of the houseboat.

"Do only young people live here?" Abigail asked, taking a big bite of the fruit. It was heavenly; it had been so long since she had had an apple, she had forgotten the taste.

"This and the houseboat docked next to us belong to orphans."

"Orphans?" Abigail's eyes widened. "Are you?"

"Yes," Shaun nodded sadly, "We all came to the boat-town without parents, so our situation is a bit different. And since school is not compulsory for children over the age of twelve, we had to learn to look after ourselves alone."

"Almost alone," Maya corrected.

"Okay, sure..."

Maya showed her around.

"We've learned a lot over the years. If there's not enough clothing for us after the foraging trips, we make our own. Some make candles, some make soap, and we've even learned to play music, so we have parties almost every night."

She said the last part louder and raised her hands in the air as if she were at a concert. A roaring boy's voice from inside the boat answered back:

"Yeee!"

"Now we can fix anything on the boat," Maya continued. "And we have our own kitchen. The chef is a Ramsey guy."

"In name only," Shaun added.

"What about the adults? Don't they help you?" Abigail asked.

"Ah, most of them think we're just hippies," Shaun smirked. "We're the only two who can have guns, because we learned how to use them before we came here..."

"But we're only assigned to guard duty," Maya finished. "Frankly, they don't even care about us anymore. If it were up to Solomon and his crew, we wouldn't learn anything new, and we'd only get menial jobs on the other ships. It's lucky that Rebecca takes on those who are of age and they can work on the fishing farm upriver."

They turned around the corner and walked up the stairs. The handshakes didn't diminish there either; everyone wanted to flock around them, so Maya navigated Abigail on a path with enough room and some to spare. Delicious smells wafted from the kitchen, teens chatted in a far away corner and the guitar-playing boy cuddled his instrument while asleep on a mattress. Abigail watched the world of the houseboat with fascination, but even she noticed that something was missing from the youngsters' lives. While for her, every day had been about training, learning, escaping for the past few years, the people here had been free to live their lives without anyone telling them what to do. *Would these be the hippies?*

They arrived at the last level, where the bridge and the terrace were located, protected from the strong sunlight by a large awning.

"Is there anyone left I haven't met?" Abigail turned her head.

"Only one now." Shaun made a sour face.

"Oh, bro, what are you so nervous about?" Maya nudged the boy aside, then turned to Abigail with a half-smile. "Only Roderick is left, but I'd rather not say anything about him. He speaks for himself."

They were on the top deck of the houseboat. There were chaise lounges on the terrace, but only one of them was occupied: near the shade provided by the awning sprawled a half-naked, long-chested young man, barely twenty. He had sunglasses on his face, a thick strip of ointment on his nose and beside him, in the shade, sat a small table with an empty cocktail glass.

"We have a guest, Roderick, don't be rude!" Maya exclaimed. Roderick slowly raised his head and peered out from behind his sunglasses. When he saw Abigail, he sat up, but his movements were languid, as if he were doing her a favor. After taking a good look, he finally stood up and offered her his hand.

"What a pleasant surprise!" he said in a gravelly tone and prepared to kiss her hand like a real Casanova. But Abigail misunderstood his intention and acted on instinct: she squeezed Roderick's hand, pulling him towards her and twisting him round. Joints and bones creaked and cracked, and the boy cried out in pain.

"Oh, my God!"

"What are you doing?" Abigail asked, ready for a fight, as Roderick flailed with his free hand.

"Okay, okay, time out. Damn it..."

Abigail released Roderick, who shook his hurt hand with a pained expression. Maya and Shaun burst out laughing.

"Gosh," Roderick groaned, but forced a casual grin on his face. "Stand back, no one's going to hurt you here."

"Sorry," Abigail said, blushing.

"Don't apologize," Maya stepped closer. "That's how you treat the unmannered. You did very well!"

"Thank you, Maya, I'm fine. It's kind of you to ask," Roderick spread his arms. He seemed to have forgotten the whole affair, but was still massaging his fingers. "My name is Roderick, the leader of the gang."

"Interim leader," Shaun corrected, and Roderick shrugged.

"Same thing. And as you can see, I've got a lot of work to do, like teaching respect to some people."

"You're going about it the wrong way, Roderick." Maya rolled her eyes. "You do have things to do, like fixing up the speedboat Rebecca got us a month ago."

Maya pointed to the battered speedboat swaying beside the multicolored waterhome. Looted gear was still in the speedboat, among it a massive anti-material rifle, of a size which Abigail had never seen before and which could shoot a bullet larger than her palm. *Jeez, these kids couldn't even load it, nevermind use it...*

"If we can tinker with it," Maya turned to Abigail, "we can arrange our own foraging trips to the northern cities."

The streamlined, thirty-foot runabout was already well beyond the crest of the wave, but it really did look ideal, with a powerful engine and room for almost a dozen people. Abigail was, of course, puzzled for a moment.

"The adults won't let you go with them?"

"At most, Roderick can go, but he's no big help to them," Shaun chuckled. The subject of the joke blinked like an uncomprehending puppy, then snapped his fingers and wagged his head.

"Why don't you get our guest a drink, Shaun? How can you be so careless?" Roderick stepped closer to Abigail, his voice deepening in a way that was more comical than seductive. "Would you like something to drink? A nice cocktail?"

Abigail's face brightened.

"I'd like something cold, but I don't want to be any trouble..."

"Oh, come on! You heard her, Shaun," Roderick nodded his head towards the kitchen downstairs. "And while you're at it..."

"Screw you, Roderick! I'm not getting you anything. You're a big enough chump to fetch your own!"

Maya laughed louder and louder, and finally Abigail smiled as well. She was sure that the youngsters were teasing each other, as if it were a daily routine, and neither of them seemed offended by the other's words. And she liked that very much. She always imagined something like that when she was lying alone on her favorite mattress on top of the RV at the edge of the car-maze. Then she wondered what Cassius would think if he saw this. He would surely freak out at this laxity. *Pedantic old man...*

"Where was I?" Roderick raised a finger to his chin.

"On the schedule for the boat repairs," Maya interjected.

"All right, all right, I promise I'll get on it tomorrow. Not that a week or two makes that much difference."

Maya looked at Abigail and resumed her role as an information desk worker.

"Solomon promised that if we brought back valuable items from our foraging trips, they'd help us build our own farm one day," she explained, almost without taking a breath.

Shaun, meanwhile, returned with a glass of something cool to drink and, with a broad, proud grin, handed it to Abigail. She took a sip and closed her eyes for a moment in surprise. She had never drunk anything so delicious, with flavors doing a sweet dance in her mouth. Maya, of course, continued her single-minded harangue:

"So it would be nice not to delay any longer, Roderick. Next year we can have our own crop if you don't screw it up."

"I told you I'd do it."

"Don't the adults give you food?" Abigail asked after opening her eyes.

"They do, it's just that we want to be able to stand on our own two feet. It's nice that we get the best catch from Rebecca, but we're a bit tired of all the fish. And we have a lot of plans that Solomon thinks are stupid. He said if we got our own farm, we could do whatever we wanted."

"Of course, that's not without its dangers," Roderick interjected.

"No risk, no reward!" Shaun said dryly before continuing with a wry smile. "I know you're a bit scared, Roderick, but believe me, we can do it."

"I don't know, wise guy! Unlike you, I stand for sanity."

"And laziness," Maya growled, and without waiting for Roderick's reply, she turned back to Abigail. "By the way, I hope you're hungry, because we're having a big feast today."

"Of course." Abigail's eyes lit up. "I'm starving."

"That's good. And you'll finally get to meet Rebecca."

Maya pointed off into the distance: another speedboat was skimming the surface of the sunlit river, heading straight for them. Abigail raised an eyebrow when she noticed that there was only one person in it.

"Come on, let's go down and say hello!" Maya nudged her sideways and was off. Abigail glared once more at Roderick, who winked charmingly, before Shaun gently steered Abigail in the right direction.

They jogged down the stairs to the first floor.

As the speedboat approached, Abigail gradually made out the

woman driving it. At first she saw only a baseball cap and sunglasses, then the woman's slender frame in jeans and a loose-fitting T-shirt. She looked like she had just stepped out of an old commercial. The speedboat docked and the woman swept off her hat as she jumped onboard and the wind caught her raven-black hair.

Shaun and a few of the boys unloaded the boxes from the speedboat, which were overflowing with fish, and Maya leaned closer to the raven-haired woman, then whispered something in her ear. The woman's face brightened.

Abigail was eager to meet one of the patron saints of the youngsters, but she noticed something that disturbed her more than it should have. Some of the older people from nearby ships were moving towards them, and not just the ordinary townspeople, but the armed guards who were leaving their posts one after the other. Meanwhile, the youngsters started to hand out the rations.

This isn't going to be good, she thought, but then Rebecca appeared in front of her and before Abigail could offer her a hand, the raven-haired woman hugged her. By then she had forgotten her worries.

"Welcome to the boat-town, my dear!" Rebecca said. "I hope you know you're safe now!"

Abigail smiled and sighed. *I hope I'm not only safe, but finally home...*

HAPPY HUNTING!

1.

The Alpha was next to the Beta's dead body. Blood seeped from its right arm where one of the large-caliber bullets had struck it and murderous fury burned in its unharmed eye. The pain returned as the adrenaline drained out, but that was no longer its concern. It only gazed at the female.

The devastation around them was immense: the asphalt was scarred by bullets, and dead members of the pack lay everywhere. Only a few were still alive. One was feasting on a mangled boat-towner beside the overturned jeep, but the Alpha didn't care. The smell that had followed them all this way still stung its nose. It was as clear as if its owner were hiding behind the nearby billboard. It was surely part of its past, someone who had been close, but there was no memory of who that person was. Everything was jumbled; thoughts were not coming together in its mind.

The smell led the Alpha straight to the boat-town. Its muscles tensed, and it wanted to swing into action immediately, to throw itself into the pleasure of destruction without thinking. The Alpha could feel the beating of its heart as it quickened and for a moment everything blurred.

A strange feeling took over its body, a mixture of revenge and helplessness. It was just enough to create surprise. Nothing like this had ever happened before.

The Alpha raised its head and noticed another vehicle – one its former self would have known as a black jeep. A white-robed silhouette stepped out of the jeep and began to examine the broken-down SUV, the car where not so long ago the pack had slaughtered a semi-transformed young man.

The surviving members of the pack snarled as they prepared to attack, but the Alpha's roar held them back.

It was saving this prey for itself.

It wanted to ease the rage and the pain that wracked its body. It roared into motion, covering the vast distance as fast as it had ever done before. Its mouth watered, adrenaline flooded its every inch, and its fingers spasmed. One hundred yards, fifty, twenty...

The Alpha fell to the concrete like someone yanked by a rope. It shook its head in disbelief and tried again, gathering strength and flinging its tortured body at the man standing beside the jeep, who was fumbling with his strange gloves. Yet again, it bounced off the invisible wall protecting the white-robed man.

The Alpha began to understand what was happening, but refused to give up the fight.

It rose and moved forward with deliberate strides, cutting the distance between them inch by inch. Every muscle in its body was in agony. The Alpha struggled, but to no avail. Its steps slowed and at last it could no longer lift its legs.

"Well, well, well," the white-robed man said, looking at the Alpha. "When God closes one door, he opens another. You're a fine specimen... Just as strong as I need you to be."

The white-robed man lowered his arm and flashed a scowl at the boat-town bathed in the mid-morning sun. His fingers toyed with his wedding ring for a moment, then he shook as if coming out of a dream. He gave one last twist on the device strapped to his hand.

The Alpha cried out, but this time a strange sensation ran through its body instead of pain. It was as if a mysterious force was calling it to the white-robed man, while another was keeping it within a few paces of him. It dropped to its knees, claws scraping the asphalt, saliva dripping from its snarling mouth.

The white-robed man leaned over.

"What do you think about some old-fashioned revenge?" he asked with a broad smile, then looked over the Alpha's shoulder.

From the valley, the remaining members of the pack came running, equally as drawn by the green-flashing device.

"Of course," he continued, "we are too few to attack, but it is only a matter of time. Backup is on the way!"

The white-robed man straightened and took a deep breath. Turning his face to the sunlight, he stepped over to the broken-down electric car and took a scarf from the passenger seat. The pregnant woman's scarf, which he then threw in front of the Alpha.

"The woman and her child are mine! The rest is yours."

The Alpha grunted and hunched, eyeing the man towering over it. It heard the words and knew them, but its consciousness drew no connections; their meaning was unknown.

"Ah, of course, how stupid of me! You probably don't understand any of it. Never mind... we'll work it out. When the others are here."

The white-robed man held up his gloved hand. The pack roared and gathered around him, but try as they might, they could not resist the invisible force. The Alpha snarled and looked at its peers.

2.

By mid-afternoon there were more than a hundred of them waiting in the trees, silent and ready to attack. The Alpha stood in the front row, among the unknown ferals. Short of breath due to its wounds, but still standing straight. The white-robed man crouched at a respectable distance, observing the waterfront. The device glowed green on his hand. The ferals watched him with their teeth gritted, but the device would let no one approach.

A boat appeared near the colony with a lone man in it, who steered the loudly humming skiff towards the watchman on the pier. In the daylight, it was clear to see that the colony was anchored to the shore by a number of thick wire ropes and that there were small and large pieces of wood floating down the river.

The Alpha looked up at the tower-crane on the bank, its jib almost reaching over the boat-town. So many ways to get in.

The white-robed man cracked his neck and stood up. He walked over to the Alpha, who was watching the glove flashing green with its remaining bloodshot eye. Its body struggled, but no matter how hard it tried, it had no chance to overcome the device.

The boat, meanwhile, approached the bank at a brisk pace. Norton gave the device a twist, and the ferals' bodies shuddered. The Alpha felt the change in its spine, the sudden freedom, and was about to start forward, but the man stopped it with another twist.

"Expendables first," the white-robed man growled and shuddered as one by one the Greenhorns and Deltas descended into the river or clung to the cables. He gave a sneer, whispering as he glared at the boat-town. "I have come to bring not peace but the sword. For I have come to set a man against his father, a daughter against her mother..."

The white-robed man looked at the Alpha.

"Happy hunting!" Then he waved and headed for the pier to distract the watchmen.

When the grip of the beast repellent loosened, the Alpha's sight cleared and the pain ceased. It took a deep breath and immediately set off towards the tower-crane. Kept in motion by a desire to kill, the thought of its prey made its mouth water.

A MAN AGAINST HIS FATHER

1.

By afternoon, the colony had fallen silent, the way it would if everyone had retired for a siesta in the late August heat. Cassius had a strange feeling; he could sense the calm before the storm in the sultry air. Even the characteristic smells had disappeared, as if a gentle breeze from the north had swept everything from the decks of the ships. After his visit to Solomon, a young boy brought him lunch, but Cassius's attempts to get information about the boat-town or its leader were in vain, and the boy left after a few brief words. The cruise ship hallway was empty. No footsteps could be heard, and the children were no longer playing outside.

Cassius tried to gather his racing thoughts, but they were shattered again and again by worry. All he could think of was that he had permanently chased Abigail away, and that he could not undo their argument. He sat down on the bed and put his weapons beside him. On his other side was the flat metal box wrapped in a striped linen rag. He opened the misshapen, rusty lid and looked at the pile of junk. The lucky dolphin bracelet of colorful pearls...

...the pendrive that held his past...

...the yellowed, crumpled postcard of the island they were headed to. The island where he had spent so many summers and which he had told his wife so much about.

He softly placed Megan's necklace on top of the other objects and closed the lid. He shut his eyes and gave in to fatigue. The emptiness drew him under, except there were no dreamscapes. He saw nothing, not Nia, not Lucas and Molly, not anyone else. Nor did he hear his wife's voice; no one spoke to him. *This whole thing wasn't worth it...*

He woke to the sound of someone knocking gently on the cabin door. Cassius's eyes snapped open and he turned his head in the direction of the noise. The midwife was standing in the doorway with Hope in her arms, wrapped in a clean swaddling cloth.

"Luckily the other moms have enough milk so we were able to feed her," Josie began, then stepped closer to show him the baby. "And she's got fluffy, soft clothes to make her comfortable, but... she'll need someone to look after her."

Cassius got up heavily and stepped closer. With a sincere smile, he glanced at the swaddled baby, who was squirming with eyes closed, her little finger held up to her rosy cheek.

"Is there anyone here who could help?" he asked, after touching Hope's brow.

"The orphans are taken care of by Rebecca and the youngsters, but the boat-town isn't a safe deposit box where you can just drop off what you don't need."

A blush of shame poured down Cassius' cheeks. He nodded, while cursing himself for even asking. His promise to Megan was on his mind, a promise he could not break.

"Yeah... I just thought that in the beginning... The wild out there is no place for babies."

Josie snorted and shook her head.

"No one is going to chase you out of here at gunpoint! If you're not dangerous, Solomon won't throw you out. Where are you running off to so fast?"

"It's what we're used to."

"But not her," the midwife glanced at Hope, then placed the baby in his arms. "She's just arrived and I'm sure she'd like to get to know her new home."

Cassius gently took Hope in his arms and greeted the baby with a soft rocking motion, and she seemed to smile at his touch. *You have your mother's nose, Jellybean.* The subtle, sweet smell of the baby reminded him of the first time he had held his son in the same way, and how he had looked forward to the arrival of his little daughter. He would have given his life just to protect them, but in the end he failed. And so would he fail with Hope, because it was down to luck that Abigail – his only success – hasn't been taken away yet. And now he was about to lose her too...

"What can you tell me about Rebecca?"

Josie shrugged her shoulders.

"She's running the upriver fish farm, which is probably the most boring job in the boat-town. But there's a reason the boss doesn't insist on her presence. She and Solomon had a row, so it was best for everyone."

"And the orphans?"

"They're exactly what they should be at their age. Useless and curious. They find it hard to fit in, and that surely doesn't sit well with a lot of people."

"Let me guess. John?"

The midwife looked the other way.

"John doesn't know what it's like to lose your family and be left alone. Solomon... and most of the people here do, so they're more understanding when it comes to the kids."

Cassius recognized the shadow passing across the midwife's face, was meant to hide a painful memory from her past. He had seen that veiled expression on others' faces too many times during their journey.

"Boy or a girl?" he asked quietly when Josie took the baby back from him.

"Boy," she said after a long sigh. "He was thirteen the last time I saw him."

"What happened?"

"We got separated from each other... not long before I came here."

"I'm sorry..."

"Don't be, because now I know he is in safe hands." Josie wiped her eyes. "The other part of our team reached the colony in Key West, and he is there with my friends. So I'm counting the days until I can see him again."

"Key West?" Cassius raised an eyebrow. "Haven't heard about them."

It seemed logical though. The islands in the Florida Keys were connected to the mainland by a highway almost a hundred miles long, and the bridges were easy to control and close.

"We managed to contact them in early summer. A man and a woman are in charge, and now they're nearly as many as we are," the midwife continued. "Solomon planned to visit them and promised that I could go with them."

"I hear that Solomon promises many things. The question is, will he keep his word?

Josie sneered.

"I know what you're thinking, but Solomon is the leader we need. Without him we'd have fallen apart long ago."

In the distance, strange muffled noises grew louder. Cassius cocked his head and raised his index finger to gently shush the midwife. He heard a shriek, then a crack of gunfire, to which Josie reacted with fright.

"What was that?"

Cassius hurried to the window and looked out. All hell had broken loose on the boats attached to the portside of the cruise ship. People were running headlong towards the inner part of the boat-town, looking back desperately at the riverbank. Then he caught sight of the first feral; a Delta had jumped from a thick wire rope onto the deck of one of the barges and immediately threw itself at one of the fleeing boat-towners. Cassius staggered back, ready to run.

"We're under attack!"

2.

Abigail had always wanted this: to be welcomed the way Rebecca and the kids had welcomed her. Like a family member. She straightened her back happily; she had already forgotten her doubts. *What could go wrong in a place like this? The boat-town is a fortress...*

After unloading boxes full of fish from the speedboat, Rebecca picked up a battered backpack, unzipped it, and showed Roderick the loot. There were MP4 players and chargers in the bag, the cables coiled like snakes in a pit. Roderick blinked in puzzlement.

"What am I supposed to do with all this?"

"Well, you could look at them and if some can be repaired, you could fix them."

"Wow," Shaun gaped at the gadgets, taking one out of the backpack. "There could be anything on these."

"Just not boomer music, that's all I ask!" Maya chuckled.

Roderick made a wry face. Rebecca gave him a broad grin and patted him on the back.

"I know you've got one more item on your list, but you'll manage somehow, kiddo."

Abigail smiled as she watched them from the background, and a happiness came over her like she had never felt before. It was as if she had finally found her home after a long journey. She sighed with relief, but something was still missing to make her happiness complete. *Perhaps someday Cassius would see that all this running around was nonsense*, she thought, but then she shook her head. *No, I won't worry about it now, screw the old man if he's going to be so stubborn!*

She glanced over at Soxy's box, still surrounded by a guerilla group of small children, not giving the pup a second's peace. But Soxy seemed to be thrilled by the interest and was happily licking the children's hands. Rebecca crouched down by the box, and listened to the orphans who constantly cut each other off. Abigail was reminded of Megan, and a strange unease came over her.

She was sure the woman and her baby were both all right, so she swept the frightening thoughts away and swore she would go straight back to the cruise ship to see them. *I should probably go now, after all...*

Someone screamed in the distance, then the crack of a rifle shattered the afternoon calm.

Abigail raised her head, her fingers instinctively tightening on the Browning slung over her shoulder. The youngsters flinched, hands clasped over their mouths, and turned towards the noise. Rebecca straightened up and glanced around with a worried look. No matter how they tried, they saw nothing. The events were obscured by the boats anchored close to the riverside.

"What was that?" A murmur ran through the crowd.

The people on the other decks also stopped, but at that point their faces showed only curiosity, not fear. Someone headed over to see what had happened. Maya and Shaun moved closer to each other, and Roderick spread his arms.

"What the heck..."

He didn't get the chance to finish.

The first scream was followed by others, this time clearer, then the cries were drowned out by the sound of gunfire. The first fleeing person ran out through the door of a barge superstructure and rushed headlong as far away from the chaos as possible. Abigail tried, at first without success, to make out what the man was shouting. Slowly, she began to catch words from among the desperate shouting.

"Run... They're here! They're..."

Rebecca and Roderick exchanged glances, and the youngsters whispered helplessly. The fleeing person was finally close enough for them to hear better:

"The fer... The ferals are here!"

Abigail's eyes widened in horror and her face paled, but her honed reflexes took control of her body within moments. She slung the Browning from her shoulder and swung immediately towards the stern of the multicolored boat, hoping to see what was happening on the bank side of the colony.

As she ran, she firmly pushed aside the puzzled youngsters and took one last glance at Soxy. Even she herself was surprised to hear the order ringing clearly in her head: *Now, just concentrate on your task! The puppy will be fine...*

After a few leaps, she reached her destination, but what she saw made her shudder. The colony was under attack by a horde of ferals, most of them still gathering on the riverbank, many others crawling across thick cables or emerging from the water. *How is this possible?* The ferals had avoided the water whenever and wherever they could, yet now it seemed as if they had overcome all fear and plunged into the river, only to cling to fallen logs and dangling wires as they approached the boats. She heard an approaching speedboat, then the warning alarm went off.

Panic broke out in the boat-town. The petrified people began to run, crushing each other as they made their way towards the ships in the middle of the river.

The watchmen tried desperately to bring down the attackers,

but they had no chance. Without a second thought, the ferals threw themselves at those standing nearby. Screams turned quickly into gurgles of blood.

Maya and Shaun appeared beside Abigail. The siblings watched the scene with their mouths wide open, but Abigail didn't think twice about what to do. She raised the Browning and aimed it at one of the ferals. The scope's reticle crossed directly over the chest of the Gamma climbing aboard. *Four bullets!* It wouldn't be good to waste them.

"It's too far," Shaun snarled, but Abigail shushed him angrily.

"Quiet!"

Shaun winced and swallowed hard.

Abigail took a deep breath and forced steadiness into her shaking hands. She pulled the trigger as soon as she could. The bullet tore through the air at the speed of three-thousand feet per second...

...but it missed. She had three bullets left, plus eight in the Glock. *Damn!* She could almost hear Cassius in her head. *I've told you, Abigail, you're not ready yet.* With a lump in her throat, she realized that he was most certainly on the cruise ship where the ferals were headed, rampaging through everything and everyone that came their way.

Someone screamed on the neighboring towboat. Abigail spun around and she caught sight of a Gamma and a Delta emerge and jump down to the deck of the vessel. The youngsters huddled together and began to back away while the ferals became emboldened by the panic. *Oh, no!*

Abigail's muscles tensed, her legs swinging faster than a thought. All doubts were out of her mind. She raised the Browning and fired the last three bullets into the Gamma closest to her, the most dangerous-looking of the two targets, but she only managed to wound the attacker.

The ferals roared, the Gamma in pain and the Delta with bloodlust. Abigail didn't bother with the Glock; she threw herself over the railing, and when she landed on the towboat, she drew her machete and slashed the wounded Gamma with three quick slices.

With the final spin she came face to face with the Delta hurtling towards her. Swish-swish, and the feral collapsed lifelessly, its deformed head falling into the river.

Rebecca and the youngsters had only just realized what had happened. Stunned, their faces white as a sheet, they watched Abigail, who stood gasping, her body drenched in sweat, her chest heaving.

"Wow!" Roderick moaned.

Abigail hurried to Rebecca. She expected neither appreciation nor gratitude. She had no time to spare, but she couldn't just leave them. She had to know they'd be all right until she returned... hopefully with Cassius by her side.

"What is your plan B? Just in case the ferals did get into the boat-town?"

Rebecca was lost for words. She was still in shock from the attack.

"We need to disconnect the houseboat and get as far away from the colony as possible!"

"How long will that take?" Abigail asked impatiently.

"A few minutes... five... ten... maybe..."

"Then do it! I'm going back to get Cassius!" She glanced at Shaun and Maya. "Every bullet counts, you hear me?"

The siblings nodded, their eyes sparkling as their initial fear was replaced by excitement. Rebecca, meanwhile, looked nervously at Abigail.

"What if you don't get back in time?"

"Then go... and take care of Soxy! If anything happens to him," she hissed, glancing ominously at Shaun, "I'll squeeze your privates so hard you'll feel my fingernails in your throat!"

The crowd watched the scene helplessly, as if no one knew what to do. A strange feeling came over Abigail, a mixture of determination and anger. Adrenaline was pumping through her veins, and she wanted to slap the youths one by one. *So this is what it's like to be Cassius... To think of everything, to say everything twice...* And then she understood something she had thought was clear to her. *You behave differently when you're responsible for someone...*

What a pain in the ass it is, and you still must do everything, even if the others don't like your decisions. Even if the risk comes at a price. *You make different decisions, you think differently.* Kind words and a nice smile are meaningless. It's about survival.

"Come on!" she yelled at the paralyzed youngsters.

The crowd dispersed in fear. Everyone went about their tasks.

Boom, boom, boom!

Abigail turned towards the boats near the riverbank. From the increasing screams and gunfire, she knew where she had to go.

3.

Cassius was mentally prepared for the worst when he threw himself out the door of the cruise ship, arriving at the deck corridor on the starboard side. He swept his gaze around, his Glock raised high, his finger on the trigger guard, then waved to the midwife waiting in the hallway, who stepped out into the light.

The boat-towners were fleeing in a frenzy towards the other end of the colony. There was no sign of the ferals yet, but he could hear the distant rattling and stamping of feet, the crunching of bones and the screams of death. He held out his hand and helped Josie step over to the barge moored beside the cruise ship, praying that Hope wouldn't fall from the midwife's trembling hands.

He glanced quickly toward the multicolored boat, which was rocking on the river many barges and towboats away. No matter how hard he tried, he couldn't see Abigail anywhere in the crowd. He shook his head, trying to gather his thoughts. *She'll be fine... She's had good training...*

"What's the plan in case of an attack?" he asked Josie, who was watching the panic unfold with bated breath. "Tell me you have a bloody plan!"

When someone screamed nearby, Josie hugged the baby closer.

"We must head for the boats in the middle of the river. That's where they'll rescue us."

Cassius turned in the direction indicated; he had only to follow the crowd with his eyes. Solomon had just jumped from his yacht to the neighboring boat and was giving orders over a loudspeaker. Two men were standing beside him, waving the escapees with spectacular gestures towards the two most distant houseboats, already half-filled with shivering women and children huddled together.

However, defense wasn't the only thing the boat-town was prepared for. The men were given guns, and they were fastening a flamethrower to a sturdy woman's back. From the top of the nearby vessels, watchmen tried to take down the ferals getting over the cruise ship. So far, they were holding out.

"Not completely useless," Cassius muttered to himself, and gently gripped the midwife's arm so that Josie would look only at him. "Run as fast as you can, and I'll cover you!" His grip then got even tighter. "Look after Hope! Do you hear me?"

The midwife nodded.

"And what about you?"

"I have to find Abigail," he replied, pointing towards the multicolored boat.

A terrifying guttural sound roared above them. Cassius looked up just in time: a Delta was about to leap from the first floor of the cruise ship straight onto the barge. He fired without a moment's thought, and barely a second after the Glock clicked empty, the Delta banged lifelessly on the metal, which gave a huge thud from the impact. Before they could breathe a sigh of relief, three Greenhorns stormed out of the cruise ship hall.

Cassius drew his machete and cried out. With a contorted face, powered by fury, he rushed at the ferals and put all his strength into his brutal slashes. Each of his attackers was struck once, and that was enough. When he lowered his blood-slicked weapon, the Greenhorns lay in pieces on the deck, close to the perforated Delta. He rubbed his injured, aching shoulder with his clenched mouth. *Pull yourself together! This is no time for pain!*

Another shadow loomed in the cruise ship doorway. Josie screamed, but it was only an old boat-towner with broken and taped glasses. The old chap froze, gasping for air, and raised both hands at the sight of Cassius clutching his machete. It all seemed comical.

"Don't hurt me..."

"Really?" Cassius thundered, laughing out loud to bring the last of his strength to the surface, then grabbed the old man's arm and shoved him towards Josie. "Help her! Go!"

The old chap shook his head, as if he couldn't believe what he was getting himself into, but then a gruff, thick voice growled at them. It sounded as if a hurricane was about to strike.

"What the hell is going on here?"

They turned immediately in the direction of the sound, which proved to be John approaching from the yacht with half a dozen armed men behind him, including the kid with the high and tight haircut and the shaggy-haired man. All of them carried machine guns and cartridge belts on their shoulders. They had a whole arsenal of ammunition boxes and grenades. An impossible mission awaited them.

The old chap with the broken glasses lowered his head and stepped back. John didn't even slow down, just said, "What are you waiting for? Get out of here!" He cocked his gun and signaled to his men to keep moving.

"Of course, John, we're out of here." The old chap grabbed Josie's arm and, with his head down, pushed her.

"Hey, wait!" Cassius stepped in front of the gunmen, ignoring John, whose anger was all over his face. "We should cover the escapers! Otherwise, the ferals will slaughter everyone," Cassius pointed around, but John angrily shushed him.

"We've got other things to do if you hadn't noticed, my friend!" he hissed, but he took one of the rifles off his shoulder and forcefully thrust it into the old chap's hand. "Cover them! We'll try to stop them bastards on the other side. If they get through the cruise ship, we're all dead!"

The old chap took the gun with a petrified look on his face, then glanced around nervously, dreading the possibility of having to use it. He was clutching the weapon as if he were a retired accountant facing the Apocalypse. It was obvious that it would do no good; the old man would not be able to cover the escapers.

"You have no chance," Cassius continued. "You're rushing to your own destruction!"

"Move aside, or I'll move you!" John snarled, except that he didn't wait for Cassius to move, but struck the surprised man in the stomach with lightning speed. Cassius fell to his knees. "I won't say it again: if you want to live, stay out of our way! You run wherever you want to, but we are not afraid to die. We've got a great adventure ahead of us, haven't we boys?"

The vague, uncertain answers were not nearly as enthusiastic as the confident question, but John didn't care. He adjusted the weapons slung across his shoulders and moved on, followed by his trembling mates, who were constantly looking back. As they disappeared down the cruise ship hallway, the old chap with the broken glasses glanced at the gun in his hand, dropped it in disgust, and started running towards Solomon. He waved wildly, so as not to be left behind.

Josie swallowed hard with a frightened expression and blinked at the struggling Cassius.

"I think I'd rather stay with you."

"Awesome!" he growled, picking up the discarded rifle from the floor and quickly checking the magazine. *Seven.*

They set off. The number of escapers had decreased, but the sound of grunts and cracking bones could be heard moving closer and closer to their position. He let the midwife pass in front of him, his eyes scanning their surroundings, looking for Abigail. He was hoping she would be waiting for him on the multicolored boat.

4.

Abigail's heart was in her throat as she raced into the cruise ship hallway and ran to the room where Megan had been taken. But the cabin and the bassinet in it were both empty, and she had no idea where Cassius was. After their last argument, she had stormed off without another word passing between them.

She looked desperately into the neighboring cabins, and when she found no one in them, she cried out like a lost child searching for her parents. She didn't care that it might put her in danger.

"Cassius!"

No answer. The hallway was empty.

Fear and panic flooded her mind, a paralyzing echo that she would not find him in time. *I shouldn't have behaved like that...*

A rustling sound came from down the hall. The door to the last cabin was open, and the light from inside was broken by a moving shadow. Someone or something was in the room. *Calm down! Concentrate...*

Slowly, she pulled the Glock out of its holster.

By this time, the crunching of teeth biting into living flesh, the spurting of blood, and the moaning of a victim were clearly audible. Abigail's hand tightened on the gun as she approached the cabin with caution. She braced herself for the worst: that she would be trapped in the narrow hallway fighting against a Gamma or a Beta.

She shuffled quietly across the worn wall-to-wall carpet, slowed down for the last few feet, and prepared herself for the final pinpoint step. She pushed her gun ahead as she turned, her eyes looking for threat.

Thank God, it's just a Greenhorn!

The feral feasting on the prone boat-towner reacted with lightning speed. It rolled over and leapt up, deftly side-stepping, so the first shots missed. Abigail didn't panic. Keeping her gaze on the Greenhorn, she pulled the trigger three more times, and the feral fell face down on the threshold. It never moved again.

Before she had time to catch her breath, a guttural roar came from the other end of the hallway, followed by a deafening noise. The pounding of feet. She turned and gasped loudly. Her chest clenched with fear as half a dozen ferals burst into the dim hall, then started towards her, pushing each other faster and faster, snarling and spurting bloody spittle.

Abigail took a few steps back in shock.

Someone grabbed her shoulder. She immediately spun, ready for a fight, but it was only John standing behind her, holding a bunch of grenades stringed on a wire. He angrily shoved her behind him.

"Run, if you want to live!" he said, then pulled out the safety pin of a Lemon and threw the cluster grenade at the attacking ferals.

He didn't need to tell her twice. Abigail ran out into the open air, to the port side of the cruise ship. The sunlight blinded her for a moment, but she didn't stop. She could hear John trotting behind her along the corridor, and in the last few yards, the heavyset man even pushed her to take cover.

Bang! The walls shook as the grenades exploded, the shockwave knocking them down. Abigail fell to her knees and scrambled over the deck of the neighboring barge. John slumped against the railing. Pain rolled across his face, but then he shook himself and stood up.

"Get out of here while you still have the chance!" he ordered her, but she could hardly move. John, like someone who accomplished his mission and was ready for another one, ignored her and headed off towards the destruction with his shotgun held high.

He had barely gone ten steps when a meager monster threw itself at him from the cover of a huge water barrel. It was not even up to John's waist, yet it attacked as aggressively as a Tasmanian devil. Abigail screamed, but there was nothing she could do. The feral was a child, transformed only a few days ago, and she recognized it, having seen it somewhere before. At the quarry, when they'd first met Megan and David... it was the skinny kid the others had called Sammy, but there was no sign of the timid, frightened boy she'd seemed before the pack attacked. It had yellow bloodthirsty eyes, its mouth wide open, and its fingers tensed with the spasm that tormented its body. Before the heavyset man could dodge the attack, Sammy bit into his thigh, clinging to its prey like a parasite.

John's hand swung, and he struck down on his attacker with the butt of his rifle, sending the skinny kid crashing to the metal floor with a whimper. Before it could get up, John was already aiming, and fired the entire magazine into Sammy. The metal clinked as the bullets tore through the fragile body, even as John screamed in pain.

Then silence fell. A stunned silence, as if the world had gone still around them. His cry echoed in Abigail's ears, with everything in it: anger and fear, rage and despair.

The rifle finally fell from John's hand and landed beside the feral's body. He looked up in hopelessness at Abigail, then blew the air out of his lungs, bowed his head and stepped off the boat...

...straight into the churning river below. By the time Abigail groaned, he was out of sight.

"No..."

She crawled backwards until her hand hit something. Startled, she turned around. Three bodies wrapped in white sheets lay on the deck of the barge, close to each other. They were dead, awaiting their last journey on earth before submerging into the deep. The sheet had half slipped off one of the bodies, revealing its face to Abigail.

It was Megan.

5.

They reached the multicolored boat safely and found Shaun and Maya guarding the ramp to the deck. The teens watched them approach with wide-eyed wonder, but before they could speak, Cassius was already standing in front of them.

"Where is Abigail?" he asked.

"She's gone to look for you," Maya panted, and pointed towards the cruise ship. Cassius swore under his breath.

"How long ago?"

"A few minutes..."

A raven-haired woman appeared beside them. Though Cassius had never seen her before, he was almost certain she was Rebecca, the patron saint of orphans. Her hands were shaking, but she held her ground, and in a trembling voice she gave orders to the youngsters who were separating the multicolored boat from the colony. She shouted towards an older, handsome-looking boy who had just jumped down from the stairs to the deck and was running towards the stern.

"Roderick! What's up with the engine?"

"We're on it! I'll unhook the speedboat, it'll only get in the way..."

"No!" Maya raised her hands. "Abigail's gonna need it."

Cassius led Josie aboard the houseboat, and, after making sure the midwife and Hope were safe, turned to run back for Abigail.

A thunderous roar stopped him. Thick claws scraped the side of the houseboat as something grappled upwards in a frenzy. Seconds later, the youngsters were screaming and backing away at the sight of the Gamma climbing on board. The feral took aim at a little girl crouched by Soxy's box.

Cassius immediately stepped towards the Gamma. While shouting to draw the attention of the attacker, he fired three bullets into the feral, hoping that would be enough. He was surprised when Shaun appeared beside him and also lunged at the Gamma. Maya, with Rebecca, came up beside the curled-up girl and selflessly pulled her and Soxy to safety.

The Gamma collapsed, its spasmodic claws tearing open the deck's wooden lining. Cassius took aim at the feral's twitching jaw and fired his fourth bullet straight into its maw. The Gamma sprawled lifeless, and the crowd sighed in relief.

The muffled explosion of grenades was heard from the cruise ship and the sound of screams intensified. Cassius's head jerked up, but he asked no questions. He sent one quick glance at the still terrified girl clutching Soxy and was off to get Abigail.

6.

Abigail cried out when she saw Megan's lifeless body. The world ceased to exist around her. She knelt beside the corpse and gently touched the petrified face. Her tears kept falling.

"No... Oh, God, no!"

Her mind was strangled by grief and guilt. She thought of not being with Megan in her last moments, but stupidly, like a sullen child, storming off because she had felt like it. *I was selfish*, she blamed herself. *I was selfish again!*

The woman was dead, and who knew what may have happened to the child. *God, please let the baby be all right.* She raised her head in desperation, and as her eyes broke away from Megan's face, reality returned: on the side of the cruise ship, ferals climbed the upstairs corridors, throwing themselves at the poor folks who had waited too long to flee their homes.

A Delta rushed towards her, but Abigail was unable to move. The feral was picked off by a surviving gunman. She glanced in the direction of the gunshot and saw the kid with the high and tight haircut who had just fired his weapon. He was being pounced on by a Beta and torn to pieces. *A Beta*, she thought, but her muscles wouldn't obey. She strained against her palms and gathered all her strength. She pushed herself up, trying not to look at Megan.

The wind blew the white sheet away, and the fabric covered the petrified face, hiding her from the shocked girl for good. Abigail wiped her eyes and straightened up. Stumbling, she turned around. *I must get back... Cassius will be there, I know it!*

Footsteps clattered behind her, but she turned too late to see who it was. She was struck with a mighty blow that sent her flying back to crash with a thud against the edge of the barge's trough-shaped cargo hold and plummet into the depths below. She gasped for breath as she fell on an empty pallet, dizzy from the blow to her head and overwhelmed by a deep, unquenchable nausea. The sound of the attack was drowned out by the ringing in her ears. The world spun around, but in her mind the order echoed. *Get up! Come on!*

Survival mode finally brought her back to reality at last.

She stood up and scanned her surroundings for her attacker. Bewildered, she looked up to find Norton towering over her. The beast-repellent gloves flashed on the mad scientist's hands and there were dark circles under his eyes, as if the device were slowly draining the life from him.

"Well, well, well... look who's here." Norton drew a demonic smile across his lips. One by one, ferals appeared beside him, snarling and snapping their teeth as they tried to pounce. The beast repellent wouldn't let them attack.

Abigail began to back away.

"What the hell do you want from me?" she shouted, but her voice lacked power. She was still gasping for breath.

Norton braced himself on the ledge, then swung over and jumped into the deep, facing Abigail from only a few yards away. At least a dozen ferals were already panting above him; even the Beta appeared.

Abigail desperately turned her head around. No matter how far she retreated, more and more ferals came up beside her. She saw no way out.

"You know exactly why I'm here!" Norton bared his teeth. "I've come to finish what I started..."

The Beta pushed aside a couple of Greenhorns and scrambled up to the ledge. It was so close to Abigail that it would have taken only one long leap to reach her. It sank its steel claws into the metal, which bent with demonic force. She groaned in fright and had a brief look back. She was five yards away from the end of the cargo hold, a steep wall with nowhere to go, one which stretched so high it seemed impossible to climb.

Norton must have guessed what she had in mind, for he stopped and raised his hand with the beast repellent glove.

"Are you ready, my dear?"

Abigail knew her time had come, but all her doubt vanished and only one order remained in her mind. *Attack!* She threw herself upon the unsuspecting Norton, and was so quick that for a moment he didn't understand what was happening. He looked up in surprise while adjusting the gadget, just in time to see the fist heading for his face. His cheekbone cracked, blood splattered, and Abigail didn't stop. She battered his stomach and threw herself aside when the mad scientist retaliated. She screamed at the top of her lungs, ecstatic at the sight of Norton's anguished face.

"Get screwed, jackass!"

She grabbed the hand wearing the beast repellent glove and slammed it against the wall of the cargo hold. Abigail felt an inexplicable force run down her spine and then the resonance stopped.

The gadget's display cracked, some of the wires were torn out of place, and the diode that had been flashing green went out for a moment...

...only to come back to life with an eerie red glow.

Norton stared paralyzed at the fuming, sparking beast repellent, then up at Abigail, who reacted faster than he did. Without thinking, she started running towards the end of the cargo hold and the steep wall. She didn't look back, but she could see the ferals targeting Norton and hear the mad scientist's desperate pleas.

"No... no, you can't do this now! Nooooooooo!"

Abigail quickened her pace to give herself enough momentum to climb the steep wall. *Maybe I can do it.* The ferals roared, and as the restraining power of the beast repellent slowly but surely diminished, they grew braver, shifting their gaze from the mad scientist to her. Somehow, though, she was sure they wouldn't attack her first. Unfortunately, she also knew that when they were done with Norton, she would be next. *I have to get out of here!*

She prayed for a few extra seconds and some luck. At the end of the cargo hold, she took a big leap and swung her body, but no matter how much she stretched, she could only reach the ledge with her fingertips. *No!*

She started to slip and thought she would fall back down, but at the last moment, someone grabbed her hand firmly.

Cassius pulled her up. Abigail landed on her feet, trying to balance with her hands, but he didn't let her fall. Before she could hug him, Cassius grabbed his machete from where it was propped against the side of the ledge and struck down on an attacking Delta. Joy nearly burst from her lungs.

"Let's get out of here!" Cassius said, and she nodded happily. She took one last glance at Norton, who had stopped adjusting the flashing red gloves and looked up.

Anger and helplessness burned in the mad scientist's eyes. He gritted his teeth, then clenched his jaw as the Beta sprang to pounce on him.

"So be it." Norton closed his eyes before disappearing into the swarm of ferals.

Abigail stretched out with pride and defiantly lifted her chin.

"Fuck your evolution!"

7.

Abigail and Cassius rushed through the cruise ship as fast as they could, and when they reached the starboard side, they were faced with devastation. They were shocked by what they saw. Cassius had experienced many things in his life, but this horror made even his stomach clench. He had to hold on to the railing to keep his balance.

The bodies of the slaughtered boat-towners and the corpses of the ferals that had been shot now lay on the decks of the nearby ships amidst discarded belongings and toppled furniture. Blood and flesh were everywhere and the persistent wailing was accompanied by the distant sounds of mauling.

As the gunfire died down, the ferals were able to cross unhindered to the starboard side of the cruise ship. There was only one person who could have stopped them: the sturdy woman, carrying the converted M2 flamethrower, who had just staggered over to the barge opposite them. A Greenhorn rushed at her, and she pointed the barrel of the device at the feral and pulled the trigger to set it alight. The Greenhorn scrabbled and whimpered, disappearing like a burning torch into the gap between the vessels. She spun around in search of more targets, shaking like a jellyfish. *Good heavens, she'll burn us up if we're not careful...*

Cassius slowed and pulled Abigail closer to him. He scanned the path ahead and the potential dangers. It was a matter of moments before he had to decide which way to go.

The yacht seemed the easiest option, but Cassius trusted neither the woman nor her flamethrower. He knew that there was enough fuel in the weapon for at most four or five more shots, and that the ferals lurking nearby had probably noticed the spectacle. But the multicolored boat rocking north was much further away.

"What are we waiting for?" Abigail asked, and was about to move on. He pulled her back. Just in time.

A Gamma threw itself from the first floor of the cruise ship onto the barge. The seven-foot feral leapt over the trough-shaped cargo hold running down the middle of the vessel and landed beside the woman fiddling with her flamethrower. She turned desperately towards her attacker, but was too late and had pulled the trigger in vain. The Gamma hit her hard, and she flew yards away, trailing a stream of flame, and ended up on another ship, among barrels marked FLAMMABLE.

Cassius pulled Abigail to cover.

"Watch out!"

The colony was rocked by a huge explosion as infernal energy was unleashed among the barrels. Fire erupted, the metalwork of the ship roared, and the windows of the superstructure shattered. The air pressure knocked them down, scorching their faces.

Some of the barrels flew up from the subsequent detonation, and crashed like blazing comets into the surrounding boats, which were instantly engulfed in fire and black smoke.

The linked ships began to tumble, setting off a terrifying chain reaction, their agony accompanied by the banging and friction of metal.

Abigail coughed.

"Now what?" she asked, holding her hand to her face. They struggled to get to their feet.

Cassius grabbed Abigail's arm and they started to run towards the multicolored boat. At the cabin windows, they lowered their heads and crossed the first boardwalk to the neighboring barge. They dodged the machinery and bollards in front of them, jumped over the ropes, and ran as fast as they could. When Abigail discovered a woman hiding behind a pallet, shaking all over, she helped her up and shouted at her to run too. Cassius glanced in the direction of the yacht, where he spotted Solomon.

The head of the colony pushed the last of the escapees onto the yacht, then turned back towards the colony to check that no one was left behind. For a few moments he watched the flames, which raged with such force that they caused the damaged boats to sink.

Solomon wiped his brow with the back of his hand, spat furiously, then boarded the yacht. His men untied the ropes and set off to follow the two houseboats, which were already moving away.

Cassius gave Abigail a big push.

"Don't slow down, come on!"

When they jumped onto the next barge, a guttural roar sounded from above and a huge shadow shrouded them. They looked up at the same time, their faces frozen with terror.

It was the Alpha. The monster had thrown itself from the arm of the tower crane above, from a height of around a hundred and fifty feet, to land directly between them. They jumped aside. Abigail screamed and Cassius pushed his back against the railing. Reflexes overcame panic, however, and they raised their weapons simultaneously, then both unloaded their entire magazines into the Alpha. Most of the bullets ricocheted off the horn-hard skin, but one ripped into its thigh.

The Alpha cried out in pain, its strong fingers tensing in agony, then it pulled itself together and straightened up. It looked down at them with sparkling eyes. At that moment Cassius had the chance to observe the wounds that covered the feral's body. It was missing an eye from the previous encounter with Abigail and torn skin hung from the surrounding area, covered with dried blood and mud. Her shot had torn through a few teeth and its left arm clutched the wound in its abdomen. Even so, the Alpha was still life-threatening, and as soon as it regained its strength, it attacked.

Or seemed like it was attacking.

Cassius instinctively threw down his empty gun and grabbed the first object that could be used as a weapon: a long metal pipe. He braced one end against the wall and raised the other like a spear in front of him, just in the nick of time.

The Alpha, hurling itself at its prey, could no longer dodge and impaled itself. The metal pipe ripped through its stomach and pierced its body along its spine. Its face contorted, its grunts mingled with almost human-like cries, until rage finally overcame suffering and the Alpha smashed the pipe in two with a single blow before striking Cassius with a backhand. He flew several yards and thudded up against the metal plating of the deck, his momentum stopped by a bollard on the other side of the barge. As he landed, the leather-bound notebook fell out of his pocket and slid off the deck, disappearing into the deep.

The Alpha fell to its knees, its nails scraping the metal decking. It howled sharply, like a wounded wolf, its jagged teeth gritted in pain.

Cassius struggled to his feet, searching for Abigail. She was standing on the other side, watching him in shock. The Alpha crouched between them prevented her from running to get help.

Abigail took a desperate step forward, not knowing what to do.

"Run!" Cassius screamed from the top of his lungs.

It was their only chance; it was Abigail's only chance. He couldn't let anything bad happen to her, and he figured that if this was the moment to sacrifice himself for her, so be it. *Besides*, it crossed his mind, *what a crazy idea it was to think of hanging out on a beach.*

Abigail couldn't move and she shook her head in silence. Tears welled up in her eyes.

"What are you waiting for?" Cassius snapped at her.

But it seemed too late to escape. The Alpha stood up with an agonized whimper and swept its gaze over them, eyes glowing with rage and hatred. Cassius unhooked his machete from his back and slammed the blade against the metal wall of the superstructure so that the feral would focus only on him.

"Go!" he clenched his teeth as he looked at the girl. Abigail backed away, but still refused to listen. He pointed towards the multicolored boat. "They need you..."

The gigantic demon straightened up, its chest puffed out, the muscles bulging beneath its skin tensed. It was at least three feet taller than Cassius. It seemed obvious that, despite its severe injuries, it was too much for even two of them to handle.

"You can't save everyone... For once in your life, listen to me!"

The Alpha snapped its teeth at the girl, and Cassius slammed the metal wall once more.

"Please..."

And Abigail finally reacted, disappearing into the cover of the superstructure moments later. *At last... at last she listened to me!* Cassius smiled. He was ready. He knew that he could no longer delay his doom, for it stood before him, looking down at him like the Cyclops at Ulysses. The Alpha's nostrils quivered as it inhaled his scent. Saliva pooled in its mouth, dribbling down its blood-and-mud spattered chin, but for some reason it hadn't yet attacked. Cassius tightened his grip on his machete.

"Well, here I am!" he shouted. The Alpha dropped both arms to its side, and the demonic snarl disappeared from its face. *What the hell is it doing? Why doesn't it strike?*

Meanwhile, the ships, caught in the fire and smoke, tilted dangerously, the chains holding them together tightened, and the boat-town shook.

The Alpha fell to its knees again, only a few yards from Cassius. He accidentally dropped his machete, and even though he tried to catch it, the weapon slipped too far away. The deck shuddered and rippled beneath them as the sinking ships began to drag the others down.

Cassius glanced at the Alpha and he spotted something. A dirty, damaged watch was clamped on the feral's left wrist. It was the only thing it had on. It wore no clothes or shoes to identify who the rampaging monster might have been long ago. The only thing it was wearing was the watch, with its glass broken, its dial damaged, and its faded, half-ripped strap cutting into the Alpha's skin.

It was a disgusting sight, but he couldn't take his eyes off of it. The strap sank into the unhealing wound like a river running through a canyon, digging deep into the pale red, festering skin.

But Cassius wasn't concerned with the wound, only the watch. The watch he still recognized after all these years. He would have recognized it after a thousand years. The damaged American A-11 was his. It had been given to him by his father, and from the moment his son was born, he had wanted to pass it on. And he had, in the first hours of the Breakdown, the last time he saw his family.

Even then, in the midst of the explosions, he remembered clearly the moment when he took off the watch and strapped it to his son's thin wrist as a farewell.

Cassius paled at the recognition, his shoulders slumping as he glanced at the Alpha. Behind the demonic features, he searched for the familiar child's face, and though he couldn't find it, the word burst from him anyway.

"Son..."

8.

Abigail ran as fast as she could. She jumped over to the tugboat, but landed badly and twisted her ankle. She ignored the excruciating pain and thought only of reaching the multicolored boat.

They need you... You can't save everyone...

Fear made her stomach churn and panic clenched her throat in an iron fist.

When she could no longer stand the stinging, dirty sweat pouring into her eyes, she wiped her brow. Breathlessness did not slow her down. Cassius' words echoed in her head. She was about to cry.

For once in your life, listen to me!

She turned the last corner. The sight before her made her heart stop for a moment, then start to beat faster. *They left me here!* The houseboat was now far away from the colony, the youths on board standing and blinking anxiously at the burning boat-town. They covered their mouths with their hands as they spotted the girl.

"Abigail!" she heard from somewhere below, but she couldn't see who was calling to her. She took a few steps forward.

The battered speedboat, with Shaun and Maya in it, was rocking alongside the tug. The siblings waved and shouted to her in relief.

"Come on, hurry up," Maya burst out. The teens could barely scream over the noise of the dying boat-town and the coughing, clattering sound of the engine. "I don't know how much longer this tub can last!"

Abigail clambered onto the railing, but before she could throw herself over the edge, the tugboat rolled beneath her. She squeezed her eyes shut and held on tightly until the quake subsided enough for her to gain momentum and jump onto the speedboat rocking below. Shaun had to catch her, or she would have tumbled into the river.

"Where is he?" Shaun asked, but Abigail didn't answer, she just stared ahead. He grabbed her shoulder, but she looked up at him blankly. Her thoughts were flooded with memories in a split second.

The bodies of the woman and the little girl in the warehouse. Trying to picture the calm in their slowly freezing features. *I did what was right!*

Soxy's siblings she had to leave behind. *We can't even help ourselves, never mind others!*

The look in Trevor's eyes, glimmering with fear and disbelief. *I told you, Abigail, you're not ready...*

David's last look, resigned to his destiny. Megan, who waited so eagerly for her baby to be born, and who sacrificed her own life so that her child could live in a better world.

Abigail knew the deal, she wasn't a schoolgirl who needed to be told how to survive the Silent Zone. They had to take care only of themselves, without taking risks. *The aim is to survive...but at what cost?*

Maya pushed Shaun aside and snapped at her brother.

"Let's go!"

But before he could steer the speedboat towards their safety,

Abigail grabbed his hand.

No!

We must always try!

"Help me!" she said uncompromisingly, and picked up the anti-materiel rifle propped against the seat of the speedboat. However, the weight —over twenty-five pounds — made her stumble back. The .50 caliber semi-automatic GM6 Lynx was a sight to behold, even if it *was* a bit dusty and worn, she had no doubt that she could take the Alpha down with it. *This has got to work*. The thought echoed in her head. She checked the magazine. Five rounds.

"You want to go back?" Shaun asked, stunned.

"I do!" Abigail nodded. "We're not leaving anyone behind!"

If the wiseass thinks he can sacrifice himself for me, he's got me all wrong!

Shaun and Maya exchanged looks before finally moving into action, helping Abigail heave the rifle aboard with loud snorts. When they were done, Abigail climbed back into the tug and took one last look at the siblings.

"Don't wait for us!" she ordered, then put the Lynx on her back and headed into the fray. For the first few steps, she felt as if she were in a slow-motion movie, her spine straining under the weight, but then she gained momentum and stumbled across the deck. She found the ladder to the top of the superstructure and with a hell of an effort, she worked her way up.

More and more explosions shook the boat-town. A searing shockwave ripped through the decks. The tug began to surge and rubble fell everywhere.

Abigail finally managed to regain her balance. She dropped the rifle from her shoulder. The weapon banged hard on the superstructure's rooftop, and she fell to her knees. She looked around and immediately spotted Cassius standing on the next barge, about fifty yards from her.

He and the Alpha stood facing each other, the deck swaying beneath them as if an earthquake had struck. The billowing smoke sometimes hid their shapes.

With a single press of a button, Abigail released the locked barrel, deployed the bipod, and propped the rifle down, pointing it straight at the Alpha. She lay down behind the gun and was settled in an instant. She slowed her breathing and glanced through the scope to find her target. She tried to shut out her surroundings: the screech of metal and the echoes of further detonations. The wind blew a thick cloud of smoke towards her, ash and rubble falling without a pause.

She chambered a round and watched. The boat-town shook again. The Alpha and Cassius disappeared behind the smoke.

9.

Cassius straightened up and looked at the Alpha as if he were staring at a ghost. His body was paralyzed with his denial. *It can't be, it's some kind of bad dream*, he thought, then his face flushed with anger and shame. All he could focus on was that he hadn't been there for his family in their final moments. Who knew what suffering they must have gone through, or how scared they were, and he wasn't there to protect them.

I failed them!

The yellow glow of the Alpha's eyes pierced into his, and for a moment it seemed as if they would stand facing each other until the end of time. They didn't move even when another explosion shook the boat-town. The flames spread, unstoppable, and the smoke gathered around them as torn cables caused some ships to drift away from the rest of the colony.

His skin was burned by the heat, his throat scratched by the ash he breathed. The barge surged wildly beneath them, but Cassius kept his balance.

I failed my son... I deserve what's going to happen to me!

The Alpha took a hesitant step forward. Its shoulders slumped, its right hand gripping its belly, blood oozing between its fingers.

"And now?" Cassius yelled at it, then spread his arms wide. "Now what?

A Gamma clung to the barge from down below and started striding towards him. But before Cassius could swing for his dropped machete, the Alpha was already moving, catching the leaping Gamma in midair. In a flash, it tore the assailant apart, then threw its head to the ground and stepped on it.

Skin ripped, bone cracked. Bits of blood and brain splattered the deck. He was dizzy with the sight and had to hold on.

The Alpha turned back towards him and slowly began to approach. Cassius didn't know what to do. He shook his head, as if trying to chase away a foolish thought. *No, that can't be my son! He is dead!* Yet he could not attack it, nor could he find the strength to fight it. He searched the Alpha's gaze, trying to divine what was going on in the monster's mind. *Yes, a monster! IT ISN'T MY SON!*

He backed up a few steps, but then someone whistled. The Alpha snapped its head up and snarled.

10.

I cannot fail!

When the Alpha appeared in the reticle, all doubt vanished from Abigail's mind. She focused only on the task at hand, her jumbled thoughts clearing. She pressed her finger against the trigger guard.

I've done it a hundred times, and I've proved a hundred times that I can do it.

The Alpha was struggling to hold on, the injuries had worn it down, but it was still a mortal threat. For a moment, its figure faded behind the swirling smoke. When it reappeared, she knew she had to act.

Now is the time to shoot. The order echoed in her head, but another voice immediately interjected. *Take a deep breath...*

Abigail pointed the reticle at the Alpha's chest and calmed her breathing. The rocking of the tugboat didn't slow for a moment and she was tortured by the smoke and heat.

The chains securing the tug snapped and the vessel started to drift away from the colony.

The order rang in Abigail's head. *NOW!* She gave a whistle and when the Alpha stopped and looked up, she slowly but surely pulled the trigger. Just as Cassius had taught her, as if scratching a line on a board with chalk.

The rifle roared like an old lion about to slay its final prey. The muzzle blast drowned out all other sounds, and the barrel pushed back, so hard that the gun slammed against her shoulder. She thought it would hurt more, but the sensation sent an unprecedented rush through every part of her body. *Yes!*

The bullet whizzed over the deck and slammed into the Alpha's chest, tearing skin and bone to shreds with incredible force. The Alpha fell back and helplessly collapsed. Its blood covered everything around.

Abigail could see Cassius's head jerk towards the blast, but she didn't wait for him to react. She jumped up and clung to the railing, leaping from the top of the superstructure. In the meantime, she yelled out, hoping he would hear her.

"Cassius, run!"

11.

Cassius could hardly believe his eyes. When the bullet smashed into the Alpha's chest, the feral fell back and cried out, lying on the ground. The painful howl lasted only seconds, however, and the beast pulled itself to all fours before struggling to its feet. Its lungs wheezed as it gasped for breath, blood oozed from its wounds, and its knees buckled. As the flames drew closer, they bit into its back, causing the Alpha to scramble forward, its legs faltering.

He heard Abigail's cry.

"Cassius, run!"

The Alpha also noticed the girl leaping from the superstructure of the drifting vessel. The feral snarled in fury and was on the move, ready to hurl itself at Abigail. No matter the distance, and no matter that it was barely dragging itself. It had a thirst for blood and revenge.

Cassius could not let that happen. He threw himself to the side, picked up his machete, and struck at the monster's shoulder with such force that when the sharp blade hit bone, his hand was nearly torn off. The pain made him see stars, but he didn't close his eyes or look away. He wanted to know if it was the killing blow.

"I'm sorry, my boy..."

The machete sliced through flesh and blood spurted, but despite the hellish effort, the bushwhacker was lodged in the Alpha's collarbone. The blow to its body brought the feral to its knees, and a feeble gurgle came from its mouth as if it were its last breath.

The cruise ship creaked with a deafening sound, then began to lean against the barge they were standing on. Explosions continued and as the fire devoured everything around them, the colony fell to pieces.

Cassius took one last glance at the Alpha writhing on the ground; the yellow, glowing eyes were fading. *Goodbye, my boy!* Without a word, he stepped back, then turned and started running. But not fast enough. Before he could dive into the river, the cruise ship capsized onto the barge, sending him up into the sky. And then straight back down.

Right into the churning, debris-filled river. Within a matter of moments, he was engulfed in the cool foam, sucked into the depths, nearly unconscious from shock and lack of air. His awareness was sinking faster than his body, but he didn't fight because he didn't want to fight anymore. His muscles went limp, the air left his lungs, then everything around him turned black.

He could no longer hear the sounds of destruction, the rushing of the water, the screams...

There was simply silence, and floating in the middle of nowhere. It seemed as if he had spent his entire life in this dark emptiness, but the command to open his eyes kept going through his head.

Cassius resisted for a while. It might have been seconds, or even hours.

Finally, he obeyed.

He was standing on the island, the island he had fought so hard to reach. It was summer, and hot, a real late-August heatwave, where the sun is still scorching, even as it fades. He gazed at the distant horizon and the endless stretch of water, his bare feet sinking into the sand, his face caressed by the light breeze of dusk.

He knew he was not alone because every time his thoughts returned to this place, he was never alone. Then he heard her voice. In his dreams he only heard her voice.

"Jake!"

Cassius expected to see no one this time either, but when he turned around, he found himself looking at a happily smiling face. The face of his wife, a face they had traveled tens of thousands of miles to find since the Breakdown, all in vain.

There was no one there but her. *Susan...* She closed her eyes and let the wind play with her cheeks.

“Beautiful!” she whispered, looking at the landscape, and smiled as something occurred to her. The lines dancing at the corners of her lips gave away that she was up to something naughty. “Not exactly Key West, but still, it'll do.”

Key West? Why did she say that?

The realization burst into Cassius's mind like a tornado. A spark of hope. The determination to continue the years-long search, because if there was a corner of the Silent Zone he hadn't been to and hadn't explored, he couldn't stop looking. He couldn't give up until then.

Wake up, the command in his head said, and he came to. He was at the bottom of the river, and he knew he had to get to the surface somehow. *I have a job to do.* Cassius summoned all his strength and started to swim. Towards the light, which meant life for him. It seemed unreachably far, but then a hand gripped his and pulled him to the surface.

It was Abigail.

12.

They searched for survivors until sunset, then anchored in the upper reaches of the river for the night, setting up sentries to prevent being ambushed in the dark. But the area was quiet, with only the occasional sound from the blazing ruins of the colony as the ships slowly sank onto the river bed.

Abigail and Cassius had both made it to the shelter of the bobbing speedboat, then the siblings took them to the multicolored boat, where they could finally catch their breath and dry off. For a long time neither of them spoke. They just stared at each other, as though they couldn't believe they had finally escaped. He playfully ruffled her hair and hugged her briefly.

After the sun dipped behind the distant horizon, they were served dinner, and when they had gorged themselves on fish, they were finally able to smile. And Abigail met Hope at last, when the midwife handed her over to Cassius with a grateful expression. The baby looked healthy and strong, and it was a bittersweet thought that their strange family had again grown by one.

"You'd better raise the li'l pooch to be an obedient bloodhound!" He glanced with feigned sternness at Soxy, to which Abigail replied with a vigorous nod.

It all seemed to go well from that moment on, but Cassius couldn't shake the thought that had been in his head from the first moment of his rescue.

Key West... Why the hell can't I get that colony out of my head? He tried to remember if they had had any contact with the area. Anything that might give him reason for hope. His wife had volunteered with a local organization before college, even made friends, but most of them had moved away. Still, what he saw underwater, half-conscious, was not a fantasy, but a memory. *What are the odds that, in the midst of the chaos, Susan had not gone with the crowd, but had chosen a specific destination, no matter how uncertain?*

At the beginning of the pandemic, the archipelago was mostly sought by people who wanted to find a way out of the Silent Zone by boat. Few thought that a place that was unsustainable could survive for long. Unless you were content to fish between hurricane seasons.

What are the odds... He knew there was only one way to find out.

Even though Abigail was also exhausted, she helped Rebecca calm the little ones and put them to bed. With most of the men-at-arms lost in the attack, Cassius taught the volunteers a few tried-and-true tricks and took the first watch on the multicolored boat. He wouldn't have slept well anyway.

The first morning after the attack was all about reorganization, and much to Cassius's surprise, he and Abigail were invited to a brief meeting with Solomon, Rebecca, Roderick, and a few other elderly boat-towners. When asked what he had to say about Norton and his gadgets, he passed the torch to Abigail and let her tell them in detail what they had seen at the mad scientist's house.

Abigail was quite surprised at this, and although she suffered a little stage fright to begin with, she ended like someone who had been giving such briefings all her life. Cassius watched her with pride, and had not the least doubt that she would stand her ground, wherever he was, and whatever happened to him.

Thirty minutes later, the first scout team was being organized to Norton's house, for which Abigail had volunteered. The task was to take inventory of everything they could use and figure out what to do with the assets piled up there. This time Solomon didn't object and, to Abigail's surprise, Cassius said nothing.

The last item on the agenda was the question of reconstruction, and it was quickly established that on their own it would be difficult, even if Norton's assets were used. There was not much left of the boat-town and too many people were lost in the attack.

"We'll have to find a way to reestablish contact with the Key West colony, but the radio hub was destroyed along with the cruise ship," Solomon said. "We're gonna need their help."

"That's a problem for tomorrow," Rebecca interjected. "For now, we have more important things to do."

The others nodded in agreement, and that was the end of the discussion. Cassius waited until the majority had dispersed, then stepped over to Solomon, who was still sitting in his seat, staring worriedly ahead of him.

"I wouldn't wait until you've got a new radio wired up before contacting them."

The head of the boat-town stood up and cracked his neck. He looked long into Cassius's eyes, as if he couldn't decide what to expect from this conversation.

"Perhaps you've got an idea?"

"I think it would be an ideal task for me. I need a speedboat and supplies. Water, food, ammunition... enough for one man."

Solomon scratched the top of his head.

"We are grateful for your warning of the attack, but we are far from giving you the keys to the town as a token of our gratitude."

"You may not have noticed, but you no longer have a town,"

Cassius bared his teeth, then paused for effect and changed to a more conciliatory tone. "You know I'm your only chance. Your squad looks pretty thin, so either you wait until someone can train the available manpower, or..."

"Okay, I get it," Solomon gestured, then closed his eyes wearily. When he opened them after a deep sigh, he pointed towards Abigail, who was talking to Rebecca. "And what does the girl say to that?"

"Let me worry about that."

Solomon gave an impassive nod.

"We'll load one of the boats, but don't expect any princely comforts," the head of the boat-town said, and Cassius snorted.

"I've never had it so easy."

13.

Cassius leaned against the railing and watched the scout team get ready to go to Norton's house. He held Megan's necklace in one hand and the flat metal box in the other, wondering how to tell Abigail what he was up to. Finally, it was she who made the first move.

"You're even quieter than usual," she said when she stopped beside him. A wry smile curved the edge of her mouth. "No nagging, no telling me I'm taking a dangerous journey... No restrictions, no parables..."

"Who am I to defy a strong, independent woman?" he spread his arms.

"Hahaha... What are you up to? And let's skip ahead in time to the point where you tell me."

They both laughed. Cassius straightened his back and nodded. He was searching for the strength within himself.

"I'm proud of you for fitting in here... I mean that!"

Abigail's face turned serious and her nose wrinkled angrily.

"And what about you? Is the boat-town not up to your fancy expectations? Or perhaps..." She wanted to continue, but bit off the sentence.

"Yes, it is."

"So?"

"I need to travel for a while before I lay down my arms for good. I need to find out one more thing so I can go fishing somewhere peacefully, or try to teach idiots how to survive an encounter with a Greenhorn."

She didn't look at him, instead watching the river heading south. The first fat tear appeared in her eye, but she quickly wiped it away, trying to ignore her feelings. But her voice gave her away; it was thin and unsteady.

"And where do you have to go that can't wait?"

"Key West."

"What makes you think you'll find Susan there?"

"I don't know... She was a smart woman who probably realized she couldn't run away to Mexico."

Abigail pointed her chin defiantly at him.

"And if she's not there? Are you gonna come back?"

"I am, even if she is. I'm gonna check out the colony, and if it's safe enough, who knows, maybe the whole boat-town can move there. Safer than hanging around here."

"Then let's stop playing games and go together. The boat-town can wait a few weeks."

Cassius smiled proudly, but when he looked around, he shook his head.

"This is the place you need to be. They need you. And at least this way I can be sure that when I come back... because I will... this place is going to be even safer than Fort Knox."

"I still don't understand why you're not coming with us to Norton's. With those gadgets, you wouldn't even need guns."

"I guess I'll stick to the tried-and-true methods where I can," Cassius said.

They hugged each other, longer perhaps, than ever before. Finally, he pulled away, looked into her sparkling eyes, and winked encouragingly. Abigail didn't want to hide the tears now.

"Are we happy?" Cassius asked, and Abigail nodded.

"Yes, we are!"

14.

One of the speedboats was half loaded with supplies and filled with enough fuel to get Cassius to the port, where their sailboat was waiting for him.

So he might as well make good use of that stupid plan, Abigail thought as she watched him, calculating how long the journey would take. *How long will he be gone?* He could reach the bay quickly in the speedboat and get the sailboat ready in a day or two, but instead of a nearby island, he would have to sail a little further. Many hundreds of miles further...

After he was finished packing, Cassius took another look at Hope and got a photo from Josie of her son. He looked closely at the features of the long-faced boy and handed the photo back.

"His name is Matthew," the midwife said, "and till you're back with the news, I'll look after Hope."

Cassius nodded, but before he could get into the speedboat, Maya appeared beside him. She leaned her weapon against her shoulder and raised her chin at him in a way that made Cassius think for a moment he was looking at Abigail.

"My brother and I would gladly join you!"

Shaun, who had been lurking in the background, looked up with a deathly pale face.

"What?"

"Never mind him!" she waved. "He wants to come as well, he just didn't dare ask."

Cassius scratched his nose and stifled a laugh that was about to burst out.

"And tell me, what's all this bravado about?"

Maya shrugged.

"A little adventure can't do us any harm. Besides that, I don't know anyone in the boat-town who can teach us what Abigail knows... and we want more than just being on watch."

Cassius sniffed, then glanced at Abigail. They smiled at the same time, and she gave him permission with a slight wave. She knew he would need the company, perhaps more than the two siblings would. After all, Megan was right: this was her purpose in life. To help. To stay and hope instead of running.

It wasn't long before Abigail was standing on the deck of the multicolored ship, watching the speedboat pull away. The scout team was finally ready, Roderick alone scratching the back of his head in concern.

"I still don't understand why it's not a good idea to bring everything here and then I'll check out the stuff. Just because..."

Abigail's bittersweet smile disappeared from her face, and she must have looked so sternly at the boy that he quickly closed his mouth.

So that's how it feels... Inside, of course, she was laughing about it, and thinking that now she would have to make unpopular decisions, too. Decisions that not everyone would like. *It's time to grow up.* But she had no problem with that. She felt ready for it.

"It ain't a wishing well," she said to Roderick, and with a decisive gesture she took off his sunglasses. "And it ain't a fashion statement."

15.

The speedboat was bouncing over the waves, heading south. Cassius turned inward as he steered, and though he seemed to be concentrating on the route, his mind was racing in all directions. Behind him, Shaun watched the passing landscape with wide eyes, and Maya grinned happily.

When they reached the billboard where the river ran closest to the road, Cassius suddenly slowed down. The siblings looked at him, puzzled.

"What happened?" Maya leaned forward.

"Is something wrong?" Shaun swallowed hard. His face looked first frightened, then curious.

Cassius steered the speedboat towards the riverbank and stopped, a safe distance away from the thing he had noticed. He slung his loaded rifle over his shoulder, adjusted the machete on his back, and jumped out of the boat. The teens followed, blinking widely, and as they tried to keep pace, they stared meaningfully at him. But they got no answer to their questions; they would have to find out for themselves.

Someone was lying on the riverbank: it was John, one hand clutching the bite on his thigh, the other digging at the ground. He was barely conscious, his body was trembling, and as they drew closer, Cassius recognized the signs of transformation. The dark streak running up to his skull, the muscle spasm, the grunting. John's yellowish eyes glanced up. Though he was a man of vitality, it had taken only a day for the virus to take over his body.

"Oh my God," Maya gasped, putting her hand over her mouth. "What shall we do with him?"

Cassius walked closer, and although he saw some recompense in the situation, he said nothing. He just watched the limp body and wondered. He chewed over the possibilities, then looked at the siblings.

"Lesson number one: never wait for someone to transform. The sooner you put them out of their misery, the better for everyone."

From the pale faces, Cassius concluded that the message had hit home. He leaned his rifle against a nearby tree and drew his machete. John watched him with bulging eyes.

"Sorry, but we can't waste any bullets!" Cassius said, then nodded his head at John's boots. They were barely used. "Nice pair. May I have them?"

THE END

ABOUT THE AUTHOR

Viktor Csák is a Marketing Diamond Award-winning copywriter, a scriptwriter for international commercials, and has contributed to a number of non-fiction books.

Welcome to the Silent Zone is his first novel. The film rights sold prior to publication.

Viktor lives in Hungary, and runs a small creative company.

Printed in Great Britain
by Amazon

30202534R00225